MW01133889

For Paul and Louise Schmidt

Jack Fernandez
6 Dec. 05

Café Con Leche

A Novel

By

Jack Eugene Fernández

authorHOUSE™

1663 LIBERTY DRIVE, SUITE 200
BLOOMINGTON, INDIANA 47403
(800) 839-8640
WWW.AUTHORHOUSE.COM

First published by AuthorHouse 01/25/05

ISBN: 1-4208-1907-0 (e)
ISBN: 1-4208-1906-2 (sc)

Library of Congress Control Number: 2004099891

Printed in the United States of America
Bloomington, Indiana

This book is printed on acid-free paper.

NOTICE: While some of the events of this novel are historically true; viz, the Tampa cigar workers' strike of 1931 and the shooting in the Circulo Cubano, I have changed the names of the parties. I moved the Circulo Cubano shooting of 1934 to 1937. Except for Mr. Perry Wall, the former mayor who addressed the striking workers in 1931, all the other characters in the story have sprung from my imagination and are not based on any persons living or dead. The headlines that begin each chapter are mostly from archives of the Tampa Tribune with a few from the New York Times. I have edited most of them.

ACKNOWLEDGEMENTS: Several kind people have helped me throughout this project. The late Professor Willy Reader of the USF English Department read the manuscript and offered excellent professional advice on style and diction. Several other generous persons read the many drafts. They include my three sons, Jack, Jr. Albert, and Rudy, Professor Marvin Alvarez, Lazaro Hernandez, Jay DeLotto, Ángel Rañón, Edward Turos, Chip Harmon, Clinton Dawes, Mary Lynne Ziegler, Tony Pizzimenti, and Mark Pizzimenti. All graciously offered helpful suggestions. My most important critic and editor was my wife, Sylvia, who read every version and found time to offer encouragement along with detailed notes and comments.

I also thank René González, who furnished the photo of Ybor City for my cover from his private collection. This photo of Ybor City's *La Séptima* (Seventh Avenue) was taken in the early 1930's.

1 - MATANZAS, CUBA, MAY 1930

*

Nazis Win Six Million Votes

*

Ness's Untouchables Hammer Al Capone

*

Machado Takes Over Cuba

*

Wall Street Bounces Back

*

To know that don Ignacio was an important man one had only to view his house atop a green, fertile hill south of Matanzas. Massive stones, stucco and wood in striking contemporary angles, broad terraces, sprawling formal gardens, and the long, royal palm-lined driveway from the street made it truly a place to impress.

With his face of iron don Ignacio stood on his third floor balcony and exhaled a billow of smoke. Lifting his gold watch from the vest pocket of his white linen suit, he recalled the morning his father left Cuba twenty-five years earlier. They had fought, but they smiled that day and embraced. Now, looking down the corridor of time the reasons had faded, leaving only crumpled bitterness. With yellowed face and bent hands the watch ticked with the urgency of a tired heart. Don Ignacio rubbed his thumb across the gold cover as if it were a sacred relic and took a deep breath and thought how his father would have loved the *don* before his name.

Still caressing the watch don Ignacio returned through the French doors into his study. The balcony wrapped around two sides, and both inner walls displayed his massive collection of books on white shelves. His father had read them all; he had read few. White doors and wood trim accented sky-blue plaster walls and varnished oak floors. Beneath the east balcony spread a magnificent garden with flower-lined stone paths cutting the grassy slope into precise geometric figures accented with palms. Along the back of the garden stood the fruit trees that had sated the childhood appetite of don Ignacio's son, Pablo. Beyond the garden, the Castle of San Severino and the Cathedral of San Carlos towered over the city of Matanzas as reminders of long-disintegrated Spanish power. The north balcony overlooked Matanzas Bay and, beyond, the Florida Strait, where the Gulf of Mexico generously warms the frigid Atlantic. With night whispering across the earth like the memory of slain conquerors, the cool eastern moon rose ghostlike over flickering city lights.

Near the northeast corner of don Ignacio's study stood a massive oak desk and high-backed judge's chair. The desk was bare except for an antique lamp, a crystal ashtray, and a framed photograph of four-year-old, towheaded Pablo standing between his parents, holding their hands and looking up adoringly at his father. In the photograph, don Ignacio, in his mid forties, gazes sternly into the camera with a glare of absolute authority. Doña Inez, in a clinging black brocade dress and a broad-brimmed Cordovan hat to protect her pink-white skin from the brutal tropical sun, looks away with head tilted back to display her handsome chin, aquiline nose, and haughty smile. Chestnut-colored hair combed back into a tight Andalusian bun and a string of pearls accent the seductive glamour of the woman who seems to be in her early twenties. In the corner behind don Ignacio's desk stood a hand-carved triangular table made from an oak felled near don Ignacio's father's birthplace in Spain. The only object on that table, a humidor, also had belonged to don Ignacio's father. On the far side of the room, near the library, an oak conference table with leather-seated oak chairs served for meetings with managers and overseers.

Enveloped in cigar smoke, don Ignacio looked out beyond his garden to the paradise hungry Spaniards claimed centuries after the Indians had. He cared little that those Indians existed only as genetic sprinklings throughout those conquerors' descendants, for he understood the price of progress and felt that, except for filling the land with African slaves, Spaniards like his father had developed the island with foresight and efficiency.

But don Ignacio's immediate challenge was more personal: to divert his son from disaster. He knew it would not be easy, for every time he tried to talk seriously to Pablo, the young man would smile irritatingly and change the subject. In that smile Pablo's mouth would stretch into a V, and his cheeks would push his eyes behind slits. Not that Pablo was homely. On the contrary, but when his father saw that smile, he knew Pablo would ignore his advice.

*

Pablo's thoughts raced as he marched across the deep, red-carpeted, arched hallway, oblivious of the large family portraits hanging on either side. His eyes were fixed on the end of the hall where a large window framed the golden glow of the dying day and where narrow stairs would lead him up to his father's study.

The young man rehearsed his defense as he scurried down the long hall, remembering the freedom he felt at college, as if his cage had been opened. Despite its harsh climate, Notre Dame had taken him to her bosom and allowed him to make new friends and explore hidden talents. He had especially enjoyed philosophy in the class of an elf-like priest who taught as Socrates had, with questions and more questions that drove students to scrape their brains for crumbs of ideas they could paste together into insights. He recalled announcing that he would major in philosophy and don Ignacio staring at him with the stony look that Pablo had come to know well. After Pablo's well-reasoned defense, don Ignacio had simply unsheathed his ultimate weapon: "Waste your time on unanswerable questions if you wish, but I will not support it. Understand?" Pablo turned to economics and business and came to enjoy those subjects, but the incident left a scar to remind him of the difference between a foot soldier and a general.

Pablo made the turn onto the stairs, his thick, honey-colored hair bouncing as he took the steps by twos. Two inches shorter than his father, he stretched to stand tall. After one month on the job he felt confident, but his father's summons had raised the specter of the old man on his balcony reaching down a magisterial finger to make mundane adjustments with deistic ease.

Tall and still handsome in his early sixties, don Ignacio looked more German than Spanish with neatly trimmed sandy hair graying at the temples, blue eyes, and thick brown moustache turned up in imitation of Kaiser Wilhelm. Standing ramrod straight on his north balcony, eyes on the custom-made cigar in his fingers, he took another puff. Pablo entered as don Ignacio raised his head to exhale a great plume that hung like a pronouncement between them.

"*Hola, Papá.*"

Don Ignacio rubbed the watch again and slipped it into his pocket.

"You love that watch, don't you, Papá?"

"It will be yours one day, Pablo. It was my father's and his father's before him."

"I wish I had known him. He must have been quite a man."

"He was demanding at the wrong times and weak when he should have been strong."

"He fought with the rebels," Pablo said, egging his father on.

"Only once, to capture escaped slaves." Don Ignacio bit down on his cigar. Then turning to his son with a fresh smile, he took the cigar between his fingers. "Let's get down to business, Pablo. You have impressed my managers."

Pablo shrugged and smiled.

"Notre Dame was worth the cost. Americans understand business. Anyway, I'm glad you are fitting in." Offering his son a cigar from his humidor, he motioned for him to sit.

Following his father's ritual, Pablo rolled the cigar between his thumb and three fingers to feel its packing, carefully removed the band bearing his father's florid signature *Ignacio Iglesias*, struck a match, and lit the cigar with a long draw.

"Your mother says you're still seeing the González girl."

Pablo said nothing as he blew out the blue-gray smoke.

"Not serious, I trust."

"You know Mamá; she doesn't like any girl."

"She said you mentioned marriage."

"Uh-huh." Pablo tried to be nonchalant, but the question was laced with danger.

"Son, you are embarking on a complex career. Marriage would be a distraction."

"I waited till I graduated as you asked."

"You're barely twenty."

"Twenty-one, Papá; Mamá wasn't even seventeen."

"That was different. The man is the breadwinner. You must know many women before you can make an intelligent choice."

"I don't need to. I love her."

Don Ignacio's jaw tightened; his face assumed the stony, impassive visage of a field general. "Don't you think it's time you grew up?"

"What are you asking?"

"I'm <u>telling</u> you to forget her."

"Why? Why don't you like her?"

"Not her, Pablo, the match. With all the fine women in the world …"

When Pablo opened his mouth to speak, don Ignacio barked, "Don't interrupt! She isn't … you know?"

"Oh, Papá!"

"I understand how you feel, Pablo. She's attractive, but that is irrelevant. Understand?"

"No, I don't."

Pablo had never challenged his father so directly. Not accustomed to explaining his decisions, don Ignacio looked away. "You have met her family, I trust?"

"You're not still mad at her father?"

"Her father is not the problem."

"What, then?"

"They simply won't do." Seeing the confused stare on his son's face, don Ignacio continued, "Your mother spoke with Father Isidro yesterday. The church keeps genealogical records on prominent families. Father Isidro had very little on hers." Holding up his hand to silence his son, don Ignacio's voice sank to a whisper. "Little, but not nothing."

He rose and turned to face the balcony again. Turning suddenly to his son he said, "It's Consuelo's mother. Understand?"

Pablo's confusion tripped on itself. "She died three years ago."

"You remember her, the nose, lips; undeniably African."

"She was beautiful. People can't all look like Swedes."

Returning his gaze to the bay, don Ignacio sucked hard on his cigar and blew out a massive cloud of smoke. "You will not degrade my posterity. Understand?"

Pablo recalled his mother bragging about his blonde hair and blue eyes. "What about the Moors? They occupied Spain for centuries."

"Never Asturias!" Don Ignacio strained to remain calm.

"Are you sure none of them sneaked in for a little fun?"

"Don't skirt the issue."

"There's no issue, Papá. I don't care about all that." He stood as if to leave, though only out of exasperation.

Standing to his full height, don Ignacio looked down at his son, pointing with his chin and speaking through clenched teeth. "Have you no regard for our family? After all I've done for you. Do you have any idea what your education cost?"

"Sure."

"I won't have it, understand? I need you at work, giving it your best effort."

"You make me feel like a traitor."

"You're courting treason."

"After all your talk about ending slavery, you really hate them."

"Not true. We owned slaves, and we worked hard to free them at great cost. But not hating them does not mean I'll tolerate them in my blood. Understand?"

"You're a racist!"

"Remember who you're talking to!" Don Ignacio paced to the balcony and back. "All that out there could be yours. Understand? My father came here with nothing and built a business. I raised it to the largest in Cuba through determination, hard work, and self-denial. I will not turn it over to a ..." Don Ignacio paused a moment. "To a dimwit who follows any skirt who wags her lure before him. Of course she's attractive. Fine! Get her an apartment; have her, but no marriage! Understand?"

"Is that what you do, Papá?"

"Of course. I'm a man."

"So it's all right to make babies as long as they don't carry your name?"

Pablo recalled an evening when he was a child, trying to make conversation at supper. "How big is our cane farm, Papá?" he had asked, hoping to bring him out of his silence.

His father had looked up out of his thoughts. "Very big, son. One day I'll take you around it." Then he had returned as if to a meditation.

Many years had passed before Pablo realized that other married couples did not have separate bedrooms. Of course, he thought. Women are commodities, like money and power, to provide a service. No wonder Mamá's the way she is.

"You're a hypocrite, Papá."

"And you're wasting your birthright on a woman." Don Ignacio waved his arms out the window expansively. "Take a good look at the stakes."

"What are you saying?"

"Simply this: marry her and you'll no longer be my heir. Understand?"

"You can't disown your only son."

"Can't I?" Don Ignacio stared into his son's eyes.

Searching his father's countenance for an atom of regret or doubt, he saw only hardened steel.

Turning to face the sea again, don Ignacio said, "You have my terms."

"You bastard; you and your terms can go to hell!" Pablo dropped his cigar on the ashtray, turned and walked out of his father's life.

*

Pablo spent the next day wandering around Matanzas, driving up one street and down the other and finally headed to the beach and then into the hills with his arms and legs disconnected from his brain, wondering what to do and how to tell Consuelo: We could wait for a while, I suppose. Maybe Papá will change his mind. But he would always be pulling the strings; I'd dangle forever.

He stopped at the tavern of an old friend for lunch, but his friend was not in, so he ate alone and drove off. With a full stomach and an empty heart he drove leisurely through the lush country, as gray memories rose out of the dusty past: of remaining with his mother in Havana when don Ignacio moved to the sugarcane plantation in Matanzas. Pablo knew his father did not have to run the business from its hub, as he had said. Then, when the new home in Matanzas was completed, his absences became longer and more frequent. Pablo wanted so much to move with him, but his mother would not allow it. She had insisted he stay in Havana to attend the American School.

"To speak English well," she had said. "To raise you above the masses."

Pablo smiled recalling the panic of that morning on his way to his first day in school: "But I don't understand English, Mamá."

"Neither does anyone else. Have faith."

Señorita Dolores was sitting at her desk when he walked in her room. In Spanish she asked the students to line up along the walls. One by one she called the name of each boy on her roll and assigned him a seat. So far so good, Pablo thought, hearing her speak Spanish. His desk was by a window on the second row. When his cousin Benito took the seat next to Pablo, they both giggled.

When all were seated, Señorita Dolores began: "Good morning, boys. *Repiten*: Good morning, Miss Dolores." *Otra vez*, "Good morning, Miss Dolores."

The boys were surprised and delighted. They answered feebly at first, then loudly. She was good at finding cognates. The boys had understood everything she said. For the rest of the day they talked to each other in their strange new language.

7

Finally recess, when Pablo spotted the pretty little girl. She was standing in the shade of a large cedar with the fingers of one hand clutching the iron fence that separated the girls' school from the boys'. In her other hand she held a paper bag. She smiled beautifully at Pablo and he walked over.

"Good morning. My name is Consuelo. What is your name?" She had her face pressed through the fence and still held the bar.

His voice came out in a whisper. "Pablo."

"How are you, Pablo?"

Pablo felt stupid, but he answered, "Bery well," and laughed.

Consuelo took a cookie out of the paper bag and offered it. "Cookie?"

"*Gracias.*"

"English, please." She smiled, holding the cookie out of his reach.

When Pablo said, "Thank you," she handed him the cookie and they both smiled as he took a bite. When Benito came up Pablo pushed him away, but Consuelo was already holding a cookie through the fence. "In English, please," she said. Pablo walked to a bench under the large tree to sulk. All the while Consuelo and Benito talked her eyes sought Pablo's. Pablo had no idea how attracted he would become to the cute little brown-haired, green-eyed girl.

That afternoon Consuelo told Pablo that her father had brought her to school that first day and that he owned a sugar cane farm near Matanzas. Pablo had heard of him and knew he was not as rich as don Ignacio. The two men had known each other most of their lives.

His father and Consuelo's had been friends. Her father had come from Asturias as had don Ignacio's father. Twice don Ignacio had tried to buy González's farm. Pablo could not comprehend his father holding a grudge over that, but he knew they were not close.

Pablo always liked Consuelo's parents. His father's recent accusation had never occurred to him. And who would not love her, he thought, the way she throws herself into life.

Because Consuelo lived in a modest home near Pablo's, they played after school most days. Pablo soon realized that she enjoyed pitting Benito and Pablo against each other. By the time they finished high school, it was clear that Pablo had won her. Benito liked her too, but he soon realized she was in love with Pablo and gave up. Pablo and Consuelo could not have said when they fell in love, for it had grown gently, like a flower opening its petals, from children pushing and laughing to sweethearts holding hands on their way to school.

His ruminations had led Pablo to a high ledge overlooking the Caribbean. It was a favorite spot when he had to think or when he did not want to think.

Things could be so good for us, he thought. Her father wanted her to become a teacher. Her mother was more pragmatic, envisioning Consuelo, wrapped in the delicate silk of a fine education, marrying a young man from one of Havana's leading families, like me. It has all happened, but somehow the scene has turned ugly.

Then there was the day he received his acceptance to Notre Dame: He ran to Consuelo's house before he told his mother. Too excited to ring the doorbell, he knocked on the door and kept knocking until she opened.

"Look," he said, out of breath and holding the letter. "I'm in!"

She smiled and said nothing. He thought she would be happy, but her face revealed something else. She led him to a chair on the front porch and sat beside him.

"Please," he said. "Now you'll have to apply to Saint Mary's so we can be in the same town."

"It's no use. They don't even accept Florida State, where my cousin is. 'It's not what good girls do,' they say."

Pablo knew she had argued with her parents and had told them they were old-fashioned and that women should be as educated as men, but they would not budge. In a whisper, she said, "Don't tell, but I applied anyway."

"But Florida's too far," he said. "At least try."

"Honest, Pablo. I have."

The following week her letter came. "Florida State College for Women, Admissions Office," she said aloud. Trembling, Consuelo ripped it open and found an acceptance and a music scholarship. Señorita Teresa, bless her heart, Consuelo thought. What a letter she must have written!

Armed with her cousin's precedent and a scholarship, she amassed all her powers of persuasion and waited until after supper that evening. When the maid came to clear the table, they moved to the living room, a bright room with a large window opening to the terrace. Consuelo's father walked her mother out and placed a cushion behind her as she sat down.

"Are you comfortable, Carmen?" he asked.

"Yes," she said, picking up her embroidery hoop and needle. Juan González took his place in his high-backed wing chair and lit a cigar.

Consuelo told them of Pablo's acceptance to Notre Dame to assure them they would not be together. They talked most of the evening. Her mother would occasionally stop sewing and lay her head back to rest.

Once she asked Consuelo to bring her a glass of water. "Would you prefer juice?"

"No, thank you, dear," she said, continuing her embroidery. Consuelo disliked pressuring her, knowing how bad she felt, but she plunged ahead. She showed them the letter and talked of Señorita Teresa's faith in her. She told them the courses she would take and how many hours she would be spending at the piano. As usual, Juan said little except to ask a question now and then. Most of the time he listened with wrinkled brow and chewed on his cigar. Consuelo knew he was imagining problems his daughter would face in a strange country.

After two hours of questions and comments that revealed serious misgivings, Consuelo was beginning to weaken, watching her mother sewing with such labor. Her full lips and nose harmonized with her wavy, black hair, and her emerald eyes seemed to droop from long suffering. Thin and emaciated, Carmen looked tired and frail. Consuelo looked into her eyes trying to remember the exotic beauty of an earlier time. Carmen must have seen Consuelo's determination crumbling into disappointment, because she unexpectedly laid down the hoop and needle.

"After all, Juan, it is a woman's college. We must remember she is our daughter and we have taught her well; she knows right from wrong."

Hearing that, Juan simply gave up, smiled, and congratulated her. Consuelo rushed to embrace him and then her mother, saying, "I'll make you both proud. I will. I will."

"We already are," Carmen said. Consuelo felt she loved them more that moment than she ever had. She was an adult and they understood.

*

For the next four years, letters flew between the two sweethearts like threads on a loom. With things said in letters that would not be said aloud, absence wove its magic. Carmen's sudden death after Consuelo's first year in Tallahassee threw Consuelo into depression. Her mother had always been sickly, but Consuelo was not prepared and felt guilty for leaving her. Calmly sitting with her father one evening a week after the funeral, she announced solemnly that she would stay home in the Fall.

"That's a generous offer, but unnecessary; I'll manage. I still have the business to entertain me."

"I've decided, Papá."

"I've never denied you, until now."

"It's what I want, Papá. I need time."

"Death is the most natural thing in life. We deal with it by living, not by stopping our lives. I'm only fifty. You treat me as if I were a rickety old man, *un viejo chochando*."

Consuelo waited until the last day before deciding. Pablo spent nearly all his time with her that summer. Seeing her so troubled and knowing she truly wanted to finish school, he encouraged her to go. "We'll finish together and then get married."

For the rest of the summer vacation they were inseparable, to the pleasure of Juan González and the anguish of Ignacio and Inez Iglesias. Doña Inez made her displeasure clear from the beginning. Ignacio guarded his opinion as an experienced tactician; that is, until the night he confronted his son.

*

Small ripples lapped their feet as they walked. Neither noticed that the green water of Varadero Beach was losing its hue as the sun drained into the horizon behind them. A bird flew high overhead, effortlessly, in a long, graceful spiral, as if relaxing before retiring. Pablo's white trousers were rolled up to his knees, and his tie was pulled loose and his collar unbuttoned. Consuelo's light blue blouse felt loose. The mild breeze would occasionally ruffle it and balloon out her white pleated skirt. Both of them looked down as they walked, stepping around the large, sharp shells that could cut their feet. Matanzas loomed in the distance to the west, to the north only water and America.

"I can't," he said.

"But it's the highlight of his life."

Pablo said nothing.

"Don't they approve of me?" Her lip trembled.

"My father's from another century, a tyrant to the bone."

"Please, Pablo."

Pablo continued several steps, knowing he could not keep it from her. "I know it's stupid, but he thinks … that you have Negro blood." Regretting the words as they spilled past his lips, he wanted to reach down to the water and wash them away.

"I thought so," she said calmly.

"I love you and all your ancestors."

They walked quietly for a long time. Finally Consuelo stopped, looked directly at him. "I was afraid to tell you."

"You don't have to." He wanted her to know how angry he was at his father, but he was confused. His father had planted the dark seed in his brain, and now the thought of corrupting his lineage was growing like a tumor.

Consuelo began: "My mother's grandfather owned slaves. He was from Asturias like your grandparents. The cane farm we have was originally his. With his Spanish wife he had three sons, all born here. He also had a daughter with a mulatto slave, who died giving birth to my grandmother. My great-grandfather's wife felt terrible for the mother. She didn't know the baby was her husband's. They named the baby Clarita because of her light skin, and they eventually adopted her.

"When his wife died, my great-grandfather told Clarita the whole story. Clarita wanted to know all about her mother, and he obliged. He told her that her mother was beautiful with large brown eyes and that she was half white. When I was a child, Clarita told me it was the most wonderful day of her life.

"Clarita had a music box that played a Strauss waltz. I'd lift the lid and start the music, and we would dance. I remember sitting and talking on our swing, while she peeled oranges for me. Sometimes she would sing to me in the most mellow, alto voice. She was the one who sparked my interest in music. She loved her father, but she spoke very lovingly about the mother she never knew. Clarita married an Asturian her father brought from Spain and bore him five girls. My mother was the youngest and the only one that looks even the least bit African. I was eleven when Clarita died."

"I never noticed it," Pablo said. Throughout her story, he drank in the beautiful olive-skinned, fine-featured woman with bobbed light brown hair and long slim neck. She was white in every detail and alive in every gesture. When he looked into her green eyes he felt he would fall into a bottomless spring. Pablo stopped and embraced her.

"Thank you, Consuelo. They were good people. What more can we expect of our ancestors?"

After a long embrace with the warm incoming tide caressing their feet, he said, "I'll talk with Father Isidro. He owes me. We'll have a simple wedding for your family and a few close friends."

"What'll I tell my father?" But before he could answer, she stopped him. "I know; the truth."

"He'll guess anyway, and it's better to admit it. Then we'll move to Florida. Benito's there. You'll like Tampa; it's full of Cubans. I'll find work and we'll live our own lives."

"Tampa?"

"He's disowned me."

"He hates me that much?"

"Not you; it's … No matter. I don't want to face questions and insinuations. He'd make our lives miserable. You liked Tallahassee. Tampa's bigger and better. You'll love it."

"What about your mother?"

"She wouldn't approve if I married the queen of Spain."

Consuelo looked down at the water for a long time. "We'll call it off."

"Because of the money?"

"You know better than that, but you can't just throw it away. We'll wait. In time he'll change his mind." She began to cry. "I love you, Pablo. That's why I can't marry you. You'd end up hating me."

"It's you I love, not his money. I wouldn't accept the old bastard's generosity now if he came crawling. No. I'm leaving, and you're coming with me."

Consuelo looked into his eyes and saw more ambivalence than determination. "Why don't we wait a few days?"

"What for?"

"All right."

*

The furniture in Consuelo's Matanzas home was classic Spanish – heavy wood with aged gold cushions and several tables and lamps. Juan González was born in Matanzas and had always preferred it to the house in Havana where they moved when Consuelo started school. When Carmen died, Juan moved back. The chandelier was a wedding present from a friend of his: wrought iron with small light bulbs that look like candles. A carved wooden-railed staircase led to the second floor with three bedrooms and bath. Beyond the stairs on the first floor was a formal dining room and beyond that a kitchen. Sandwiched into a city block, the house was long and narrow with the only windows in the front and back walls. Consuelo never got used to a bedroom with no windows. That's why she preferred the bright, white kitchen that opened onto a small, walled-in terrace filled with flowers, a small lawn, and banana trees in the rear. That small garden had been the center of her life, especially when Clarita had lived with them.

During supper, Juan González said little, waiting for Consuelo to reveal the wedding details in her own time.

After finishing their soup, she said, "We want a small wedding, just you and our closest relatives and one or two friends."

"I thought you wanted a big wedding with music," he said.

"He doesn't want a big fuss."

"Pablo?" Juan asked.

"No, we …" But it was too late to cover up her blunder.

Her eyes filled when his face drooped.

"Don't worry, Consuelito. I had the same problem, but my parents came around. You know how they loved your mother."

"Not this one. He's disowned Pablo."

"The old tyrant! Fine, then! A smaller wedding means a bigger wedding present."

"You're wonderful, Papá, but I've saved the worst for last. Pablo wants to move to Tampa, Florida. His cousin Benito lives there."

Knowing her father, she expected strong objections.

"That's just a few hours by ship, Consuelito. I'll come up every chance I get."

"I feel terrible leaving you; like when Mamá died."

"Just another part of life, Consuelito; quite natural. But you will always be here." He put his hand on his heart.

Consuelo stood and hugged him.

"Wasn't your old college roommate, Lizzy what's-her-name, from Tampa?"

"Yes. It'll be good to see her again."

*

To ensure the privacy Pablo requested, Father Isidro arranged the ceremony in a small, side chapel in the Cathedral. With bare, windowless, stone walls and high ceiling, the room reeked of old world gloom. Even the flowers adorning the small altar and Consuelo in her mother's white wedding gown could not brighten the darkness in their hearts.

When the ceremony ended and the small party moved out of the chapel, Consuelo said, "Pablo, I'd like to stay a few minutes. Do you mind?"

"What is it?"

"I just want to talk with Father Isidro."

"I'll go with you."

"No. I'll just be a minute."

Pablo walked out to talk with the others and Consuelo went inside.

"Father, I'm worried. You know Pablo's parents opposed our wedding. They wouldn't even come."

"Yes, my child."

"Will you give me a special benediction?"

"But I've already done that."

"Please, Father. I'm afraid."

"Of course." After performing his blessing he said, "Don't worry, Consuelo. Pablo's parents are very strong people. But you must follow your heart without fear." After thinking a moment he said, "You won't repeat what I've said, will you?"

"No, Father, and thank you."

That evening, sitting on the balcony of their room in the Hotel Inglaterra overlooking the Prado and El Malecón in the distance, Consuelo could not shake off the heavy feeling in her breast. "To our new lives together," she said, raising a glass of champagne. "May it last forever."

They did not speak of his parents.

*

His mother looked stern when she walked in on him three days later. With the shades up, light flooded the large bedroom. Pablo had shoes lined up along the floor near the bed, and stacks of clothes and two half-filled suitcases lay on the large bed. "I assume these are still mine?" he said, continuing to pack.

Doña Inez always dressed well and weighed herself down with sparkling diamonds on her neck, wrists, and fingers. That morning, wearing a black satin dress, she seemed wrapped in an air of indignant resignation. "How dare you talk to your father that way?"

Pablo did not answer.

"You'll stay and do what he says."

Familiar with her aloof commands, Pablo ignored her and kept packing. Doña Inez was a handsome woman if not beautiful. With rosy-white complexion, which she protected from the sun, and fiery hazel eyes, she would be considered attractive anywhere, but in the tropics she stood out as a Nordic beauty. She glared, trying to appear threatening.

"Sorry you didn't make the wedding," he said.

"I didn't feel welcome."

"You had no right to go to Father Isidro," he said, standing to look at her. "How dare he spread such gossip?"

"He's afraid of your father."

"*Que maricón!*"

"What horrible language to use with your mother! Don't you want to know who you're marrying?"

He said nothing and bent over again and laid two shirts over a layer of underwear.

"What will become of me, Pablito?"

"You've got Papá."

"You belong here with me."

"I belong with my wife."

"How cold and ungrateful!"

"What's wrong with getting married? It's normal."

"Abstinence is more normal and more healthy. It's the way of Our Lord."

"Shouldn't we use His gifts?"

"Use, indeed!" she said. "How revealing. God's gifts are not to be used; they are for creation, not recreation. Young people today live for one thing only."

"We're in love."

"You're in heat. All she wants is your money."

"You've forgotten, Mamá. Papá decided to take it with him."

"You're used to high living, Pablito."

"I'll be fine."

"Don't make me ill. We didn't have to spend all our time in bed proving our love. Your father's a decent man, content with a celibate life."

Pablo stood shocked, as she turned to the window with icy composure. In that pose her makeup stood out like paint on a statue. Her painted eyelashes reinforced a hardness Pablo had seen many times. Papá had mistresses, he thought. His father's infidelity now took a different shade: Poor Papá twisting his life to fit a wife's warped morality. Her candor and cruelty seem normal, yet different. She had always pampered him, going to extremes to satisfy his childish whims. But he could recall other times: yanking him away from a little girl he was playing with, and surreptitiously pinching his tiny arm because he asked for candy and people were looking. With a heavy foot she had cleared his path of every flower, pulling him by the hand. For the first time in years Pablo recalled a recurrent dream in which he was drowning.

"Mamá, I can't touch bottom."

"I can accept your lavish life style, but I cannot forgive squandering your life on that woman. After giving you everything, this is my reward."

"Consuelo's a nice girl; I'd never find a better wife."

"The Blessed Virgin should be your model."

After a long silence he said, "Really, Mamá, why don't you like her? She wants to love you."

"I don't need her love, and neither do you."

Her gaze twisted her face into a dark caricature of seduction. Pablo shuddered. Feeling like a little boy he turned away, put another shirt into his suitcase, and then stood again.

"Do you remember the day I was born?"

"How can a mother forget the birth of her only child? It was horrible."

"I thought having a baby was supposed to be wonderful."

"I was only seventeen and terribly confused when the pains woke me. By noon I thought I was dying. I had no idea what was happening. I panicked. If my mother had not been there, I would have died." Tears ran down her shallow cheeks. "I knew God had inflicted that pain for a reason. I promised Him I would forsake all worldly pleasures and devote my life to you."

"Why, for heaven's sake?"

"I didn't know how ungrateful you would turn out."

After a long silence trying to decide if he should ask, "Is it true you didn't marry Papá until afterwards?"

"Who told you that?"

"It's a simple question."

"I resent the insinuation."

"Then it's true?"

"It's not what you think. I didn't even know how it happened."

"Don't tell me it was a miracle."

Her face twisted into rage.

"Such an old trick, Mamá, so unworthy. When I overheard that story years ago, I didn't believe it." After a few moments he asked another question that had always bothered him, "Is Papá my father?"

"You filthy good-for-nothing!" She rose as if to leave, then stopped. "You're a mule like him."

"I don't mean to hurt you, Mamá. I just don't understand your hatred."

"Some day you'll understand my love," she said. She paced to the window and back, watching him pack. "How do you expect to live?"

"With my savings and a generous wedding present from Consuelo's father. We'll be fine until I can find a job."

"What about me?" she asked sobbing. After a few moments she regained her composure. Feeling sorry for her Pablo embraced her.

"Your father is not a bad man, but he's hard, often even cruel. Don't be like him, Pablito. Stay."

"It wouldn't work, Mamá. Maybe I am like him."

"What will you do?"

He smiled and embraced her again. "I'll stay in touch," he said and kept packing.

She said no more and left the room.

*

As they approached the gangplank, Pablo felt a tug at his sleeve. It was his mother. "Take this," she said, pulling him out of the line and handing him an envelope.

"I'm glad you came, Mamá. What is it?"

"What do you think? And it's from me, not your father. My father left me well fixed. He didn't want me to be dependent on such a hard man. I think you're making a grave mistake, but I can't stand by and see my baby boy starve."

He embraced her and said, "Come, say goodbye to Consuelo."

Without answering she walked away.

"Please, Mamá," he said, trying to hold her, but she was gone.

A warm breeze blew across the bright afternoon when the gangplank lifted with a band playing and people waving and shouting to family members and friends. Standing at the railing in a neatly pressed white linen suit, Pablo held Consuelo's hand. As if to assure a bright beginning, she wore a white dress that modestly revealed a lovely figure. They waved goodbye to her father on the dock. As the ship disengaged and slowly drifted into Havana Harbor, Pablo spotted his mother at the edge of the crowd. Standing erect, she was holding her broad brimmed blue hat against the breeze, and her cheeks were wet with tears. Pablo and Consuelo smiled and waved and squeezed each other's hand. Looking into Consuelo's eyes, Pablo saw only sadness. He knew she would follow her husband as any good Cuban wife would; his fortune would be her fortune; his destiny would be her destiny. With her clothes, personal possessions, dishes, and all the other things she thought they would need, she was ready for a new life. Pablo submerged his anger and, with the will that he inherited from his father, resolved to succeed.

As the ship sliced its way through the calm water, Pablo and Consuelo strolled to the other side of the ship for a last view of the magnificent Morro Castle as it shrank into a tiny speck. The bustling city, which an hour before was all they could see, now came into focus as a comprehensible unity and then gradually receded into a silent gray smudge on the long green coast. As the afternoon swelled, a white mist swallowed their homeland, and the turbulent waters of the Florida Strait heaved them toward their new shore.

2 - YBOR CITY – THE NEXT DAY

*

Buying Wave Sweeps U.S. Markets

*

Source Of Radium Rays Discovered At 'Heart' Of Atom

*

Japan Determined To Keep Troops In Manchuria

*

Exhausted Reichsbank Outlines Debt Policy

*

Benito Iglesias met their ship at Port Tampa with his Model-T touring car and drove Pablo and Consuelo the ten miles to his home in Ybor City. On the way he showed them the main business district of Tampa. Benito talked with excitement about home. "How's the depression there?"

"Hard to tell," Pablo said.

"That's the Courthouse. Isn't it beautiful?" Benito slowed as he passed a typical southern courthouse square with a statue of a Civil War soldier and another of a World War I soldier. Sidewalks crossed the lawn in imitation of the Confederate flag, and sable palms added to the southern charm. Benito's comments tripped over each other.

"Really glad you're here, Pablo; and you too, Consuelo. You haven't changed since first grade: pretty as ever. You'll love Sara. She's a joker;

you never know what she'll say. Tell me about Matanzas. It's been two years since Papá's funeral. How are Tía Inez and Tío Ignacio? They never show their age. Good stock, those Asturians."

Leaving the main downtown area, they passed a huge cylindrical tank behind the railroad station.

"Supplies gas for the whole city. Now we're in Ybor City. Fourteenth is one of the main streets. The Cuban Club is two blocks up, but we'll see that later. This is La Septima. It's the main drag."

To Pablo and Consuelo, Ybor City looked more Cuban than American. They passed restaurants, cafés, a drug store, a grocery store, a barbershop, several clothing stores, hardware stores, doctor's offices and gambling houses along Seventh Avenue. Benito pointed them out as they passed. Most had signs in Spanish.

"Look! *La Placita Cubana*," Pablo said with a laugh, "Tropical fruits! Could be San Rafael Street in Havana."

"What's that?" Consuelo asked, pointing at the massive, red brick building.

"El Centro Español," Benito said. "For the Spaniards, like the Circulo Cubano. There's also El Centro Asturiano and L'Unione Italiana. Each one has a clinic, pharmacy, library, bar and game room, and they give picnics and dances. They're the centers of Ybor City life."

"Why is there a Cuban town in the middle of an American city?" Consuelo asked.

"Cigars," Benito said. "In the late 1800s a man named Martinez-Ybor came here, built a cigar factory and a bunch of houses for his workers, and Tampa erupted like an exploding cigar." He laughed loudly.

"But why Tampa?" Consuelo asked.

"First they tried Key West to avoid the Ten Years War, but labor troubles drove them out. Our weather's like Cuba's, good for working tobacco."

"Is Ybor City part of Tampa?" Pablo asked.

"Sure. It's a barrio east of town bordering the bay. To the north and east there's nothing but pines and palmettos. When a few hundred Cubans and a handful of Spaniards got here forty-some years ago Tampa was a Cracker village. Before long, Sicilians started coming. At first, the Latins outnumbered the Crackers, but now we're only about a third. Did you know that Tampa produces more cigars than Cuba?"

"You like Ybor City," Consuelo said.

"Yes, and so will you."

By this time Benito pulled up to the curb in front of a large frame house several blocks north of Seventh Avenue and honked his horn. The son of doña Inez's brother, Benito was Pablo's first cousin and the same age as Pablo. Moved by a spirit of adventure, he had come to Florida to make his fortune instead of attending the university. He and Pablo looked like brothers, both Nordic in appearance. Stocky and sporting a thin brown moustache, Benito was still chattering when he hopped up to his front porch, where Sara was waiting.

Sara wiped her hands on her apron and reached out to kiss each on the cheek. "I've got Cuban rum waiting," she said. "Come in, please." The living room was bright and cheerful with large windows and light colored, stuffed furniture with sedate, floral cushions. The windows were all open, and an oscillating fan on a small table moved the mass of warm air around the room like vaporous molasses. Leading them into the kitchen she poured out her pleasure at meeting them as she handed each a drink. Here too, a fan hummed. "Sara's parents moved here just before she was born. She's a native American," Benito said.

"And proud of it," she said.

"But you sound like a Cuban," Consuelo said.

"Of course. I didn't learn English until I went to school. I met Benito at a Cuban Club dance. It only took a year to trap him. A man in his business always brings home the bacon."

"I keep my little chicken well fed," he said, patting her ample fanny.

"Finish your drink, Romeo," she said.

"Where's Gene?" Benito asked.

"Asleep, but he wakes up with a bang. You'll hear him."

When they had finished their drinks Consuelo said, "How about a walk before it gets dark. I'd like to see more of Ybor City."

"Great!" Benito said.

Sara walked them to the front door and said, "Supper's at seven."

"We're taking you out," Pablo said, over his shoulder.

"Nonsense. Now scram and be back by seven."

Benito led Pablo and Consuelo along Twelfth Avenue to the corner, where they turned right five blocks, through streets lined with houses and occasional stores. It was difficult to walk along Seventh Avenue as people stopped to talk and blocked the sidewalks. Cars parked along the curb and two sets of trolley tracks left little choice for automobiles except to follow the trolley cars. Cars honked their horns at other cars or at pedestrians or simply to proclaim their presence; rumba music blared out of shops, and La Septima throbbed. People walked in and out of stores, spilled onto the street, dodged cars and trucks. Trolley cars clanged along steel tracks, ringing their warning bells. Street vendors yelled out their goods: devil crabs, candies, fritters, fried green plantains, boiled tripe and kidneys.

People hung over their second-floor balconies watching the passing scene. A woman shook out a small rug as the newcomers passed underneath; two others talked across the street from one apartment to the other. Cafés and restaurants, coffee mills, and bakeries emitted a medley of scents that enveloped the newcomers.

"Isn't it great?" Benito said, smiling.

Inside the large window of Las Novedades Restaurant a large man with thick black hair sliced ham off a leg for Cuban sandwiches. With the grace of an artist, the man stopped to stroke the long, narrow knife on his steel as he smiled through the window at Consuelo.

Benito said, "He's a Spaniard. Learned that slicing baloney."

Inside, the roar of the crowd was deafening. Waiters rushed past them carrying plates stacked along their arms or taking orders and then yelling them to the men behind the bar.

"There's a table near the bar," Benito said. As they worked their way back, Pablo and Consuelo smiled at the bustle. It was as if they had never left home.

"Doesn't anybody here speak English?" Pablo asked.

"Even some natives don't," Benito said.

After a long wait, the waiter stopped at their table and stood scowling, obviously impatient. Benito asked for three small glasses of orange juice. The man shrugged in disgust and walked off. He returned in less than a minute with the juice, and Pablo and Consuelo drank chuckling at the grouchy waiter.

"We're lucky he didn't pour it in our laps," Benito said.

Before leaving, Benito bought some Spanish sweets, and they resumed their stroll, in and out of the narrow side streets, talking and window-shopping. Automobiles inched along, blowing their horns at the slightest provocation, dodging trolley cars and pedestrians. As they turned into Fourteenth Street toward Eighth Avenue, they passed a gambling casino. It was a small store with a counter along the back wall that had numbers painted on the surface and a roulette wheel on the wall at one end. "They throw bolita here," Benito said. "It's a lottery. Watch. The proprietor puts those numbered balls in the bag and ties the opening. Now he shakes the bag and tosses it back and forth and into the audience." When the tossing had gone on for a minute, the bag flew back to the proprietor who caught it by one of the balls and held it as his assistant cut that ball out of the bag. When the ball was free, the proprietor called out the winning number. A large woman jumped up shouting, "I got it! I got it!" and pushed her way to the front to collect.

"A good place to lose your salary," Consuelo said.

"As my mother said, gambling expresses '*La esperanza del pobre.*'" Benito said. "The hope of the poor. We hear the Cuban lottery too, every Saturday at 2:00. The radio screams it out of every house in Ybor City. It can drive you nuts."

"I saw it once in Havana," Consuelo said. "One young boy yelling out a number, and another yelling out the prize."

"Here, you make your bet with the neighborhood bolitero, the numbers peddler."

Pablo laughed as they walked around that block to Seventh Avenue. "Come, I want to show you the Ritz Theater. I love the long, semi-dark entry hall. By the time you get to the movie, your eyes are used to the dark.

"Reminds me of a cave I saw once," Pablo said. "It had no end or bottom."

He had stared into the dark passage for several seconds when the usher looked at him quizzically and Pablo turned. From there they crossed Seventh Avenue to see what was playing at the Casino Theater in the Centro Español on the next corner. "The Centro uses it mostly for movies now," Benito said. They crossed Seventh Avenue several times to look at store windows, mostly clothing stores. In front of Kress Department Store a man sold devil crabs out of the white box on his bicycle handlebars. The middle-aged man, neatly dressed in white and wearing white gloves, picked up one of his deep fried crab croquets with his tongs. He placed it into a piece of waxed paper in his other hand, cut a gash along the length with the tongs, and squirted hot sauce into it from a small bottle. When he handed it to the woman, she took a monstrous bite as she handed him a nickel.

"The odor's enough to drive me crazy," Consuelo said.

"His name is Miranda. His devil crabs are the best!" Benito said. "I wish we weren't eating so soon. Try one sometime. He's always here."

As they passed the stately L'Unione Italiana, they heard two men conversing in Sicilian. "I can make out an occasional word," Benito said, as they continued on.

"Where's the Catholic church?" Consuelo asked.

"Our Lady of Perpetual Help; the kids call it OLPH. It's right down the street on the way home." Benito led them to the large, simple brick church. "It's not fancy, but you'll like it. The pastor's a Spaniard, but he's OK."

When they walked into the church Consuelo genuflected, made the sign of the cross, and knelt in a pew while Pablo and Benito walked around. When they had seen enough, Pablo motioned to Consuelo and they left. "What were you praying for?" Pablo asked.

"Happiness."

Lazily, they wound their way home, where Sara was waiting on the front porch. "It's about time!" she said. "Supper's ready." They took their places in the dining room as Sara prepared each plate. She scooped a large pile of rice that covered the plate and then laid slabs of pork roasted with garlic and oregano on top of the rice and beside that, also on the rice, thick slices of fried ripe plantains. On smaller plates she arranged tomato slices with onion rings and olives over them and then doused them with olive oil and a little vinegar. Finally she brought out a large platter stacked with chunks of Cuban bread cut into small pieces and a smaller dish with a large dollop of room temperature butter.

The dining table seated six. Along the outside wall, two large windows facing similar windows next door seemed to compete for air. Gene's high chair was pulled up to the table where he sat smiling and stuffing his mouth with hands full of whatever was on his plate.

"How old is he?" Consuelo asked.

"Almost two," Sara said. "I can't wait for him to talk. All he does now is point and grunt." At that Gene looked at his mother, smiled, and grunted.

When they had eaten their fill they sat and talked. Finally, Sara brought a large flan out of the icebox. "Is there anyone who doesn't like flan?" she asked. Pablo rubbed his belly and held up one hand as if refusing, and then took two helpings. After supper Pablo and Benito retired to the porch with glasses of Spanish brandy and Cuban cigars while their wives washed and dried the dishes. Benito rocked his son in his lap. Soon the women joined their husbands, and the foursome spent the rest of the evening chatting and watching fireflies. Occasionally a passerby would interrupt them with the familiar," *Adiós.*"

"*Adiós,*" Sara said.

"It'll be back to normal before the end of the year," Benito said.

"I agree," Pablo said.

"It better," Sara said. More than anything else, the short, chubby young woman with the short, wavy coal-black hair and piercing, deep brown eyes liked straight talk. Her strong speech was buttressed with strong neck, legs, and arms and an ample chest. She had a solid way of walking; instead of the usual delicate, feminine swaying, her stride was muscular and determined in a way that was uncannily attractive. While they talked, she leaned over the railing and yelled out, "*Oye, Manolito!* Your mother will kill you if you don't get home. She's probably crazy looking for you." The boy frowned and slowly walked home, not daring to defy such authority. Returning to her chair she continued rocking and fanning herself with a newspaper, stopping only when a neighbor passed. "How's your husband?"

"The same," the passing woman said, rocking her open hand.

"Say hello for me," Sara said, as the woman walked past. With most neighbors that passed she started a conversation. It was not enough merely to say, "*Adiós*," as everyone else did.

Tired of the talk about the depression, her curiosity erupted: "Benito says your father owns most of the cane in Cuba. Why would you come to Tampa?" She stopped rocking and looked into Pablo's eyes for his answer.

"We wanted some adventure," Pablo said, nonchalantly. Consuelo was praying he would not mention his father's opposition to the wedding.

"I hear you and Tío Ignacio had a fight," Benito said. Seeing Pablo's shocked expression Bentio added, "Your mother wrote."

"I wouldn't call it a fight. You know Mamá. What did she say?"

"Just that. She didn't say why," Benito said.

Pablo hesitated. "It's personal."

"Then you're staying?" Sara asked.

"If we like it," Pablo said.

"What'll you do?" Sara was not ready to drop her inquiry.

"Find a job."

Pablo's curt answers only fueled their curiosity. Sara stopped her questioning when Benito gave her a stern look. "I'm sure you'll find something," Benito said. "It's tough, though."

"How'd you get started?" Consuelo asked.

"The land boom was at its peak; people weren't afraid to spend money."

"Still with the food distributor?" Pablo asked.

"You bet. I didn't like it at first, but people always have to eat."

Sara took Gene inside. "It's this little man's bedtime," she said.

"What about the factories?" Pablo asked.

"That's where I'd start," Benito said. They sat for a while saying nothing, drawing on their cigars and sipping their brandy.

"The first thing we need is a house," Consuelo said.

"You came to the right place," Benito said. "Sara knows everybody and everything in Ybor City."

"You bet," Sara said as she returned and took her seat. There's a house for rent on the next block. Amparo Cuervo's husband died last year and she's living with her parents."

"How's the rent?" Consuelo asked.

"We pay five dollars a week; I think Amparo wants the same. It's cheaper near La Septima, but you're better off here. La Septima's noisy, and you won't like those cigar box houses. Tell her I sent you."

The next day, after helping Sara with breakfast and the dishes, Consuelo left to check on the house. She walked up the steps of a bungalow one block east of Benito's house. "My husband and I are looking for a house to rent. Sara Iglesias sent me here."

"Sara's a jewel. Sure. Four-fifty a week furnished as is."

"When can we move in?"

"It's ready. Anytime you want."

"May I look around?"

"Sure." The woman took her into every room and explained that the house was only ten years old. "It's in very good shape."

After a few minutes, Consuelo agreed and gave the woman a month's rent in advance and took the keys.

That afternoon, she took Pablo to see the house. It was identical to Benito's. The porch had a swing, several rocking chairs, a table, and various clay pots of geraniums on the stubby, square brick columns that held a heavy wooden railing around the porch. The front door opened into the living room with large windows facing the porch and the narrow side yard. Sandwiched in between the house and the neighbor's stood a lush mango tree. Beige cushions filled a white wicker sofa and two chairs. A door on the left opened to a bedroom, which also had windows onto the porch and the other side yard. Leading back, the hall opened to a dining room on the right and another bedroom on the left. They decided to use that second bedroom because it was closer to the bathroom and more private. Beyond the dining room, the hall led to the bathroom on the left and the kitchen on the right. At the back a long screened porch stretched across most of the back of the house with a small spare room on the left side.

"Nice place for a romantic supper," Consuelo said. "And look, mango, orange, and avocado trees. Isn't it great?"

*

A piano now became Consuelo's priority. Over the next few days she found she could explore the city by streetcar. Following ads in the newspaper she located several piano stores on south Franklin Street. One had a small Knabe grand that she liked, but at five hundred dollars, she hesitated. The next morning Sara dropped by to see if Consuelo would accompany her to the grocery store. Consuelo had not finished unpacking, and boxes were strewn along the hall. "No time for food; I'm looking for a piano," Consuelo said, "but they cost a lot more than I expected."

"Hortensia Manresa. She lives on 14th Street and 8th Avenue, caddy-corner from the barber shop," Sara said. "She has one for sale."

"What kind?"

"I don't know nothing about pianos, but it's supposed to be a good one and she needs the money. I've got to get going. Say hello to Hortensia for me. Poor thing, they're having a rough time."

Consuelo had no trouble finding the tiny house. When she introduced herself, the old woman led her to a beautiful, mahogany, upright Chickering. It was out of tune, but Consuelo liked the tone and the action. After playing for a few minutes, she said, "This is a very nice piano. Why are you selling it?"

The old woman was sitting in a ladder-back chair with a cigar box in her lap filled with tobacco cuttings, and she was rolling a cigarette. As she finished licking the paper and smoothing out the cigarette with her fingers, she said, "My husband is not working; we need the money. And my rheumatism won't let me play anymore." She held up her hands to show swollen joints. Then she reached toward the table by her chair and picked a match out of a box, lit it, and drew on the cigarette with the flame under the tip.

"It sounds and feels like a grand," Consuelo said. "What are you asking?"

"Fifty dollars?"

"That's not enough." She had expected to pay at least twice that much and counted ten ten-dollar bills into the woman's trembling hand.

"I'll make some café con leche," she said, moving toward the kitchen. Before Consuelo could object, she had disappeared into the dark hall. While she was gone Consuelo continued to play. In a few minutes the old woman returned with two pitchers.

"How do you like it?"

"*Clarito*. Lots of milk."

"You play very well," she said, as she poured a little coffee into the cup and filled it with milk. "I only played popular music."

"It'll be good to play again."

"This is all I have," she said, setting some cookies on the small table.

"It's almost lunch time."

After she sat, the old woman talked continuously: "My husband lost his job at the factory because his fingers wouldn't move fast anymore. We came from Cuba in 1889. There was plenty of work, but life was rough. La Septima was dirt with wooden planks for sidewalks. It was on the edge of a swamp. It's been filled in. Once in a while somebody would spot an alligator. It was exciting, but, of course, we were young; you know how it is."

During a break in the monologue, Consuelo stood. "I'll have someone pick it up in the next day or two. I'll let you know."

"I'm always here," the old woman said. "And thank you."

The next morning a man and his son drove up to Consuelo's house in a large truck bearing the letters, "*EL MEXICANO,*" painted on its sides. They laid out their planks and rolled the piano out of the truck onto the sidewalk and then up the planks to the porch. "Where do you want it, lady?"

"In the living room," Consuelo said, holding the door open as the men pushed the lumbering hulk past her. "Against this wall." With the sounding board facing the back living room wall, she hoped to keep down the sound. "You don't sound Mexican," Consuelo said.

"I'm not. I bought the truck from a Mexican."

Consuelo could not wait for them to leave so she could indulge herself. Now if that tuner will just come as he said he would, she thought.

Pablo dragged in that afternoon and sat at the kitchen table.

"Any luck?"

"None." He sat with his face in his hands.

"Notice anything different?"

"What?"

"The living room."

He got up to look. "I walked right past it." Striking a few keys, he said, "Now it's a home." He put his arms around Consuelo and kissed her. "Play something for me?"

"Not on an empty stomach. Supper's almost ready."

After eating and stacking the dishes to wash later, she played for over an hour and almost made him forget that he still had no job.

The next morning a young woman knocked on the door. "I'm María Rodriguez from next door. We enjoyed your playing last night."

Consuelo invited her in. "*Café con leche?*"

"I've had breakfast, but … sure, why not?"

Consuelo put some water on the stove as they talked. When the water was boiling, she took it off the heat and added the coffee, stirred it, and poured it through a flannel strainer. As Consuelo poured the coffee and milk, María said, "*Oscuro, por favor.*" Consuelo added more coffee to darken it, and the two sat in the kitchen and talked about Cuba and Ybor City and the experience of moving. "We were both born here," María said. "My husband's a cigar maker. My father came with don Vicente

Martinez-Ybor in 1886. Sometimes he drives us crazy talking about the good old days."

Consuelo smiled.

"He's nice, though, and handy."

After a few days, with other neighbors dropping in to compliment her on her music, she began to play with her windows open. Before long she was a local celebrity. Neighbor women would request selections for the morning's practice as if it were a daily recital. Consuelo loved the attention and the women's taste: "You played a fast piece last evening," the woman across the street said. "The one with the scales. It goes . . ." and she hummed the tune.

"Chopin's Minute Waltz?"

"I love it," the woman said. She sat down on the sofa as Consuelo began the rippling sounds of the introduction. With the final downscale crescendo, the woman stood and applauded. *"Estupendo!"*

Consuelo played mostly classical music, but sometimes, to please her audience, she would break out a rumba or a dansón. Other times she would play Spanish music, usually her favorites, Granados or Albéniz. Some neighbors would even sit on her porch to listen.

One morning about a month after they had moved in, a delegation of women knocked on her door. Surprised to see such a group so well dressed, she invited them in. One of them, an older woman wearing a white dress, white gloves, and a hat with flowers, looked around the living room and said, "We'd like you to give a piano recital at the Cuban Club. I'm in charge of events for the coming year; these ladies are my committee. We think you would draw a good crowd."

"I only graduated last year. But if you really … Yes, I'd love to. I'll need time to prepare."

"You decide a date and let us know," the chairwoman said. "A few weeks before, we'll post announcements all over Ybor City and West Tampa. It'll be a sell-out."

"Do you have many piano recitals?" Consuelo asked.

"This will be our first."

"Maybe I could do Cuban and Spanish music."

"Wonderful!"

Consuelo went immediately to María's house to tell her. "Great! I'll bring all my family. Excited?"

"Oh, yes. I'm beginning to like it here. People are friendly."

María smiled.

29

"I wish Pablo could find something. It's funny. At first I hated the place and he loved it. The trip was awful. All I did was throw up. Poor Pablo was so kind and patient. Now he's the unhappy one."

"The Florida Strait's treacherous," María said. "I had the same experience when we went down."

"Pablo spent most of his time at the railing with the wind in his face, looking for land. When Key West appeared, he ran to tell me. I could barely stand, but I followed him."

"Is he worried?"

"He's talked with two-dozen cigar owners. He hasn't said so, but I think he's having second thoughts."

"Thinking of going back?"

"I wouldn't mind, but he shouldn't return defeated."

"A college graduate should be able to find something."

*

That afternoon, Consuelo met Pablo at the door. "How did it go?"

"Nothing new."

Well I have a nice supper, baked fish. Come into the kitchen while I get it ready. A man came by selling them this afternoon. Caught them this morning. Now sit down and stop worrying."

"I hate to complain, Consuelo, but this shirt, well, someone at the café said I must have slept in it."

"I'm sorry, dear. I've never had to iron men's clothes." Seeing how flustered she looked, he returned to his all too familiar litany: knocking on doors, talking with friendly men and being told, no. Finally he stopped and put his face on his fists.

"Oh, Sara was here this afternoon," Consuelo said. "Benito says Vila and Fernández lost their bookkeeper last week."

"One of the few I haven't seen."

"Also, I've been invited to give a recital at the Cuban Club."

"That's wonderful, Consuelo. When?"

"Whenever I'm ready. I'll have to practice like mad."

"You know, all these failures make me wonder if I was too harsh with Papá. Feels like he's getting even."

Consuelo kept working on the fish, getting it ready to put into the oven. "I told you we should have waited."

He embraced her. "I'm sorry. I'm not thinking straight. I meant that maybe I could have had you and the inheritance."

"That would have been nice," she said, turning to the stove.

"I've hurt your feelings."

"Not really. Fighting with a parent is serious stuff. I'm lucky; my parents were always good to me."

"Mine weren't always bad," Pablo said.

*

Pablo stewed nearly an hour before the door opened. The distinguished man with thick brown hair wore a celluloid wing-tipped collar with a bow tie and a dark suit and seemed to be in his early fifties. "I am Gustavo Vila," he said, extending his hand and ushering Pablo in. His large office with varnished panel walls reaching high ceilings had two large windows overlooked the bricked-in yard where trucks brought shipments in and out of the factory. "My partner, Agustín Fernández, retired last year, so I have to run the factory alone. Then, last week my bookkeeper left after eighteen years. *Hablas Inglés?*" he asked.

"Yes. I think I can pass for a native."

"Good. That's useful. Tell me about yourself."

After summarizing his college background, he added, "I can do accounting or anything in business."

"Any experience?"

"A short time in Matanzas sugar cane."

I lived there when I arrived in Cuba," Vila said. "It was quite a change from Barcelona, but I liked it. How do you find Florida?"

"Primitive, but exciting."

"Do you expect to return home?"

"This is home now." Though he was far from certain, Pablo tried to sound emphatic.

"Got a place to live?"

"Yes, a house on Twelfth Avenue."

"Fine. When can you start?"

"Tomorrow. Today if you wish. Thank you, don Gustavo. I won't disappoint you."

"Tomorrow then, eight o'clock sharp."

3 – AUTUMN 1931

*

Kentucky Miners Starved And Beaten

*

Atlanta Mayor Urges Revolt On Prohibition

*

Chinese Seek Soviet Aid In Manchuria

*

*Alabama Governor Frees 65 Convicts
Thanksgiving Morning*

*

*Former King Alfonso XIII of Spain prevents his son, don
Jaime of Bourbon, from marrying the girl of his choice.*

*

On Saturday morning, November 8th, Pablo walked out to his front porch to get his morning paper, slipped it under his arm, walked back to the kitchen, sat at the table, and unfolded the paper. The headline screamed out: *Officer Shot, Others Hurt In Clash With Communist Mob.* When he read the headline to Consuelo, she said she had heard loud noises that could have been gunshots. Pablo resumed reading as Consuelo went next door to ask María if her husband was involved.

"Yes. The police started the riot, then wouldn't let anybody leave without being searched," María said.

"What was it about?"

"The union wanted to have a parade and the police wouldn't let them. Free country, bah!"

"Where is he now?"

"The Labor Temple. They're all pretty shaken."

"The newspaper says it was a communist meeting," Consuelo said.

"Crackers see communists everywhere."

Consuelo returned as Pablo was folding the newspaper and laying it on the table.

"I'm going to stop at the café to see what's going on." On his way out Consuelo related what María had said.

*

Since beginning his job with Vila, one coffee shop had become his favorite hangout. After supper most evenings he would go there for an hour or two of conversation with the cigar makers and occasionally a game of dominoes.

The sign hanging over the door read *Café Cubano*. The windows on either side of the front door were dusty and plastered with a small menu and Cuban Club posters announcing next week's dance, an upcoming picnic, and a beauty contest. Recognizing several cigar makers through the window, he entered the dark cavern where two lights hanging down the middle of the high ceiling spread a dull, brown glow. A fascinating pattern of cubes in white, gray, and black made the tile floor look three-dimensional. High in the back wall a loud fan tried vainly to suck out cigar smoke. Another wall between the main room and that back wall hid a private room where the owner served liquor to well-known customers. Along the cream-colored wall behind the ancient, varnished bar that ran to the back was a wooden counter with a cash register surrounded by displays of candy, chewing gum, cigarettes, and an assortment of cigar boxes with their colorful labels offering grateful relief to the dullness. At the front window behind the bar stood a man much like the one at Las Novedades, slicing ham off a bone with great delicacy. Stacked like small logs of firewood at the edge of his cutting table stood a neat pile of Cuban sandwiches containing ham, pork, cheese, baloney, pickle and, if requested, lettuce, tomato, mayonnaise, and mustard, all placed between sliced, nine-inch pieces of Cuban bread cut from the yard-long loaves.

Domingo, the owner, sandwich maker, and bartender, was a fifty-year-old Spaniard with thick, black hair, thick eyebrows, a heavy black moustache that hung over his lips, and long sideburns. He was slightly over five feet tall and wore a white apron marked with mustard and coffee stains. His wife Rosa prepared the café's soups, fried plantains, and fritters in their apartment upstairs and helped her husband downstairs during busy hours. The only other family was a skinny gray cat, named Osvaldo, whose only duty was to control the mice population.

Bent wood chairs and marble-top tables on black metal frames filled the rest of the café. Behind the bar near the back wall, a gas stove kept a pot of garbanzo bean soup steaming. The odors of soup, sandwiches, and the less pleasant ones that emanated from the small toilet at the rear intensified the anxious atmosphere. The small place would have had little charm were it not for the cigar makers who brightened it with conversation. Because it was just a block from the Vila y Fernández factory, many of its workers frequented the place.

Silence spread over the café as the aristocratic, white-suited, obviously management young man walked in. Pablo leaned on the bar and pushed back his Panama hat, and said, "*Café solo.*" He lit a cigarette, looked around, and said, "*Hola, Jacinto.*" The older man was standing at the bar sipping coffee from a saucer.

"*Que pasa?*" Jacinto, tall, barrel-chested, well-dressed, and in his early sixties, sported a well-kept, rust-colored, handlebar moustache, long sideburns, and graying, light brown hair parted in the middle. His large, deep-set, blue eyes gave people the impression that he was staring.

"Read about the riot?" Pablo asked.

"The police broke it up before it started," Jacinto said. "No warning, nothing; just started shoving. When our men pushed back, they started swinging their clubs. Arrested everybody on the platform and a few others. It's a known fact they're with the factory owners. What's so damn terrible about a parade?"

"What kind of parade?" Pablo asked.

"Solidarity," Jacinto said.

"The paper says they're communists," Pablo said.

"Bullshit!"

"It's not bullshit," the large mulatto said from the far end of the bar. Pablo had seen him before, but had never spoken with him. Matilde preferred to remain at the periphery of the café's social life. "They don't hide it," Matilde said. "They get their orders from Moscow. Also, Jacinto, they shot one of the cops."

"Don't believe everything you read in that rag," Jacinto said. "I'm a union member and I'm no communist."

"The police broke into their headquarters after the riot," Pablo said, "and arrested a man."

"Who was it?" Jacinto asked.

"Somebody named Crawford. They got lots of stuff: shotguns, rifles, boxes of shells, mimeograph machines and a truckload of pamphlets."

"He's right," Matilde said. "And a Soviet flag." Matilde barely moved his head as he talked.

"Maybe," Jacinto said, "but they talk sense. The owners don't give a damn about us. This new union wants us to own the factories. Not a bad idea, if you ask me."

"Something for nothing, eh?" Matilde said, smiling and turning to face Jacinto.

"There's talk about a sympathy strike for the people in jail," Sarna said. The thin, middle-aged man, whose nickname means "mange," had walked to the bar from one of the tables and sat vigorously scratching his crotch.

"Damn fools don't remember the last strike," Matilde said, looking at Pablo. "You were here, Jacinto. Tell them about it."

"It was bad. Nobody wants a strike. Really think they're Russian agents?"

Matilde stood. "Do you know any of them or where they come from?"

Jacinto sat silent, his blue eyes boring into the large mulatto.

"Well I do," Matilde said. "The leaders come from New York, Chicago and Latin America. Most aren't even Latins. Another thing: why do they need guns and Soviet flags?"

The large, sloppy mulatto was grossly overweight, but his enormous shoulders and slightly over six-foot frame revealed a powerful body. With his shirttail out, he looked more like a hobo than a cigar maker. Two years older than Pablo, he looked ten years older. He had medium-dark skin and tight, curly, black hair, but his thin lips and aquiline nose favored his European ancestry. Moving like a giant sloth, his words flowed like honey. With a deep bass voice, he commanded attention with a word or two. Jacinto did not like to argue with him, but he could not bring himself to give in: "Was it fair to cut our salaries? Ten percent ain't peanuts."

"What's fair? Not this depression." Matilde looked at Pablo. "Sure they cut our salaries."

"Whose side are you on?" Jacinto asked.

"On the side of keeping my job," Matilde said. "Would you rather they fired ten percent of the cigar makers? Instead of trying to understand what was happening, we got mad." Matilde poured some of his coffee into the saucer and took a sip. "And what did we do? We turned to the new union. Those slimy communists were just waiting for a crack so they could gouge the hell out of it."

"What do you suggest?" Pablo said.

"Keep working and keep up the pressure without shitting in our plate."

*

The lector's voice boomed across the room as one hundred and forty cigar makers worked elbow to elbow at their individual tables on the Vila y Fernández factory floor. Light beams cut across the large room as the lector read from don Quixote de La Mancha. Upstairs, pickers segregated the raw tobacco leaves into stacks according to size, quality, and use. Because their job was to get the most out of the tobacco, pickers earned the highest pay of cigar workers. To provide good, indirect light, pickers worked on the north side of the building, which, like all factories, was laid out in an east-west orientation to allow lots of good lighting for this delicate, demanding job.

In a room near the warehouse, strippers, usually women and children, removed the main stems from the leaves and stacked the two leaf halves on their laps according to whether they were right-handed or left-handed. These stacks went to the cigar rollers.

On the main floor the bunchers formed cigar innards by placing long rough leaves in one hand, shaping them, rolling them roughly into a cylinder, and placing them into a mold that held ten such bunches. The skill lay in making the bunch tight enough to burn smoothly and loose enough to draw well. The mold had two halves with ten carved spaces. The two halves fit into each other sandwiching bunches into the molded spaces between. When he had filled the mold, the buncher would fit the two halves together and put the combined contraption into a press to squeeze the bunches into shape until they dried out.

Later the roller removed one bunch at a time from the mold, laid it on a half leaf spread carefully on his cutting board. Catching the end of the leaf around the lighting end of the bunch, he rolled the bunch diagonally over the leaf until it was covered neatly. Depending on whether the leaf was left-handed or right-handed, the roller had to roll the cigar with his left hand or his right. Workers who were not ambidextrous ended up doing other jobs. Finally, the roller finished the mouth end by trimming off the excess piece of leaf with a broad, rounded blade called a *chaveta*, and rounding it onto the head with a little paste. Finally, he cut the lighting end to size in a guillotine-like apparatus and stacked it in a hexagonal holder that held fifty finished cigars.

In another room, the selector chose cigars for boxing on the basis of color so that all the cigars in a box would have a uniform color and appearance. Selectors's pay was slightly lower than pickers'. Spaniards almost always held these jobs and that of foreman. The most menial job was the banders who put the labels on cigars before boxing.

*

The day after the riot, don Gustavo burst into the bookkeeping office. "Did you hear about the riot?" The office had desks for two men during good times, but Pablo was their only bookkeeper now. The bookkeeping office was next door to Vila's office on the first floor. It was a spacious room with large windows on one side overlooking the courtyard where trucks brought in raw materials. Pablo's desk had a lamp and a telephone. A filing cabinet stood next to the desk.

Hunched over his work Pablo turned to face don Gustavo when he heard the door open. "The Tribune has pictures of the leaders," Pablo said.

"What nerve!. They wanted to march downtown to celebrate the fourteenth anniversary of the Soviet Union; through the Scrub. The Scrub! No wonder the police stopped them."

"What's the Scrub?"

"The Negro neighborhood between here and downtown. They'd like to stir them up too."

"Why are they celebrating a Soviet holiday?"

"They're communists! Any excuse to make trouble."

"I didn't know cigar makers were communists," Pablo said. Having heard the cigar makers' version of the incident, Pablo wanted to hear the other side.

"Most aren't. When times are hard, this rabble pop up like boils. They blame us for the depression. They aren't a union; they're political troublemakers trying to bring down the government."

"I've heard talk of a strike," Pablo said.

"Some are already out, but not here, thank God. The old timers haven't forgotten the last one."

*

The workers had been at their tables for two hours when the lector arrived with his newspapers, books, and magazines. He stopped to chat with a cigar maker as he strode to his platform that overlooked the floor. In a booming, clear, baritone voice he began with an editorial from the Morning Tribune:

"Individuals and groups who are insidiously or openly engaged in agitating disorder and fomenting anarchism should turn back the pages of Tampa's history to a chapter years ago. The city had suffered month after month from a paralysis of its chief industry. The strike was due entirely to the pernicious activities of a small circle of troublemakers, interested in promoting and prolonging the strike for selfish gain.

"One bright morning their followers awoke to find them missing from their accustomed haunts. They had not been lynched, lashed or incarcerated. They had simply been induced to take a vacation, a change of scene and air, without return tickets.

"The constituted authorities of Tampa have usually been found adequate and capable of dealing with malefactors of this stripe. When the authorities have not been sufficiently powerful, the American manhood of the city has always risen to the occasion.

"In the present manifestation, we believe, and we hope, that the law and its officers will furnish all the corrective treatment required."

As the lector went on to another article, the workers began to grumble. "When was that?" Sarna asked.

"1910," Jacinto said. "The police picked up a group of union leaders, took them to Ballast Point, and put them on a boat to Honduras."

"What happened?" Sarna asked.

Jacinto shrugged. "They dropped them on a deserted beach, and we never heard from them again."

"Trapped and eliminated like animals," Sarna said.

Across the table from Jacinto, a very thin man they called Huesito looked up. "They're actually telling people to take the law into their own hands."

With all the murmur from the floor, the lector had to stop reading and ask his audience to keep quiet.

"That's not all," he continued. "Another article says three of the men under arrest may be deported." Then he read that article. By the time he had finished, the roar had submerged him.

A week later, the lector read an article from the morning paper about two children, brother and sister, ages fourteen and sixteen, who had been arrested at the riot on November 7th. With a voice crusted with irony and anger, he translated aloud into Spanish:

"The children have filed suit alleging false arrest and imprisonment. The mother and oldest sister were among the seventeen arrested that day. The suit also included a complaint for the son's arrest yesterday while he was attempting to take pictures of the accused as they were escorted into the courtroom. The police confiscated the boy's camera and turned him over to juvenile authorities. They later released him to the custody of his father." The reader stopped to say, "What have we come to when they jail children?"

*

Gustavo Vila frequently passed among the workers, stopping to talk with some on his way. On Friday morning, the day after Thanksgiving and three weeks after the riot, the reader had not arrived and one of the cigar makers was reading aloud from that morning's Tribune. The story described a meeting of cigar manufacturers held the previous day in which they had agreed unanimously to discontinue reading in all factories as a means of curbing communist agitation. The article noted that workers in seven of Tampa's largest factories had already walked out. The owners had decided that the trouble was originating from the reader's stand, "… where fiery communistic translations from anarchistic publications are constantly poured into our workers."

Don Gustavo was in the middle of the floor when he realized what was happening. One of the more intrepid cigar makers rose from his table.

"Is this true, Señor Vila?" he asked in a sharp, nasal, high-pitched voice.

In a raspy voice Vila said, "The strikers are protesting the arrests of the 7th, but the strike isn't hurting the city government or the police who made the arrests. It's hurting the factories they work for. We had nothing to do with those arrests. Is it fair to punish us?"

"Is it fair to take away our only glimpse of the outside world?" the same man asked. "They're mistreating men, women, and even children because we want to be heard. What recourse do we have?"

"We have to protect our businesses and your jobs," Vila said.

All eyes came to rest on Matilde working at the end of one of the rows of tables. After keeping silent throughout the reading and the discussion, with great deliberation and a profound sense of drama, the large mulatto put away his chaveta and other tools, wiped off his cutting board, and stood. In his resonant bass voice that could have erupted from the bowels of the earth, he said, "You all know I have resisted the strike. It will hurt our families, our industry, and our city. But it's obvious that they won't stop as long as we give in to their tyranny. The time has come! To the street!"

With a roar of approval the entire work force rose and moved out. Within minutes the floor cleared out with workers mumbling insults at Gustavo Vila, who remained rooted to the spot.

"Tyrants! We won't come back until the lector returns," one man said from the midst of the crowd.

When Pablo heard the ruckus, he lifted his head from his ledger and walked into the hall. Men poured down the stairs and out the wide, factory portal like a great wound bleeding into the street. Many of them had wanted to join the strike. Pablo wandered down the hall until he found the janitor.

"They've walked out," the man said, throwing down his broom. "Me too."

*

El Rubio, a completely bald man in his mid-fifties, had worked for years next to Matilde, and they were old friends. He admired Matilde, but he did not want to strike. Hesitating when he reached his apartment above Silver's Department Store, he ascended the stairs slowly.

"I already heard," his wife said.

"I ha-a-ave to go to the Labor Temple to see wha-a-at's going to happen."

"I can tell you: we'll be eating corn meal and rice," she said.

"It w-o-on't last long."

"One day is too long. You have a short memory: ten months of corn meal and rice." She threw a pot across the kitchen. It fell to the floor and spun loudly before it stopped.

"I'd be-be-better go. We'll have to vo-vo-vo-vo-ote," he said, and turned and walked down the stairs and headed for the Labor Temple.

Jacinto arrived just as his wife was starting to prepare lunch. "You're early," she said.

"We've walked out," he said, walking to the stove and raising the kettle lid. "Ah, stew, my favorite."

Angelina said nothing and bit her lip as she continued cutting an onion.

"I'm sorry, Angelina, but everybody went out. I had no choice."

"We managed before; we'll manage again."

*

The Labor Temple was a shell of a building. From the outside it was plain stucco with columns at the entrance. The main room was a single, two-story auditorium with windows on all sides that provided the only light during the day. Looking so solid from outside, it seemed rickety inside, as if a wind could blow the walls in. Rows of folding chairs lined the floor in front of the speaker's platform, which rose three feet above the floor.

The walls of the giant room vibrated with the roar of hundreds of voices yelling their approval as President Sánchez paused. "We must be prudent," he continued. "The last thing we want is to start a revolution. The riot of November 7th should be a lesson. We want first to protest the arrests of three weeks ago, and second to protest the removal of the lectors. But we must make our protest with calm and intelligence. Our Executive Committee proposes a 72-hour strike to show we are moderate and don't want to ruin our factories. On Monday morning at this time we'll return to work."

The crowd was silent at first, but after a few seconds voices began to shout, "He's right!" and "Three days!"

Tall and thin and wearing a rumpled tan suit, the President lifted his glasses off and straightened his tie as the crowd yelled. When they subsided he continued: "We'll need our members to walk down La Septima and ask store owners to close in sympathy with us. We'll ask them not to sell even bread. With the people of Ybor City and West Tampa behind a brief, orderly strike, the owners will know we're responsible but serious." The crowd cheered and stamped their feet in approval. "Go out and tell your friends and families that this will not last long. We won't hurt our families, our bosses, or the city. We must show that we're not communists and that we care for our city and our country. Long live America!"

President Sánchez stood at the podium smiling, obviously enjoying the cheering.

The atmosphere at the Café Cubano was not as clear. The day was cloudy, and in the semidarkness every table vibrated under pounding fists. "The bastards treat us like paid laborers. We're artisans; we know our craft better than these sons of whores."

"They want to keep us ignorant."

"Profits, that's all they care about."

"Spaniards are the same the world over. Nothing good ever came out of Spain."

Those who had not lived through the war with Spain recounted old stories they had heard as children:

"When the Cuban farmers would not support their tyranny, the soldiers went into the countryside and burned every farm, crops and all. My grandparents had to move to Havana to keep from starving."

"We need men like García."

"What a man!"

As if no one had ever heard the story, one man recounted it: "A bullet could blind him, but it could not stop him. When he was able to get on a horse again, he galloped onto the field. 'Point me at the enemy, then let my horse go,' he said. At the signal, he charged into a pack of Spanish soldiers, his sword flying, hacking in all directions like a madman! Scared the shit out of them. The cowards turned and ran from the crazy, blind Cuban with the flying sword. *Que hombre!*"

"Both sides did wrong," Matilde said. Everyone turned to him and began to yell objections. Matilde remained on his barstool, sipping his beer.

When the abuse stopped, Jacinto answered. "We're free men here, Matilde. We don't have to take their abuse."

"I don't like it any more than you do, but let's keep our minds on today and not on warmed-over memories."

Ignoring Matilde, El Chulo spoke up. "They can't treat us like that no more. This ain't Cuba. Maybe we should take over their factories. We are the factory!" Young, tall and handsome, El Chulo wore a thin moustache and hair that curled at the neck, a loosely fitting white silk shirt open at the collar to reveal a gold cross, and tan trousers that did not conceal his bulging manhood when he walked. Before long, he stood. "Got a heavy date tonight, *caballeros. Hasta luego.*"

When most of the crowd had dispersed, Jacinto returned and found El Rubio talking with Domingo at the bar. Matilde was still sitting at the far end.

"These Crackers treat us like ni-ni-iggers," Rubio said, as he swirled his coffee cup.

"They wrote the constitution for themselves, not for us," Jacinto said, sitting at the next barstool.

"Like ni-ni-niggers," El Rubio said.

"I wouldn't stand for it," Matilde said, calmly without turning.

"Don't be offended, Matilde. It's ju-u-ust that these pe-eople don't think of us as Am-m-mericans. Jacinto and I were born here, but to them we're for-or-oreigners."

"The Negroes in the Scrub were born here too," Matilde said, "and their ancestors since they were kidnapped in Africa."

"It just shows what kind of people we're dealing with," Jacinto said.

"Just like us," Matilde said. "What have we been saying about Spaniards? And the Italians? If one of them marries a Cuban, he's ostracized. People are people everywhere."

"It's not the same," Rubio said. "Sure, w-w-we have our disagreements, but in the end w-w-we stick together."

"We have to survive," Jacinto said.

"Our good friend Pablo could become one of them if he left Ybor City and changed his name. He could easily pass for white," Matilde said.

"What do you mean, pass; he is white, and so are we," Jacinto said.

"But you don't sound white and you don't act white or dress white," Matilde said. "With those sideburns and moustache, and your accent, Jacinto; you too, Rubio. You natives are really foreigners. Of course, you could take lessons in talking Cracker and learn to dress and cut your hair. Maybe you could become one of them at that," Matilde said.

Realizing that Matilde had no such option, and if he did, it would move him to the Scrub, Rubio said, "Enough of this bul-ul-ullshit. How about some dominos?"

"Not for me," Matilde said. "Time to go."

*

On Saturday, cigar makers moved through Ybor City stopping to talk with each storeowner, asking them to close for the weekend. It was not a march, but a quiet, amorphous mass that filled the spaces of Ybor City like a vapor. They did not have angry faces as they spoke with people; they approached the task lightheartedly, stopping everywhere to chat or joke about the serious situation.

By 6:00 that afternoon, Ybor City was deserted. Bakeries did not make bread that night, and even the movie theaters closed. Only the cafés and restaurants remained open. Saturday's paper carried a report of the cigar makers' three-day strike, stating their walkout had been orderly. It also reported a second meeting of factory owners, in the midst of their pre-Christmas rush, to counter the workers' action by announcing that those who walked out were no longer employed.

On Sunday, from 10 o'clock until 1:30, the Labor Temple shook with fiery rhetoric. The consensus of opinion finally came down on returning to work Monday morning. If they were locked out, they would return to the Labor Temple for further discussion.

The highlight of the day was a speech, the only one in English, by past mayor Perry G. Wall, whom the cigar makers knew and respected. In a conciliatory speech he said he would have allowed the parade. As to those in jail, he assured his audience they would get a fair trial. He also said that lectors should be allowed only if they read material approved by competent authorities.

*

"You should have seen them. Looked like a swarm all over La Septima," Pablo said.

"Sara was here this morning. Benito was with them and said it was a big party."

"Yeah, but scary. A mob like that could easily have turned violent."

"Are you with the workers?" she asked.

"Sure, but I'm in management. I've got to be careful."

"What are you going to do?"

"I'm not on strike."

4 – CYNTHIA

*

35-Hour Week Could End Unemployment

*

Loan Corporation Officers Indicted

*

Louisianan Kills Another In Heat Of Political Argument

*

American Legion To Intensify Americanization Plans

*

Consuelo's excitement reached a new level as she walked into the doctor's office. Seeing only three other women in the waiting room, she relaxed. All three watched her walk in, sign her name at the desk, and sit. The only window had the blinds closed, so one would not know that the day was sunny and bright. A lamp at each of three corners poured out a warm, sanctuary-like glow. Consuelo picked up a magazine from the table near her and turned the pages with one hand, tapping scales on the armrest with her other hand.

Soon after she sat down, the nurse called one of the women, and Consuelo looked at the clock on the wall. Fifteen minutes later, the nurse called in the second.

The third, an older woman, turned to Consuelo: "You're next. I'm waiting for my daughter."

Finally, the nurse opened the door, motioned to Consuelo, and ushered her into the examination room. "Please remove your clothes and put on this robe," she said. "The doctor will be right in." Within a few minutes the doctor appeared at the door with the nurse and asked how she was feeling. Past middle age, he was short and his pronounced belly stretched his white hospital jacket. His metal-rimmed glasses hung halfway down his nose as he passed his hand over his large, nearly bald, head.

"I'm fine, doctor. Maybe this time?"

He asked her to lie on the examination table. When he had finished the examination he asked her to dress and come to his office. Consuelo dressed and walked down the short hall to his office. "Please sit down," he said.

"Well?"

Smiling broadly he said, "No doubt about it."

Making the sign of the cross she said, "Thank God ... "You're sure?"

"About two months, I'd say."

"Oh, thank you, Doctor Chávez.

"I had nothing to do with it," he said, and handed her a pamphlet. "Read this and come back in a month."

With that miracle tucked into her heart she left his office and walked out the door dreaming of how she would tell her husband. Our baby, she thought, the first of our family born in America. The consuming depression was grinding out new bottoms each of those last days of 1931, but Consuelo acknowledged no depression. At that moment a new human being, a miracle, was growing inside her. On her way home, she stopped at the church to light a candle. She thanked God for His gift and, after a few minutes looking at the stained glass windows and musing over the miracle of the virgin birth, she went home.

She was still planning how she would tell Pablo as she opened the door. He always avoided the topic, saying only that they should wait, but she knew he would be thrilled. It had finally happened! "We're going to have a baby," she'd say, but that seemed ordinary. "You'll soon be a father." But that, too, would blunt the moment's edge. "Can you guess what I have?" Too vague. She spent the rest of the day searching for the right words.

When Pablo walked into the house with the latest news of the strike, she was standing over the kitchen sink, her face baptized in sunlight. Standing at the kitchen door, he looked past her and said, "The factory owners fired the strikers. They're crazy."

She listened patiently, hearing little, thinking only of her news.

"Why are you smiling?" he asked.

"I saw Dr. Chávez today."

"Anything wrong?"

"Oh no," she said, smiling broadly, toying with him.

"Well then?"

"We're going to have a baby."

Pablo stood frozen as Consuelo waited, expecting his burst of happiness.

"Oh no!" he said finally, and spun around.

Consuelo's smile went slack as she stepped around to face him. Putting her arms round his neck, she said, "What's wrong?"

"Haven't you been listening?"

"We'll be fine. We've got money."

Pablo kissed her cheek. "I'm going to wash up."

His father's words echoed in his brain: "Set her up in a house, enjoy her." As he took off his shirt and bent over the washbasin, he thought about cigar makers sitting around a domino table. "That's entertainment; work is serious," he thought, "like the difference between a mistress and a wife." He looked into the mirror thinking his father may have been right. I'm stuck here, he thought. I should have thought of the future. He dried himself and put on a clean shirt and tie, cursing himself for his stupid clinging to principle. He fumbled the knot he was making in his tie and pulled it out and started over. She wasn't the only woman, he thought, but she was my choice. Why is it always painful to do the right thing?

He slipped on his jacket, put on his Panama hat, and walked out of the house.

"Where are you going?" she asked, as she followed him out the screen door. "Supper's on the table."

No answer.

Through tears Consuelo watched her husband's figure recede as he hurried down the sidewalk and turned the corner. She must have stood transfixed for several minutes before she noticed the woman on the porch across the street looking at her, scowling. Consuelo went back in.

*

Pablo headed toward La Septima as if hypnotized. Nothing came into focus with the confusion that surged in his brain like a tropical hurricane. Turning onto La Septima, he bumped a woman pushing a stroller, seeing neither the baby nor its mother. Without looking, he crossed the street in front of a driver who screeched his brakes and honked. All he heard was the horn's long "Ah-uuuuga!" He continued past Sixth Avenue and the noise until he found himself in front of the notorious house on Fifth Avenue that someone had pointed out to him. The streetlight's sick color fought the fading red of the setting sun. He walked to the corner and turned and continued around the block until he stood once more before the large two-story house. It was not unlike other houses in Ybor City: large, two-story, white frame with white painted brick columns on the front porch. He expected to see a red light in the window, but saw only heavy drapes. He pushed the gate and walked up the front steps to the porch and knocked.

"Hello, handsome," said the middle-aged woman with dyed black hair and a thick Cracker drawl. She was overweight, but her creased-lined face held echoes of distant beauty.

"Come on in."

Pablo took off his hat and entered.

"Looking for somebody in particular?"

"No."

"I'll take you to one of our prettiest girls."

He walked ahead of her up the stairs past a door that opened into a small, dark room. Stopping, he asked, "In here?"

"Not that closet. We save that for our Cuban customers," she said with a sneer. Feeling the sting of a loud slap, she found herself against the wall. Regaining her composure, she rubbed her cheek and said, "I'm sorry. You're so blonde and all." When Pablo turned to leave, she grabbed his arm. "Don't go. You'll like Cynthia. Come on now. Don't hold a grudge."

Pulling him by the hand, she opened a door at the end of the hall. "Cynthia, I've brought you a handsome Cuban man. Treat him good now." When the older woman left, the young redhead turned away from her dresser mirror and walked to where he was standing and looked him over. "Ain't never seen you before."

Thinking only of escape, Pablo could not speak.

"Relax, sugar. I ain't seen nobody all day. Sit down."

Calmed, he faced her again. A tinny rumba from a Havana station was blaring out of the radio by the bed.

Seeing Pablo frowning at the radio she reached over and turned it down.

A red-shaded table lamp diffused the room's only light onto the pink panel walls and the nondescript-colored rug with an elaborate gold pattern that Pablo could not decipher even after staring down at it for several moments. A dresser with a pitcher in a pan stood beside the double bed. The only other pieces in the room were a rocking chair and a small cabinet with a music box, a package of Chesterfield cigarettes, and an ashtray. The heavy drapes that covered the single window added depravity to the anxious atmosphere. Pablo shuddered, as if he had fallen into a vortex of evil.

"I've never been in a place like this before."

"I know, sugar. How about a shot?" she said, taking a bottle of brandy from inside the small cabinet.

"Thanks."

"Well, sit down," she said, helping him take off his jacket and loosening his tie. Hanging his jacket on a hook behind the door she said, "Might as well be comfy." She poured his drink, handed it to him, and sat on the edge of the bed, smiling as Pablo stared back. He was sitting with his hands in his lap.

Cynthia's blue eyes sparkled and her long red wavy hair hung over her shoulders. Though her makeup was overdone, Pablo did not mind. Her low-cut, snugly fitted, silky dress accentuated every nuance of her sumptuous body. Except for the shoes and the gold cross on a thin chain around her neck, it was the only thing she had on as far as he could tell.

As if to break the ice, she smiled. "A lot of white Cubans prefer mulattas."

Pablo stiffened and put his glass on the table. But before he replied, he thought again and decided not to take offense. Her directness was shocking but attractive.

"Why?" he asked, as if she would know better than a man.

"Damn if I know. Forbidden fruit, I reckon. Men like strange stuff once in a while."

Pablo resisted arousal. "Aren't you drinking?"

"Ain't allowed when we're on duty."

"Maybe we could meet sometime when you're not on duty."

"That'd be nice, but it ain't allowed neither."

"I'd better go."

"We're just gettin' acquainted. I ain't got nothin' better to do, with this damn strike."

"I shouldn't be here."

"But y'are. What's the matter, sugar? Little wife holdin' back?"

"Just the opposite."

"Well that's a new one," she said, pushing back her long hair. For the first time she exposed more than a trace of impatience. "Just what the hell's your problem, then?"

"She just told me we're having a baby."

"Then what the hell you doin' here? What kinda man are you?" She extracted a cigarette from the pack on the cabinet, tapped it hard, and lit it. "Sorry. Ain't none of my business. Actually lots of fellas like you come here, but usually their wives are futher along. Don't worry; you cain't knock up a pregnant woman." She laughed. "Men are sure funny."

She got up from the bed. "Maybe you oughta go. This don't feel right."

Pablo finished his drink and stood. Taking some bills out of his wallet, he held them out.

"No charge."

"Could I stay a while and just talk? I'll pay."

"Why not?" She sat on the bed again.

"How about another?" Pablo asked holding out his glass.

She reached for the bottle and poured him another and returned to the bed holding one knee up with interlocked fingers.

"I'm a bookkeeper in one of the factories. The strike hasn't hurt me, but it probably will. With the depression, we can't afford a baby."

"Folks manage," she said, drawing on the cigarette.

He took another sip. "My family cut me off in Cuba."

"How come?"

"My father … didn't approve."

"Oh?" A malicious smirk spread over her face.

"I don't want to get into that," he said stiffly.

"What the hell're you wasting my time and your money for if you don't wanna screw and you won't say what's ailin' you?"

After a while he said, "What you said a few minutes ago about men liking mulattas; my father thinks my wife has African blood."

"Aha!" She smashed her cigarette into the ashtray. "Bet he gets a little black stuff once in a while."

"Don't be disrespectful." He immediately felt stupid.

"Sounds like he ain't too respectful. Prob'ly told you to get some on the side and forget about marryin' her. Right?"

"This is too personal."

"It is, sugar, but you cain't run from it. I think you're worried about the baby's looks and your old man shittin' a brick."

He got up and put his tie around his collar, took his jacket off the hook behind the door and walked out of the room. Cynthia was still sitting on the edge of the bed. She stood, poured herself a glass of brandy, and lit another cigarette.

A minute or two later the older woman opened Cynthia's door. "That fella' stormed outa here like the house was on fire. What happened?"

"Just another poor sap screwin' up his life. Nothin' outa the ordinary."

*

It was well past eleven o'clock and Consuelo was rocking on the front porch watching the neighborhood lights die out one by one when a Model A Ford drove up. The large mulatto got out of the driver's side and went around to the passenger's side, opened the door, and lifted Pablo out. Carrying Pablo to the front porch the huge man seemed to envelop Pablo like a bear holding a sleeping child. He stood Pablo up by the banister and looked at Consuelo standing at the door. "Matilde Gómez at your service, Señora," he said, bowing with a flourish. Then, seeing tears streaming down her cheeks, he added, "He's had a few too many; that's all. You've got a very gloomy husband."

Consuelo reached in and turned off the living room light. "I'll take him," she said. Pablo held the banister with one hand and his wife's shoulder with the other. His white linen suit was rumpled. "Come on, Pablo." She said, putting his left arm around her shoulder and her right arm around his waist. His knees buckled and he could not find the handle, so she opened the screen door for him. When she turned to look back, his deliverer was standing at his open car door watching them.

"I'm sorry I was rude. You're very kind, Mr. Gómez, and I'm grateful."

"Have no fear, Señora Iglesias. He'll have a headache in the morning, but he'll survive."

Inside, Pablo fell into the living room sofa. With some straining she raised him and walked him to the bedroom where he flopped into bed. As she removed his shoes and socks, his eyes suddenly opened and he tried to sit up. Instead, he flopped over the side and vomited on the floor making awful, wretching sounds. When he finished, he lay there for a while, spent and puffing, and then rolled back onto the pillow.

"I'm sorry," he said and pushed his hair back. "I'm no good ... a failure."

"Quiet now. Go to sleep," she said in a soothing voice as she finished undressing him.

"You're too good to me. I don't deserve ..." Then he passed out of consciousness.

Seeing that he was asleep, Consuelo went to the kitchen and brought back a mop and a bucket and cleaned the floor by the bed. On her way back to the kitchen, she heard noises in the hall. Following the sounds to the bathroom, she found Pablo standing in the dark with one hand on the wall, urinating on the floor next to the commode. She moved him gently to correct his aim and, when he had finished, walked him back to bed. Several times during the night she heard him walking, once to the kitchen, where he drank some water from the faucet making loud slurping sounds. Each time, he returned to bed and almost immediately began to snore.

*

The next morning Pablo sat down to his breakfast of buttered Cuban bread and café con leche wearing a black suit. "Sorry about last night."

"What happened?"

"I found some friends from the factory. I guess we drank too much."

"Mr. Gómez was kind and gracious."

"Who?"

"Matilde Gómez, a big mulatto."

"Where did you see him?"

"He brought you home."

"Oh."

"Don't you remember?"

"Obviously not."

"You're not yourself, Pablo. Is it the strike?"

"What else? It's not so trivial, you know." He dunked his bread in the coffee splashing some over the side of the cup; then he pushed away from the table to see if any had spilled on his suit.

"I know it's important, dear." Consuelo knew there was more. "Are you going to work?"

"Don't I have enough without getting fired?" Consuelo started to cry. She was standing over the stove.

"What now?"

"I thought you'd be happy. I didn't plan it."

"Me neither." He finished his coffee and left the table. After footsteps she heard the screen door slam.

*

When Pablo got to the factory that Monday morning, he found two armed guards at the door. "What's this?"

"You may pass, Señor Iglesias. The factory's closed to strikers.

Gustavo Vila was at his desk when Pablo walked in. "Glad to see you, Pablo. Sit down."

With his head throbbing, Pablo was not fully aware. "I knew the workers would object with the lectors gone, but why lock them out?" he said, as he pulled a chair closer to Vila's desk.

Vila sensed that Pablo was distracted. "We have no choice."

"The work's pretty boring. They need the distraction."

"They spoiled a good thing by bringing in communists."

"But it's only three days."

"They picked the best time for us. We're ready to ship; this break will save us money, and they can't afford a Christmas without salaries."

"But why punish them?"

"This isn't the first time we've argued about lectors, but this time they're finished." Seeing that Pablo did not respond, don Gustavo went on. "You've got to show strength; otherwise, as soon as they fill their bellies they'll be singing the same song. You've seen the books. You know how sales have dropped. We had to cut wage rates back in January." Seeing Pablo sitting with his head in his hands, Vila said, "You don't look well, Pablo."

"I'm embarrassed to tell you; I had too much to drink last night."

"Celebrating?"

"No . . . Well, yes. My wife is expecting a baby."

"Well that's certainly worth celebrating. Congratulations."

"Thanks."

5 – STRIKE – NOVEMBER 1931

*

Miami Bank President Arrested

*

NY Probe Continues on Bootlegger Protection Racket

*

World Sitting On Powder Keg Says Former Secretary Of War

*

Chinese Army Advancing On Captured City

*

"Bastards!" Jacinto said.

"Quiet, *El Presidente* is speaking," El Chulo said. Two thousand people crammed into the Labor Temple that Monday morning, and several hundred more huddled around loudspeakers outside. This meeting was not as raucous and loud as the one that called the strike. With the workers locked out the situation had taken a dark turn. Most of the men were sitting in the great, unlit room with only the windows to illuminate the proceedings.

"The owners announced last Thursday that we had to pick up last week's pay at 2:00 Saturday as usual, or we'd have to wait until next Saturday," President Sánchez said. "I'm happy to report that very few of you went to get your pay. Now the owners have locked us out as they promised. We're here to decide our next course of action."

When President Sánchez sat down, the secretary took the podium to describe how little money remained in the union treasury. When he had finished, Matilde Gómez asked to address the assembly. A rumble rose from those who did not want him at the podium and from those who did. Apparently oblivious or possibly inured to such reactions, the large mulatto ascended the stage with ponderous movements. He stood silent as the crowd murmured. Finally, seeing that he would not speak until the noise diminished, the crowd quieted down. When the hall was quiet, he began:

"With Christmas approaching we can expect hard opposition from the owners. Their warehouses are stocked and they're shipping. Any cigars we make now won't be sold until next year, so our strike isn't hurting them; on the contrary; we're saving them money. They understand our strike is a gesture of sympathy for those in jail and a mild protest against removing the lectors. It was only for three days, one of which was a Sunday. Yes, they understand our strike and our motives. They also understand we have no bargaining power. They have it all, and they want our lectors. They're afraid of the ideas the lectors pour into our heads. But they are mistaken. We are intelligent. We can evaluate ideas. We know what the communists want. The owners also know the communists are gone; they just want to make sure they don't come back. They have no faith in our ability to distinguish fact from fantasy. The fact is the lectors are gone, and the owners will not take us back until we are hungry enough to accept it unconditionally. We should tell them that if they open their doors we will work without lectors."

A roar of disapproval drowned him out. He waved his massive arms to signal he was not finished. After several minutes they calmed down and he resumed.

"We must accept it. They will try to use the strike to get rid of those they consider troublemakers. If we return unconditionally, I assure you they will purge many of us. For this reason, we must tell them we accept the loss of lectors, but we demand they take us all back, every one of us. All or none!"

The crowd erupted into cheers. It took several minutes to quiet them.

"How many of you would return only if they take us all back."

Hands went up in a grand crescendo until every hand was up and voices were reinforcing their vote, "*Si! Si!*" With the tumult bringing the meeting to a standstill, Matilde slowly walked down from the podium and back to the floor where his coworkers shook his hand and embraced him.

Before the crowd could disperse, President Sánchez took the floor. As he was about to adjourn the meeting, a large group of junior high school children burst into the Labor Temple carrying banners supporting the strike and yelling and laughing and chanting as they marched past the podium.

The secretary went to the President and said, "What the hell is this?"

"I don't know, but I'll find out." Sánchez stepped down to the floor. "What's going on?" he asked the students.

"We marched here from school in sympathy with the strike," the student leader said. "Our parents are out, and we want to help."

"Then go back to school," Sánchez said. "You'll just make things worse." He returned to the podium and asked for volunteers to walk the children back to their schools. Over fifty adults volunteered and ushered the children out of the Labor Temple. The children followed their elders out of the temple, embarrassed and angry. By the time they had assembled outside, they were chanting again as they marched back, some to V.M. Ybor School, others to West Tampa.

"I'd like to meet with the Executive Committee for a few minutes," Sanchez said. "The general meeting is adjourned."

As the meeting broke into random groups, some stayed to talk and others walked home or to one of the cafés. On the floor, in front of the stage, Sánchez assembled the committee in a circle and told them they should let people know they had nothing to do with the students' strike. After some discussion, they decided to prepare a statement to the school board with a copy to the newspapers. The statement assured the public that the union deplored the disturbance in the schools and that they would cooperate in keeping the schools open.

By late morning, the owners announced they would not open their factories until order prevailed. But, contrary to their previous announcement, they would allow workers to pick up their pay envelopes that afternoon.

That evening, the mayor called a small group of Tampa business leaders to his office. The proceedings of their meeting were kept secret, as were the identities of the attendees. The Tribune report was brief and candid:

"A secret committee of 25 outstanding citizens of Tampa, whose appointment was authorized by a mass meeting of 300 citizens, went to work last night. They will deal with the radical element in Tampa. The membership will not be disclosed. A survey of the situation is before the committee.

One group will investigate radical attempts to spread communism in the schools. The other will deal with the cigar strike. Reports show that 90 percent of cigar workers do not sympathize with the communists."

*

"Things are looking up," Gustavo Vila said, as he opened Pablo's door. He sat down and puffed on his long cigar.

"The Mayor's secret committee?" Pablo said.

"That's what it takes."

"Sounds like the Ku Klux Klan."

Vila laughed. "Precisely!" Vila was excited and stood and paced around the office. When he stopped, he put his arm around Pablo's shoulder. "Look, son, there's not much to do around here. Take a long lunch hour, but be back by three when we start shipping." Pablo looked at his boss and asked if he was sure. "By all means."

Putting on his jacket and hat, Pablo left Gustavo Vila looking out the window. Pablo walked down the steps of the factory trying not to think about the pregnancy. He walked down the busy street smiling and nodding at people he passed as he wandered. He did not want to face Consuelo's belly and its dark possibilities and was relishing the noise, traffic, and alluring smells of Seventh Avenue. With the strike in full force, the streets were crowded. After walking for half an hour, he found his way to the Café Cubano.

Matilde abruptly interrupted his conversation with another man to size up the slender, handsome, golden-haired Pablo in his white linen suit and Panama hat. To Matilde he looked like a Cuban politician. "Good to see you made it, Mr. Iglesias." The mulatto's ample belly rubbed against the bar each time he reached for his black coffee. With massive shoulders, arms the size of some men's legs, and enormous hands, he looked more like a stevedore than a man whose bulky fingers were nimble enough to roll small, delicate cigars. His cigar had gone out, but he continued to chew it, occasionally rolling it from one side of his mouth to the other, seeming, at times, almost to swallow it. With his necktie pulled loose and his shirt tail out in back, he looked as if he had just finished some hard labor.

"You don't remember?" Matilde asked with a broad grin.

"I went to one or two places, but . . ."

"You were pretty far gone when you got here."

"Did I make a total fool of myself?"

"Not total. Don't worry; you weren't alone. We're on strike; what's your excuse?"

Pablo tried vainly to remember something, anything.

After waiting for a response, Matilde continued. "You were concerned about your wife, I gathered."

"Did I say that?"

"No. You kept saying that you love her, but in a very sad way."

"What else?"

"Nothing worth mentioning; just alcoholic ramblings."

"The strike isn't going well."

Matilde took the cigar out of his mouth, looked at it, and picked off the remaining ash with a match. "We're nothing in their eyes," he said, snapping his fingers. After relighting it, he gulped down the rest of his coffee. "But that won't affect you."

"Thanks for bringing me home. My wife said you were very kind."

"*Coño!* You really were out," he said with a loud laugh. "At first you seemed disgusted, but then you began to talk about how good it is here, where races can mingle without prejudice and other crap like that."

"Isn't it so?"

"In Ybor City, to a point, but nowhere else."

"I hope I didn't say anything ... "

"Don't give it another thought. Come on back. I'll buy you a cognac. I owe you four or five from last night," Matilde said.

"I've sworn off." Pablo held his head.

Matilde laughed. "That too will pass. How about another coffee?"

"Thanks."

"*Dos cafés,* Domingo." Then returning to Pablo, "What are you doing here anyway?"

"Vila gave me some time off. This better end soon. I've got a baby on the way."

"It won't hurt you."

"No, but I won't keep my job long unless everybody goes back to work."

"We'll lose this one," Matilde said.

The men in the Café Cubano were quiet. "They'll get a fair trial," Pablo said. "We've got to trust the courts to do the right thing."

"I trust the mayor's secret committee. They'll fix things like they always do, with a lynching or a kidnapping."

"Lynching?" Pablo asked.

"Why do you think they're secret? You've heard of the Ku Klux Klan? They're secret too."

Chagrinned, Pablo looked down into his half-empty cup and said nothing, recalling his similar comment to Vila.

"If the secret committee does something illegal, do you think they'll get a trial, fair or otherwise?" Matilde asked.

"I can't believe it would come to that."

"The owners will ruin our Christmas and they'll win, but they'll never own us. Tell Vila that when you go back … no … forget it." His words had revived the other men, who voiced agreement.

Out of the corner of his eye, Pablo saw something move near the back of the café. It was Osvaldo playing with a mouse. The mouse was lying still, apparently wounded and tired, with the cat's head just inches away. Every few seconds, Osvaldo would poke at it with his paw. When the mouse tried to run, Osvaldo pounced on it until it stopped squirming, then stopped to wait for it to try to escape again.

An old memory intruded: Pablo's mother is walking him to school. As they pass Consuelo with her mother, Pablo slows and says something to her. His mother yanks his hand so hard his arm hurts the rest of the day. He starts to cry and looks back at Consuelo. She seems about to cry too.

Osvaldo again poked at the mouse. When it started to run, Osvaldo pounced. Pablo wondered how long before the cat would end his cruel game.

As the men continued to talk excitedly, ignoring Pablo, he put down his coffee cup, placed a nickel on the bar, and turned to leave.

Matilde pushed the coin back. "My treat."

*

Unnerved, Pablo walked four blocks down Seventh Avenue to the Columbia Restaurant and back. When his wandering finally led him to the factory, he saw the light on in the office and heard loud banging. He walked up the entrance stairs past the office and up to the floor, where a man wielding a crowbar was ripping boards off the wall where the reader's platform had been attached. The unpainted slashes on the wall screamed out the message. Pablo walked into Vila's office without knocking.

"You're not wasting any time," he said, before Vila was fully aware of his presence.

"Sit down, Pablo."

"It's not right, Gustavo."

"Business is down. These people have to learn."

"You're making me an accomplice."

"You work for me, remember." His tough businessman's heart pulsed through his words.

"I know that, Gustavo, but I don't feel right."

"Do what you must, but remember, you're management. I promised your father I would help you, but don't push me." Seeing Pablo's shocked reaction, Vila instantly realized Pablo did not know. "Take the rest of the day off and think it over."

"Did you say …?"

"Not another word. Go home and relax. Better yet, take your wife to supper at the Columbia Restaurant as my guest. Now beat it." Vila pushed Pablo to the door.

On the street Pablo thought, That explains it. Like a caged animal, he wanted to flee; the urge was unbearable. On the heels of that primitive thought followed a desire for Consuelo, the source of his agony and his happiness: So soft and loving, so beautiful. She'll make sense of this mess; perhaps relieve my anguish.

It was well past one o'clock; he thought about his house, the wide front porch where he and Consuelo had spent so many pleasant evenings planning their future, and the back porch where they had made love. He knew she'd be standing at the door wearing her lovely smile no matter how bad her day had been, her flowerbed brimming with zinnias, gardenias, and azaleas. Stopping at the florist shop he had often passed but never noticed, he opened the door. I'll make it up to her with flowers, he thought. The only other customer was a well-dressed young, red head wearing a gold-colored, flapper's dress. She was facing the counter, so Pablo could not see her face. His heart jumped when he saw who it was. In street clothes Cynthia was even more striking than before. Nearly as tall as he, perfectly formed, with no excess make-up, she looked demur with her blazing hair gathered in back. In the daylight her slight freckles made her look girlish and wholesome.

"Hello," he said, moving beside her.

Saying nothing, she took the box that the sales clerk had wrapped, paid him, and left. He kept an eye out the window to see which way she went and told the clerk, "I'll be back."

Pablo followed her for two blocks until she stopped at a store window. As he reached her she said, "Are you following me?"

"Why no. Well actually, yes. Why the cold shoulder?"

"It ain't good for business to talk to clients on the street." After a few silent moments, "Well, we cain't just stand here. Come on by … in about a hour."

"I don't know."

"Suit yourself, sugar." She turned and walked away.

For the next hour Pablo could think of nothing but Cynthia. He decided to go home by way of the flower shop, but when he got there, he kept walking. What's wrong with talking to a neutral party? He thought. She might have some good advice. Within minutes he was standing at the house, still debating, when she walked past him and onto the front porch. Turning and smiling, she said, "You comin'?"

Pablo followed her like a puppy to her room.

"Get comfy while I pour you a shot."

"No thanks. I had enough last night." He removed his jacket and tie and hung them behind the door.

"So, you got pickled. What'll it be today? More talk or action?"

"Can we start with a little talk?"

"Whatever you say, sugar." She removed her hat and shoes and began to undress. "Mind if I get comfy?"

When she had removed her dress and was about to loosen her brassiere, he came up behind her and put an arm around her waist and turned her to him. "I can't take this any longer," he said, embracing and kissing her deeply. She pushed him away. "You sure? I ain't too comfy with pregnant daddies, you know."

"Don't talk." He kissed her again as he finished unfastening her brassiere and moved her against the bed. She sat on the side of the bed and began to unbutton his shirt. By the time she finished, he was shaking and could barely stand. "Oh, Cynthia," he said, and pushed her onto her back, as the room dissolved into the moment.

A few seconds later, she began to laugh. "You got too excited, sugar. You gotta learn to pace yourself." Pablo rolled over on his back to regain his breath and his composure.

"Now get dressed and go on back to your wife. I ain't got nothin' she ain't got." She raised herself up on an elbow. "And leave two bucks on the cabinet." Like a little boy Pablo dressed silently, walked to the door, and laid the money on the small cabinet. "I'll be back."

"I wouldn't, sugar. Ain't worth it."

*

Pablo found the Café Cubano nearly empty with Matilde and another cigar maker nursing their coffees at the bar. "Can we talk?" Pablo asked Matilde, "privately?"

"Sure." The large man smiled as he lumbered to the back of the café. "Did you convey my sentiments to Vila?"

"That's not what I want to talk about, but he's taken down the reader's chair."

"*Cabrón!* I heard a carpenter was there this morning."

"I want to ask you something personal."

"You haven't killed anybody or held up a bank, have you?" Matilde smiled.

Not sure he was joking, Pablo said, "You married?"

"Five years."

"Children?"

"No." Matilde's face turned serious.

"How old are you?"

"How old do you think?"

"I'd say thirty-five."

"I'm twenty-four, two years older than you."

Having seen information travel with the speed of light in Ybor City, Pablo did not bother to ask how Matilde knew his age. "Have you ever … you know?"

"So! You've found something on the side. Well, it's not mortal unless you catch something."

"Don't joke. I'm serious. My wife's a wonderful woman, beautiful, intelligent, kind."

"I'll say." Matilde's lilt irritated Pablo.

"She's pregnant; don't you understand? I'm worried."

"So you found a cutie with no strings. *Una puta?*"

Pablo had to restrain his temper at the use of such a foul word to describe Cynthia. His reaction was exactly as Matilde expected.

"On Fifth Avenue?"

Pablo felt naked before this all-knowing mulatto for whom Pablo's predicament was no more than a trivial incident. Before he could respond, Matilde continued, "I bet it was either Christine or Cynthia. They're the stars around here."

Pablo put his hands over his ears as if to shut out the words.

"Now, now; it's not that bad, but she is a whore. You can't fall in love with a whore." Every time Matilde used that word it enraged Pablo more, and seeing its effect, Matilde hammered it all the harder. "Forget about her; go home to your pretty little wife, unless, of course, you plan to completely louse up your life. You're already hurting yourself with Vila by hanging out here. Now go home and pretend nothing happened. Soon, you'll realize nothing did."

When Domingo came to take their order, Matilde said, "Bring me a beer. Don Pablo's leaving." Then to Pablo, "And don't be noble; she doesn't want to know."

"You didn't answer my question."

"It's none of your damned business."

Pablo rose and shook Matilde's hand with a look of sorrowful gratitude. "Thank you."

"Shut up and get the hell out of here."

*

"What beautiful roses," Consuelo said.

"We're dining at the Columbia Restaurant tonight."

"That's so extravagant."

"Gustavo's treat; we'll eat like rich people."

"Why?"

"I'll explain later. Now get dressed. It's almost dark, and we have the whole evening." As he went to the bathroom to wash up, his thoughts raced: Matilde's right. It was over so fast; just mechanical; can almost say it didn't really happen at all. And it'll never happen again. I could have squandered everything. Only two years older, and so wise. If only Papá … So he wrote to don Gustavo. Maybe Papá's not so tough after all."

*

Seeing Pablo pass his office, Gustavo Vila went to see him. "How was supper last night?"

"Excellent. I hope we didn't leave too high a bill."

"You're a good investment, Pablo. How do you feel about our conversation yesterday?"

"You're right. I'm management, not labor."

"Good!" Vila slapped Pablo on the back. I've got good things lined up for you. You've worked hard these past months; the books are up to date; the shipment is finished. Take the rest of the week off. Relax and enjoy the weather."

"Why, thank you. Sure you can spare me?"

"I can handle an empty factory," Vila said with a wry smile.

Pablo headed for the Café Cubano to find Matilde. He felt good about the way he had handled Vila. On his way he bought a newspaper. Not seeing the large mulatto in the café, he asked Domingo if Matilde had been there.

"He's usually here by now. I don't know. Maybe he has some business, or his wife needs him to do something. You know how good Matilde is about helping people. One day I asked him if he would watch the café for me while I took my wife to the doctor. What do you think he did? He took over and washed dishes and made fresh coffee and cleaned the whole place. I wouldn't have asked him except that my wife was very sick with a pain in her stomach."

Domingo followed Pablo to a table, still talking: "We thought it was her appendix, but it wasn't. The doctor examined her completely and found it was only gas. When she passed it the pain went away. But Matilde didn't care that it wasn't an emergency. He helped out just as if it had been serious. I tried to pay him, but he wouldn't take money. 'Just bring me a cup of coffee,' he said, so I made some fresh for him. It was the least I could do."

By the time Domingo finished his story, Pablo was seated, reading his newspaper. "Un café solo," he said.

When Domingo brought the coffee, Pablo was immersed in a front-page article and did not notice that Matilde was casting his great shadow over him. The article read:

"Negro Who Killed Employer Lynched By Maryland Mob

"Salisbury, Md. Dec. 4 - (A.P.) - A mob tonight stormed the Peninsula General hospital here, seized Mack Williams, 35-year-old Negro, dragged him from his bed and lynched him in the Wicomico County Courthouse yard. Williams had shot and killed his employer, Daniel J. Elliot, a lumberman, and then wounded himself. Six men entered the hospital by a side door as officers guarded the front entrance. The Negro's head was swathed in bandages from the gunshot wounds he had received and was unable to stand. The mob estimated at 2000 hustled the Negro from the hospital and dragged him to the courtyard. Yelling as he appeared, the mob quickly threw a rope over a lamppost and several men pulled him off the ground.

"Half hour after the lynching the mob cut the body down, placed it on a pile of boxes and burned it."

Pablo was pale as he looked up. Seeing Matilde's massive head, he folded the paper.

"Don't bother. I've seen it. They killed him twice. They would have found him guilty anyway."

Pablo could think of nothing to say.

"There's a neighborhood just a few blocks from here, where Negroes live in filthy shacks like animals," Matilde said. "Between Ybor City and downtown. They call it the Scrub."

"I've never seen it."

"The main streets from Ybor City to downtown Tampa skirt around it."

Pablo sensed a delicate pain rising in Matilde's eyes.

"Things aren't the way you think, but you have something else on your mind," Matilde said, weary of an old theme.

"I just wanted to thank you for the good advice. I had never been with a woman like that. I bought Consuelo some roses and took her out to supper."

"*Muy bien!* Now what about Vila?"

"Nothing new, except that they're determined to get rid of the lectors."

Matilde was silent for a few moments. "Every strike hardens the owners. We're just machines to them." Matilde seemed to be debating with himself as he relit his cigar. "You've seen the men turn to me, even though I'm not a union officer."

"Who's president?"

"A white Cuban named Raúl Sánchez. A nice guy, but he's not even a good buncher. He beat me twice in a union election."

"Because of race?"

"City officials spread the word that they wouldn't tolerate a Negro in that position. If you don't believe me, just ask any of the white Cubans they lobbied."

"What about the owners?"

"They didn't mind having somebody they could control."

"And the workers?"

"They voted; Sánchez won."

"That's awful."

"Let's take a walk," Matilde said, standing.

"Where?"

"It's too nice a morning to waste in this hole."

"You know, Matilde, I've never felt comfortable with Vila. He treats me well, but something about him ..."

"He's an owner."

"I just found out he hired me because of my father."

"You didn't know?"

"The old man disinherited me. I guess he felt guilty."

"What are you going to do about it?"

"Ignore it for now and start my own business as soon as I can."

"Now you're talking like a man with his brains in his head instead of his penis."

Pablo laughed loudly, something he had not done in days. He put his arm around Matilde's shoulder. "Come to my house for lunch."

"Better ask your wife. She wasn't too happy with me the other night."

"She'll be delighted."

"I'll have to tell Zoraida."

"Eleven OK?"
"Fine."

*

Consuelo was not happy. The thought of that unkempt, sweaty man with his belly straining his buttons, carrying her clean, handsome, drunk husband had been too embarrassing. "Why didn't you warn me? I didn't have time to go to the store. All I have is rice and eggs."

"How come? What have you been doing?"

"I went to mass this morning and stayed to talk with Father López."

"You've been to church a lot lately."

"Father has helped me a lot; he understands."

"Understands what? Was it about me?"

"No!" She went to the kitchen.

"Uh-huh. Well, rice and eggs are fine," he said as he followed her. "He'll be here any minute."

"How could you do this?"

"He's a good man. You'll like him."

When Pablo heard heavy footsteps on the porch, he jumped up from his chair and met Matilde with his upturned smile and a handshake. "This is your home," Pablo said, with a formal gesture.

Usually calm and in control, Matilde seemed nervous holding his crumpled Panama hat in his hands. Walking into the living room, Consuelo said, "I apologize for lunch. Pablo didn't warn me."

"Anything you make will be excellent, Señora Iglesias."

Under Consuelo's gaze Matilde feel like a bug pinned to a board. She tried to smile and make him feel at home, but his size and appearance repelled her. Being obviously black and just as obviously white sounded a disturbing dissonance. His vein-laced dark eyes made him look menacing, as though he could appear some night out of a dark alley and strangle a person with those bear paws. Though she tried not to show her feelings, they resonated with her every word and movement.

"Please sit down while I finish," she said, and went into the kitchen, lit the gas under a frying pan, and poured in some olive oil. When the oil was hot, she cracked eggs into the pan two at a time. While she waited, she ladled huge piles of white rice into three plates and finally laid two eggs on top of the rice in each plate. On the table were a platter of fried, ripe plantains, a platter of Cuban bread, and a lettuce and tomato salad over which she had poured olive oil and vinegar. When it was ready she called them in.

"I love the smell of good oil," Matilde said. "It's wonderful."

As they sat down Pablo said, "Matilde is the unofficial leader of the cigar makers, and not only in our factory. He spoke at the Labor Temple this weekend. I told you last night about how he laid me out at the Café."

"We're newly arrived and newly married and new at life. Now we're expecting a baby. It's a lot to grasp in so little time."

"You're as gifted as your husband … and a lot prettier."

The compliment caught Consuelo unaware; she resented the blush she felt spilling over her face. "I guess this strike is hard on all of you. I hope for your family's sake that it ends soon."

"We all do, Señora Iglesias."

"Please call me Consuelo." As the words slipped out, her jaw tightened and she looked down at her plate.

"Matilde thinks the industry is doomed," Pablo said, as he cut up his eggs to let them seep into the rice.

"You can't stop progress," Matilde said. "But progress brings its losses. Machines can't duplicate our craft, but the cheap cigars they produce will ruin the industry. As Karl Marx said, machines dehumanize. When everything is machine-made we'll become so detached from reality that people will think oranges and eggs come from grocery store shelves." Seeing Consuelo smile, he said, "I've said something funny?"

"I was thinking about eggs coming from store shelves.

"Have you read Marx?" Pablo asked.

"Das Kapital. Long and boring, but well worth the effort."

"Are you a communist?" Consuelo asked.

"Absolutely not! But, like all mistaken geniuses, he said some good things."

"Like what?" she asked.

"That workers would become squatters with disembodied hands, divorced from the feel of a hand-rolled cigar, the firmness of a job well done. How can you take pride in your work when you're only part of a machine? Like being a puppet. My grandfather harvested his tobacco leaves, cured them, and rolled the cigars at home in the evenings. Every week, a broker came and took them to market. My grandfather couldn't strike when the leaf was poor, but he could brag he made the best cigars in his village. It wasn't efficient, and the cigars weren't uniform, but they were his. My grandmother helped and so did my mother and her brothers and sisters. A handmade cigar is that, the work of human hands and a human soul. Marx doesn't advocate returning to old ways. He thinks workers should own the factories, but workers argue when they have no power; imagine the chaos if they were in control."

"Did your grandfather ever work in a factory?" Consuelo asked.

"Yes, during the war, Rebel soldiers burned his farm. They had to move to Havana and almost starved. He finally found work in a small factory. With no land, they couldn't grow food." Matilde stopped and shook his head. "But that's another story. We complain when the leaf's bad. What can the owner do? It might have spoiled in the ship or at the dock. Everybody blames somebody else. The factory system is efficient, but it pits factions against one other."

"Rebel soldiers?" Consuelo asked. Weren't they with the poor farmers?"

"Yes, but the big boss, General Gómez, decided the only way to beat Spain was to destroy the Cuban economy. He tried to bring agriculture to a halt."

"Horrible!" she said. "But getting back to Marx, what's the solution?"

"I wish I knew."

"How will the strike end?" Pablo asked.

"The lector's gone; we'd better accept that before we lose more."

6 – ZORAIDA – DECEMBER 1931

*

Hoover Delivers State Of The Union

*

Federal Prohibition Agent Held In Alabama Lynching

*

Two Tampa Gambling Houses Close Mysteriously

*

Split Along Party Lines Looms Among
Anti-Prohibitionists

*

On Thursday night, December 3ʳᵈ, the executive committee of the Tampa Tobacco Workers Industrial Union ordered demonstrations at the Regensberg factories in Ybor City and West Tampa. It was the communist union's bold attempt to seize control from the older, more established union. Within an hour the order spread throughout Ybor City and West Tampa. With the news so widely known, word easily found its way to City Hall. The police chief immediately dispatched policemen to the two factories to wait for the demonstrators.

When the demonstrators began to appear at the Regensberg factory in West Tampa the police emerged from their squad cars.

"Remember, men, we're after the communist leaders only. Go easy and use your heads," Lieutenant Taylor said. "Now take your stations and don't let anyone into the building." Thirty-eight years old and battle-scarred, the seasoned, police veteran led his men with confidence.

As the crowd grew Lieutenant Taylor led his men cautiously onto the factory yard.

A loud voice yelled out, "All right; form a column and begin the parade like we said. Don't worry about them."

The strikers spread around the building like a giant amoeba in full view of the police, yelling to the few workers inside, "Come out! United we'll win!"

The police moved in with clubs in their hands, yelling for the crowd to disperse. "This is an unlawful assembly, Liertenant Taylor said. "Go home and nobody will get hurt."

But the amorphous crowd continued to march, now with taunts and jeers. Seeing the demonstrators on the verge of erupting into a full-blown riot, Lieutenant Taylor ordered his men back. At the squad car, he radioed headquarters. "We're outnumbered. Send reinforcements. ... How many? ... At least 500 ... No, I don't see any guns."

With the police apparently in retreat, the crowd gained confidence. Their jeers grew louder. "Keep it up," their leader said. "Don't be distracted."

Within minutes, six patrol wagons screeched in with sirens blasting, and a horde of police and deputies in civilian clothes erupted and quickly assembled on the yard near the street. A plain clothed deputy named Adams, stocky and muscular, slaped a blackjack into the palm of his hand. "Let's get those red bastards," he said.

"Take it easy, Adams," Lieutenant Taylor said. "We don't want to drive the rest into their ranks."

"Bull!" Adams said. "They're all reds."

"We need your help, Adams, but you follow orders or stay out," Taylor said.

"I take my orders from the twenty-five," Adams said.

"There's no time to argue," Taylor said. "You deputies get behind the uniformed policemen and follow me."

The police marched toward the building with the deputies close behind. As they approached the crowd, the strikers stopped marching and surrounded the police. One of the deputies, a short, fat man, sprang out swinging his club at the strikers yelling, "Communists bastards!" When the strikers retaliated with their fists, the other deputies and the police rushed in. Some of the policemen tried to separate the strikers from the deputies. Others, agreeing with the deputies, joined them, swinging their clubs viciously. A policeman grabbed a striker, who bit the cop's arm and clamped on. The cop hit him on the head twice with his nightstick before the man fell groaning. Standing over the man the policeman saw blood spreading through his sleeve. Another striker found an old wooden chair near the building, smashed it against a tree and tossed pieces to others saying, "Use this."

Solidly swinging their clubs, the more disciplined police left bloody men scattered on the ground.

Having identified one of the communist leaders from photographs, a policeman grabbed the man and threw him into a patrol wagon. Other cops did the same. It took only fourteen minutes for the police to gain the upper hand.

The lieutenant looked around at dozens of bloody strikers and a few policemen lying crumpled on the ground. The patrol wagon bulged with ten of the leaders including three women.

"We'll take them," Adams said.

Ignoring him, Lieutenant Taylor said, "Take them to the station and book them for rioting. No bond." Then he turned to the crowd. "It's over. Now go home."

Two of the patrol wagons with the arrested strikers drove off. The remaining police and deputies stayed at the scene until the crowd finally dispersed; then Lieutenant Taylor ordered his men to their cars.

*

A similar scene was occurring at Regensberg's Ybor City factory: Police deployed when demonstrators began marching around the building chanting for people to come out.

"Stop those men," Captain Wilson yelled. "They're trying to get into the building." Four policemen rushed to a stairway on the side of the building. Three strikers struggled to break open a locked door. Pulling strikers back off the stairs any way they could, the policemen forced their way to the door and pushed the strikers back down the stairs. Two officers remained to prevent another attempt. Within minutes, the strike leader yelled, "Hold it, hold it."

Motion stopped suddenly.

Turning to the police he said, "We have a right to demonstrate."

"This is an unlawful assembly," Captain Wilson said. "Vacate the premises. By order of the Mayor."

"Why is the Mayor with the owners and not the workers?" the man asked. At these words his followers begin to yell agreement.

"The Mayor must keep order. A demonstration like this could spark another riot."

"That's right," the strike leader said. "And you'll be the one who sparked it. We're not making trouble. We're just asking the workers inside to come out and join us. There was no violence till you showed up."

Turning to two officers at his side, Wilson said, "Take him."

The crowd moved closer as if to resist, but their leader turned to his men, held his arms up, and said, "Don't start anything. It's what they want." Then he calmly walked to the two officers and gave himself up.

Captain Wilson held the strike leader until the crowd had dispersed and then tells him, "I'm not going to charge you. Now go on home."

News spread that the executive committee of the communist union had ordered a noon raid on two other factories. When the news reached police headquarters, the riot squad, armed with riot guns, got ready with squad cars and other automobiles parked outside the police station ready to move the instant they got word that marchers had appeared. This force also included special deputies supplied by the secret committee of 25.

Nerves were taut when the clock struck twelve. Minutes passed; the police waited.

"Let's go, Lieutenant."

"Relax, Johnson. The last thing we want is to start something."

By 12:30 the riot squad got out of their cars. It was clear the strikers had changed their minds.

*

After the first riot three weeks earlier, the Tampa Tobacco Workers Industrial Union moved their headquarters from the Labor Temple to a secret location. Following a tip, the police stationed themselves on Seventh Avenue down the block from the building suspected of housing the new headquarters.

Shortly after 3:00 P.M., Captain Wilson said, "OK, Hernández. We're all here. Move in."

The undercover detective, a tough-looking man of thirty-four, with black hair and piercing brown eyes entered the building. Wearing an open collared white shirt, a seedy suit coat with unmatched trousers, and work shoes, he looked like an unemployed cigar maker. Chewing a cigar he walked into the office toward the man working at a cluttered desk. "What's your name?" he asked.

"*No hablo ingles,*" the man said.

Detective Hernández restated the question in Spanish.

"Who are you?" the man asked.

Hernández pulled out his wallet and flipped it open to reveal his badge. The thin man with brown hair and bushy moustache stood staring at the badge.

"Herrera."

"Where from?"

"Cuba."

Detective Hernández then told Herrera to hold his hands behind him, and he handcuffed him. Then he called in the rest of the police waiting outside. Showing Herrera a search warrant, they searched the small, windowless office.

"What is this?" one officer asked, holding a cigar box stuffed with money.

"I don't know."

"We're going to find out. It'll go better for you if you save us the trouble."

"This week's collection, the local defense fund."

"And this?" Hernández asked, opening a file drawer full of cards. "Each has a name. Who are they?"

"Members."

"And these," another policeman asked pulling two fistfuls of slips of paper out of one of the desk drawers.

Hernández translated the question.

"New members," Herrera said. "We haven't put them on cards yet."

"Get him out of here, the captain said. "We'll finish interrogating him at the station." Then addressing his men, "Grab all the stuff you can carry; we'll come back for the rest."

The membership cards contained the names of 3500 cigar makers; 1500 additional names were scribbled on the paper slips. The police also confiscated files that contained letters sent to and from operatives in Mexico, Puerto Rico, and South America. The crude, homemade Soviet flag hanging near Herrera's desk consisted of a red linen field bearing a crossed sickle and hammer in white.

The newspaper the following morning quoted the Chief of Police: "The evidence gives us a complete picture of the communist organization. The membership cards will be of interest to the federal immigration department because I am convinced many aliens are enrolled with the reds. Wholesale deportation proceedings may be the outgrowth of the government's investigation."

*

Tall, with a voluptuous figure, and brimming with sensuality, Zoraida wore her thick wavy black hair under a kerchief in the African style. With large, light brown eyes, slender nose, full lips and white even teeth, she reflected the seductive inscrutability of a wild animal. Through her pale skin oozed the mystery of the Tropics. She called herself a mulatta, but revealed little about her life, even to Matilde. When he asked, she would smile and nuzzle up. "What does it matter, *mi amor*? I am who I am, *tu mulata*. I was born that night we danced in Havana, the night we made ourselves one." Matilde had never been able to resist her untamed, feminine magnetism, nor did he try. He felt married to a feral cat of the jungle.

Their house stretched back along the narrow lot, a long rectangular frame structure with a metal roof. A smaller rectangle, within and halfway back along the side of the house, enclosed two bedrooms. The bedrooms separated the remaining space into a living room in front and a kitchen at the rear with a passageway joining the two running beside the two bedrooms. It was the pinnacle of architectural simplicity. Horizontal, grooved pine boards painted a glossy cream color lined the inside walls that rested on a varnished pine floor. A hand pump next to the kitchen sink just inside the window supplied water. The back door opened to a tiny yard jammed with papaya, mango, banana, and avocado trees planted by an earlier occupant. On the left side stood the privy.

Their second bedroom was darkened with heavy window drapes and had only two pieces of furniture. One was a table with a two-foot-tall statue of Saint Barbara holding a chalice in one hand and a sword in the other. A vase of flowers stood in front of the statue. On a second table, several carefully coiled necklaces of the Santería religion lay next to a small tureen that housed the mysteries of the Cofá de Orúnla, the only initiation conferred upon women by the high priests of Santería.

After praying to Saint Barbara, Zoraida moved to the second table, bent down and opened the mystic tureen and extracted the sixteen cowrie seashells, called caracoles in the religion of Santería. The caracoles were small, flattened seashells with a pushed-in opening on one side that resembles a tiny mouth. Zoraida said some words in the African tongue and cast the caracoles on the floor mat. "Speak," she whispered. Only three of the shells fell with their mouths facing up. She sat transfixed before the caracoles as she waited for the saints to speak to her. When she heard footsteps on the porch, she quickly put the caracoles back into the tureen, tidied up the altar, and walked out.

Matilde was walking faster than usual. When she saw him she stood. "Oh, I'm glad you're not hurt."

"Police broke up a demonstration at Regensberg," he said, as he walked up the steps to the porch. "How did you know?"

"I heard. For what they did that?"

"The strikers tried to march around the factory." He sat on the heavy banister and lit the cigar he had been chewing.

Zoraida stood at his side with her arm around his waist, pressing her breast against him. "*Mi amor,*" she said melodiously. Feeling she was not wearing anything underneath, Matilde pulled her around, looked into her eyes and kissed her. "Better," she said. "You need your mulatta. *Vamo',* it's time to eat."

Matilde walked back to the kitchen and sat in one of the four, straight-backed chairs at the table. On the far wall hung a framed print of Jesus with a crown of thorns.

"I have your favorite, boiled corn meal with garlic."

Matilde smiled at his wife's attempt at humor. "It's only been three weeks. Are we reduced to cornmeal already?"

"There is no ill that does not bring some good," she said.

"The bolitero has been here," he said.

"Don't worry yourself, *mi amor*. It will please you when my number comes out."

"*Coño*, Zoraida. I've told you a hundred times. I can't afford it now."

"What's going to happen?"

"They're tightening the screws. And they've got help, that secret committee of 25 sons of whores."

"Looking for Marxists?"

"*Claro.*"

"The only ones who care for the workers."

"They only care for themselves," he said.

"Throw out the owners: I believe in that."

"*Ay, Zoraida, que inocente.*"

"*No, amor*. The innocent is you. He who lives on the generosity of others will die disappointed. The owners will squeeze all they can until the workers finally accept Marxism and throw the capitalist vultures into the street." Zoraida's eyes radiated wrath. Standing over her husband as one prepared to fight, her chest heaved.

"You're right about one thing: that committee will do anything to purge the communists."

"And your friends?"

"A few believe as you, but the majority just want a free ride."

"All good must come through violence, Matilde. The capitalists will never willingly give up their plunder. Barbarians!" she said, turning toward the stove.

"That secret committee worries me."

"And they call us savages!"

"I don't understand how the Mayor can resort to vigilante action. This is supposed to be a country of laws."

"*La ley del embudo*," she said, with a cynical grin. "The law of the funnel: for me, the big end; for you, the small end. Liberty is the big end, Matilde, and it is for the rich. While the rich are with us, we will have no liberty." Turning, she put a pot under the pump, filled it with water, and set it on the stove.

"This is depressing, Zoraida."

She walked to him and kissed him. "It is not good to dwell on such things."

Matilde sat silent.

With a strange fire in her eyes she said, "I've consulted the caracoles."

"You know I don't believe in that crap!"

Ignoring him, she continued. "I cast them, and three fell facing up. That's the oracle, Oggundá, 'Arguments bring tragedies.'"

"And what is that supposed to mean?"

"The strike will end; the workers will win and lose." She spoke softly and gravely.

"It doesn't take caracoles to figure that out!" he said, getting up and walking into the hall. "Why can't they tell you which number to play?"

"Come back." When he stopped, she put her arms around his neck.

He kissed her tenderly. Pressing herself against him, he passed a hand down her back as far as it would reach. "You still excite me the way you did that first day. There's a violence in you, Zoraida, that's very sexy."

"You speak like a god." When she laid her head on his shoulder, he lifted her gently as if she weighed nothing and carried her to their bedroom.

*

Matilde was lying on the bed almost asleep looking out through the sheer drapes. The long green leaves of a mango tree shattered the sunlight into shards that flitted around their bedroom. He reached for the cigar he had left on the table next to the bed. It was out, so he took a match out of a large box and reached down and struck it on the bottom of the iron bed. He could not help thinking about Pablo.

Young, white, educated, and a safe job, he thought, should be enough for any man. With his beautiful wife expecting a baby, his world should be perfect, at least in the view of a striking mulatto. He cannot appreciate how we are different or how we are the same.

After exhaling smoke toward the window, he looked at his wife. Her hair was spread across the pillow like a black halo. She was smiling.

"You are worried?" she asked, turning on her side to face him.

"Pablo Iglesias is a strange one, down one day and up the next."

"*Indigestión de bien estar*," she said, raising her head and pushing a pillow beneath it.

Matilde laughed as he drew on the cigar. "Sick on too much wellness," he repeated. "He thinks he has troubles."

"It is human to have troubles, *mi amor*."

Sensing his depression returning she said, "Don't let it drown you, my love. Disappointments don't kill, but they corrode. Each must live his life. With life there is always hope."

He smiled and kissed her again.

"Now I must cook."

"I've got a library book to finish. I'll be on the porch."

When Matilde got to the front door with the book in his hand, he was surprised to see a man standing on the porch. It was the cigar maker who lived across the street and who had barely spoken to Matilde or Zoraida since moving there over a year ago. The man hesitated, especially when he saw Matilde's frown through the screen door. He was about Matilde's age and had been a neighbor in Havana. With erect posture this imposing man was well over six feet tall. Not handsome, but rugged looking, he did not scowl at Matilde the way he usually did; instead, his eyes were on the floor. Anger rose in Matilde at the sight. Waiting in vain for the man to speak, Matilde finally asked what he wanted. Almost inaudibly he said, "My wife is in labor. I don't know what to do." Matilde knew what he wanted, but waited for him to ask.

Hesitating, the man said, "I hate to disturb you, but … Zoraida is a midwife. We're desperate."

"I'll tell her."

Zoraida was walking toward him when he turned. "*Vamo'*," she said. Wearing a large necklace of blue and pink beads worn by the initiates of Oba, and her Santería ritual tureen in her arms, they ran across the street.

"That *cabrón* knows us well enough when he wants something," Matilde mumbled, remembering a day when they passed on the street. Matilde had greeted him and the man had ignored him and walked past. Zoraida had to hold Matilde back. "Don't, my love. He's not worth it."

"*Hijo de puta!*"

"He who will not enter my home ejects me from his," she had said. Then, pulling him by the hand, "He may be shy." The soothing quality of her voice calmed him more than her words.

Matilde was still standing on his porch as Zoraida went into the neighbor's house. "With all our white neighbors only Zoraida can help."

*

"The situation looks bad," Matilde said that evening at the Café Cubano. A handful of the usual cigar makers were there, sipping coffee, saying little. Next to Matilde sat a man they called El Gordo, a short, rotund man in his early fifties whose ruddy face seemed about to explode. Jacinto and El Rubio were sitting at a table playing two-handed dominoes. Osvaldo was crouching, sneaking up on something near the back door.

"Vigilantes kidnapped a man yesterday. They beat him and left him in the woods."

Matilde sounded as if he were talking to himself. Instead of his usual oratory, he was delivering a soliloquy into his coffee cup as if seeking answers in the opaque brew.

"The Sicilians are leaving the factories, selling vegetables in pushcarts, anything to stay alive. They've got it rough too, but they're smart enough to get out."

"We're craftsmen," El Gordo said.

"And if we don't get back to work soon, we'll be crap eaters," Matilde said. "You can't get more milk by starving the cow."

"We have our pride. They can't treat us like day laborers." Jacinto slammed down a domino.

"If we don't get back to work soon, we'll be sweeping streets," Matilde said.

"What about the le-e-ectors?" El Rubio asked, laying down his last domino to win the game.

"They'll install radios to entertain us with inanities," Matilde said. "Jacinto, what did you have for supper last night? And you, Rubio, when was the last time you took your wife to a dance? Face it, *caballeros*, it's over."

*

Every table and barstool of the Café Cubano was occupied on Monday morning, and all ears were focused on El Chulo, dressed as if for work in a suit and tie. With his hair combed back neatly and his hat pushed back, he held a cigar in his teeth as he read. In his most stentorian voice he was imitating a lector by translating the newspaper into Spanish for his friends. "The manufacturers will gladly welcome workmen for whom we can provide work, but on an open shop basis. They will refuse to deal with any organization with communist affiliations and will not permit reading in the factories. Collections from the workers will not be permitted except to help a fellow worker in distress."

"How nice!" El Chulo said. "First we asked them to hire us all even if only for one week, then for one or two days. *Coño!* It's Christmas! What the hell do they want?"

"To cut some of us out," Matilde said.

"Wh-wh-wh-what do we do?" El Rubio asked, feeling the pain of the strike and the futility of resisting.

"We're men," El Chulo said, "not mice."

Sarna, the thin man in his mid-forties with an unruly mane of brown hair, was sitting on a stool scratching his crotch. "I've got to feed my family," he said.

"That is a man's first responsibility," Matilde said in his slow drawl.

"Let me read something," Sarna said, opening a newspaper-like publication.

"The Tampa Tobacco Workers Industrial Union endeavors to organize all tobacco workers, with the shop as the basic unit and democratic centralization as the guiding rules. Our union realizes that successful struggle can be conducted only when all workers in the industry are united nationally and internationally with workers of all other industries to combat capitalistic exploitation throughout the world. We are affiliated with the Trade Union Unity League, militant leader of the trade union movement in this country. The Trade Union Unity League in turn is affiliated with Red International of labor unions. Throughout these affiliations we are a part of the working class united front against the entire system of capitalistic, wage-slavery and oppression."

"That's the Tribune; the owners' mouthpiece," Jacinto said.

"This is not the Tribune; it's the pamphlet the communists passed out before the riot. Maybe you should've read it," Sarna said.

*

Fifteen hundred workers gathered in the Labor Temple on Thursday afternoon, December 11th. It was a somber meeting with little noise and few speeches. The sun shining in one of the high windows cast a bright beam on the platform, like a massive column leaning into the wall. Tiny dust particles performed their lively dance in the light beam, converting the workers' temple into an eery cathedral. Some of the men looking at the light beam seemed to be praying. At the end of a short presentation by President Sánchez, the workers unanimously agreed to return to work on whatever terms the manufacturers might impose and to maintain their union, from which, as Sánchez put it, "every bit of the red has been wiped out."

That evening, the manufacturers met with the Secret Committee of 25. The next morning's Tribune carried their statement, which included the question, "How can they take a stand without knowing the manufacturers' conditions for reopening?"

Reflecting the Secret Committee's advice, the manufacturers' terms appeared under the headline, "Manufacturers Unanimous." They spelled out briefly and clearly the six conditions under which they would reopen their factories: (1) No reduction in wages. (2) Hiring based on need, with each factory hiring as many as they could. (3) They will deal only with individuals. (4) No lectors or distribution of literature or speeches. (5) Factories operated on principles of true Americanism. (6) Foremen would be present at the factories on Saturday afternoon and Sunday morning to sign up workers who want to work.

That Saturday afternoon, the line outside the Vila and Fernández factory stretched half way around the block. Some men left smiling with their jobs restored; others left grumbling after being told they would not be rehired. When Jacinto stepped to the desk on the sidewalk outside the factory, the foreman said, "*Hola, Jacinto.* I already have you down." Saying nothing, Jacinto took a step and waited for Matilde who stood next in line. "Sorry, Matilde," the foreman said.

"What? There's some mistake," Matilde said.

Jacinto came back to the foreman. "This man worked hard to prevent the strike and to convince the workers to return."

"Sorry. Orders. Vila says he was an instigator."

"I instigated more than he did. Keep your shitty job," Jacinto said, chin thrust out and fists on his hips.

"M-m-m-me too," El Rubio said, standing behind Matilde.

"Don't be stupid," Matilde said. "That won't help." He turned and walked away. Jacinto went after him. "They can't do this. It's unfair."

"You can't afford to be noble, my good friend," Matilde said. "And don't let anybody else be stupid."

Jacinto and El Rubio stood on the sidewalk as Matilde walked away with his head up as if he had won a battle.

*

When Jacinto walked into the factory Monday morning and saw the scars of the lector's amputated platform, tears filled his eyes. Though he knew it, seeing it and realizing what they had lost was too much. Saying nothing, he sat at his table, unwrapped his tools, spread a half leaf of wrapper on his cutting board, removed a bunch from the mold, and began quietly to work.

El Rubio said nothing to his fellow workers as he sat at his customary place. There was little talking as workers filed in as if to a funeral.

"Where's Matilde?" El Gordo asked, seeing his neighbor's table empty.

"They didn't rehire him," Jacinto said.

"Why not? He argued against the damn communists!" Sarna said.

"We told the foreman all that, but he wouldn't budge," Jacinto said.

"Are we going to take it?" Sarna asked, standing up and looking around.

"Sit down," Jacinto said. "Matilde knew people would feel that way. He said not to be stupid."

*

Matilde spent most of the morning rocking on his porch looking at the neighborhood. The day was cool and clear and the sky an endless, regal blue with clouds so thick and substantial he wanted to reach up and stir them with his fingers. The light poles and houses looked like sharp sculptures cut out of the clouds. A bird landed on an electric wire across the street and brought the scene back to life. The only sounds he could hear came from La Septima's automobile traffic filtered through two blocks of houses and trees. He tried to read, but could not concentrate. As he reviewed events of the past weeks, nothing made sense. It can't be racial, he thought. Other Afro-Cubans are working. His powers of insight failed him. As he sat and rocked, he looked into the eyes of all who passed on their way to work. Their wives had to face him too when they opened their front doors. It was a useless gesture, but he wanted them to face the irrationality of the strike. He had known what the owners would do, but he did not expect to be a victim.

"*Vamo'*," Zoraida said. "You look like an idiot sitting there."

"Maybe I am."

"I have lunch on the table."

"We just had breakfast."

"Four hours have passed. Come, your mulatta needs you. Tomorrow the sun will rise again, and you will find something."

"Where?"

"Somewhere there is a shop owner who does not care about unions or politics if you make good cigars."

"Maybe tomorrow. Today I'm going to wallow in my misfortune."

7 – SAM - 1932

*

Al Capone Convicted Of Tax Evasion

*

Spain Riots

*

Paris Mob Battles Police

*

Amateur Night Attracts Large Crowd

*

Pablo had been looking out the dining room window for several minutes hoping that it wouldn't rain. As Consuelo walked in carrying a tray of fried steaks covered with fried, chopped onions, Pablo could not take his eyes off her belly.

"What's wrong, Pablo? You've been sitting there since I started cooking."

"Nothing. I'm fine."

She laid a steak and some onions on his plate. "Your favorite," she said.

He cut his steak and ate for several minutes without looking up or saying anything.

"You're not worried about the baby, are you?"

83

"Stop asking stupid questions. I told you nothing's wrong."

"I know better, Pablo. I can't help if you won't tell me. Father López says married people must talk out their problems."

"I thought you said you weren't complaining about me." Slamming down his fork, his wineglass fell over and broke. His eyes frightened her. "Don't you understand? It's the strike, the depression, and bringing a baby into this godforsaken world. Otherwise, everything's perfect." He picked up the broken glass as she soaked up the spilled wine with a towel.

"You've changed," she said.

"I guess you're stuck with me."

"Why so angry? We were so happy."

"Maybe you are. I'm miserable, but that's life."

"I wish I could do something," she said, coming around the table behind him and putting her arms around his shoulders.

"Vila's given me every boring job in the factory, whole days of inventories and trial balances. I'm a flunky. Understand? How the hell am I supposed to be happy?"

She backed away.

"The trouble with you is you've never had to face the real world. You have no idea. You're not qualified to talk. Just do your job and I'll do mine. Understand? And stop nagging." He rose, put on his jacket and hat and walked out into a drizzling rain.

Looking down at the uneaten food on the table, Consuelo wept.

*

In ten minutes Pablo arrived at the Café Cubano looking for Matilde. Not finding him, he sat at the bar and ordered a cup of coffee. Before he had finished it, Matilde walked in. "Come into the back room," Pablo said. When they were alone at the small table, Pablo asked in a whisper, "Vila blames you, doesn't he?"

Matilde looked at Pablo suspiciously. "That's what I hear. Why?"

"He never chats the way he used to. He gives me every crappy job in the factory."

"That's not my fault, I hope," Matilde said.

"No. It's our friendship."

"Aha! Partners in crime you mean."

"I don't know. He hasn't said anything, but he's very cold."

"Welcome to the legion of alienated cigar workers." Matilde called Domingo and asked for two brandies. "We'll drown our sorrows together like brothers, my aristocratic accomplice."

"It's not funny, Matilde. What'll I do?"

"Find something else."

Pablo looked at the smiling man who was clearly far worse off. "I'm sorry, Matilde. I'm not used to this."

"You're the product of a mediocre education, Pablo. You've never had to find your next meal or face failure with dignity. I, on the other hand, have been to the best university. I'm terribly sorry for you."

Pablo could not imagine Matilde's life. He drank his brandy and put his hand on Matilde's shoulder. "You're a good friend, Matilde."

The rain had stopped when Pablo found his way home sober enough to walk and drunk enough to evade conversation. Consuelo was sitting in the living room when he walked in. She looked at him quizzically without commenting. He saw her staring at him and said, "Before you say anything, I've had a few, and I'm going to bed."

*

Pablo was not far wrong about Gustavo Vila. The old man never forgot that electrifying moment when Matilde called for the walkout, and he hated him. Convinced that Pablo bore watching, Vila considered firing him, but decided to keep him in view and in his debt.

At home the Iglesias's lives had congealed into deafening tedium: after a bath and supper, Pablo would walk to the Café Cubano to talk or play dominoes with the cigar makers. Lonely, Consuelo tried to counter her husband's morose demeanor with bright thoughts of her baby. She spent most afternoons crocheting blankets and booties and doing all the things expectant mothers did to while away the days and hours waiting for their babies. In the evenings she read or listened to the radio. She played the piano less now. Pablo attempted to drown his loneliness in a river of anonymous friends who offered, at best, only distraction.

One bright light appeared in the form of a letter to Pablo. It had been forwarded from Matanzas. He looked at it, didn't recognize the sender's name and laid it on the table by the sofa.

"Aren't you going to open it?"

Without answering Pablo picked it up, opened it and unfolded the letter. As he read, a smile crept over his lips. "Some guy named Marvin Burke; graduated two years before me. He's trying to form a Notre Dame alumni group in this area."

"How did he get your address?"

"The school gave him my parents' address; my mother sent it on."

"Sounds interesting. Maybe he can help you."

"That'll be the day."

*

That evening Consuelo was sitting on her porch when Sara dropped by. *"Hola Consuelo. Como estás?"*

"The baby's kicking like mad. It shouldn't be long."

Sara sat in one of the rocking chairs. "Benito's at the Cuban Club as usual. You'd think these men have enough of each other at work."

"I know. Pablo too."

"I haven't seen you lately. You're not *that* pregnant."

"I haven't felt like socializing."

"Anything you want to talk about?"

The offer brought a burst of sobbing. Sara put her arm around Consuelo and helped her into the house. "That's it. Let it out."

"It's Pablo. We hardly talk. He says he's worried about having a baby with the depression and all. He won't say it, but I think he's blaming me for losing his inheritance."

"Want to tell me what happened with his father?"

Consuelo hesitated. More than anything else she wanted to share her burden; it had become too heavy to shoulder alone. "It's very personal, Sara, but I know I can trust you. Pablo's father didn't want him to marry me."

"Why not?"

"My great-grandmother was a slave."

Both women sat silent for a while. Consuelo was overcome with fear that she had committed a grave error and that Sara would tell Benito, Pablo would find out, and he would be furious. As she thought she imagined him leaving her. Her imagination was at the boiling point when Sara broke the silence:

"We already knew. Pablo's mother wrote us."

"Then everybody knows."

"I don't think so. She made us promise not to tell anyone, even you, unless you brought it up. I'm not sure why she told us, but I'm glad she did. Someone close should understand what is going on."

Consuelo nodded.

"Pablo really told the old man to go to hell?"

"Something like that. He gave up everything for me. It was flattering that I meant so much to him, but now I can't stand the coldness."

"You don't know men, Consuelo. He was just showing off his *cojones*. Men have a thing about *cojones*."

Consuelo could not help laughing. "You think so?"

"That's right, and I think he's worried the baby might appear colored."

"God! I never thought …"

"They're the kind that digs up ancestors when their kids get married."

"I know. The priest told them."

"Priests! They're not normal men. Pablo will come around. Don't worry. As soon as he sees his beautiful baby, he'll be himself again."

"Think so?"

"Sure."

"If only my mother were alive."

"Pablo's mother wrote she was thinking of coming to help."

"Oh, my God. She hates me."

"You're going to need somebody after the baby comes."

"You don't know her, Sara. Please don't tell Pablo. He'll encourage her."

"Benito already told him."

When Consuelo put her face in her hands, Sara picked up the crocheting Consuelo was working on. "Let's see what you're making. These socks are beautiful. He'll love them. That's a lucky baby, Consuelo." She took Consuelo's hands. "What about the recital?"

"I can't think about that now. My heart isn't in it. All I can think about is this little package."

"Nothing wrong with that. Sorry, Consuelo, but I've got to go. I'll come back." Sara rose and walked to the door.

"Thanks, cousin."

*

Two weeks before the due date, Pablo's mother wrote to say she was coming to help with the new baby. When Pablo got home that afternoon, Consuelo met him with the letter. "Did you invite her?" Consuelo asked, after he had read the letter.

"You'll need help, Consuelo. Who would you ask?"

"She can't stand me."

"Nonsense. It's not personal; she wouldn't be happy with anybody. Don't antagonize her and she'll be fine."

"It'll be awful." She started to cry.

"She's coming, understand? Make the best of it and try to be gracious."

Not wanting to ask for time off, Pablo asked Sara and Benito to meet his mother at Port Tampa. Doña Inez walked down the gangplank

87

wearing dark glasses and a broad-brimmed hat that shaded her entire face and shoulders. She hugged her nephew and then turned. "You must be Sara."

"Happy to meet you, Inez." Sara looked the older woman up and down. In a dark brown dress, long string of pearls and diamond-studded gold brooch, the older woman looked like royalty. Wearing a simple cotton dress, Sara felt a tinge of embarrassment.

"Is Pablito very unhappy?" she asked Benito.

"I don't think so. And how are you and Tío Ignacio?"

"As well as can be expected. And Consuelo? Too busy to meet her husband's mother?"

"She didn't want to risk the long drive, Tía, and Pablo couldn't get off work. Consuelo's fixing lunch for us."

"So she's learned to cook."

"She's a very good cook, and she has a nice room for you."

"I hope so."

Sara looked at Benito with raised eyebrows. "Well, we might as well get going. We'll show you some of Tampa on the way, Inez," she said.

"Just another provincial American town. I've seen more of them than I care to recall."

*

Consuelo fixed the front bedroom for her mother-in-law—a single bed, dresser, table and rocking chair ready for the baby. She wanted to do everything she could to make her happy. She even bought new curtains for the spare room.

When doña Inez walked in and looked around she said, "I see you don't expect me to stay long."

"Please stay as long as you can, Inez," Consuelo said, hoping to prevent complaints to Pablo.

"Since you have no mother to help you, I thought someone should be here."

"Not a day passes that I don't miss her." As Consuelo spoke, doña Inez inspected the house with looks of disdain.

When Pablo walked into the living room that afternoon, he turned his head and showed his cheek for her to kiss. "How was the crossing?"

"A little rough, but I managed to keep my composure."

"Consuelo was sick all the way. It's amazing how she got well as soon as her feet touched land." His V-shaped smile pushed his eyes out of sight.

"Your father sends regards, Consuelo," she said.

"How's Papá?" Pablo asked.

"The depression has him down, but I'm sure you're not concerned about that."

"How can you say that, Mamá?"

"You look good, Consuelo."

"I feel good. The baby kicks quite a bit these days."

"Oh, what awaits you! I'm glad I only had to go through it once."

Not wanting to hear her mother-in-law's horror stories, Consuelo excused herself to finish supper.

"If you don't mind, I'll bathe, and then fix drinks," Pablo said and went to his room, leaving his mother alone in the living room. In fifteen minutes he returned wearing his white linen suit, white shoes, and a blue tie. "Now I feel better. How about daiquirís?" Both Consuelo and doña Inez nodded, and he went into the kitchen. When he returned with the drinks, he sat beside Consuelo on the sofa.

"May your delivery be easier than mine," Inez said.

Pablo lifted his glass, tipped the others, and said, "To the depression. May it soon end."

"It's devastated your father's business. He's beside himself with worry."

"We've been lucky, Inez. Pablo has a good job."

"For the time being," Pablo said, showing discomfort.

Consuelo wondered why that would anger him.

"Have you decided on a name?"

"Not yet," Consuelo said.

"It would make your father happy if you called him Ignacio."

"When do we eat?" Pablo said. "I'm hungry."

"I thought you wanted to talk a while," Consuelo said.

"We can talk and eat," he said, his eyes menacing.

When Consuelo stood, Inez and Pablo remained seated. From the kitchen, Consuelo could hear her mother-in-law's not so subtle tones.

"Your father needs you, Pablito."

"He has his problems; I have mine."

"Married life isn't what you imagined, is it?"

"I'd like to show you the Gulf beaches. They're beautiful."

"I thought Consuelo was afraid to drive in her condition."

"She loves the beach."

"I see. What a cross you have, Pablito."

"Please, Mamá, try to like her. And stop talking about the horrors of childbirth."

"She'll find out soon enough."

"Supper's ready," Consuelo said.

Pablo and his mother followed her in.

When Pablo started to eat, Inez said, "Don't you say grace any more?"

"Of course, Mamá." They bowed their heads, as he repeated the prayer he had learned as a boy.

After a few minutes, Inez said, "Well, you two don't seem very happy about the baby."

Consuelo looked at Pablo.

"I'm worried about the depression, that's all. My job could end any time."

"Consuelo said you have a good job."

"She doesn't understand such things," he said, looking at Consuelo.

The rest of the meal passed silently with Inez occasionally stealing glances at Pablo and Consuelo.

When they finished their coffee, Pablo stood. "I'm sure you want to discuss women things. I won't be late, Consuelo," he said and kisssed her forehead.

Inez sat in the living room while Consuelo finished the dishes. Then Consuelo invited her out to the porch. It was a warm evening with enough people walking past to entertain them.

"Pablito's distracted. What's wrong?"

Consuelo rocked for a while before answering. "Poor Pablo. He's afraid of losing his job. And now with a baby coming …"

"I never saw an expectant father look so sad."

"He's bogged down."

"Is it his father?"

"Pablo never discusses him. I think he wants to leave the factory, but with the poor economy …"

"It would help to ease up on him."

By that time Consuelo had had enough chipping away at her emotions. Standing, she said, "I'm very tired, Inez. I'm going to lie down and read a while. Please feel at home and make yourself comfortable."

Without removing the bedspread she fell into bed with a magazine, but couldn't concentrate; her thoughts whirled: I thought the baby would calm him … if only I could ask him directly about what Sara said, but it would make him furious. The more she thought, the angrier she got: A man should love his baby no matter what he looks like. Look at that ancestor who took in my grandmother and loved her because she was his daughter. He had real *cojones*. I may forgive his selfish fears, but I'll never forget. Never!

Inez interrupted Consuelo's frantic argument with herself to say that a friend had come to visit. When Consuelo got to the porch, she saw the most beautiful and exotic woman she had ever seen.

"I am called Zoraida Gómez. I am the wife of Matilde Gómez, a friend of your husband."

"Of course. Your husband is very kind."

When Inez offered to warm some coffee for them, Consuelo, surprised, said, "Thank you, Inez."

"I wanted to know you and to ask if you wish to know if it is a boy or a girl," Zoraida said.

"Can you really tell?"

"Oh yes, and much more. Let us go inside."

As Consuelo stood, Zoraida looked her over. "Looks like a boy, but we'll see." Inez met them in the living room.

"Zoraida thinks it's a boy."

"How interesting," Inez said, turning to look out the window.

Zoraida asked Consuelo to leave the room and close the door. While she was out Zoraida took a kitchen knife and a pair of scissors out of an apron pocket, removed two of the sofa cushions, and placed the knife under one cushion and the scissors under the other. Then she called Consuelo.

Consuelo returned with anticipation, feeling like a little girl about to open a gift.

"Sit on one of these two cushions," Zoraida said pointing.

"Which one?"

"You decide."

Hesitating, Consuelo looked at the cushions and at Inez, who raised her eyebrows in boredom.

When Consuelo sat, Zoraida smiled, "Aha!" Then she asked Consuelo to stand. When she did, Zoraida lifted that cushion exposing the knife and then the other. "The scissors would have meant a girl." She said with great solemnity.

"I hope you're right," Consuelo said.

"Time reveals all. In the religion of Santería, destiny begins before birth in heaven. We are all children of the gods. Race, language and place of birth are not important to them."

When Consuelo said she knew nothing about Santería, Zoraida said, "Through Santería, it can be foretold which god is protecting a child even before he is born. Anytime you wish to know, come to me." Hearing the song of a mocking bird coming in the window, she said, "How celestial! You must play number 97 on *bolita*. Now I must go. If I can serve you, Consuelo, please call." Then handing Consuelo a piece of paper containing her address, Zoraida said goodbye and walked out as calmly as she had entered.

"I've seen that trick before," Inez said. "Just superstition."

"What was that about the number?"

"Ninety-seven is mocking bird, more superstitious nonsense."

*

Pablo was poring over a ledger when the old man who lived next door, María's father, broke into his office. "Your wife. It's time," he managed to blurt out, panting. "You'd better go. I just told the doctor."

"Please tell Mr. Vila," Pablo said, grabbing his jacket off its hook and running out of the factory and down La Septima. People stopped to look at him with his jacket under his arm running for all he was worth.

He found Consuelo in a rocking chair on the porch, calmly talking with doña Inez.

"Don't worry, Pablo. I'm fine. The doctor's on his way."

Pablo was out of breath when he sat on the banister and stared at the floor. He felt like a condemned man. "When?"

Just then the doctor drove up in his 1929 Buick touring car with the top down. In no apparent hurry Dr. Chávez lifted his bag off the front seat and walked up the steps to the porch. "How do you feel, Señora Iglesias?"

Consuelo smiled, and looked quite relaxed. "Good. The pains started about an hour ago; they're every five minutes."

"There's time, then. Let's get you inside and get things ready. You are Consuelo's mother?"

"No. Her *suegra*."

"Come in. I'll need you."

"I'm afraid I won't be much help. I can't stomach these things."

Turning to Pablo he said, "Wait out here in case I need to send for something".

As Pablo rocked, he saw the most attractive young woman approach. Swaying as she walked, she held her head high atop her tall frame. When she turned into the yard and walked up the porch steps, Pablo stood.

"I am Zoraida, Matilde's wife," she said, standing close enough to make him self-conscious. "I heard Consuelo is in labor; I've come to help."

Pablo shook her hand. "Matilde's a good friend. I'm happy to meet you finally. Consuelo told me you had dropped in."

He called his mother to the door.

"Come in, Zoraida," she said. Pablo remained at the door as she vanished into the darkness; then he sat again overwhelmed by Zoraida's beauty and thinking she could pass for white."

Before long, doña Inez came to the door. "Come, Pablito; I've warmed the soup Consuelo left for you."

"I'm not hungry."

Lifting him by the arm, she said, "It's chicken soup. I can't vouch for it, but you'll feel bad if you don't eat something."

Pablo sat at the table, looked at the soup for a few moments and began to eat. He had not realized how hungry he was until that moment. Eating voraciously, he turned to his mother to say something as Zoraida walked into the kitchen.

"The doctor needs towels," she said, in a mellow voice and smiling at Pablo.

"In the bathroom, over there," Inez said.

"Thank you." Zoraida disappeared into the bathroom and reappeared a moment later. Her movements were fluid, effortless.

"What an attractive woman."

Immediately sensing her intent Pablo said, "She's the wife of a very good friend."

"I know. Maybe she would come to work for us. We'll need a maid. You can't expect me to cook and scrub like a common servant."

"We'll find somebody else."

"But Zoraida's perfect. She seems competent." Doña Inez's tone was seductive.

"How's it going in there?" he asked.

"Don't worry; Consuelo is fine."

Again Zoraida appeared. "The doctor would like some café solo. May I fix it?"

"Of course; over there," doña Inez said, pointing.

"I'll make enough for you." She filled a pot with water and put it on the stove. When it came to a boil, she added the coffee, stirred it, and poured the mixture through a flannel colander into a kettle. She poured two cups for them and disappeared with the other. Pablo tried his best to appear uninterested, but he was aroused watching this gorgeous woman glide around the room. She moved with eloquence, as if carving out the space she passed through.

As soon as Pablo finished his soup, doña Inez led him back to the porch. "I'll call you when the ordeal is over," she said, opening the screen door.

Pablo had just lit a cigarette when Sara appeared with a dish of stew. "I thought you might want to eat tonight," she said with a malicious smile. "I don't imagine your mother cooks."

"She helps in her own way."

"Well, just in case, some of the neighbors will bring food the next few days."

"I hope you didn't say bad things about her."

"I'll take this in and see how Consuelo's doing."

When the doctor emerged an hour later, Pablo jumped out of his chair.

"It'll be a while. I have to go to my office."

"Anything I can get for you?"

"No. I have some things to do. There's plenty of time."

The doctor returned in half an hour, finished his cigarette, and put it out as he walked up the front steps. "Don't worry, she's fine," he said, and went in.

Having smoked his last cigarette, Pablo walked to a store on the next block to buy more. By now his mouth tasted sour and rotten with all the smoking. His whole body felt rotten as if he was bringing more rottenness into the world. He hated the thought and pushed it out of his mind, but it kept returning. When he returned he stopped to look in and then sat on the porch. Half an hour later he walked back and bought the Tampa Times and La Gaceta and sat on the porch. He read them both thinking it would take his mind off what was happening. While he was reading, Sara came out.

"What happened?" he asked.

"Everything's fine. I've got to tend to Gene and Benito. I'll be back later."

At seven o'clock, Pablo was standing on the sidewalk, hoping to talk with anyone that passed, when Dr. Chávez came out and said, "I thought you'd gone."

"Is she all right?"

"You have a healthy boy."

"I didn't hear anything. Aren't they supposed to cry?"

"He's not a loud mouth, but he's fine: robust and hungry."

"And my wife?"

"Anxious to see you."

Pablo's heart raced wondering what he would do if the baby looked strange with his mother there to see his reaction. Horrible!

He abruptly shook Chávez's hand, thanked him, and rushed into the bedroom. Consuelo had the baby in her arms. "Isn't he beautiful?"

It was as if a ton had been lifted from Pablo as his panic dissolved. Aside from the normal redness, the baby was indeed perfectly white with light blonde fuzz on his head. Pablo poked at his cheeks, but he only moved his head and kept sleeping. Pablo burst out laughing. "How do you feel?"

"Better than I expected."

"How long will you be in bed?"

"A couple of weeks. You'll just have to wait on me." She was smiling.

"What about Zoraida?"

"She was wonderful. The doctor didn't want a midwife, but he needed help, and she knew exactly what to do. Just holding my hand was a big help. And she was right; it is a boy."

"Where is she?"

"Cleaning up."

"I'd like to thank her."

Consuelo held his hand and said, "Later."

Pablo stayed for over an hour talking quietly so as not to bother the baby. Zoraida came in to tell him that Consuelo should rest. Pablo looked at Consuelo, and she said, "Let him stay a little longer."

Pablo couldn't stop staring at his son, stroking his head and pushing his finger into his hand for him to grab. Every few seconds he would burp or make a gurgling sound, and Pablo would break out laughing. When doña Inez came in, Pablo hugged Consuelo and said he would be back in a while.

"Is Zoraida still here?"

"She had to go," doña Inez said. "Like a primitive, she went to play the number for baby on the lottery."

"In Ybor City they call it *la bolita*."

"What number is baby?" Consuelo asked.

"Who knows? It's one of their superstitions. The number she should play is twelve,"

"What's that," Consuelo asked.

"*Puta*."

Not wanting to argue with his mother, Pablo winked at Consuelo and smiled, hoping she would get his meaning and said, "I'm going out. I've got to hand out more cigars than Ybor's got."

*

Stopping at a store on Seventh Avenue, Pablo bought a box of expensive Cuban cigars and hurried to the Café Cubano, where a handful of men were drinking coffee or playing dominoes.

"I've got a beautiful boy," Pablo shouted as he opened the door, "Blonde hair, blue eyes, and well endowed."

Matilde smiled from his stool as he poured some coffee into the saucer, blew across it, and sipped. Pablo shook his meaty hand, embraced him, all the time thanking him profusely for his wife's help.

"Zoraida was wonderful. What an amazing woman!"

"I know, I know," Matilde said.

After passing out the cigars, Pablo told everyone to move into the back room where he bought a round of cognac. As he went around the room handing out more cigars, each man congratulated him, shook his hand, and slapped his back. Everyone had something to say as Domingo passed among them handing out glasses of cognac.

"Leave the bottle," Pablo said.

"I know how important this day is for you," Huesito said. The old man looked like a long, thin bone under a thick mane of gray hair. He was so shy that his speech surprised them all. He raised his glass and said, "To your little family."

They all raised their glasses: Jacinto, Huesito, El Rubio, El Chulo, El Gordo, and Sarna. Sitting away from the table with his chair leaning against the wall, Matilde also raised his glass.

"Thank you all," Pablo said. "Now: To my good friends." Again they all raised their glasses. "And now, we need another round," Pablo said, as he refilled the glasses.

Before long they were laughing and slapping each other and filling each other's glasses. Pablo had no memory of his recent suffering. It was as if he had never worried about the baby.

Matilde had said little since Pablo's arrival, but seemed to be enjoying the camaraderie from a distance. On several occasions, Pablo walked to him to say, "I have a son, a blonde boy, the image of me."

"That's wonderful," Matilde said, each time. "I am thrilled to the bone, my young friend."

Soon, inhibitions dropping like leaves of autumn, Pablo approached El Rubio and patted his bald head. "Rubio, you must have had blonde hair when you were young."

"That's not how he got that nickname," El Chulo said. "He used to drive us crazy talking about the long blonde curls that hung down to his shoulders when he was a little boy."

"Well it's t-t-true," El Rubio said, still frowning. Turning to Pablo he said, "At least I don't dress like a ma-ma-ma-male whore."

El Chulo said, "I don't look like most of the hicks you see in Ybor City. And I dance like Rudolf Valentino. Women die to dance with me."

When El Gordo began to pat his enormous belly, the crowd broke into roaring laughter.

Finally, Matilde spoke up: "From this day forward, Pablo, your name is *El Blanco*."

Looking at the large mulatto who was leaning back on his chair, Pablo asked, "Why?"

"Your white linen suits, white shoes and Panama hats. You are El Blanco, and that's final!" Matilde said with stifled anger. Then he picked up the bottle and poured another round.

Pablo ignored his tone for the moment.

"Why no nickname, Jacinto?" he asked, turning to the tall, robust, well-dressed man.

"My young friend, you have something to be proud of, but you are only a novice. My first wife bore me six children before she died of TB. Two years later, I married my second wife, who had ten of her own. At the end of our second year of marriage she had a baby who died at birth. What name could you devise for me? *Pueblo? Mundo?* No name suffices, I'm afraid. So before you engage in nicknaming me, you have a way to go, don Blanco."

"My God," Pablo said. "How could you to marry a woman with so many children?"

"My mother bore eighteen. Fourteen didn't seem out of the ordinary."

"You're a saint, Jacinto," Huesito said.

"Or a *comemierda*," El Chulo said.

Jacinto stood. "I demand an apology."

"This is a celebration, *caballeros*," Pablo said.

"Of course I apologize, Jacinto," El Chulo said. "I was trying to be funny, but didn't make it. And to prove my sincerity, I'll buy the next bottle. Domingo!"

Before long, swirling in brandy's warmth, the conversation returned to birth. "It's a law of nature," Jacinto said.

"What's a law of nature?" Sarna asked, one eye closed and the other drooping.

"That all the characteristics of a baby come from the father. Conception is very complicated," Jacinto said. "During conception, the father's seed implants itself in the mother's womb. The mother only provides nourishment, a nest as it were, for the father's seed to mature in."

"Now wait a minute, Jacinto," Pablo said. "I've studied biology and I know the woman's egg is fertilized by the man's seed, as you call it. The baby is a combination of both."

"That only proves professors know very little, my young friend," Jacinto said. "Eggs?" he asked. "Men have *huevos*, not women." Laughter interrupted Jacinto's image of a woman with testicles. "What I told you is established medical science. When you've lived as long as me, you will realize we ancients have wisdom you can't find in books. As the saying goes, 'the devil knows more because he is old than because he is the devil.'"

"I'll write to my professor right away," Pablo said, chin on his fist.

"C-c-c-come on, Jacinto. He's right. No one b-b-believes that crap anymo-mo-mo-ore," El Rubio said, when the laughter died down.

"What do you say, Matilde?" Jacinto asked. "You are our sage."

From his chair, the large mulatto had been listening and shaking his head. "My father was a Spaniard; I never met him. He planted his seed and left the garden to tend itself, apparently more interested in the planting than the fruit. Now I know what he looks like. I see him every morning in the mirror."

"Wisdom doesn't necessarily come with age, Jacinto," Sarna said. "You must have learned something from living so long."

"That's right, El Chulo said. "I look more like my mother than my father; I have her eyes and hair."

"You should have g-g-gotten her clothes," El Rubio said.

El Chulo stood as if to attack El Rubio, but before he could say anything, Matilde added, "What Jacinto means to say, Pablo, is we should respect our elders, even when they're full of shit. One thing we all respect is fatherhood and the new father in our midst. He has a very lucky son."

Tears flooded Pablo's eyes. He walked to Matilde and embraced his massive shoulder. "I'm lucky to have a friend like you."

"You'll feel more rational when the cognac evaporates from your brain," Matilde said. "But thank you anyway."

*

Matilde drove up to Pablo's house and helped him out of the Ford. Pablo was not as drunk as the first time, but Matilde would not trust him to get home safely, afraid he might end up with Cynthia. El Chulo had fallen asleep in the back seat of the Model A. Doña Inez was on the porch waiting for Pablo. She knew it was Matilde from Consuelo's description and waited on the porch.

"He's not that drunk; he's been celebrating. Forgive me; I'm Matilde Gómez. You must be his mother."

With icy voice she said, "Bring him in, please."

Matilde walked his charge into the house. "May I see the baby? Pablo couldn't stop talking about him."

Saying nothing Inez went into the bedroom, looked down at Sammy, and mumbled icily, "I won't let that ... man ... inside. Why would he want to see a baby anyway?" She lifted the baby out of his bed and laid him against her shoulder. As an afterthought she picked up a diaper and leaned him back to tuck the diaper between his face and her shoulder. In the process, the baby's head flopped backward. Frightened, she grabbed his head and dropped the diaper and said, "Spoiled brat!" Then she bent down, retrieved the diaper, stuffed it as best she could between the baby's head and her shoulder, and walked out to the porch. Not wanting to hand the baby to Matilde, she turned so he could see the baby's face over her shoulder. Matilde's face grew serious and his eyes watered. He could barely talk. Finally, as he turned to leave, he said, "I see why Pablo is so happy. He's beautiful."

When Matilde reached the curb, Pablo shouted from inside, "I don't know when I've had such a good time, or such a good friend. Thanks again, friend."

"Save it for tomorrow when you rejoin the living," Matilde laughed. "I hope you can remember the fun you've had. Now I've got to get El Chulo home before he wakes up and wanders off."

*

Pablo rose to greet his wife lying next to him with a broad smile and a warm embrace. "Careful, Pablo. I'm holding the baby."

"I know. The hug's for him too. What a beautiful boy."

"I'm glad you're happy. You've worried me."

"Let me hold him." Consuelo passed him the baby, who moved his head and opened his eyes and seemed to look straight at Pablo. "See, he knows me. And look, he has blue eyes."

"All babies have blue eyes, Pablo. They change later."

"His won't change. They'll look like mine. Jacinto said so." Then he kissed her. "By the way, we can't keep calling him baby."

"What about Ignacio?" she said. "It would please them."

"I like Samuel. It's biblical and universal, and it's a good, manly name. We'll name him after 'Uncle Sam'"

99

"I like it, but are you sure?"

He lifted the baby so they could both see him, and said, "*Buenos días, Samuel.*" They laughed.

"I think I'll call that guy from Notre Dame today," Pablo said as he got out of bed. "It's time I made contact with the outside world."

*

The mood at the factory was not as cheerful. Pablo stopped in to see Gustavo Vila and handed him a cigar. "Consuelo had the baby yesterday, and they are both doing well. We've named him Samuel."

"Congratulations, Pablo. That's wonderful, but we've got a lot of work. The new shipment of tobacco is in and has to be inventoried and recorded. Also, a shipment of cigars is ready to leave. That has to be taken care of too."

"Right away," Pablo said, as he turned and went out into the hall and into his office. It was obvious that his standing with Vila had deteriorated, but with his mind clear again, he could begin to look around. Through his work he had met several accountants in the downtown firm that periodically audited the V & F business. Working closely with them he felt they liked him. Feeling his ablaze with new vigor, he telephoned one of them and asked if he could come down to talk about openings. The man was pleasant, but his answer was unequivocal. There were no openings or even distant possibilities because they were not filling vacancies. Pablo called an acquaintance in another firm and got the same response. Even these rejections did not depress Pablo. He took out Marvin Burke's letter and dialed his office. After introducing himself, they chatted briefly about their Notre Dame days. Finally, Pablo said he would be interested in helping organize an alumni club and would like to meet him for lunch.

"Got a car?" Marvin asked.

"No."

"Then let's meet tomorrow noon at Las Novedades."

Unsure of what good it would do, Pablo would at least meet someone in a different circle. Sure that the cigar industry was doomed, he felt his best chance lay in the Anglo community.

Of medium height, robust, with short, jet-black hair, blue eyes, and ruddy complexion, Marvin was standing just inside the restaurant entrance when Pablo walked in. Conversation started with a burst and continued enthusiastically for the whole hour.

Marvin said he liked yellow rice and chicken, so they both ordered it and a small salad and iced tea. Pablo was at his brightest, talking about the cigar industry and its impending fate.

"I handle large tracts; citrus groves mainly and some cattle land," Marvin said. "People got burned during the 1920s land boom. They paid hundreds of thousands, sight unseen, for parcels they can't sell now for a hundred. Some are still holding on, but most of them can't. They're trying to unload just to keep food on the table. Anyway, I help them, and when I see something really hot, I buy it. You won't believe what you can buy for five or ten bucks an acre. When things improve, and they're bound to, I'll cash in."

With the money his mother and Consuelo's parents had given them, Pablo easily visualized possibilities. Consuelo had hoped not to touch the fifteen thousand dollars except in an emergency, and so far they had spent less than five hundred. If Marvin was right he could buy a grove without making a serious dent in his nest egg. He could sell fruit and later, when values rose, he would sell the land.

When Pablo told Marvin about his experience in the Cuban sugar cane industry, Marvin lit up. "If you have money you don't need for food, you're in a position to make plenty. Of course, you shouldn't use dough you'll need any time soon."

"How have you done?"

"I've been at it five years; I'm still afloat."

Glancing at his watch Pablo said, "My God! I'm late. The hour's flown."

Marvin Burke picked up the check over Pablo's objection. "Come see my office in Brandon. I'll show you around."

"Where's Brandon?"

"About ten miles east of Tampa. Just take Seventh Avenue and turn right on US 301 to route 60, then left. You can't miss it."

They parted, agreeing to get together about the alumni group as Pablo walked toward the factory.

*

Consuelo was thrilled. "I saw one the other day for under five hundred. We don't need anything fancy, but a new car would be nice," she said as she pushed herself away from the table. "Especially if you'll be driving people around."

"You're way ahead of me."

"And I think buying land's a good idea. What are we saving for?"

"Marvin seemed honest, and he sounded sincere."

"Let's do it."

101

"Who is this Marvin?" Inez asked. "Do I understand you are going into business with a stranger after leaving a million dollar sugar business at home?"

"Oh … Mamá. I thought you were taking your siesta."

"With all this turmoil?"

Don't worry, Mamá. I won't put up any money right away."

"I am neither deaf nor stupid. Why would he take you in if he did not expect something in return?"

"He wants my expertise."

"What expertise?"

"Pablo is very talented, Inez," Consuelo said, as sweetly as she could without erupting. "I have every confidence in him."

"Each fool to his folly. And you leave a paying job for this? Your father would never trust someone he just met." Inez was waving her hands and arms like a windmill and slapping her thighs. "This is crazy; first you abandon your inheritance and now you abandon a paying job."

"That's enough, Mamá. I'm not Papá. I left Cuba to run my own life. That's what I plan to do."

Walking out Consuelo said, "I feel tired, and Sammy's calling."

"I knew this would happen, Pablito."

"Nothing's happened," he said.

"But it starts. What kind of wife would encourage her husband to follow such a foolish scheme?"

"Don't blame Consuelo, Mamá."

"You fool. She is dragging you down even lower."

Looking down the hall to Sammy's room Pablo said, "Don't worry, Mamá. We'll be fine."

He left her standing there and walked into the baby's room, where Consuelo was lying on the bed staring out the window. "Don't feel bad," he said. "She means well."

Without looking at him Consuelo shook her head silently. He sat beside her on the bed, bent down and caressed her cheek, and whispered, "I'm excited, Consuelo. Let's not let her ruin it. I have to get back to work now. I'll telephone Marvin right away to arrange a meeting tomorrow."

*

Pablo pulled his shiny, new, dark red 1932 Ford sedan into the parking space in front of the Marvin's building. It was an abandoned filling station with potted plants where the pumps once stood. Marvin was on the telephone when Pablo entered; he motioned for him to sit. Pablo looked around the small room. Though he had refurbished it to look like an office, it still looked like a filling station with a large glass wall facing the front and a door in the middle. The toilet was outside, behind the building. Marvin sat at a desk and had two chairs for customers, a filing cabinet, wastebasket, and a coffee percolator. When he hung up the phone, he rose and shook Pablo's hand. After several minutes of joking about almost missing Brandon because it was so small, Pablo found himself getting into Marvin's three-year-old Chevy and driving into the heartland of orange country.

"This is great land for oranges," Marvin said.

"But it's mostly woods."

"When you clear off this hardwood hammock, you have prime citrus land. It has good drainage and it's rich. Sandy pine forest is poor because a few feet beneath the surface there's a layer of hardpan that holds water. Oranges can't take that."

"Hardpan?"

"Clay."

Every once in a while they passed a developed grove hung with green fruit. "What beautiful country! I like it."

By the end of the afternoon, they had agreed to work together. Marvin figured Pablo could entice Latins from Ybor City. "I can't offer you a salary. I don't get one myself; just commissions."

"I'll let you know in a few days. I have to think it over. Leaving a paying job is serious business nowadays," he said, thinking that he would have to live on savings for a while.

That night, it was obvious Consuelo had given the matter much thought: "Your salary's thirty dollars a week. We'll live off our savings. Even if it takes a year that's only fifteen hundred and sixty dollars."

"I don't know if I've got the nerve, but I like it."

"By the way, your mother wants to hire a maid, and I agreed."

"Do you have anybody in mind?"

"Sara knows somebody."

"Do you know her?" Pablo was afraid it might be Zoraida

"No, but Sara knows everybody. It's just for a few weeks."

"OK."

*

Within a week doña Inez announced she was returning home. "You have help now; you don't need me anymore."

"We wanted to give you a tour of Florida," Pablo said.

"I'll be back to normal in a few more days, Inez," Consuelo said. "I'm sure Ignacio missies you."

103

"And I'm sure you want to be alone again," Inez said.

Pablo glared at Consuelo and turned to his mother. "Consuelo and I both appreciate your help, Mamá.

"Of course, Inez. Thank you very much," Consuelo said.

Two days later Pablo drove his mother to Port Tampa. "I really wish you could stay longer, Mamá. Don't you enjoy Sammy?"

"I'm not good with infants. Besides, Consuelo wants her house back."

"Has she said anything?"

"She didn't have to."

Pablo did not want to defend his wife knowing his mother's unswerving disapproval. "We'll try to get down soon so you can see Sammy."

Inez did not respond. Neither said anything else on the way. When they arrived at the port, Pablo carried her bags to the ticket counter. She showed her return ticket to the attendant. Seeing that she had a luxury suite, he smiled and tipped his hat and said, "I'll have someone show you to the gangplank."

"No need," she said and turned and walked there with Pablo. At the gangplank Pablo leaned down and offerred his cheek for her to kiss. After the perfunctory kiss she walked up the gangplank and disappeared inside. Pablo waited to wave goodbye, but she did not appear, so he left.

*

Consuelo felt liberated the following week when she could spend the whole day out of bed and moving about. That Sunday, Pablo drove Consuelo and Sammy to Brandon. Marvin and his wife Suzanne met them at the office. After introductions, the two couples talked, as Marvin drove them around the Brandon area. "There's no real center, but it's a nice, quiet, rural community," Suzanne said. "We'd planned to live in Tampa, but this was too beautiful to pass up."

At noon, Marvin drove them to his home. "You're having lunch with us," Suzanne said. The two women became friends almost immediately as they hovered over Sammy. Suzanne confided to Consuelo that they wanted a baby, but no luck.

After lunch, Marvin took Pablo for a walk and a cigar around the grove. Pablo had brought Marvin a box of V & F's best. Handing it to him he said, "I'd like to work with you."

"Terrific! You won't regret it." They spent the rest of the afternoon talking about business opportunities, looking at county maps, marking existing orange groves as well as promising, uncultivated land. It was late afternoon when Pablo and Consuelo began to gather up Sammy and all his things.

"I'll have to give notice," Pablo said.

"Whenever you can," Marvin said, as Pablo started the Ford and began the trek back to Ybor city.

*

The following morning Pablo stopped at Gustavo Vila's office wondering how the old man would react. When he told him his plan Vila erupted. "That's good," he said. "When you came to me, I took you in as one of my own. I kept you in a position of trust during the strike, but you turned your sympathy to the workers. If your father had not been a close friend, I would have fired you."

"Then I've saved you the trouble. I wanted to resign when you said my father had intervened, but with the new baby I couldn't. Now we're both free of obligations."

When he got to the door, Pablo turned. "I shouldn't leave without thanking you for helping me get started. Regardless of your reason, it was generous of you, and I'll never forget your generosity."

Startled by Pablo's gesture and seeing that perhaps he had misjudged him, Gustavo Vila looked at him for a long moment and then rose from his desk and walked around and extended his hand. "Thank you, Pablo. That makes me feel better." Then he embraced the young man. "I liked you from the start. I would have hired you anyway. Your father helped me when I was getting started. My partner Fernández was starting this factory in Tampa and needed money. I had always wanted my own business, and with no one else to turn to, I approached your father. He went over the prospectus and talked with Fernández. A few days later we closed the deal. Without him I wouldn't be here. When he wrote me about you, I was happy to reciprocate. I wasn't supposed to tell you."

"What did he say?"

"Only that you'd had a disagreement. No details."

"It's personal. He's been a good father, but too demanding and rigid. I did what I had to."

"I understand. When will you start your new job?"

"In two weeks. I didn't want to leave unfinished work here," Pablo said.

"Finish it this week, then take a week off with pay as my gift for the baby," Vila said. "And let me hear from you when you can."

*

Consuelo was nursing the baby in the living room when Pablo arrived. They had not had a vacation since they arrived. Delighted to hear that Pablo had a week off, she said, "How about a day or two at the beach?" Still wary of Pablo's moods, she was afraid to set him off, but Pablo agreed without a second thought.

After supper, Pablo went to the Café Cubano to tell his friends about his new job. Matilde's reaction surprised him: "After worrying yourself sick about losing your job, you're leaving it for one with no pay?"

"It's a gamble, but all life is a gamble."

That gamble was not available to a man of mixed race in Florida. A move into the Cracker world would land him in the Scrub. He knew that for Pablo, who could easily enter the main stream of American culture, the ethnic attractions of Ybor City would soon fade. But that community was the only one Matilde could hope to inhabit with self-respect. But there was much more to Matilde's anger. Pablo's exuberance at his son's appearance was the first hint of what had been bothering him all those months: not only did his son have to be healthy and beautiful; he had to be purest white.

With only eight years of formal schooling, Matilde loved books and, as a child, read every evening when his work was done. He learned quickly, and his talent showed itself early enough for him to discover that such talent bore so few benefits. Intelligence had illuminated the height of the barrier and the stark contrast between the worlds it separated. Matilde knew his own father was rich and powerful, but he had never tried to meet him. It did not matter, he had told himself. He lives on the other side of the barrier. Pablo's intelligence, on the same side, could lead him whereever he chose to go. Matilde often thought that ignorance was better, for ignorance would obscure the breach between him and people like his father and Pablo. Like a dwarf or a hunchback, Matilde was a troubling anomaly in the normal world. Oblivious, Pablo hoped to sustain their stillborn friendship. Matilde cursed his useless intelligence and wanted to curse Pablo's advantage, but could not. In spite of all his analyzing, he had come to feel like a brother to Pablo.

8 - NEW BUSINESS - 1933

*

Roosevelt Signs Antiprohibition Bill

*

Lakefront Home – Five acres of beautiful lakefront, 300 feet frontage on state highway, 5-room house, hot water, lights and telephone, lots of shade. 35 minutes drive from Tampa. Price $1250, $625 cash, balance arranged.

*

Farm, $2250 – 10 acres, mile north of Brandon high. 12 miles from Tampa post office, all cultivated, good bungalow of six rooms and screened porches, garage, barn, etc., fine oak shade trees around the house – ideal for poultry and fruit. Good terms.

*

5 Acres – House. 5 acres, 3 acres high land. 2 acres planted trucking land, 3-room house, close to road 17 and Six Mile Creek. Price, $900, $25 down, $12.50 month.

*

*Big Bargain in close-in place, one acre of land and
livable unfinished house, very rich muck soil within
Tampa city limits. $600 with some terms.*

*

For over a year Pablo had driven through the area alone and with
Marvin until he knew it as well as any native. Sometimes he took
Consuelo on his jaunts to show her the potential of that part of Florida. He
had had a few prospects and had bought two small tracts for himself, but
had not yet earned any commissions. Consuelo was beginning to worry,
imagining his mother's reaction. Pablo knew his luck would change and
remained as cheerful as ever. He had not bothered to get a realtor's license
because Marvin offered to carry out transactions for him. Marvin hinted
a few times that Pablo would be better off with his own license, but he
never pressed. Pablo always smiled his V-shaped smile and changed the
subject.

In April of 1933 Pablo's luck finally changed over a small, five-acre
farm in a high, dry part of the county. The farm had gone mainly to
sandspurs and palmettos and sold for $2,500. His commission was $125,
more than a month's pay at the factory, his first success in real estate.
Consuelo met the news with a hug.

"Some Sicilian," Pablo said. "It was the strike. He got tired of fighting
battles he didn't understand. All he wanted was to grow vegetables like
he did in Sicily. Said no matter what, people have to eat. He knew the
land was poor, but he said he could make something grow." Pablo held the
check for Consuelo to see. "How do you like that?"

The check was all the encouragement either needed. Pablo felt like a
prospector finding a gold chip on a gravel road. Each sale reinforced the
feeling that money could be made even in hard times.

*

"Where's my boy? Where's he hiding?" Pablo asked, running from
room to room a few days later. Hearing the boy's squealing and laughter
coming from his bedroom, Pablo crawled after him on all fours and caught
him as he tried to scoot under the bed. They tussled a while, and then
Sammy said something.

"What's that, Sammy?"

"*Caballo … Caballo.*"

"Oh," Pablo said, getting on hands and knees as Sammy climbed on his back.

"Giddy-giddy," he said, slapping his father's behind.

As much as Pablo enjoyed Sammy, the ritual had become tiresome, especially when Sammy kept repeating, "*Mas, mas,*" over and over until Pablo had had enough and put him down.

"*Caballo, Papá?*"

"Later, Sammy. I have to talk to Mama."

In the kitchen, Pablo reported his latest news as he stood over the stove and lifted each pot's lid. "Nothing today except another beautiful piece of land. When it's cleared it'll be great for oranges"

"Did you buy it or sell it?"

"Neither. I found it. Now I've got to find a buyer."

"And Marvin?"

"He hasn't sold anything in weeks, but he's not worried. Time for a bath before supper?"

"Sure."

He kissed her and went to the bathroom. Soon he returned in his new gray, pinstripe suit carrying his new gray felt hat. "Glad it's finally cooling off."

"With that suit you're not a Cuban anymore. You look like an American."

"Don't you like it?"

"Of course. You're in business now; you should dress like a businessman."

"I hadn't thought of that," he said, not wanting to admit he had. "So you like it?"

"Very much, dear."

After supper, he sat in the living room with Sammy for a few minutes and recounted his day: "I drove through the woods until I found a dark forest, just like in the fairy tales."

"*Caballo, Papá?*"

Pablo had had enough of that word. He turned to Consuelo. "Sammy's straining to stay awake, Mamá."

"I've got to bathe him."

"I won't be late," he said, kissing them. Then he left for the Café Cubano.

By ten-thirty he had been there almost two hours and the crowd had thinned. Two ancient men were watching four others play dominoes. Pablo put on his hat and walked home.

As usual, Consuelo was waiting in the living room, reading a novel. "Have a good time, dear?" she asked.

"All right. Ready for bed?" She knew what his smile meant and got up and put her arms around his neck. Pulling her close, he kissed her. When he backed away to look at her, they were both breathing heavily.

"Come," she said, leading him to bed.

Pablo could not stop staring as she undressed. "You've gotten even more beautiful."

She slipped into bed and pulled the covers back for him. "Don't talk. Just get in here."

Pablo finished undressing and slid in beside her. At once they were in each other's embrace, groping hungrily at each other. When she turned on her back and pulled him to her, he said, "Just a minute." Turning to the small table by the bed, he opened the drawer.

"You don't need that."

"No need to gamble." He knew she didn't approve, but he pretended not to notice, imagining that in a moment she would not mind.

*

Dark blue clouds inched over the land from the eastern horizon as Marvin and Pablo sat in their filling station office trying to decide whether to call it a day or sit out the storm. As Marvin was about to get up, an old pick-up truck rolled in and parked under the roof. A sorrowful-looking man got out and knocked on the door. He held his straw hat in his hands as he walked in. Even from several feet away, Pablo could see the dust and scratches on his steel-framed glasses. With a face deeply tanned and creased and with thinning, pure white hair, the man appeared to be in his late sixties. He wore a pair of overalls over a white dress shirt buttoned at the collar. Barely over five feet tall, he looked even shorter the way he stood bent forward at the waist.

"Mr. Iglesias?" he asked in a surprisingly strong baritone voice, looking at both of them.

"Yes, sir. What can I do for you?" Pablo said.

"My name's Stewart. I seen your ad in the Sunday paper. I got an orange grove I need to sell."

"I'll be happy to list it and do all I can to sell it. Please sit down, Mr. Stewart." Marvin moved to his desk and busied himself as Mr. Stewart continued. "I'll need some information," Pablo said. "You know, location, size, description of the house, price, etc."

Mr. Stewart sat by the desk. Pablo took a form out of his desk drawer and began writing as the old man described the property. The 20-acre grove had a three-bedroom house facing the road and 19 acres of temple oranges. There was a small garden and an abandoned windmill. The house had electricity and water supplied by a tank reservoir filled by an electric pump at the well.

"Is it producing?"

"Yes, sir. I sell the fruit to a processor in Lake Alfred. We been living off it for years; that is, until my wife passed on."

"I'm sorry."

"I'll be honest, Mr. Iglesias. Since last year's freeze, it don't produce like it used to. And since Ruth passed on, I ain't got the spirit to work it the way it needs." The old man's eyes dropped and he sat shaking his head.

"We'll do our best. What are you asking?"

"I ain't got no idea. I bought it twenty years ago. Paid three hundred dollars and cleared it myself. I reckon it's worth more now."

"I'm sure it is. Suppose I follow you there and take a look."

"Sure," the old man said, "If you don't mind the rain."

They ran to their cars through the downpour that fell like bullets out of the black sky. After turning off and driving half a mile north along an unpaved road they arrived. Pablo had to slosh through mud and navigate deep puddles. They came to a stop at the house, and Pablo motioned that they should wait in their cars for the rain to slacken.

Through the deluge the house stood like an apparition in the gray day. The darkly beautiful setting riveted Pablo to the spot. He remembered a schoolmate's house on the outskirts of Havana. It was during a deluge like this that Pablo had first seen that house. He came to love the place and its fruit trees, but mostly he loved the family's warmth. The boy's mother always offered goodies and seemed to really love Pablo. He had fantasized about moving to that house with his friend's family.

Within minutes the sun reappeared as if the rain had been a big joke, and the house came alive. With the sun reflecting off each leaf, the green of the grass and plants and trees revived; flowers erupted into full color. Sitting back from the road about two hundred feet, the white frame house was nestled in beds of azaleas, gardenias, and hibiscus. In the front yard stood twin date palms. In back, a giant jacaranda rose out of the earth like a fountain to shade the back half of the house. In back stood a barn and behind that a large fenced-in area with a chicken coop. A wide porch wrapped around the front and north sides of the house.

"Come on," Mr. Stewart said, jarring Pablo out of his reverie. Mr. Stewart led Pablo through the grove, pointing out some of the freeze damage and one large grapefruit tree near the center. "I planted grapefruit first, and they was going real good until the big freeze of 1917. This is the onlyest one left. When I replanted temples, I didn't have the heart to pull this one out. It gives all the grapefruit a family can use."

After showing the grove, Mr. Stewart took him to the barn, which had an old tractor and some disking equipment. "I used to keep a cow, but it was too much, milking her twice a day, ever' day of the year."

Inside the house, the shades were drooping and frazzled, the sink was stacked with dishes, and clothes and shoes littered the living room. "I ain't no good at housekeeping. My wife kept it right homey, though."

"It's a comfortable home," Pablo said, his heart beating with the thought of living there. "We could start at $4,000. That's high, but the house is in good shape. Electricity and plumbing are important selling points."

"That's a right smart high," Stewart said.

"Let's give it a try. I won't turn down any offers without talking them over with you."

"Fair enough," Mr. Stewart said, as he extended a calloused hand that surprised Pablo with its firmness.

*

"That's way too high," Marvin said. "You'll scare people off."

"We can drop it later. Marvin, the place is beautiful. Anybody who sees it will want it."

"It sure would help the old boy."

"Poor old geezer's pitiful. If it doesn't sell, I may buy it." Until that time, Pablo had been working for Marvin. Having paid for the ad, Pablo considered this his first independent deal. Marvin didn't think it would sell at that price, but he said, "I guess experience is the best teacher."

It was after supper and Consuelo and Pablo were sitting in the living room. "I can't get it out of my mind. You should see it, Consuelo. It's beautiful. Needs a little work, but what a place for some lucky family."

"Sounds like you'd like it."

He nodded.

"We'd be pretty isolated."

It's a farm community, good people, honest, friendly. You should've seen him. So humble."

"Would you farm it?"

"No. Some company picks the fruit, hauls it away, and pays cash."

*

Weeks went by with only two inquiries. Both prospects bristled at the price. When Pablo asked the second one to make an offer, the man said he couldn't come anywhere near that price.

Pablo ran another ad dropping the price to thirty-five hundred dollars. Three weeks passed with no inquiries. One afternoon he stopped at the grove. When he summarized the situation, Mr. Stewart said, "Just get whatever you can, Mr. Iglesias. I don't want to mess with it no more."

"Would you take $2,000 cash?" Pablo had not planned to make an offer, and his words seemed to jump out of his mouth.

"Sure."

"I'll draw up the papers and bring them back tomorrow morning," Pablo said, and walked to his car.

"Papers?"

"I'll buy it. My wife will love it."

"I'd like that," Mr. Stewart said, "knowing a young family would live in it."

Pablo drove straight to his office and drew up the contract and arranged for transfer of title. As he was working, a man came in. "Mr. Iglesias?"

Pablo detected a northern accent. "Yes. How can I help you?"

"I'm interested in that property you advertised in the paper, the $3,500 orange grove. Sounds pretty good. I'd like to see it."

Pablo's heart sank. Before he could think it through he said, "It's sold. I'm sorry."

"Too bad. Sounded like just what we were looking for. Ohio winters are getting to us. You got anything else?"

"Not right now, but I should soon. Why don't you check back in a few days?"

"We're heading home next week; we'd like to find something before we leave."

Pablo could not wait for him to go. "Check back day after tomorrow."

That night Pablo told Consuelo about his offer.

"Did he accept?"

"We're signing tomorrow."

"Poor old man."

"It's a good deal for him."

"What about schools?"

"I haven't checked. I'll look tomorrow. Soon as I can make some repairs, we'll move in. You'll love it."

He kissed her. Consuelo seemed unconvinced, but said, "I'll adjust. Sammy will like it."

Not wanting to press the issue Pablo said no more.

Driving home the next evening, Pablo sang all the way. The Ford flew down those country roads like wind through trees. The red-smeared evening lit the western sky over La Septima. Red brick cigar factories punctured the dying sky.

"I'm finally out!" he yelled.

Passing open fields and swamps and hammocks, the area felt free as air and sun. He had walked its trails and smelled its flowers and dipped his hand into its waters and seen its birds and bears and gators. And he had met its locals -- bankers, businessmen, mechanics, a man who owned a general store and tavern. He liked them and they seemed to like him. He knew they'd never take him for a Cuban from his looks and speech, only when he said his name. I'll call myself Paul, he thought. That's it. Paul and Connie and our blonde son, Sammy: perfection."

He pulled up to his house and parked. Hopping up the steps, he threw wide the door, left a package on the sofa, burst into the kitchen, where he laid a large, ripe orange on the table.

"You bought one orange?"

"Didn't buy it."

"You bought the grove ..."

He stood over his booty like a child with a new toy. "Twenty acres, temples, and at my price."

Consuelo looked unbelieving. He sat her down and held her hands across the table. "You'll love it."

"Tell me everything."

"A nearby grove brought $135,000 eight years ago. I looked it up last month. This is a gift of the depression." Thoughts tripped over each other. "Remember the freeze year before last? Cut the owner's crop in half. He didn't replant, so he lost again the next year. Then his wife died, and he lost interest in farming."

He went through the whole story about listing it at too high a price and then lowering it.

"I wanted to help the poor old guy. He had become morose and hard to talk to. That's when I offered him $2,000. I told him I could afford to wait until times got better and he couldn't. I almost lost it, though. When I got back to my office and was filling out the papers, another guy showed up ready to pay the full $3,500. I swear I didn't know what to do. I couldn't let it go. Without thinking, I told him it was sold."

"Then what?" she asked, not wanting to believe what she knew was coming.

"I closed with Mr. Stewart this morning."

"Without telling him?"

"Why should I?"

"It's unethical."

"It's business."

"Taking advantage of a poor old man down on his luck? How cold, inhuman; it's revolting."

"That's unfair, Consuelo. Times are tough. I haven't sold a thing in weeks. I can't turn a good deal down for sentiment."

She turned away.

"My job is to support my family. Yours is to run my house, not to nag. Understand? Times are tough; it's dog eat dog; every man for himself."

For a few moments they glared at each other.

"And while we're at it, no more babies. I won't be tied down. Understand?"

Consuelo's face tightened. She put her tight fists on the table. Through clenched teeth she said, "How dare you?"

"That's my decision. There's nothing to discuss. Understand?"

Pablo recalled the months of worry. Then he said, "Come on, Consuelo, can't we enjoy what we have?"

He reached for her hand again, but she drew back. He stood and put his arms around her waist; her arms hung limp at her sides. He felt he would drown in the green of her eyes. At that moment he realized how much he had hurt her. "We'll do fine. Leave business to me. We're lucky to have Sammy."

Pablo knew a Cuban wife would not defy her husband. "Look, it's a beautiful house with lots of windows looking out on trees and flowers. It's perfect tranquility. I won't have to drive far and it'll be great to leave this crowded neighborhood. Sammy will love the country and so will you when you get used to it."

She stood motionless, as if petrified.

"Wait here," he said, and ran back to the living room. "Fruit is not the only thing I have."

Lifting a bottle out of the paper bag, he popped the cork and poured. Straining to act festive, he raised his glass, "To our new adventure."

"To poor Sammy," she added, with a sullen look.

Pablo calmed himself with the belief that she would get over it. He stayed home that evening and talked more than he had in a long time. Throughout his excited chatter, she listened in stony silence. He wondered what she was thinking, but he dared not ask. When they went to bed, they lay face up as he talked about all the things they could do in the country and about Sammy growing up in the clean, country air, and meeting

American boys to play with and going to school away from the noise and bustle of Ybor City. When he turned to face her she had fallen asleep.

*

Pablo reached the office early, eager to tell Marvin. He tried to read the paper as he bit his nails. When Marvin arrived, Pablo exploded before he had closed the door: "I got the grove!"

"This morning?"

"Yesterday. The twenty acres I was trying to sell."

Marvin tried to talk, but could not squeeze in a word.

Stumbling on his words Pablo told the story leaving out the detail about the buyer.

"That's awfully cheap."

"The old man's happy."

"Going to resell it?"

"No. We're moving there." Pablo could tell Marvin was annoyed.

"OK, Pablo, but to survive you'll have to sell something."

"I may sell it later."

"I guess this calls for celebration," Marvin said. "I'm buying lunch, but first I have a new listing I'd like you to see."

*

That night, after supper, Pablo walked to the Café Cubano. He knew he would have to say goodbye soon, but he was not yet ready. As usual, Matilde was smothering a barstool, nursing a cup of café solo, spilling it into his saucer a little at a time and sipping. Domingo finished wiping the bar and began to straighten out the bottles under the mirror behind the bar. Four men played cards at the back table.

"*Coño!*" Jacinto said. "I can't win a single hand."

"The mo-o-oon is full," El Rubio said.

"What the hell does that have to do with anything?" Jacinto asked.

"Everything," El Rubio said. "The stars di-dic-tate our lives. Don't you know anything about astron-n-nomy?"

"Astrology, not astronomy," Sarna said, starting to deal a new hand.

"You're both going to see stars if I don't win soon," Jacinto said, slapping his hand on the table. Looking up he said, "*Hola Pablo.* Where have you been?"

"*Hola caballeros.* Anyone want to buy some land?"

"On what ass does the turtle sit?" Sarna asked.

"I can get you terms. Anyway, I've bought some, and I'm planning to move there as soon as I fix it up."

"Don't like us anymore?" Matilde asked.

"It's a temple orange grove."

"What do you know about far-ar-ar-ming?" El Rubio asked.

"My father owns cane fields outside Matanzas, remember?"

"My uncle has a dairy, but I can't milk," Sarna said.

"Let's see if you can deal," Jacinto said.

When Pablo asked Matilde how he was doing, he said, "Not bad. No major problems."

"The hardest part will be leaving my friends," Pablo said.

"How's that beautiful son?" Matilde asked.

"Bright and lively. Follows me around. I never expected to enjoy him so much. Of course he's still a baby. I can't wait till he's old enough to play ball."

"Enjoy him now, Pablo. Children are God's greatest gift. Compared to them, nothing matters."

The sadness in Matilde's words startled Pablo. He knew Matilde had no children, but he detected another, different sadness, but he was too pleased with himself to inquire. I'll talk with him later, privately, he thought. "How about a cognac?"

"No thanks, Pablo. Time to go." Draining his cup, Matilde lit his cigar, turned to his comrades. *"Hasta mañana, caballeros."*

"You haven't heard, Pablo," Jacinto said after Matilde had left.

"What?"

"They let him go last week."

"I thought he was set at that small factory."

"Business dropped off, and he was the last one hired," Sarna said.

"What's he going to do?"

"Vila spread the word; nobody will hire him," Jacinto said. "For a while he did odd jobs, anything to pay the bills," Jacinto said. "We wanted to take up a collection, but he wouldn't let us. He's working at the Cuban Club."

"Doing what?"

"Cleaning."

"Horrible!"

9 – A DEATH OR TWO - 1937

*

*Four Confederate Veterans
Attend Memorial Services Here*

*

*Women Read News, Not Pie Recipes,
Says Mrs. Roosevelt*

*

Bathing Suits More Conservative This Year

*

Rail Workers' Pay Cut Restored

*

Pablo spent the next year trying to convince Consuelo to move to Brandon. She held out saying that she did not want to be so isolated while Sammy was still a baby. "What if he needs a doctor or a hospital?"

When he complained about his long drive to Brandon, she argued that he spent the day driving anyway. Pablo used every argument he could dream up, but when it came to Sammy, Consuelo was a granite tower, and he eventually gave up.

Aside from that disagreement, Pablo and Consuelo managed a calm life during the next four years. Her greatest antagonism came from his cautious lovemaking, which seemed distant and callous. By avoiding carnal contact he had shriveled in her eyes. But she resolved to adapt, though it offered one more aggravation.

By the spring of 1937 they had settled into a routine. With the image of a house in the country before him, Pablo would not buy one in town, so they kept the rented house on 12th Avenue. Consuelo stayed home with Sammy, doing all the things that filled women's lives in those days and finding solace in the church, which offered divine understanding, but little human intimacy. And when nothing else would lift her spirits, she would sit at the piano.

Accepting the inevitable, Pablo enjoyed Ybor City's social life. No longer part of the Latino world, he still enjoyed the inhabitants of the Café Cubano with their familiar accents and mannerisms. Though the depression dragged on, his business remained solvent. Sales were scanty, but provided a reasonable living, and he managed to acquire several parcels at bargain prices. He never invested savings unless an outstanding deal presented itself.

*

Fourteenth Street was packed with people as Pablo approached the Cuban Club. The April sun was still high at 5:30, and a cool breeze eased the four-block walk from his house. The sidewalk seemed to be filled with people apparently headed in the same direction as Pablo. As he drew nearer to the club the crowd grew. Pablo saw people moving up the front stairway and had spilled out onto the second floor terrace. He had never seen the white-trimmed, beige brick building so full of people since the Cuban opera buffa that came to town months before. The crowd was lively but orderly, milling about outside the club and into the street as they spoke to each other with vigorous gesturing and arm waving. The outdoor terrace on the second floor was slightly more boisterous. The first person Pablo recognized was El Chulo.

"What's going on?"

"An open board meeting in the auditorium. People are mad as hell," El Chulo said. "It should be very interesting!"

"I'm a new board member; I'd better get up there and see what's going on," Pablo said. "Are you coming?"

"I wouldn't miss it."

Pablo inched his way through the crowd. As he walked from the sidewalk onto the broad stairway that led up to the terrace, he passed a man who was trying to ascend with his wife hanging on him.

"*No, Pedro, no!*" she pleaded. "There's going to be trouble."

"Quiet, woman."

"*Por favor, Pedro,*" she said, crying. "They're liable to do something crazy."

"Excuse me, Madam," Pablo said.

"You see, woman? You're blocking the stairs. Stop nagging and go home."

"You'll see!" she said, turning and leaving the scene.

As Pablo passed them, he heard the man mumble, "Henpecking woman."

At the top of the stairs he pushed through another argument. "But Papa, he's trying to help us; Moreno's denying us the clinic."

"Fine. Vote your conscience, but be careful," the father said. "This fight goes beyond the doctor."

"I don't care about Vallarte or the President. It's Dr. Ramírez and the men out of work. They're the ones."

Pablo listened as he walked, trying vainly to piece the scene together into a coherent whole. He decided not to take sides because whichever side he took, he would alienate the other. He even thought about returning home. He could say his son was sick. But curiosity had overcome prudence.

Pablo had never been involved in Cuban Club affairs. He joined the club when he arrived in Ybor City, but never used the club's clinic. He preferred to choose his doctors and pay the cost. His logic was simple: What can you expect from a clinic that charges a dollar a month for unlimited medical care for an entire family? He rarely missed the parties, picnics and dances, though. It was Marvin who suggested running for office to expand their business into the Latin community.

Following Marvin's suggestion, Pablo had volunteered. Having no ties to any of the factions, the blonde, handsome young man easily won a seat on the Board of Directors. He had heard about a doctor being fired, but he knew no details and had formed no opinion. Judging from the crowd and the arguments, members seemed strongly divided.

He had to push his way through the crowd to get in. Three or four men blocking the door to the lobby were debating whether Moreno should have fired the doctor. "We can't afford it. If you can't pay, you're out," one man said. "Otherwise, the club will go broke."

"Nonsense!" another said. "What can it cost to help old members until they get their jobs back?"

"It's just not good business," the first man said.

"Don't you give a damn about your fellow cigar makers?"

Before the first man could answer a third said, "Thank God for Vallarte."

Pablo finally elbowed his way into the crowded auditorium. The curtain exhibited a pastoral scene of workers harvesting tobacco in the Cuban countryside. A podium stood on the stage in front of the curtain. The stage, which rose about four feet above the floor, opened into the wings and dressing rooms. The only access to the stage from the audience was through a small, arched opening on either side of the stage that led up five steps to the wings. Pablo heard a man say there were over five hundred people there. All the doors and the large, high windows on the outside wall were open to let in the cool breeze and the cloudless April day. Trying to find the board members, Pablo spotted various scattered throughout the audience. The roar was deafening. Pablo found a seat and heard a strong voice behind him rising above the others. "He's gone against the constitution. Hiring and firing is a board decision. Moreno's a dictator." When Pablo turned to see who it was, he recognized a fellow board member, a loud, abrasive man named Luis Vallarte. The short, stocky man in his early fifties wore his black hair neatly combed back and sported a thin, black moustache. He flailed his arms and slapped one fist into his open palm as he spoke. "This would never have happened if they had elected me."

"What's on the agenda?" Pablo asked.

"The firing, of course," Vallarte said. "Where do you stand?"

"I don't know. This is my first board meeting."

"I know that; but where do you stand on the firing?"

"I'll tell you when I've learned what's going on." As he turned to face the stage, Pablo thought, I won't be pushed by him or anyone.

"You should have informed yourself before the meeting. All you'll hear today is lies." Then Luis Vallarte turned to the man next to him and resumed his conversation.

Pablo was enjoying listening to the commentary crackling around him. In the seat in front of him a man spoke with great passion.

"He's a butcher. I took my son to him last year for a swelling in his arm. Ramírez barely looked at it. Without saying anything to his mother or me, he turned to the nurse and said, 'take him down, I'll cut into it and see what the problem is.' When I told him he could cut into his mother, he said I was ungrateful and walked off."

"What happened to the boy?" his friend asked.

"I took him downtown to an American doctor. He bandaged the arm and told us to keep it soaked with warm Epsom salt solution. In a week it was fine. Just think if I had let that butcher cut him up."

The man next to Pablo tapped him on the arm and said, "Don't believe everything you hear."

"I'm new to the board. What do you think?"

"I'm on the board too, but I want to hear more before deciding." It was the first objective opinion Pablo had heard. "Jorge Del Río at your service," the man said.

President Moreno walked onto the stage and stood behind the podium. Some of the audience applauded, and hearing that, others began to boo. The tall, stocky man was wearing a Cuban, light tan, linen suit and looked commanding as he held the podium and looked over the audience. Smoking a long, dark cigar and waiting for the noise to die down, he passed his hand through his thick, light brown hair. "Please come to order," he said, laying the cigar on a dish. "Some board members requested this open meeting, and I complied. I ask you to remember that we're here to transact business in an orderly manner. I'll recognize anyone who wishes to speak, and that person will have the floor for a reasonable time. I'd like everyone to listen quietly while each person speaks. I will begin by presenting the facts of the case."

Someone yelled out, "We know the facts. Let's vote."

The president ignored the comment and resumed. "A large number of members have complained to me and some of the board members about Dr. Ramírez."

"A lie!" another voice said. "We like him."

"Gentlemen, we can't have a serious discussion without order. Everyone will have his turn." When the chatter subsided he continued: "Dr. Ramírez has been treating nonmembers and prescribing medicines from the pharmacy. We cannot afford such generosity. He is not paying the expenses; the members are. When I spoke with him Dr. Ramírez told me he would continue to treat anyone who needed him. He said he didn't care whether they paid or not. That was intolerable, so we fired him. I know that some of you don't agree with this because Dr. Ramírez has helped you. I'm not saying he's incompetent. The problem is he's not suited for the job. He's a good man and a good doctor, but he has poor business judgment. Our clinic exists to serve our members. I believe Dr. Ramírez will be better able to serve people in private practice. Those are my reasons. Now I open the discussion to the board or any members who wish to speak."

Luis Vallarte was the first to stand and begin speaking before the president formally recognized him.

"I completely disagree with what you say; we can easily afford to treat unemployed members. But there is a more formal issue: you have no authority to fire or hire without the board's approval. It is against our club constitution. I don't know your real reasons for firing Ramírez. Those don't matter anymore than the reasons you've just given. I demand you present the matter to the Board of Directors for their vote as required by the constitution."

As Vallarte sat down, the crowd erupted into a cacophony of applause, cheers, boos, yelling, and laughing. Someone threw a paper airplane that glided onto the stage near the feet of the president, which brought a wave of laughter.

Waving a sheaf of papers, President Moreno tried to quiet them. "This is our constitution. I defy you to show me where it says that the board must vote on hiring and firing."

Again Vallarte rose. "I have a copy too, Moreno. I'll read it to you. 'Medical personnel will be appointed and terminated by the President with the consent of the Board of Directors.' That's clear as glass."

Again the crowd yelled and paper airplanes, the sport of the day, filled the air. Several minutes passed before President Moreno could respond. "Several board members agree wholeheartedly with me."

"You didn't ask me or any board members I know," said Vallarte. "Here's our new member, Pablo Iglesias. Did you ask him?" Pablo sank into his seat. "I demand to know who you consulted." Not wanting to be drawn into a political fight before hundreds of people, Pablo did not look around.

Out of the corner of his vision Pablo saw Matilde at one end of the side section near the stage. Calmly rising, Matilde asked to speak. When Moreno recognized him he began: "Fellow members, no good will come of this meeting. There is too much emotion and too few facts for us to decide anything rationally. I move we adjourn and let the board meet in private."

Vallarte was still standing as the crowd began to boo. He yelled, "I'm still waiting for an answer, Moreno!"

Ignoring Matilde's motion, Moreno responded to Vallarte. "I will not give names. That would violate their confidence."

Matilde moved calmly to the aisle, walked to the lobby exit and disappeared.

"Perhaps you should worry about Dr. Ramírez's reputation and the well being of our members," Vallarte said. "It's obvious that you don't give a damn about either, as long as you have your books neatly balanced. Why are you so interested in bringing money into our club? Or is that where it's going?"

A woman in the second row stood. *"Sinverguenza!"* she yelled, waving her fist at the president, and the crowd roared.

Feeling that the meeting had degenerated, President Moreno threw down the papers he had been waving and yelled, "If the membership is going to permit their president to be insulted, I adjourn this meeting," and walked back stage.

At that moment six or seven men in the audience followed Vallarte into the small arched doorway at the right of the stage. Intending to take control of the meeting, Vallarte instead attacked Moreno. He and his friends knocked Moreno to the floor and began beating and kicking him. Immediately five of Moreno's friends appeared in his defense. Some of them pulled Moreno into a small room backstage. Vallarte and his followers forced their way in, pushing and grappling, and Vallarte grabbed Moreno again and both fell to the floor. When Moreno's allies saw that Vallarte was pounding their friend, they jumped on Vallarte.

Not knowing what was happening backstage, the auditorium went wild. Some tried to squeeze into the backstage area; others threw soft drink bottles and anything they had in their hands at the stage. Fists flew, but when they heard shots everyone froze, and a woman's voice rang out from the wings, "They've killed him!" Backstage, the only man who did not get up was Vallarte. Moreno, his face bleeding, stood. Vallarte's friends and his wife tried to help Vallarte. One of Moreno's associates slipped out the back door and drove away. Vallarte's friends carried him out the back stage door and walked around the building and across the street toward the Cuban Club Clinic on the next block. A doctor had run backstage, examined Moreno, and pronounced the cut superficial. Moreno's supporters led him out the back door a few minutes after Vallarte, while the clamor continued.

Pablo managed to push his way to the aisle, where an elderly man was swinging his fists wildly. Pablo ducked in time to avoid the fist. The man lost his balance and Pablo pushed him over the back of his seat. Someone yelled, "They've shot Vallarte!" Across the auditorium El Chulo punched a man in the face. The man crumpled, and El Chulo turned with his fists up looking for someone else to hit. Pablo made his way out and realized his shoulder hurt from a wild punch he did not remembered. He had jogged a block and turned in front of a cigar maker's house as two police cars screeched to a stop at the club entrance. The police stopped the men with Vallarte. By this time Pablo was nearly home.

The police expanded into the room like a pungent gas and quickly stopped the free-for-all. The two cops with Moreno saw his bloody face and asked if he wanted to go to the clinic. His friends said a doctor had already seen him. Then policemen led Moreno and his friends to the squad car. The cops with Vallarte asked where they were going.

"The clinic. Please, officer, he's been shot." Seeing Vallarte unconscious, one of the policeman went with them. The other entered the club.

Inside, the police blocked all exits and began interrogating people. Within an hour, they had finished and dismissed everyone. Outside, Sergeant Monroe asked who were the men in the squad car. "This man was attacked," one of them said. "His name is Armando Moreno. He's the club president. They tried to kill him."

"All right, all right," the sergeant said. "Harrison, you and Hoover get him to the clinic across the street. The rest of you stay in the car."

"Are we under arrest?"

"For the moment."

Vallarte was so serious that they took him into surgery immediately. Moreno told the doctor he had been shot. "No," the doctor said, as he calmly looked him over. "You've been cut." He bandaged Moreno's wound and released him to the police. "Probably a broken bottle."

The police took the detained men to the police station for questioning. No one in the auditorium admitted to seeing the shooting. Some said they thought Vallarte had tried to shoot Moreno. Others said Moreno had shot Vallarte. The animosity between the two soon became apparent, and the police stopped questioning.

At the station, they questioned Moreno. They had found no gun on him, but reasoned that he could have gotten rid of it easily enough. One of Vallarte's friends said one of Moreno's men took the gun when he left the auditorium. The officer in charge, Lieutenant Pierce, sent two men to Moreno's home to interrogate his family and look for a gun. When they returned an hour later, they brought a gun. "Mrs. Moreno said it's her husband's; it hasn't been fired," the policeman said.

After interrogating everyone the police released them. "What do you think, Lieutenant?" Sergeant Monroe asked.

"Hard to tell. Moreno could have done it, or it could have been one of his buddies. We need to find the guy who left. He could have taken the gun." Looking at his notes, he said, "Let's see … Manolo Fuentes. Send a couple of men to his house and check it out. Here's his address."

"That's West Tampa, Lieutenant. He had to cross the Michigan Avenue Bridge. He could have thrown it in the river."

"Pick him up."

The two Policemen soon returned with Manolo Fuentes and took him to a small, windowless room with only a hanging lamp. "Wait here. The lieutenant wants to ask you some questions." The only furniture was a small table and three straight-back chairs.

About twenty minutes later, Lieutenant Pierce came into the room where Fuentes had been waiting. "When did you leave the Cuban Club?"

"During the fight. I didn't want to get involved."

"By the side exit?"

"I guess so."

"After the shooting?"

"No, I heard the shots when I got outside."

"You're a friend of Moreno's, aren't you?"

"Yeah. They were beating him up, and I was trying to get him out. That Vallarte's mean."

"So you were involved in the fight backstage?"

"Not really. Look, I didn't shoot nobody."

"Uh-huh."

"I didn't have nothing to do with no shooting," Fuentes said. "I was outside."

"How did you go home?"

"In my car."

"I mean what route?"

"West on Palm Avenue to Nebraska, then to Michigan Avenue, then to Albany Street, where I live."

"So you crossed the Michigan Avenue Bridge?"

"Sure."

"What did you throw into the river when you crossed it?"

"Nothing. I didn't throw nothing," Fuentes said.

"Remember, you'll be questioned under oath later, and lying under oath is a serious offense."

"Who said I threw something? It's a lie. I didn't throw nothing."

"Take him back and hold him." Lieutenant Pierce left the room.

*

Pablo got home a little past seven o'clock.

"I'm glad you're home. I forgot to tell you about the meeting of the church ladies at 7:30. They're soliciting money for the cigar makers."

"You won't believe what I've been through," he said. "There were five hundred people at the meeting. They shot Luis Vallarte backstage; I didn't see it. He started an argument with the president."

"Did the police come?"

"Got there after I left. Had to fight my way out. It was rough. I would've stayed to help, but I didn't want to get involved with the police."

"I'm glad. Was anybody else hurt?"

"It was crazy. People were fighting in the auditorium, throwing bottles; it was a riot. I saw El Chulo knock out some guy."

"I shouldn't leave you alone with Sammy after that."

"Go and have a good time. I'll put Sammy to bed and then get some work done." Sammy was still sitting at the table reading. "Time for bed, Sammy."

"Aw, Papa, a little longer?"

"You've been looking at that book long enough. Now to bed and don't argue."

"May I have a drink of water?"

"To bed; I'll bring it."

Pablo's nerves and patience were frazzled. "Of all days," he muttered to himself. "And I have so much to do for tomorrow morning." He opened the refrigerator and poured a glass of water.

"Now go to sleep," he said, handing it to the boy, who was sitting on the edge of the bed.

"Tell me a story, Papa."

"Not tonight. It's late and I have a lot to do."

Sammy was still whining when the phone rang.

"Hello?"

"Mr. Iglesias ... Pablo? This is Cynthia. You remember me?" He immediately recognized her voice and Cracker accent. His heart was beating so hard he could barely talk. "Can you come to my house? I cain't explain why, please."

"What is it?"

"Not on the phone." Her voice was squeaky and trembling.

"I've just put my son to bed and I can't leave. My wife's gone out."

"I wouldn't call if it wasn't urgent."

Cynthia's panic unnerved him. Writing down her address he said, "Sulfur Springs? That's a long way; I'll have to bring my little boy."

"Just hurry."

The table light was still on in Sammy's room; he was pulling up the covers when his father walked in. A model airplane hung over his bed, and a pile of toys was pushed into the corner.

"Get dressed. We're going out."

Sammy threw off the covers and jumped out of bed. "Where, Papa?"

"Just hurry."

As he put on his shoes and a shirt, Pablo tried to recall the details of the Cuban Club meeting that afternoon and the turmoil and his narrow escape. He wondered about Matilde. Quietly walking out before the fight started was smart, he thought. Must have figured out what was going to happen. That man has a sixth sense.

Then he thought about Cynthia and the times he was with her. He had not thought about her lately. Such an exciting woman, he thought. I've lived up to my vow not to see her again, but it would be nice. Barely twenty, the redhead was nothing if not the sexiest woman he had ever known. Those long, shapely legs and firm body like pure desire, he mused. His agitation over seeing her frightened him. He wondered if she had called because she wanted him or perhaps she's no longer in the business and is looking for somebody steady. Pablo was in a panic of desire and fear and rage, unaccountable rage.

As he tied his shoelaces his mind switched between Cynthia and the shooting when Sammy burst into his bedroom.

"I'm ready, Papa."

Though Sammy's socks didn't match, Pablo said nothing. He lifted him onto his lap, threaded his half-pulled-out, dragging shoelaces, and tied them neatly. Sammy reached up for his father's hand, and together they walked out to the carport and into the four-year-old Ford.

The moonlight traced long, lonely shadows on the tree-lined street. In his headlights, telephone lines entangled the light like a cat's cradle against the inky sky. Pablo drove without haste. The shooting, Consuelo and Cynthia needled in and out of his thoughts as he threaded his way through the unfamiliar street looking at house numbers.

She was standing at the curb. Drawn shades made the pale green stucco house look vacant. "Pull into the carport," she said. In a blue chenille bathrobe with fuzzy blue slippers and her disheveled flaming red wavy hair, she looked wild. He glimpsed a domestic side of the hard professional who worked on Fifth Avenue. Cynthia followed the car in. Her eyes darted to the boy and back to Pablo.

"For Christ sake, did you have to bring him?"

"I couldn't leave him alone. What's the problem? Is that Vila's Cadillac?"

"Leave him and come in."

"Stay here, Sammy. I'll be back in a minute."

They walked across the dark porch to the front door. Her uncharacteristically nervous walk made her look girlish and vulnerable. Once inside the dark living room she erupted: "This is the shits! Nothin' like this ain't never happened to me before."

"What?"

"He's dead."

"Who, for Christ's sake?"

"Gustavo."

"What do you mean, dead?"

"Don't you know what that means? He ain't alive no more. And I cain't move him. You got to get him outa here."

"Take it easy; calm down. Why me?"

"Expect me to call his wife? I don't know. He talked about you once in a while."

"OK. Now calm down and tell me what happened."

"He's in my bed. Do I have to draw you a picture?" Cynthia was holding down erupting hysteria. "He musta got too excited. He'd had a few drinks; all of a sudden he started gruntin' and moanin', grabbed his chest, and fell limp. I had a awful time pushin' him outa between my knees. He's heavier than he looks."

"I didn't realize you … ah … knew him."

Even in the dark he could see Cynthia's fingers curl like talons. "You know I'm a business woman."

"Why here? What about Fifth Avenue?"

"He didn't want nobody to know. Anyway, what's the difference?"

The shades were rolled down in the bedroom, and a small table light cast long shadows on the walls and ceiling. The small bedroom was painted pink and had a double bed, a vanity dresser, a tall dresser, and a large oak wardrobe with mirrors on the doors. A half-empty bottle of brandy and two glasses stood on the night table by the bed. Gustavo Vila was lying on his side, naked, in the middle of the bed. "My God, he's gray, and his eyes are half open." Pablo reached down and closed them with his fingers.

"How long has he been like this?"

"Twenty … thirty minutes. I didn't know what was happenin'. He musta had a fit or somethin'. When I saw he weren't breathing, I panicked. Picked up the phone, but who would I call that wouldn't send the cops? I tried to dress him but couldn't. He's too heavy."

Pablo pushed don Gustavo from his side onto his back and looked down on the stubby figure. "How can you be alive one minute and dead the next?" he said, trying to remember their last conversation. Pablo lifted the old man's knees and said, "Come on, let's pull up his shorts." When they got them up to his thighs, Pablo tried to raise his midsection but couldn't at that angle from the side of the bed. He said, "OK, pull them up the rest of the way little by little as I roll him from side to side."

"Not so damn rough," she said.

"He's dead, for Christ sake. He can't feel anything."

"I don't care; take it easy."

After getting the shorts in place, Cynthia hovered over the body straightening them. Weaving around each other Pablo bumped into her and knocked her off balance. He caught her under her arms and almost pulled her robe off.

"Sorry."

"It's OK," she said with a noncommittal smile.

The head and then the arms slid easily into the old man's undershirt. They pushed the pants up onto his legs with lots of rocking.

"Push; keep pushing," Pablo said as he continued to roll the body.

"Damn it, I'm doin' the best I can," she said, puffing.

Tucking in his shirt took time, but she finally got it looking neat and smooth. A button popped off with all the pulling and tugging, and Cynthia reached past Pablo for it. As her breast brushed against his face he realized she was wearing nothing underneath. Pablo put on the old man's socks and shoes while Cynthia took a needle and thread out of a sewing box and sewed the button back on. She tied his shoelaces and then gently wiped the old man's face with a small towel and combed his hair. Pablo stood aside and watched as she attended to each detail, like a mother dressing a baby. When they were finished, he put his arm around her shoulder and walked her into the dark living room.

"I never realized how hard it is to move a dead body," Pablo said. "It's been pretty rough, hasn't it?"

"Oh-oh," Cynthia said. "Look."

Sammy was outside in the dark, looking through the screen door, rubbing his knuckles into his eyes.

"I thought I told you to stay in the car."

"I got scared."

Pablo opened the door and lifted him. "I'm really busy, Sammy. You've got to stay in the car. I'll turn on the radio and you can listen to Charlie McCarthy. How about that?"

"I guess so." Sammy was still rubbing his eyes.

Cynthia went into the kitchen as Pablo took Sammy out to the car. While Pablo and Sammy were trying to find the station, Cynthia came out with a glass of milk. "Here, Sweetie. Milk with honey, my favorite." Then she stayed at the car with him a few moments listening to the radio while Pablo went back in the house.

After a minute, she said, "We'll be right out, Sweetie. Wait here, OK?" When she returned to the living room, Pablo had disappeared. Hearing a noise in the bedroom she called out, "What's going on?"

"Got to move this dresser so we can walk him out."

Pablo had moved Don Gustavo's legs around so they hung over the edge of the bed. Then he grabbed the old man's arms and pulled him to a sitting position. "Sit on that side and put his right arm over your shoulder," he said. "I'll do the same with the left arm. Now when I say up, stand up and hold his arm. Don't let it slip. Ready, up!"

Together they lifted the body and, with short steps, walked it out of the bedroom into the dark living room and out the front door.

Cynthia said, "Don't let his toes drag on the concrete. They'll get scuffed."

They walked the body around to the passenger side and leaned it against the car while Pablo opened the door. Then they lowered the body into the front seat, and Pablo moved the legs in. Cynthia bent down and straightened the old man so he would appear to be asleep.

"Now, what'll I do with him?" Pablo asked, standing outside the car.

"Just take him someplace and say he died while you were driving."

"I got it: a funeral home. They'll take care of him and notify his wife."

"Fine," she said, "just get him outa here. And here's my phone number … in case."

Pablo looked at her quizzically, but decided not to ask. He said, "What'll I tell Sammy?"

"Just say he's drunk."

"He doesn't know about that. He's only five years old. I'll tell him he's sick."

"Fine, fine. Now go."

As she walked around the car he realized he was covered with goose flesh. I don't need this, he muttered to himself as he opened the car door and got in.

Sammy had both hands around the empty milk glass when Pablo started the car.

"Charlie McCarthy's funny, Papa."

"Yes he is."

"What's wrong with the man, Papa?"

"He doesn't feel well, Sammy. I have to take care of him. Tell you what: we'll get some ice cream on the way home. How's that?"

"Oh boy. Is the man going to have some too?"

"He's sick; I'm going to take him someplace first."

"An ice cream cone might make him feel better."

"Just listen to the radio. We'll drop him off and then we'll go home."

"After we get the ice cream?"

Pablo did not answer. As he backed out of the driveway, Cynthia, who had walked back to the front door, motioned for him to wait. She jogged back to the car, and bent over to look into the window. "I just wanted to say thanks. I didn't mean to be so bitchy."

Pablo smiled for the first time. "It's OK." He watched her walk back across the porch and open the front door before he drove off.

"What's bitchy, Papa?"

"It's a bad word, Sammy. You mustn't repeat it." He saw the living room light and the porch light go on and Cynthia smiling and waving. Pablo drove with urgency.

Sammy stood behind his father in back. He did not recognize the neighborhood. "Are we going home?"

"No, son, we're going to take this man first."

"Where?"

"Not far. You'll see." Pablo was praying that the funeral home would be open.

"Can we get the ice cream first?"

"Damn it; just shut up about the ice cream!" Sammy's bottom lip trembled as he crossed his arms on his chest and looked at his father's face in the rear view mirror.

Pablo turned onto Nebraska Avenue, passed a stop sign without stopping, and as he turned right sharply the body slumped toward him. Pablo hit the brake, the body lurched forward; the old man's head hit the steering wheel and then fell onto Pablo's lap. "*Coño!*" Pablo's first thought was that he might be hurt.

"What's the matter with the man Papa?"

Pablo swerved two or three times before he could slow down and straighten the body. Within a block, he heard a siren behind him.

"Oh no! The police!" Pablo slowed down, and when he was sure it was after him, he pulled over. He got out and met the officer at the rear of the Ford.

The officer held a flashlight beam on Pablo's face. "I was going too fast, wasn't I?" He tried not to attract suspicion but couldn't take his eyes off the handcuffs and revolver on the cop's belt.

"How much have you had to drink?"

"Absolutely nothing. Here, smell my breath." Pablo exhaled three or four times into the policeman's face.

"OK, OK, that's enough. You failed to stop at a stop sign; you were speeding and changed lanes several times without signaling."

"I'm sorry, officer; it's late and I wanted to get my little boy home." At this lame response the officer moved around to the passenger side of the car and shined his light around. Sammy was still pouting and looked away when the light hit his eyes. Then the policeman saw the slumped body with its head resting on its chest. "What's wrong with the old man?"

"Nothing. He's had too much to drink, that's all. We'd had a late meeting and were driving home."

"A meeting and he's dead drunk?"

"He had a few drinks afterwards and it began to take effect after we got going. He'll be OK. I'm taking him home." Pablo knew the story was pitifully weak, but he could think of nothing better. He could feel the handcuffs snapping shut around his wrists.

The policeman again flashed his light on don Gustavo and reached in and shook his shoulder. "This man's dead."

"All right," Pablo exhaled a deep sigh. "He died while we were driving around. Honest. I think he had a heart attack. I was all shook up and was taking him to Lord and Fernandez's Funeral Home. It's just up the street. I should have told you the truth from the beginning, but I was so nervous."

"Get in your car and follow me."

Thinking it was over, Pablo considered telling him the truth, but instead he asked where they were going.

"The hospital. They'll determine the cause of death, and if it was a heart attack, they'll certify it and take care of the body."

"Oh."

Pablo drove as carefully as he could, but had trouble keeping a safe distance behind the police car; the Ford seemed to want to accelerate on its own. He pictured a prison cell with a thief or murderer as cellmate. I'll have one phone call, but who would I call? he thought. Cynthia and Consuelo fought it out in his prison fantasies. His hands gripped the steering wheel as if he were holding back a team of horses. He wondered how Gustavo could go to a woman like that. Such an old man ... must be sixty ... wasn't a bad guy, but look at him now, just dressed up meat and bones. Funny how Cynthia fixed him up, combed his hair and all. Nice to Sammy too.

The car was no longer running away from him.

*

The emergency room took the body in immediately and determined that don Gustavo had indeed suffered a massive heart attack about an hour before. Pablo was surprised when the hospital attendant insisted on checking his blood pressure and pulse.

"A little high," she said, "but that's to be expected after your ordeal." Then she sat him down and read him a series of questions from a standard form—time of death, symptoms, next of kin, and other details—that she filled in. Pablo began to relax when he realized that she harbored no suspicions about his role in the death.

As the policeman was leaving, he said, "You looked pretty scared back there. Don't feel bad; we see these cases every week. Some guys conk out behind the wheel. Now that's dangerous. You're lucky he wasn't driving."

"He's too drunk to drive," Sammy said.

"I wish he were," the policeman said. "Drive careful now."

"Come on, Sammy, Let's go get that ice cream."

With his arm around Sammy's shoulder Pablo's thoughts fluttered over the past hour. He had forgotten the Cuban Club riot. As they started to walk out, the hospital attendant asked Pablo if he would notify the widow. "I can do it, but I think she would rather hear it from someone she knows."

"I'll stop by her house on the way home."

Standing at the front door of her Hyde Park home so he could keep an eye on Sammy, he earnestly told Mrs. Vila how Gustavo had called him to talk over some problems he was having with the cigar makers.

"I told him I was alone with Sammy and couldn't stay long. He had a few glasses of brandy and, when we were through, he asked me to drive him home. On the way he slumped over dead. I took him to the hospital. They said it was a heart attack."

Mrs. Vila showed little emotion and thanked him vacantly.

"He's had heart problems for several years. Who was he with?"

Her question unleashed a gush of memories of his trysts with Cynthia five years before; he wondered whether Consuelo ever suspected. "With me."

"Yes, of course."

Pablo could not bear her resignation. Before leaving, he took her hand and said, "Please call me if I can do anything."

"Thank you. It's late; you'd better get your little boy home. I'll have the Cadillac picked up tomorrow. It's at the factory?"

"Please don't trouble; I'll bring it in the morning." Pablo had not thought about the car. As far as he knew, it was still parked in front of Cynthia's house.

By the time Pablo pulled in at Los Helados on Fourteenth Street, Sammy had fallen asleep against his side. Pablo laid his head down gently and ran in and bought a quart of coconut ice cream. Then he gently backed out and drove off.

*

It was ten o'clock and Consuelo was still not home. Pablo carried Sammy in and managed to remove his outer clothes and get him into bed without waking him. He pulled Sammy's favorite afghan up around his shoulders and stood for a few moments over the child lying on his side, praying hands under his cheek. I wonder what he dreams about, he thought. He bent over and kissed him. After putting the ice cream into the refrigerator, he sat in the living room trying to make sense of the evening. Two deaths in one evening! Wow! Cynthia would not leave his thoughts—the way she cared for the old man's body and for Sammy. After a few moments he took her number out of his pocket, picked up the telephone, and dialed.

"I've tucked him in."

"You were terrific. Thanks."

"I told his wife that I would bring her the Cadillac tomorrow. I hope you have the key."

"Yeah, his wallet too. They fell out while we was dressin' him."

"Good. I'll take a taxi to your house tomorrow and get it."

Laying the phone in the cradle, Pablo began to plan what he would tell Consuelo. He knew he would have to tell her because Sammy would surely say something. A few minutes later she came in.

*

"The meeting was nice, but too long," she said. "I would have enjoyed it more if you had been there. Father Lopez was wonderful. We're going to take up a collection for the cigar makers who are out of work."

"Sounds boring."

"How was it without me?"

"Just another death," he said, pretending to yawn.

"What do you mean?"

"I got a call just after you left. It was from a strange woman who called about Gustavo Vila. She wouldn't say why, only that it was an emergency. I figured something had happened to him, so I dressed Sammy and drove to her house. As I suspected, the old man had died."

"Was she his lover?"

"Sure. He was dead in her bed. Can you imagine the old fraud?"

Who is she?"

"I didn't ask."

"And you went there?"

"She didn't want the police to find him there."

"Why you?"

"She said Gustavo talked about me a few times. What's the difference? He was a friend. I couldn't refuse."

"So? What happened?"

"I helped dress him and put him in the car and drove him to the hospital. A policeman stopped me when the body slumped and I swerved. I thought I was headed for jail, but no. He escorted us to the hospital."

"How did you explain a dead man in the car?"

"That he died while we were driving. He believed it."

"And where was Sammy?"

"In the back seat."

"Poor child. How could you?"

"I had no choice. I told him he was sick. He doesn't know who it was."

"What about the woman? How did you explain her to him?"

"He didn't ask. He didn't realize what was going on. All he wanted was the ice cream I promised him."

*

The next morning before starting breakfast Consuelo went out to get the newspaper. As she flipped through the pages looking for anything about Vila, Sara walked up the steps.

"*Ay, Consuelo.* Benito saw Pablo at the meeting. Is he all right?"

"Fine. He got out just before the police came. How about Benito?"

"He saw it all, the police questioning, everything." Sara sat in one of the rockers, and Consuelo joined her. "He got hit on the head, he thinks it was a bottle, but he's all right. Got a big bump though."

"Did he see anything?"

"No, but he thinks Moreno shot him. That's what's going around. Nobody will admit even seeing a gun. Typical."

"How's the man who was shot?"

"He's still in the hospital. They say it's serious, that he won't make it."

"I'll bet nobody can tell you what they were fighting about," Consuelo said.

"It's always about who has the biggest *cojones,* just like I told you."

Consuelo laughed. "Pablo was smart to get out. And you'll never believe what happened, while I was at the church meeting."

Sara perked up and sat forward in the chair.

In hushed tones Consuelo told her the story of Pablo being called to a strange woman's house to get Gustavo Vila who had died in her bed. By the time she had finished, a cynical smile covered Sara's face.

"What the hell is a man that age doing with a woman like that?" Sara asked. "Poor wife. Just another old fool showing off his *cojones.* Why did she call Pablo? Does she know him?"

"No. The old man had spoken of him, and she remembered his name," Consuelo said, as she opened the newspaper to look for Vila's death thinking, He said he didn't know her. "Here it is. Cigar manufacturer dies of heart attack."

"I'll read it when I get home," Sara said, getting up.

"Did they take Benito to the police station?"

"No. They questioned him at the Circulo. Well, I have to go."

When she left, Consuelo's eyes skipped through the column until she came to the words, "Mr. Vila died in a car driven by a friend, Pablo Iglesias, when he suffered a heart attack. Apparently, death was instantaneous." The article went on to describe Vila's business and the workers he employed. She went back and read the whole article and then went in to tell Pablo, who was in the kitchen waiting for breakfast.

"*Coño!*" he said. "Well, it could have been worse, I guess."

"How?"

"I don't know. They might have blamed me. How do I know?"

*

That morning Pablo drove his car to Seventh Avenue, parked it near the Café Cubano and called a taxi. He waited in the Café over a cup of café con leche until the taxi pulled up to the curb. He gave the driver directions to Cynthia's house and sat back.

As the taxi headed north on Nebraska Avenue, Pablo burned with desire thinking that the old man must have been keeping her. When he reached Cynthia's house, he knocked on the door. "I'm here for the old man's car," he said.

Cynthia was wearing the same chenille robe she wore the night before. "Here's the key," she said, handing it to him, "And his wallet."

"OK to come in?"

"Sure." She stepped back.

"Is this your house?"

"Naw. Gustavo's been paying the rent. I gotta move out by the end of the month."

After thinking a moment, he said, "I have a little house in Six Mile Creek you could use."

"That's pretty far."

"I could get you a car."

"Are you propositioning me?" She feigned surprise.

Not sure what to say he fumbled with his hands and hesitated. "I guess I'd like to see a lot of you."

"I wouldn't mind. How about some brandy?"

"It's a little early."

"Then why don't you just take off your tie and jacket and relax. I'll be right back."

Pablo loosened his tie and took off his jacket and sat in the sofa. He lit a cigarette and rested his head back on the cushion trying to remember how the room looked the night before. It seemed more cheerful in the daylight; the feeling of dread had vanished. She returned wearing a slip that shimmered and clung hungrily. She had combed her hair so that it stood out thickly like a red halo. "Now what would you like?"

10 – PRESIDENCY - 1937

*

Hoover Denounces Move To Pack Supreme Court

*

Ambassador Says Americans Don't Understand Spanish Civil War

*

Japanese Block U.S. Messengers At Embassy Gate

*

End of Miami Horserace Gambling? Rumors Fly

*

Senator Opposes Democrats' Pump Priming

*

Two days later the Café Cubano reeked of smoke as cigar makers bantered nervously about the riot.

"What happened to the old man?" Jacinto asked Pablo as he walked in.

"Didn't you read the paper?"

"Come on, spill it."

"That said it all. I was driving him home and he passed out. When I stopped to see what happened, I couldn't hear a heartbeat. I got nervous and a cop stopped me for speeding. When he saw the old man dead in the front seat, he led me to the hospital. That's all."

"Well then, what do you think about the shooting?"

"Anything new?" Pablo asked, happy to change the subject.

"The Tribune said the grand jury questioned forty witnesses," El Gordo said.

"Did Vallarte say who shot him?" Pablo asked.

"Yeah. Moreno," Jacinto said.

"I didn't see that," Pablo said.

El Gordo started to read from the newspaper: "When the witness said, 'I asked Vallarte who shot him …' the judge stopped him. 'Answer only the questions asked,' he said.' Why would they stop a witness from telling what he knows? A dying man's word is supposed to be evidence."

"If he knew he was dying," Matilde said, from the end of the bar behind El Gordo's table.

"But he died," El Gordo said.

Matilde turned on his stool. "From what I heard, he only realized he was dying after he woke up from the operation."

"Too bad they didn't listen to you," Pablo said.

"I hoped people would follow me out," Matilde said.

"El Chulo was in the middle of it," Pablo said. "I saw him knock somebody down."

"I wouldn't cross him," Jacinto said. "*Muy macho*. What are you going to do, Pablo?"

"Do?"

"You're on the board. You'll have to vote."

"I don't know; frankly I'm not anxious to do anything."

"I overheard Ruben Ayala yesterday at the factory," Jacinto said. "He said Moreno has *cojones* and knows how to defend himself; said Vallarte had it coming."

"So?" El Gordo asked.

"He was bragging. Why brag about Moreno unless he did the shooting?"

"I can't understand how intelligent men can kill over something so stupid," Huesito said.

"That grand jury's fixed," Jacinto said.

*

During the third day the grand jury's questions turned to Vallarte's declaration. The two directors who appeared first said that they did not know who fired the shots, but that Vallarte had named Moreno as the killer.

"Were you in the room when the shooting occurred?" the State Attorney asked.

"Yes," the first witness said.

"Did you see Armando Moreno shoot Mr. Vallarte?" the State Attorney asked.

"No, but I heard them."

"Them?"

"The shots."

The second witness said Vallarte named Moreno as the shooter, but he also said he did not see the shooting.

Mrs. Vallarte was serious but flustered when she sat in the witness chair. She fidgeted with her fan, folding and unfolding it during the questioning.

"Please tell us what happened when the riot started," the State Attorney asked.

"When I heard the shots, I ran backstage and found my husband staggering out of a small room. His face was bleeding. I asked him if he was all right. His hands were holding his side. I held a chair for him to sit on; then he said, 'Moreno shot me.' That was before they took him to the clinic."

"Did you go to the clinic?" the State Attorney asked.

"Of course. He told me he ran backstage and Moreno threw him on the floor. He felt something hard pressed into his side and heard two shots."

"Did he say anything else?"

"Yes. He said, 'When Moreno shot me, I called him a coward for shooting a man when he's down.'" Her sobbing interrupted her testimony. After composing herself she continued: "He said, 'I know I'm going to die. You'll be alone now. Save all the money you can.' A few minutes later he said, 'I don't forgive Moreno, and you shouldn't either. Make sure they punish him; he deserves it.' Then he said, 'Manolo Fuentes and Ruben Ayala were holding me when Moreno fired.'"

Every witness testified that Vallarte spoke before the operation, right after he got to the hospital. When they asked if he knew he was dying when he spoke, they all said they thought so.

The next witness, Manolo Fuentes, said, "I left by a rear entrance as soon as Vallarte and Moreno fell to the floor."

"What did you do then?"

"When I got outside I heard two shots. I got in my car and drove home."

"Another witness has testified that you were still inside when the shooting occurred," the State Attorney said.

"Whoever said that is a liar." Fuentes wiped his face with his handkerchief.

"On your way home you crossed the Michigan Avenue Bridge," the State Attorney said.

"That's right."

"What did you throw into the river?"

"Nothing. I didn't have nothing to throw."

Armando Moreno was still bandaged when he limped to the witness chair and sat with some difficulty. When the State Attorney asked him to describe what happened, he said, "I left the stage when a woman insulted me from the audience. And then I heard someone say, 'Kill the President.' Then Vallarte intercepted me behind the curtain. When we went into a clinch and fell, they struck me and kicked me from all sides until I was nearly unconscious."

"Did you hear a gun shot?"

"No."

"Did you have a gun?"

"No, sir."

"Do you know who fired the shots?"

"No, sir."

*

The Café Cubano buzzedthe following morning: "Can you believe this?" Jacinto said, raising his head from the outspread newspaper on the table. "The grand jury says, 'death at the hands of unknown parties.' Everybody in Ybor City knows who did it." He pushed the newspaper away and stood and said, "This stinks."

"Nobody won't do nothing when it's one of us," El Chulo said. "If it had been one of them, somebody would be swinging from a tree by now."

"It's not over," Matilde said.

"Don't hold your breath, my friend," Jacinto said. "What do you think, Pablo?"

"I don't know. It may not have been a deathbed statement."

"What about Fuentes? He threw the gun away," Jacinto said.

"No witnesses saw him throw it," Matilde said. "This may end as an unsolved crime."

"Matilde's right," Domingo said, walking to the table where Jacinto had been sitting. "I remember the shooting at the Centro Espanol in West Tampa. It was years ago, at least twenty. Five men were playing poker at one of the tables at the back of the cantina. No, it was near the front door. I remember, my friend Paco from West Tampa told me. He was one of the players. You all know Paco, the son of Manuel the well-digger, who was married to Nena La Loca before he divorced her and married Paco's mother. Paco's mother is a good homemaker and good to Manuel. Nena La Loca went with other men, *una puta*. Anyway, these men were playing poker like they did every Friday after work. Even when Paco was sick with a fever of 39 degrees and had to stay home from work, he got out of bed to play. But that was another time. The day I'm talking about, one of the players, Jorge Alvarez, I believe his name was, well he got mad at one of the other players, a man named Segismundo, a long time friend of his. Segismundo was a baker at La Segunda Central Bakery, you know, the bakery Juan Moré started in the nineties. They make the best Cuban bread in Ybor City. Segismundo worked the oven and was very good at his job; they say he was the best *hornero* in Tampa in those days. Well, that evening the two of them got into an argument and before long it got pretty hot. The other players tried to calm them, but Segismundo called Jorge a liar. Every time Jorge said something, Segismundo said, '*Mentiroso!*' Jorge said, 'Shut up or you'll be sorry.' When Segismundo said, 'Liar!' Jorge slammed the cards down on the table and stood up, knocking over most of the stacks of chips in front of the players. He left without saying a word to nobody. They thought he was going to the toilet, but instead he went out the front door. That's how I remember the table was near the front, because the toilet is in the back. He left all his chips and everything."

"I hope he can finish before closing time," Jacinto said.

"I thought you said there was a killing," Pablo said.

"Wait. I'm coming to that. I don't want to miss any part of the story. Where was I? Oh, yes, the others kept playing as if nothing had happened. They didn't know Jorge had gone home. And why do you think he went home?"

"He liked his toilet better than the one in the Centro?" El Chulo said.

"It's not funny. You'll soon see how serious it was," Domingo said. "Nobody knew it, but he went home to get his gun. See, he had a .32 in his bedroom under his pillow in case a burglar ever tried to break into his house. His wife didn't like it, but what could she do? Jorge was a hothead and wouldn't take nothing off nobody. That's why everybody was so shocked when he left the game without a word. They expected him to punch Segismundo, but he just walked out.

"In a little while he walked back into the Centro and went directly to the table where his friends were still playing. 'Do you still call me a liar?' he asked Segismundo. What do you think Segismundo said?"

El Chulo stood with his arms spread and said, "Please, for the love of God, shoot and put us out of our misery."

"No. He didn't say that. Anyway, how would you know, Chulo? You weren't in Tampa then. What Segismundo said was, 'Just sit down and play, liar.' Segismundo was smiling when he said it. I think he was kidding, but Jorge didn't think it was funny. Still standing at the table facing Segismundo, Jorge took out his .32 pistol, aimed it at Segismundo, with his gun arm over Paco's head, and shot Segismundo in the chest. Segismundo must have been surprised because he looked down at his chest just before he slumped over on the table and smashed his head against two tall stacks of ten-cent poker chips. Spilled them all over the floor, and then bled all over them."

"Did he die?" Pablo asked.

"Wait," he said. "That's not all."

"Oh, God," El Chulo said. "How much worse can it get?"

"Somebody called the police, and they busted into the Centro asking questions. Everybody told them exactly what had happened. When the police finished questioning everybody, they arrested Jorge and took him to jail. I forgot to tell you that right after the police arrived, an ambulance took Segismundo to the hospital, but he died on the way to the hospital. The bullet got him right in the heart. Jorge was a very good shot. He could hit a can on a fence at a hundred feet. Anyway, Jorge had a good lawyer, a man from West Tampa named Fernández, very well known in those days. Well, the trial took two whole days. They called the men who were playing and the bartender and all the others who were there that night. There weren't many, because it was still early when it happened, before the place had gotten crowded. They all said Jorge did it. What do you think they did to Jorge?"

"Took his gun away?" El Chulo said.

"No. They let him go."

"Impossible!" El Chulo said.

"No it's not," Huesito said. "It happened in 1919 exactly as Domingo said. They talked about it for years."

"How could they?" Pablo asked.

"Temporary insanity," Domingo said. "Fernández, the lawyer, claimed Jorge got so mad he went crazy, but only long enough to kill Segismundo; then he got sane again."

"Just like I told you," El Chulo said. "It didn't matter because he killed one of us. If he had killed one of them, they would have hung the bastard, crazy or not."

"That's nothing," El Gordo said. "A few years later there was a killing in the Italian Club. Four men were playing dominoes and an argument started just like the other one, but a little different. One of the men got up, went behind the bar and got a hammer. Then he came back and hammered the shit out of the guy he was arguing with. Killed him. Got blood all over the place."

"Thank God for El Gordo," Jacinto said. "He kills them quick."

"Except for the players, no one else was in the room except the bartender, an old Sicilian from Agrigento. The police came and questioned them all. One man said he was in the toilet when it happened. Another said he was tying his shoelaces and didn't see nothing. The other player said he was at the bar talking with the bartender, and neither of them saw nothing."

"What happened?" El Chulo asked.

"Nothing," El Gordo said. "They had no evidence, so they closed the case."

"See?" El Chulo said. "By the way, did anybody notice the newspaper misspelled Vallarte's name every single time? That's no accident. In every damned article they misspelled it, and they misspelled it the same way every time."

"I didn't notice," Domingo said.

"Just another example of how they ridicule and insult us every chance they get," El Chulo said.

"Maybe they can't spell," Matilde said.

As Pablo walked home that evening, glad to be alive and well and tired of killings, Cynthia flooded his thoughts: how she talked ...what she did that night and the way she was the next morning ... so willing ... I can have her any time ... no entanglement ... nobody knows.

*

Ruben Ayala assembled the next board meeting in one of the small rooms on the second floor of the Cuban Club. After debating with himself all that day, Pablo finally decided to attend. With no windows the inner room was sweltering. An oscillating fan whirred on a small table near the door. A bare light bulb hanging from the ceiling provided more shadows than illumination. Even with the fan going, the cigar smoke enveloped him like a blanket. When Ayala called the twelve men to order, he noted that they had one more than a quorum.

Sitting at the head of the table Ruben Ayala spoke first: "Armando Moreno resigned this morning as President of the club," he said. "He did not want to serve with this cloud of doubt hanging over him. We're here to elect someone to finish out his term. After that we must vote on whether to uphold or reverse the firing of Dr. Ramírez. Do I hear a motion?"

"I nominate Ruben Ayala," Fuentes said.

"I move that nominations close," another said.

"Just a moment." All faces turned to the thin man with thick white hair and bushy moustache. Jorge Del Río stroked his moustache and continued: "Moreno resigned because he was under a cloud. Mr. Ayala is under the same cloud."

"Are you accusing me, Del Río?" Ayala asked.

"Not at all. I'm simply saying that you were present at the shooting. I assume you had nothing to do with it, but as agitated as the members are, we need a neutral and unbiased president."

Several members nodded. Others maintained noncommittal silence.

"I resent that," Ayala said. "Everybody knows I'm a fair man."

"Don't take it personally. I mean no disrespect. I'm only thinking of the club," Del Río said.

"Who do you suggest?" Fuentes asked. "Everybody here is on one side or the other."

"I was thinking about Pablo Iglesias," Del Río said. Pablo had not been paying close attention, but when he heard his name, he sank in his chair. "Iglesias has not expressed an opinion about the firing. He told me at the meeting that he had not made up his mind. I think we need his objectivity to calm the waters."

Pablo remembered Del Río as the man who sat beside him in the auditorium.

Ayala frowned, but did not respond.

"Where do you stand, Iglesias?" Manolo Fuentes asked.

"The truth is I don't know enough to decide. I only learned about the firing at the meeting the other day. Besides that, I don't know enough about the club to be President."

"I could support an educated and respectable businessman who has not yet made up his mind," Esteban Cruz said. Cruz, the owner of a small factory, was short, rotund, and bald with only the slightest ring of hair around his head. His belly pressed against the table when his hands rested on its surface. As he spoke he wiped his brow and head with his handkerchief.

The discussion ran on for several minutes, during which Pablo tried to think up an excuse.

"How can I be effective without understanding the fiscal operation of the club."

"Committees handle the details," Cruz said. "I second the nomination."

Chagrinned, Ruben Ayala asked if there were any other nominations. The group was silent, so he called for a show of hands. "All in favor of Pablo Iglesias?" Nine hands went up. "I guess he's the new president," Ayala said, and sat down.

In those few minutes Pablo had grown fond of the idea. Confusing as the situation was, he liked the idea of becoming a community leader, and he could, after all, help the club. Rising, he said, "I'd like to make a suggestion about the firing. I truly have not made up my mind. Let's canvass the paying members by letter. The problem seems to be that unemployed members can't pay their dues. Providing them access to the clinic costs those who pay. The paying members should be the ones to decide."

"Do you have any idea how much it would cost to send a letter to every member?" Fuentes asked.

"The dues collectors can deliver them at the end of the month when they make their rounds," Pablo said.

"What kind of letter?" Fuentes asked.

"First, whether they want to fire Dr. Ramírez. Second, monthly dues are one dollar. We could ask for a voluntary ten cent contribution to help defray the cost of treating the unemployed members."

"I don't think they'll go for it," Fuentes said.

"Then we can't afford to treat delinquent members, and the problem will be solved," Pablo said. "I see two issues: one is whether we want to treat nonpaying members; the other is whether we want to fire Dr. Ramírez. Those questions are not necessarily related. Members might want to help those in need and still want to fire Ramírez."

Fuentes could not fault Pablo's logic. Ayala sulked under heavy eyebrows at the end of the table.

"Do I hear a motion to canvass the members as I described and ask for a ten cent per month contribution?"

"I don't see how we can lose," Del Río said. "I like it, and I think the members will pay."

"Me too," Esteban Cruz said.

Ten board members raised their hands, not waiting for the vote call.

"Motion carried," Pablo said. "Before we adjourn I'd like to ask Esteban Cruz and Ruben Ayala to help me with the letter. I will prepare a draft, and the three of us can meet here tomorrow after work," Pablo said.

Ruben Ayala brightened and said, "I'll be happy to help."

"Me too," Esteban Cruz said. "Five-thirty?"

"Fine," Ruben said.

"Five-thirty," Pablo said.

*

Sammy was asleep when Pablo sat down in a porch rocker and told Consuelo about the meeting. He did not tell her the outcome at first, but waded through the entire meeting's discussion before telling her he was the new president.

"What a surprise!" Consuelo said. "That's wonderful! I didn't know you were interested."

"I wasn't. It never occurred to me. But I started thinking: I could solve the problem better than any of them because I have an open mind."

"The letter's a good idea. The members will pay."

"I think so."

They sat, rocking and talking for over an hour about all the things Pablo could do to improve the Cuban Club and the relations among the various factions.

*

Cynthia did not wait for the end of April. With the eight-year-old Model A Ford Pablo bought her, she moved her meager possessions to the house in Six Mile Creek. It was far from luxurious, a step down from the Sulfur Springs house, but it would do. She liked Pablo and knew he would take care of her. With the ten dollars a week he gave her, she could buy what she needed and indulge some of her whims. The money was better at the Fifth Avenue house, but this life gave her more freedom, and she didn't have to put up with men who like to treat women badly.

During her last week on Fifth Avenue, before she moved to Sulfur Springs, a man had come to her. He had not shaved or bathed in days and was dirty and smelled of rancid sweat. She had seen such men before and took it as part of her trade. But when he pushed her down on the bed and tore her dress off, she knew she was in trouble. While he started to take off his pants, she got out of the other side of the bed and ran to the door, but he got there first. "What do you want?" she asked.

"You know," he said, "but my way."

"I don't think I'm going to like your way."

"I don't care what you like." He grabbed her arm and threw her on the bed again.

Cynthia again got up and went up to him with a smile. "Look, fella', I can give you a good time, but you've got to take it easy."

"I don't like it easy." He grabbed her by the arms.

At that moment she kicked her knee as hard as she could into his groin. He doubled over and fell to the floor. She didn't even hear him fall. She was out and running down the hall and down the stairs. "Get Jake," she screamed. "There's a mean sombitch in my room."

Jake had been sitting in the small room adjoining the living room when he heard Cynthia's scream. He had to duck to get through the door and seemed to fill the entire opening when he passed through. Wearing a work shirt, dungarees and work boots, he took the stairs in threes. The next minute he returned holding the man by the back of the belt so the man's feet barely touched the floor. When they reached the edge of the porch, he gave the man a push that landed him in the street with his teeth shattering against the cobblestones. Jake brushed off his hands and returned to his room.

"I think I'll take an hour off," Cynthia had said.

"Sure, Honey."

Just recalling that day made Cynthia's heart race. When Gustavo Vila suggested setting her up in her own house, she jumped at the opportunity. She didn't especially care for him, but he kept her comfortable and treated her well, if not passionately.

Half way between Tampa and Brandon, the relatively isolated Cracker community of Six Mile Creek was perfect. Pablo had bought it for the land a year earlier. The house stood back about a hundred yards from the road in an oak hammock that obscured the house from passersby. It stood on five acres of rich land that Pablo was holding. The small, furnished house had lots of windows and a front porch that opened into a living room. The unmatched pieces of furniture were enough to make Cynthia comfortable. She added color with vases of artificial flowers. There was one bedroom, a kitchen, a bathroom, a back porch and a small barn about forty feet behind the house. When visiting, Pablo always kept his car in the barn to keep it out of sight. Cynthia kept the 1929 Model A by the front porch. Sprawling oaks smothered the house in comforting shade that made the summer tolerable. With so much shade, the yard was mostly hard-packed, bare dirt strewn with leaves. Pablo could spend the night or stop in for lunch or in the middle of the afternoon or on his way home from an overnight trip, and she would be there. Six Mile Creek was a refuge that asked no questions and sought no justification; it was simply a place to be with a beautiful woman who knew how to please a man.

*

The domino game on the back table stopped and Jacinto and El Rubio stood when Pablo walked in. Osvaldo, who had been lying near the back door, slowly came toward Pablo and rubbed against his leg. El Chulo saluted.

"How the hell did you get elected?" Jacinto asked. "The last I heard you didn't even want to be on the board."

"I guess they like me." Pablo stooped to pet Osvaldo.

"You see," Domingo said. "Even Osvaldo's impressed."

"You'll be a good president, Pablo," El Gordo said. "I've never been friends with a president before."

"Wha-a-at are you go-go-going to do?" El Rubio asked.

"Try to solve the problem without shedding blood."

"Good luck," Jacinto said.

"He'll do it," Matilde said. "From what I hear, he's made a good start. I'd like to poll this group. You're all members, right?" They all nodded. "Would you be willing to pay an extra ten cents each month so the clinic can treat unemployed members who can't pay dues?"

Everyone in the café said yes. "That's good if the rest agree," Matilde said.

"How did you know about that?" Pablo asked.

Matilde smiled. "Anyway, congratulations."

"As president my first duty is to buy the drinks. Domingo!"

*

"This is even better than I'd hoped," Marvin said.

"Yeah, well, last week I was ready to flatten you for getting me into that riot," Pablo said.

"It all worked out. Let's take our wives to supper tonight to celebrate."

"If we can get someone to stay with Sammy, Consuelo will love it." Pablo was enjoying the adulation more than he expected. Everyone was happy for him. It was the first time he had done something that pleased everybody. He liked the feeling of power even if the post was inconsequential. At least he might be able to leave a mark on the Cuban community, and it wouldn't hurt business.

150

Before going home he stopped in on Cynthia to tell her. Seeing him drive in she met him at the door.

"I'm sure glad to see you," she said, putting her arms around his neck.

"Why? What's the matter?"

"Nothing. Just lonely."

"Surprise!" Cynthia brightened. He led her in and sat her on the sofa and went through the details of the meeting, ending with his election. When he had finished he saw that she looked at him blankly. "What's the matter? You're not happy."

"Sure I am. That's great."

"What's wrong then?"

"I guess I won't be seeing as much of you."

"Why not? Maybe more. This job will give me another excuse to get away from home."

"You'll see less of your family?"

"That's my problem. You should be happy for me. It's a big job with lots of prestige. And it's good for business."

"I know. I'm happy. Honest. Can you stay a while?"

"Long enough."

She smiled and stood in front of him. "Come on," she said, reaching out for his hands and pulling him toward the bedroom.

*

"Where have you been? Marvin called hours ago to see if we were going to supper. I told him to go on without us."

Pablo had forgotten, and it was clear Consuelo was worried.

"I'm sorry," he said, and kissed her. "I went to the Cuban Club to work on the letter and lost track of time." As he said this he hoped he had wiped Cynthia's lipstick off his face.

"Have you eaten?" he asked.

"I was waiting for you."

"We can still go out."

"Sammy's already in bed; I have steaks."

"I'm sorry, Consuelo."

He followed her into the kitchen. She put a skillet on the stove, waited for it to heat, and dropped two thin steaks and sliced onions into it.

"How did it go—the letter."

"We just talked about it. I'm going to write it myself and then have the others look at it. Anything else going on?"

"No. Sammy's fine. He's so bright it frightens me. Today he was reading the newspaper. When I saw him looking at the funnies, I asked him if he liked the pictures. He looked up at me and then looked back at the page and read it to me. I couldn't believe it. How did he learn that?"

"I don't know."

*

At breakfast Pablo turned to Sammy. "Have you read the paper yet?"

"Not till after you leave."

"Read me the funnies."

"OK, Papa." He read Dick Tracy with only slight hesitations and then he turned to Popeye. "Popeye's my favorite."

"How did you learn that?"

"Mama taught me the letters. I don't know. I'll learn a lot more when I start school."

"I imagine so." His father looked at Consuelo, who had watched the scene from the kitchen sink.

*

Summer had elbowed its way in by early May. The little room in the Cuban Club was hot and smelled of stale cigar smoke. Pablo turned on the oscillating fan while he waited for the other two to arrive. Esteban Cruz walked in wearing a white suit and a Panama hat. He took off his hat, laid it on the table, and sat.

"*Buenas tardes*. Ruben's talking with someone downstairs."

A moment later Ruben Ayala walked in and said, "*Buenas tardes*."

"*Hola, Ruben*. I have a draft letter for you to look over." Pablo handed each man a copy. It read as follows:

Dear Member,

As your Interim President, I write to ask for your help. Some of our members have lost their jobs due to factory closings, and they are unable to pay their monthly dues. We have two alternatives before us. The first is to drop them from the Cuban Club roll. The second is to continue to extend them and their families access to the Bien Público Clinic. The second alternative will increase the Club's expenses. The only way we can afford that alternative is if regular members are willing to contribute an additional ten cents a month to cover the cost of helping our unfortunate fellow members. This is entirely voluntary and temporary. We are not raising the dues. If you are willing to contribute this amount, please give it to the collector and he will keep a record of your contribution. If you

152

are not willing, say nothing. Please note that for this to work it will have to be nearly unanimous.

Also be aware that this request is not tied to Dr. Ramírez. His status has not been decided and will not depend on whether you contribute.

If you believe that members who cannot pay dues should be dropped from membership, please give your vote to the collector who will record it anonymously. You may also choose not to vote.

Thank you for your attention to this important matter.

Respectfully yours,

Pablo Iglesias,

Interim President

"It covers everything," Esteban said.

Ruben Ayala was still poring over the draft. "There are some things I don't like," he said, laying down his cigar. "I would change the second sentence to read, '*Some of our members have stopped paying their monthly dues.*'"

"But Ruben, that sounds as if they don't want to pay," Esteban said. "We automatically drop members like that. Perhaps we should say that only unemployed members will be retained."

"How long? We can't keep this up forever."

"That's sticky, *caballeros*," Pablo said. "The membership is not too large. We should know who's trying."

"Is ten cents enough?" Ruben asked.

"Good point," Esteban said.

"I asked the treasurer," Pablo said. "He said eight or nine percent of our members are out of work."

"Then nearly one hundred percent of the paying members have to contribute; otherwise, we lose," Ruben said.

"We could ask for more, but if a great majority of members are not behind this, it'll fail. I'm not trying to push either way; I simply want it to be clear that it's temporary and it must be nearly unanimous. If not, then we'll either ask for more contributions or cancel the plan."

"You mean that if a big majority don't want to contribute, we'll drop delinquent members?" Ruben asked.

"There's no other way."

The discussion went on another fifteen minutes in which it became clear that Ruben Ayala was still concerned. "A lot of people are depending on me to represent them. They want this thing ended without bankrupting the club," he said. "If you send this letter, people will think I approve of it."

"We won't send it if you don't approve," Pablo said.

"It's not that. I have to admit I like your plan, but I don't know …"

"If it's not right, let's fix it," Pablo said.

"Send the damn letter," Ruben said. "I'll just have to explain it to them. You've done well, Pablo. Now I have to go."

When Ruben walked out of the room, Esteban got up to leave and Pablo gathered his notes. "I never expected Ruben to walk away so meekly. If this works, Pablo, you're a genius," Esteban said. "*Hasta luego.*"

*

A month later Pablo spent most of the collection day in the Cuban Club waiting for collectors to deliver their money to the treasurer. Each collector had to visit about a hundred members to get their dues. They walked their route wearing a large leather purse that hung around their necks to belt-level. When the woman of the house saw who it was, she would come to the door and hand him her payment. The collector would sometimes spend a few minutes talking or, in other cases, simply say, "*Gracias*," hand her a receipt, and walk to the next house. On this day, Pablo expected the collection to take longer because each collector was told to give each housewife a copy of the letter and wait for her to read it and respond. By collection day, the letter's contents had flooded Ybor City and everyone had an opinion.

Fernando Cabrales had been collecting for the Cuban Club for over twenty years, and everyone knew him. He was a jolly, short man who waddled when he walked. The walking should have helped work off the fat, but he overcame the effects of walking with a voracious appetite. "Here's a letter for you, Hortensia," Fernando said.

"I've heard all about it. Here's my dollar and a dime. It could've been Manuel."

*

Fernando was the first collector to return. "Well, we did pretty well. Just about everybody gave the extra dime," he said. "And they all knew about it."

"Excellent," Pablo said, as the treasurer began to count the money.

It was six thirty when the last collector returned.

"Ninety-five percent. Not bad," the treasurer said.

Pablo slapped the man's back and laughed out loud. "That's what I was waiting for. I knew it would work." That night he contacted the board members to tell them and to say he had scheduled a meeting for next Monday at 5:30 PM.

*

At the next board meeting Pablo reported the results of the collection with great enthusiasm. "For the moment, the plan seems to be working."

"What if they don't keep up the contributions?" Manolo Fuentes asked.

"We'll worry about that when it happens," Pablo said. "Remember, this is only a temporary solution. If they don't keep it up, we'll drop members. We'll take it month by month."

"The main reason for calling this meeting is Dr. Ramírez. We can't leave him hanging. I'd like to put the controversy to rest one way or the other," Pablo said.

"We should fire him like we said," Fuentes said.

Another friend of Moreno, agreed.

"Why? Moreno fired him because he was treating nonmembers. That's taken care of," Esteban Cruz said, "at least for the time being."

"Are there other complaints against Dr. Ramírez?" Pablo asked. "If so, we must consider them. I'm sure he wasn't fired without good reason."

Ruben Ayala had remained silent through the discussion. "I know of no other reason," he said, clenching the cigar in his teeth as he spoke, "as long as the membership is willing to support delinquents."

Manolo Fuentes looked at his friend with surprise. "Well, you've certainly changed your stand, Ruben."

"A man has to change when conditions change. I agreed with you and Moreno then, but our reasons no longer exist. If things change, we'll act."

Pablo again asked if there was anything else to consider about Dr. Ramírez. Ruben Ayala's abrupt comments stifled the opposition, and no one offered further comment. "Do I hear a motion to rescind the firing?"

"I move we keep Dr. Ramírez as long as the contributions keep coming in," Ruben Ayala said.

Esteban Cruz said, "Fair enough. I second the motion."

Pablo called for a vote. The result was eleven in favor of keeping Ramírez and three against.

"Dr. Ramírez is reinstated for as long as the contributions continue," Pablo said. "If there is no further business, the meeting is adjourned."

Jack Eugene Fernández

11 - GOOD BUSINESS - OCTOBER 1938

*

Storm Hits Cuba, Florida Braces

*

Soviets Execute 13 Terrorists

*

Roosevelt Demands 6 New Supreme Court Members

*

*President's Message Shocks Stock Market
Into Heavy Selling*

*

Rebel Armies Cut Loyalist Spain In Half

*

Pablo couldn't wait to drive his new Packard sedan down Seventh Avenue that morning hoping his friends would see him. As he passed the Café Cubano and saw Domingo sweeping the sidewalk, he slowed and waved. Domingo immediately stopped to look when the dark blue sedan glided past heading west. Squinting, he saw Pablo waving. Pablo slowed down enough to be sure Domingo had seen him and then continued on.

"*Coño!*" Domingo muttered. "He must have hit the *bolita*!"

"Are you going to sweep, or are you going to stand there like a *come-mierda?*" Rosa said from the door.

"You should see Pablo's Packard. Must be rich."

"He's born to be rich."

Eyes still on the car, Domingo again said, "*Coño!*"

"Enough vulgarity. Get to work."

Pablo had just ended his term as President of the Cuban Club and declined to run for reelection. As much as he had enjoyed it, he was glad to be out. Driving down route sixty as on a cloud, he smiled at the sky, blue and cloudless as his future. Musing on the fortune he was accumulating, he turned onto a rutted trail past a massive oak. Recalling his early days in Brandon and the budding business he had built upon the rock of hard depression, he smiled. Standing under the oak, looking down to a pond, he imagined a town, complete with shops, churches, schools, cafés, and drugstores. He was carving a dream out of the stillness. A screeching blue jay swooped to warn the intruder. Pablo laughed at its effrontery. Like Consuelo's refusal to move, the jay was full of bluster, mostly flapping air. He knew she would give in when Sammy started school. Pablo used her argument against her: "We shouldn't start him in a school here knowing we're moving. We won't have rent to pay. I'll get you a car so you can drive to town whenever you want."

And he won. She knew she could not keep Pablo in Ybor City forever. "All right, Pablo. School starts next month. I'll enroll him in Brandon."

He hugged her.

As he recalled that victory, his thoughts turned to Cynthia. Hishe yearning and desire had relaxed into fulfillment. He knew her bluster veiled a deep affection, but he would not open that door. She knew talk of love would drive him away; her allure hung on the 'no-strings' clause of their arrangement.

*

After Consuelo's angry reaction to his first purchase, Pablo kept his dealings to himself. She led a quiet life, lonely, but peaceful, relishing her time with Sammy, watching him discover the natural world. Sammy instantly loved the grove with its fruits and seemingly boundless freedom. He especially liked to plant seeds and watch them germinate. All nature fascinated him. He also enjoyed listening to his mother play the piano. She would ask him for requests and then play them to watch his reaction.

157

He was soon picking out melodies. One day he began to harmonize a tune he had heard on the radio using both hands. She came out of the kitchen to watch. He smiled and played on. Though thrilled, she made no fuss. When she asked if he wanted her to give him lessons, he said that he could already play.

"I can show you lots more. We'll start tomorrow. Just have fun now."

By the time he entered school that September, he was playing small Bach and Handel pieces. In the evenings he entertained his father with songs he had learned that day. "He has your gift," Pablo said one evening.

"He's still a baby. He's bound to find all kinds of things to tickle his fancy," she said.

In school Sammy discovered arithmetic and science. In fact, all things sparked his curiosity. "How do trees come out of seeds?" he asked his father one evening.

"Each seed contains a tiny blueprint of the plant it's going to become. It builds the tree out of the food it takes from the ground and the air."

"You mean plants use oxygen like us?"

"Not exactly. Plants absorb carbon dioxide and water from the air."

"What's carbon di- . . .?"

"Carbon dioxide. It's a gas that we and other animals breathe out. We breathe in oxygen and exhale carbon dioxide. Plants breathe in carbon dioxide and exhale oxygen. Plants and animals help each other."

"That's swell, Papa.. Then the tree makes more seeds, which make more trees?"

"Right."

"Why, Daddy?"

"Only God knows that. And before you ask me where God is, I don't know that either. Now time for bed, young man."

Sammy began to speak English with his country friends. His parents continued to use Spanish at home so he would not forget, but he preferred the common lingo of his new surroundings and began to respond in English. Pablo could imagine his son growing into a business partner one day. He knew bad times would end eventually. Perhaps the rumbling in Europe would heat up; the lid could blow, and when it was over the future would spill out abundance. Then his young empire would grow.

*

Pablo and Consuelo had always attended Our Lady of Perpetual Help Catholic Church in Ybor City, mostly because of Consuelo, who had turned to the church in her loneliness. When they moved to Brandon, Pablo decided they would attend Sacred Heart Church in downtown Tampa.

"We can't. Father López is a wonderful priest. I'm so comfortable there."

"All Catholic churches are the same. You might like the new priest better."

"Don't you like O.L.P.H., Pablo?"

"You didn't like that at first, remember? You'll like Sacred Heart. It's bigger and much more beautiful. Most of Tampa's leading Catholics go there. I'll be able to make good contacts downtown, and Sammy will love the pipe organ."

Consuelo reluctantly conceded. It helped that, at their first mass, she ran into Lizzie Lockwood.

"Consuelo! I haven't seen you since graduation. Are you on vacation?" Lizzie said, embracing her in the aisle.

Consuelo felt guilty for not making contact earlier. "I live here now, actually in Brandon. Meet my husband, Pablo Iglesias and our son Sammy."

"Wow! A family and everything. That's swell." Turning to Pablo, she said, "We were roommates. She talked about you all the time."

"And I feel like I've always known you."

After a few minutes Lizzie said she was expected for lunch and had to go. "Let's trade phone numbers. Here's mine. So we can get together," she said.

In the months that followed, Lizzie and Consuelo met every Thursday for lunch at the Valencia Gardens Restaurant. Lizzie, who lived with her parents in Hyde Park, worked as a legal secretary for a Madison Street law firm.

One noon Consuelo said, "Lizzie, you don't know what a Godsend you've been."

"It's funny how things work out. At first I couldn't stand Ybor City, but it turned out fine. Moving to Brandon was traumatic. I thought I'd been lifted out of my world."

The tall, frizzy-haired blonde was not pretty; in fact, her large teeth, tiny eyes, and protruding chin gave her face a comical look, especially when she was serious. At those times, listening intently, she appeared befuddled. But she was so vivacious, intelligent, and outgoing that one quickly saw past the mask. Reaching for Consuelo's hand across the table she squeezed it.

*

At mass the following Sunday, Pablo fidgeted on the hard pew most of the hour, feeling relief each time he stood. Dark, threatening clouds hung over the gloomy Sunday. On his way out he stopped to talk with a middle-aged man outside the church. Consuelo and Sammy walked toward their car and waited. "Know who that was?" Pablo asked when he caught up.

"Who."

"President of the new bank. We're having lunch next week. We might do business."

When they were all in the Packard and driving east along Lafayette Street, Sammy said, "I sure like this car. It's like a rocket ship."

"On the open road, it flies," his father said.

"I liked the homily," Consuelo said.

"A little depressing. I've had enough of 'honor thy father and thy mother.'" Pablo said.

After a moment she said, "What are you going to do about your mother's letter?"

He shrugged.

"You can't just ignore it."

"The old man could've written."

"Maybe he can't."

"I won't crawl."

"Please, Pablo." Her eyes moved toward Sammy in the back seat.

"What do you want me to do? I'm no doctor."

"He's your father. This may be the last time."

"Everything was said seven years ago."

"Sammy might like to meet his grandfather."

"What about it, Sammy?"

"I don't know, Papa. I guess so. Is he a bad man?"

"He and Papa had an argument a long time ago, Sammy, but they're both good men."

"Then let's go, Papa?"

"I'll think about it."

*

It was drizzling and windy the day their ship docked. Consuelo had been seasick most of the time. "That's all we need, a damned hurricane to completely ruin a terrible trip," Pablo said as he walked down the gangplank.

"It won't hit here," Consuelo said, pretending to know.

"Oh boy, a hurricane!" Sammy said.

They spotted doña Inez holding an umbrella and waving from behind the wire fence. She was easy to spot in a dark blue business suit with white blouse and diamond necklace. As usual, her fingers were weighed down with diamonds.

In spite of his apprehension Pablo was glad to see her. She waited for them to walk to her and kissed Pablo and held her cheek out to Consuelo. Then she bent down to Sammy's level and embraced and kissed the boy. "How beautiful. He is your image, Pablito," she said, resuming her posture of reserve and dignity.

"He is handsome, isn't he," Pablo said smiling.

"Come, the car's on the street," she said.

"Where's the driver? We have bags," Pablo said.

"I'm the driver."

"I thought we'd stay at a hotel," Pablo said. "So we can come and go. We want to see Consuelo's father, too."

"Nonsense. What would people say? You can use my car."

Consuelo nodded and he said, "All right."

"We'll be there in an hour. I'll take you along a scenic route so you can see the changes," doña Inez said.

Havana seemed more rundown than they remembered, but soon they had entered another world. The overcast sky and drizzle added a touch of mystery to the exotic beauty of the jungle. "Things look pretty much the same," he said.

"Everything has changed, Pablito. The depression has devastated us. Your father has lost nearly everything. That's what brought on the stroke."

"I didn't know it was that bad."

"There's much you don't know, but we'll talk at home. Your business is going well, I hear."

"Can't complain."

The rain had stopped and the wind had calmed by the time they reached the outskirts of Matanzas. As beautiful as ever, the old city offered no surprises until they approached the house. Pablo was stunned. Grass and weeds had won the battle of man against nature. Dry, gray fronds hung like old men's whiskers from the stately palms along the driveway; cracks, holes, and overgrown tree roots had left the entrance drive bumpy. Gray mold covered the house, and weeds grew out of every crevice. The stone path was barely visible under the tall grass and weeds. Bare but for a wooden box of scraggly crotons, the porch colonnade was an ancient ruin.

As they got out of the car the stench of rotting fruit enveloped them. "I've never seen you drive before, Mamá."

"Necessity, Pablito. Come, your old room is just as you left it. Samuelito will sleep in the room next to mine."

Pablo led the way with two large suitcases; Consuelo carried a smaller one with Sammy's things. "The place looks awful," he whispered to Consuelo as they climbed the curved staircase.

"What a shame," she said.

"Come down when you get your things put away, and we'll have tea. I'll show Samuelito his room later."

Their room was spacious and bright with windows on two sides and a small balcony that faced north. Setting her bags on one of the twin beds, Consuelo said, "I didn't know things were so bad."

"Where are the fruit trees?" Sammy was looking out the window.

"Where's my double bed?" Pablo asked. Then he remembered his mother's warped morality. "I guess we'd better face the music." He put his suitcases on the floor, washed his hands and face and said, "Let's go."

Sammy was the first one down and found his grandmother with her silver tea set waiting in the living room. "Where's the beach?" he asked.

"A long way. But there's plenty to see here after we have our tea."

The living room rambled endlessly, bending around corners, with planters and tables and chairs placed strategically to divide the space. It seemed to be in better shape than the rest of the house. Beyond the French doors, a terrace led to the garden. The furniture was as Pablo had left it and the rugs seemed in good shape, but he noticed that several paintings were missing as he and Consuelo walked in.

"Where's Papá?" Pablo asked.

"Upstairs."

"I guess I should see him."

"You won't understand him."

"How bad is he?"

"The doctor says he can go any time. His blood pressure is still quite high."

"Things look run down," he said.

Pouring the tea she began: "With the depression, he became more secretive. He couldn't sleep. When the price of sugar began to drop, he cut production. It was costing more than it was bringing. After two years, seeing all the panic selling, he began to buy land, expecting the depression to end soon, but it only got worse. When he couldn't make the payments, he tried to sell some of his new holdings, but … no buyers. He sold his cars, paintings, everything. Got rid of our domestic help, as you can see. He borrowed money on our home, but it didn't help. He lost nearly everything. Scavengers hovered like vultures, waiting to pluck him clean. The day he sold the rum factory, he had an awful argument with his manager, blamed him for losing his empire. Imagine blaming an underling! During a furious tirade, there came a blinding moment; he stood silent, staring at the wall behind the man as if in a trance. The manager asked him if he was all right. When he got no answer and moved toward him, your father collapsed. He would have hit the floor, but the manager caught him. At first he thought he was dead, but he was still breathing. He picked him up, carried him to his car, and drove him to the hospital. After working on him for over an hour, the doctor came out and said, 'His left side is paralyzed. I don't think he'll make it.' I didn't know what to do. During the two weeks he was in the hospital I tried to learn what I could about his business. He never confided it to me, so on top of worrying about him, I had to learn all that. Luckily, Fermín understood it and helped me. You remember Fermín, your father's accountant. Well, he explained it all. This house, the fields, everything had been sold or mortgaged. I bought the small Chevrolet a few weeks ago." Throughout her tale doña Inez was surprisingly calm, sounding like a seasoned businesswoman, almost proud of herself.

"What can I do?" Pablo asked.

"Nothing. It's been terrible for me. Go now. He wants to see you."

"Come, Consuelo."

"Alone, Pablito," doña Inez said.

"Yes, Pablo. Sammy and I can see him later."

*

The man lying in the large bed by the great window overlooking Matanzas bay did not look like his father. Sallow and completely white haired, he looked more like a corpse. Even his moustache and teeth were gone. His hollow cheeks were marked with long wrinkles that ran from his eyes down to his bony chin. He held out his right hand to Pablo. "*Hola, Papá. Como estás?*"

The old man said something, but Pablo could not understand him.

"Don't talk, Papá. I've come to see you."

Don Ignacio took Pablo's hand again and pulled it toward him so that Pablo had to stand. The old man pulled him toward the right side of the bed and pointed to the small table.

"Should I open it?"

The old man nodded as best he could. Pablo opened the drawer and looked at his father. He moved his hand again pointing in the drawer.

"This?" he asked, holding up a small box with a rubber band around it.

The old man nodded again.

"Open it?"

Again don Ignacio nodded.

Inside the box was a gold watch with a gold chain attached to it. "This?"

Don Ignacio nodded and flipped his right hand toward him a few times.

"For me?"

Don Ignacio nodded.

"Thank you, Papá. I remember it well. Abuelo gave it to you when he turned over the business to you and returned to Spain."

The old man nodded, and a tear ran down one of the gullies of his right cheek.

"It was his, wasn't it?"

He nodded.

"Now I have something for you. I've brought your grandson to meet you."

The old man abruptly turned away.

"Don't you want to see him?"

The old man remained still, continuing to look out the window.

"I see. You never forget, do you? Well then, I'll give you something else. I've done well in Florida. I have a prosperous real estate business. Mamá told me about your losses. I've succeeded where you failed."

Don Ignacio turned to his son again and nodded. The right side of his face moved into a half smile that looked more like a cynical leer. Pablo's confusion must have shown, because the old man reached for his hand again. When Pablo grasped his father's hand, his father held on to it. His meaning was clear. At this point, the old man's eyes began to droop, but he did not take his eyes off his son.

"Are you tired? Would you like me to leave for a while?"

The old man nodded and closed his eyes.

*

The boy and his mother and grandmother were still sitting over the tea set. "Consuelo, I'd like to talk with Mamá alone. You show Sammy the grounds."

When they had gone doña Inez said, "Did he give you the watch?"

"Yes."

"He was very excited when I told him you were coming. He's been saving it for you. It's always meant a great deal to him, your link to his father and to Spain. He wanted to give it to you himself."

"When I told him about Samuelito, he turned his head. He doesn't want to see him."

"Don't rush to interpret. He loves his grandson, but the thought of meeting him frightens him. Perhaps he's afraid he'll love him too much. He's a mule and nothing can change him." Then thinking further, "It may also be that the boy reminds him of what he's missed in life."

"But he's had everything."

"Everything but you, Pablito. Maybe seeing his grandson would be more than he can bear. He spent his life building his empire, as he liked to call it, and now it's vaporized. I think he knows how little it meant compared with losing a son and a grandson."

Pablo thought about his budding empire. His father's grew a crop in solid earth—food to feed millions. Pablo's empire would use earth too, but his product was insubstantial. It was a wisp of reality on clouds of dreams and speculation. Pablo was a middleman, a facilitator. Let others turn over the earth, he thought. Not me. Let the money do the work.

"I'm taking Samuelito up," Pablo said.

"I won't stop you."

"Most of my wealth is in land. I have little cash right now, but I can help."

"Thank you, Pablito, but I'm fine. With Fermín's help I'm managing to pay off your father's debts. In time it'll work out. In any event, as you know, my father left me well fixed, perhaps better than you think. I could retire your father's debt easily, but he got into this; his money will have to get him out."

"You could use a nurse."

"One comes in the evenings. Your father may live on or not, but we must go on. He cannot tell you, but he loves you very much."

*

The drizzle had stopped when Pablo took Consuelo into the garden to a bench under a large avodado tree, which would provide shade if the drizzle resumed. "I always loved this spot. It seemed so generous with its shade and fruit."

"What happened?"

"He gave me his father's watch."

"Did you talk about Sammy?"

"He didn't want to see him."

"How mean."

"I was pretty mad until Mamá explained. She says he's afraid."

"I'm so tired of excuses."

"He's afraid of meeting Sammy. It has nothing to do with our argument. You should've seen his reaction when I told him how well I'm doing. I wanted to hurt him for turning away from Sammy. I thought he would blow up, but instead he smiled. He was happy for me."

"I'd like to believe that," Consuelo said.

"I'm going to take Sammy up to meet him," he said, getting up, "I'd hate to have to explain it otherwise."

"Think it over, Pablo."

"No," he said, smiling calmly. Taking her hand and walking to the house, he looked around until he heard his mother's voice coming from the kitchen. She was standing over the counter fixing a mango milk shake for Sammy. When he saw her he dropped Consuelo's hand." Come, Sammy. Time to meet your grandfather."

"I'll save the *batido*," doña Inez said.

Ignacio did not move when his door opened. "It's me, Papá. I've brought Consuelo and Samuelito."

The old man turned away from the sound. "I told you …" Consuelo said.

"Your grandson wants to meet you."

Don Ignacio did not respond. He was still facing the window. Sammy walked to his bed on the side the old man was facing. *"Hola, Abuelo. Soy Samuelito.* Don't you want to see me?"

The old man turned away.

"I'm very glad to meet you," the boy said. "I'm sorry you're sick. I hope you get well soon. I live in Florida, in an orange grove and I go to school. I'm in the first grade. We live in the country, not far from Tampa." Sammy looked at his father for approval. After a moment, he said, "If you want me to leave …"

Suddenly the old man turned and held out his hand. Sammy placed his little hand in his grandfather's and smiled. The old man twisted his lips into his version of a smile and held on to the boy's hand. He turned to Pablo and smiled at him. When he saw Consuelo, he began to weep silently and extended his right hand toward her. She walked to him and took his hand. With his eyes and his crooked smile he expressed his feelings clearly.

"Hola, don Ignacio. It's good to see you. I hope you will be up and around soon." He shook his head and she understood. "I'm very glad

we came. Sammy wanted to meet you. He's a bright musician and an excellent student."

The old man's smile sagged and his eyes drooped again.

"Tired, Papá?" Pablo said.

He nodded and closed his eyes.

*

Doña Inez waited for them in the living room.

"He was glad to see them both."

"Good. I've fixed something to eat." Then she led them into the kitchen, where they sat down to a Spanish tortilla, consisting of eggs, potatoes and onion fried in olive oil, and a tomato and lettuce salad. She opened a bottle of Rioja wine she had been saving.

"Aren't you eating, Inez?" Consuelo asked.

"All I want is warm milk and toast."

For the next hour Pablo overflowed with talk about his father and how well he communicated and how glad the old man was to see his grandson. He barely realized what he was eating. "He was nice to Consuelo too. I'm very glad we came."

Throughout his talk his mother maintained her icy composure. That evening they sat on the terrace and talked about old times, and his mother filled Pablo in on his relatives in Havana and Matanzas. It was a cool evening with intermittent drizzle. Every half hour or so, Inez would go upstairs to look in on the old man and then return. At nine o'clock, the night nurse came in.

"I'm glad to see you," Inez said. "I'll be up later."

Pablo talked about their life in Ybor City and the strike and his friends and Consuelo's recital that had not materialized, and he hoped it would soon. Then he told her about his real estate business. "Papá taught me a lot." Then the conversation returned to his father's business failures and what his mother would do if his father died.

"There will be time enough to worry about that," she said. Her detachment disturbed Pablo. She might have been discussing the weather. During a break in her monologue, she said, "To be quite frank, we have never shared our lives. But I'll miss him; I do already. It's one thing to drift apart, but quite another to see him helpless, stretched out and immobile, both of us knowing he's at the end of his days. When you lose someone close, even someone you haven't loved, it hurts. The pain has been part of my life, and it won't depart with him."

The evening had turned clear and cool. The moon suspended above them brightened the terrace. Night enhanced the house; it was crisper now,

167

as if carved out of the darkness. It reminded him how much he liked the evenings in Matanzas where there was always an ocean breeze to sweep away the day's heat. At about eleven o'clock Consuelo stood. 'It's late. Sammy should have been in bed long ago."

"But I'm not sleepy."

"Come along now," she said, as she gathered him up.

"I'll turn in too," Pablo said, rising and kissing his mother. "See you in the morning."

*

Sammy was the first one up, anxious to see his grandfather again and to tell him all about school and his friends. Not finding his grandmother in her room he ran to the kitchen where he found her over the stove. "Is it OK to see Abuelo now?"

"Eat your breakfast first."

"Then can I go?"

"After your parents come down."

In a few minutes Consuelo walked into the kitchen and kissed her mother-in-law's cheek. A minute later Pablo appeared. "Good morning, Mamá. How is he?"

"Let's have something to eat first," she said, raising her eyes to the ceiling.

Pablo turned to Sammy, "Son, would you go to my room and get my pen? I want to write a letter."

When the boy was gone Pablo looked at his mother. "What is it?"

"He died early this morning. It was almost light when the nurse came to tell me. She said he didn't move or utter a sound. He simply stopped living."

Consuelo began to cry, confused by her reaction. Pablo sat still. "Things happen so fast," he said.

"I think he was waiting for you. Every day he asked for you. I think he died happy seeing Samuelito."

*

"I never expected such a turnout," Pablo said. Besides childhood friends and business associates, dignitaries from the mayor to the provincial governor and reporters came. At the last moment before the mass began Fulgencio Batista and his entourage appeared. The dignitaries filled five front rows.

Just as the ceremony was about to start, a dark, middle-aged woman dressed in black with a black veil that covered her face entered the church

168

and sat in the back pew. Several people noticed her, and a gentle murmur rippled through the church. When a woman in the row behind Inez tapped her shoulder and whispered in her ear, Inez turned to stare back through clenched teeth. After a moment she returned her gaze to the altar.

The governor summarized in eloquent phrases Ignacio Iglesias' contributions to the Cuban economy, its industry, and to the wellbeing of his employees, who had numbered over one thousand in better times. Arrangements included interment in a freestanding mausoleum. In the presence of such important communicants, Father Isidro presided over the spectacle with trembling hands and voice. During communion, he helped himself to a liberal swig of wine trying to calm himself. Inez sat between Pablo and Consuelo; they and Sammy shared the front pew with the mayor, the governor, and the President. Her sister and brother and Ignacio's remaining cousins and their children spilled into the second pew. The procession to the cemetery stopped traffic through the center of Matanzas for nearly an hour. Flowers at the gravesite overpowered the words that were spoken, but not the sunny, cool, October morning. As Father Isidro tried, through uncooperative lips, to say something profound over the coffin, a mocking bird sang a lilting accompaniment.

When the final words were spoken and the crowd dispersed, Pablo's little family and his mother returned to her house, where doña Inez had hired a cook and server to prepare and serve lunch for relatives and close friends who would drop by. By 1:00 the house was overrun with people chatting, doing business, and a few grieving. Inez was her most gracious, holding court in a comfortable chair in the living room surrounded by her closest family. To everyone who passed she introduced her grandson Samuelito, who was enjoying the wonderful festivities. When there was no one waiting to talk to them, Sammy turned to his mother. "Why is everyone so happy? Abuelo just died."

"That's the way funerals are, Sammy. There's an old Spanish saying: *'El muerto al hoyo; el vivo al pollo.'* "

"What does that mean, Mama, the dead in his hole; the live to his chicken?"

"More or less that we must bury the dead and go on with our lives."

Consuelo's father said, "I'm glad they're here to keep you company, Inez."

"It's the least they can do after all I've been through," doña Inez said, tears in her eyes.

Pablo and Consuelo took Sammy to Consuelo's father's house the day after the funeral. Things were much more cheerful at the González home. Juan had erected a swing in his garden for Sammy and took him to fly a kite. Sammy also enjoyed his stories about his early days working in the cane fields and of fighting the Spaniards. His tales of daring and danger kept his grandson spellbound for hours. Unexpectedly, Juan would take him to the kitchen and fix him a tropical fruit *batido*. Sammy especially liked coconut. Consuelo was afraid he would gain too much weight. "Don't worry," Pablo said. "Kids don't gain like we do. He'll be back in the real world soon enough."

"Why don't we tour the island?" she said.

"My thought exactly. I'll rent a car."

Doña Inez saw the tour differently: she turned to Consuelo and said, "That's impossible. We're in mourning. You should know better."

"It was my idea, Mamá," Pablo said. "We just want to take a drive."

Again looking at Consuelo, doña Inez said, "Absolutely not! People will be coming to see Pablo and Samuelito. You have no right to take them out vacationing so soon after his father's death."

"That was not my intent," Consuelo said, startled by the old woman's attack. "We'll do it another time."

Pablo agreed to stay and said no more. Later, in their room, he reminded Consuelo, "That's the way she is. Don't be offended; just ignore her."

"I thought she was over it."

"Just rise above it. It's what I do."

During that week friends dropped in for more relaxed conversation.

At the end of the week, the visits had died down and Pablo took Consuelo out into the garden for a walk. "How would you like to spend a couple of days in Havana."

"Think we should?"

"I won't tell if you won't."

"My father would love to have Sammy. What do you think?"

"You read my mind again."

*

"Of course. We'll have wonderful time," Consuelo's father said with a smile.

"Let's keep it between us for now," Consuelo said. "Tomorrow morning all right?"

"Of course, and take your time."

Before they could tell Sammy, he said, "Let me stay with *Abuelo*? I don't care about Havana."

"I think we can arrange that," his mother said. In a few minutes they parked at the González house. "He wants to stay with you, *Abuelo*," Consuelo said.

"Good. We'll go fishing, and there's a carnival nearby, and then …"

"We have to be going, Papá. We'll hear the details later." As they pulled out of their parking space, Consuelo yelled out the window, "We'll be back in three or four days."

Liberated, they spent three days in the Hotel Nacional on El Malecón, seeing the city during the day, discovering new restaurants in the evenings, and catching shows at their favorite nightspots. Alone for the first time in years, they luxuriated in a harmony they had not felt since before their wedding. With his father's rage lifted from his soul, Pablo seemed to be enjoying life again. Consuelo did not question; she would enjoy his happiness while it lasted. They spent the late afternoon of each day with cocktails on their balcony overlooking the bay, watching the waves crashing on the sea wall. The automobile traffic was tamer than they remembered, probably, they thought, because of the depression. But the depression did not exist for them; their world had expanded into slow time, warm breezes, good food, sparkling entertainment and, above all, each other. Unconstrained and carefree, they gorged themselves with abandon.

*

On their return Juan invited them and Pablo's mother to supper for their last evening in Cuba. "It is the most elegant restaurant in Matanzas," he said, "known for their roast snapper and their stupendous *brazo gitano* (a cream pudding ladled onto a sheet cake and then rolled into a large "Gypsy's arm")." Later, at home, Juan brought out a bottle of Carlos I Brandy, and he and Pablo smoked cigars with their coffee and brandy in the patio. A few minutes past midnight Pablo, Consuelo, Sammy, and Inez drove home.

In the morning after breakfast, Inez drove them to the Port of Havana where Juan González was waiting for them. He had brought flowers for Consuelo, cigars for Pablo, candy for Sammy, and kisses and hugs for all. Finally they walked the gangplank into the liner, happy with their visit and happier to be going home. Over the railing they saw their parents standing together. Juan was waving and smiling. Stony-faced Inez was adjusting her hair.

That mostly clear, cool two weeks of October had brought relief to both Pablo and Consuelo. And once again they set off for Florida, this time with one burden lifted.

12 - NOVEMBER - 1938

*

Dionne Quintuplets' Mother Has Baby Boy

*

Senate Passes Record Army Appropriation

*

Hitler Gets 99 Percent Vote For Austria Seizure

*

Mrs. Roosevelt Defends Right Of Wives To Work

*

Years of worry and anger and apprehension seemed like a dream: they had actually enjoyed the visit to Cuba and the trip back. Now that Pablo had at last found peace with his father he could put aside the anger over his lost inheritance. Only Sammy seemed quiet and introspective, thinking of the grandfather whom he had never known and would never know. The ghost of *abuelo* Ignacio had finally become incarnate if only as a whisper of his former self. But even a glimpse and a touch of a flesh and blood grandfather was better than the ghost of one.

The grove received them like a mother with widespread arms. Sammy could not wait to climb his favorite tree, the center of his imaginings about nature and life. They had stopped at La Placita Cubana on Seventh Avenue to buy groceries. While Consuelo unpacked and prepared supper, Pablo showered and left for the office to check on messages and phone calls.

"Can't that wait? I was planning a quiet evening together. Like in Havana."

"I left some things pending. I won't be late."

After a quick phone call to Cynthia from his office he dashed off in his car to her house, ran up the porch steps, and opened the door. Cynthia met him with a passionate embrace. "I don't have much time."

"You don't need much," she said, pulling him into the bedroom.

*

Consuelo was putting Sammy to bed when Pablo arrived. "Are you ready to eat?"

"I figured you'd eaten, so I stopped at Frenchy's Tavern for a sandwich."

"But you said ... it's such a nice meal."

Looking in the dining room, he saw the table set with two plates, wine glasses, and candles in the center. He embraced her and said, "I'm sorry."

Trying to hide her disappointment, she fixed herself a plate and ate at the kitchen table; Pablo sat across from her with a cup of coffee. "Anything important at the office?"

"Not really. The usual." When she rose to take her dishes to the sink, he said, "I think I'll turn in. Big day tomorrow."

Consuelo watched him leave the kitchen, then washed the dishes with slow, heavy motions.

*

Pablo had never bothered to get his realtor's license, realizing early that he could do better speculating than brokering sales for others. He had invested much of his cash reserve and had sold enough at reasonable profits to remain solvent. Marvin executed all the transactions. Comfortable with his realtor's role, Marvin bought little for himself. The few properties he had bought earlier were still waiting for buyers, and he was feeling anxious.

The new office building they had constructed two years earlier had more space than the old converted filling station and, as Pablo argued, looked more prosperous and inviting. The new white frame building stood on the southeast corner of Route 60 and a narrow county road with a parking area along the narrow road. The front door opened into a receptionist's anteroom furnished with desk, chair, and filing cabinet.

173

On top of the filing cabinet was a small hot plate with a coffee percolator. Beside the filing cabinet stood a water dispenser with a five-gallon jug inverted over it. A large, glossy picture of a Florida scene showed a lake surrounded by a thick oak hammock on one side and an orange grove on the other. Near the edge a man fished from a rowboat. The anteroom opened into two separate offices each of about 400 square feet with two large windows. Each office had a large desk, a filing cabinet, two comfortable, leather-covered chairs, a table, and a leather sofa. Pablo had found the furniture for sale at a cigar factory that had gone out of business. A small table near the door of each office held a lamp and some real estate magazines. A toilet with lavatory connected the two offices. Behind the building stretched an acre of orange trees that had been part of a grove that Burke and Iglesias had owned for two years. They sold off all but the acre on which their office stood.

Suzanne, Marvin's wife, had volunteered for the receptionist's job. At first Pablo liked the arrangement, but soon his imagination went to work. He felt she was too close to business decisions, imagining her referring potential clients to her husband on the sly. Suzanne gave no evidence of such behavior, but the possibility was enough for Pablo.

Feeling more solidly in control of his life, Pablo decided it was time to end their partnership. Their business goals had diverged. Marvin was no longer interested in buying land, so they were not pooling their money. Pablo was not able to execute sales and was adding little to the partnership. But most important, he wanted to keep his transactions private. Armed with such rationalizations, he approached Marvin the Saturday after his return from Cuba.

"But why?"

"We're doing different things. I think we'd both be better off."

"I don't know," Marvin said. "We've done pretty well together."

"You can buy me out if you want to keep the office. It's the only property we hold jointly."

"How much are you thinking?"

"How's five thousand for my half?"

Marvin turned his head. "It didn't cost anywhere near that."

"But we've improved it. Besides, I think the town will grow toward us when the economy picks up."

"That's too much," Marvin said. "We got back our investment plus enough to build this office when we sold off the nineteen acres. Besides, I couldn't raise anywhere near that much."

"How much could you raise?"

"Fifteen hundred maybe."

"Do you think that's a fair price?"

"Hell, I don't know. I haven't thought about it. It'll leave me broke."

"What if I give you fifteen hundred for your half? That'll give you some cash to play with."

Marvin looked at Pablo with curiosity. "I don't get it. Why? And why now?"

Putting his arm over Marvin's shoulder Pablo said, "I've enjoyed it, Marvin, and I appreciate the start you gave me, but I want to be on my own. It has nothing to do with you."

"When do you want me out?"

"I wish you wouldn't think of it that way. There's no rush."

*

The triumphant feeling tightened into a knot when Pablo told Consuelo that evening after he had put Sammy to bed.

"Marvin helped you when you needed it. Why are you pushing him out?"

"I gave him the option of buying me out."

"But you've done well together."

"We don't need that much office space. It was a frivolous idea."

"So you bought it because it's frivolous?"

"The building was a good investment. I'll sell it down the road to somebody who can use it. Look, I want to be on my own. What's so terrible about that?"

Pablo did not tell her he had a potential buyer, a Tampa builder interested in developing the property. He had sparked the builder's interest by telling him that Brandon had no grocery store, and residents had to drive into Ybor City to shop.

"Look, Consuelo, I've learned a lot and it's been fun. But I want to do things my way and not have to consult him over every detail. He's a nice guy and we're still friends."

"I just think you owe him."

"No argument, but I'm not really helping him."

"Fifteen hundred isn't much."

"He set the price."

Consuelo was not comfortable, but she let it drop.

That night in bed, wanting to calm the harsh feelings, he snuggled in behind her and began to fondle her. Before long she had turned to face him and they were in a tight embrace. It was the first time since Havana.

Suddenly he said, "Wait a minute," and reached to the night table and opened the top drawer.

"Oh, not that!" she said, putting her hand on his shoulder. "Why don't you want another baby?"

"Same reason: too much distraction."

"So nothing's changed."

"Can't you understand? My business is just taking off."

"Sure that's all?"

"What else?" he asked as innocently as he could.

"Good night."

*

Pablo slept late that Sunday morning. When he walked into the kitchen and kissed Consuelo, she did not respond.

"Where's Sammy?"

"In the grove."

"I'll go get him."

"Breakfast will be ready soon."

Pablo found him under the giant grapefruit tree in the center of the grove. He was sitting in a large Adirondack chair trying to rip the peel off a Hamlin orange with his fingernails.

He handed it to Pablo. "Would you peel it, Papa?"

"Sure." Pablo took out his pocketknife, unfolded the long, narrow blade and began to peel. He watched Sammy's fascination as he started at the stem end and cut a long coil until it twisted down to the ground.

"That's swell, Papa. You made it in one piece."

When Pablo had finished, he cut the orange in halves and gave one to Sammy and began to eat the other.

"When I was a boy, I liked mangos. I'd climb one of the trees in our garden and sit on a limb and peel and eat until I couldn't hold any more. By that time the juice would be dripping off my elbows."

"Why don't we plant a mango tree?"

"Mangos freeze this far north."

"I'm glad I met *Abuelo*."

"Me too."

"Why did he die?"

"His heart was weak."

"Does everybody have to die?"

"I'm afraid so, Sammy."

"You too?"

"Sure, but don't worry; not for a long time."

"Mama too?"

"Let's talk about good things. Things we can do something about."

"OK, Papa. When are we going back to Cuba?"

"I don't know, soon I hope. Come on, let's go eat."

*

On Monday Marvin accepted the $1,500 check silently with the same look of bewilderment he had had Saturday. By the following Saturday, he had removed the last of his belongings.

"You didn't have to rush."

"No need to delay. I'll use our spare bedroom until I can find a place."

"Let's keep in touch."

"Sure." They shook hands as Marvin left carrying a box of file folders and magazines.

"If I find something good, we can still do business together," Pablo said, as Marvin closed his car door.

"Swell," Marvin said. "Give my best to Consuelo."

*

The following Monday, a cool, mid-November evening, Pablo came home smiling. It was late and Sammy was already in bed. Pablo had hired a woman to clean the building and had waited for her to finish.

"Good news, Connie," he said.

Irritated, she got up from the piano and stood to kiss him.

"What is it?"

Leaving his hat and coat on one of the chairs in the living room, he sat on the sofa and motioned for her to sit beside him.

"I just sold the office to a builder from Tampa. He wants to put up some houses and a grocery store and plans to convert the office building into something else."

"When did this come up?"

"Actually, I've been talking with him for a couple of weeks, but he agreed to the deal just this afternoon and gave me a deposit."

"How much?"

"Are you ready? Five thousand!"

"You'll split it with Marvin, right?"

"Are you crazy?"

"You knew about it when you bought him out."

"It wasn't certain, but what if I did? Business is business. You've got to be tough or be swept up like trash on the highway."

"This is trash. It's disgusting!" She stood and looked down at him. "To cheat your partner, the man who helped you. You must enjoy cheating people close to you. Like Hitler. You don't care about people's feelings."

"What are you saying?"

"Like your edict about no more babies." She was yelling.

"I'm the man and I set our course."

"Whether you're a man is debatable."

"I won't take that from you or anyone else. If I'm not man enough for you, then find somebody else."

"That's an attractive offer."

"Look, Connie, let's not say another word. We won't settle anything like this. We'll talk tomorrow."

"I don't want to talk anymore."

"Fine. Tomorrow."

*

The next morning, Pablo found Consuelo in Sammy's room, packing Sammy's suitcase. "I'm going home for a while."

"What was all that anger about last night?"

"Stay here and finish, Sammy," she said, and walked to her bedroom and closed the door, "Last night was the last straw. It's been building since we moved."

"Don't like Brandon?"

"Not Brandon, Pablo. My life."

"I don't get it."

"I'm not surprised."

"Oh, Connie … where are you going?"

"I don't know."

"Come on now, Connie. Tell me."

"My name is Consuelo. I don't remember changing it."

"Is that it? That I call you Connie?"

"You're not the Pablo I knew; you're somebody else. I don't know you. I married a thoughtful, idealistic boy, and he grew up to be an arrogant opportunist. That was my blunder."

"I'll go with you."

"Don't be stupid. It's you I want to get away from."

"What does that mean?"

"You want the truth or the *mierda* you dish out?"

He hesitated trying to stay calm. "The truth."

"The truth is, I don't know."

"That's not the whole truth."

"You're right. I've known all along why you were so worried when I was expecting Sammy. And it hasn't changed."

As if doused with cold water, he could barely speak. In a thin voice he said, "What are you saying?"

"You were afraid my slave ancestor would reach up from the grave to give us a black child."

"How could you think that?"

"I don't think it; I know it!"

Pablo sat drenched in his dark, hidden truth. And now it stared back with round brown eyes from the depths of Consuelo's heart. He sat and put his face in his hands. "You don't know how I've hated myself for that. But I couldn't help it. I love you, Consuelo, but a demon was eating my insides. When I saw Sammy I was happy for the first time since ... I know I worried you all those months. I'm sorry. I'd like to forget it, but I can't. I can't go through it again."

"So you thought our son would soil your illustrious family heritage." Still standing over him she said, "Why did you marry me?

"Please try to forgive my stupidity, Consuelo. I do love you."

"Instead of renouncing the stupidity you cling to it. I could forgive you for the past, but you haven't changed. I can't forgive a stupidity that you won't change."

"I'm trying to be honest, Consuelo. I love you. I need your strength."

"I remember your words, Pablo: 'no matter who or what your ancestors were.' That was *mierda*."

"No it wasn't."

She resumed packing. Unable to do or say anything, he walked out.

*

Consuelo arranged passage on the S. S. Florida leaving for Havana on Friday. Few words passed between her and Pablo as they drove along the beautiful, curving, Bayshore Boulevard. Consuelo did not see the ornate mansions with their broad, columned porticos that lined the boulevard on the right, nor the calm waters of the bay to the left, nor the grand Centro Espanol Hospital set back on its broad lawn. Her eyes were focused straight ahead as if on a dark future. Wearing a broad, blue hat and matching dress, she reminded Pablo of their crossing eight years earlier. But now he saw a mature woman who was even more beautiful. At that moment Pablo could not imagine his future without her. As he tried to reconstruct the disasterous discussion of the previous few days, he

179

searched his memory trying to understand her anger. His thoughts turned to himself and the good living he had provided for her and his son. What else could she possibly want? he wondered. Many people would be happy with one child. Why couldn't she be happy with Sammy, such a beautiful, intelligent child?

The tiny voice from behind interrupted his rambling thoughts: "When are we coming back?"

"I'm not sure," his mother said, "but we're going to have a beautiful vacation at Abuelo Juan's home. And we'll visit the beach and do all the things you liked the last time."

Sammy tried to smile. Pablo said nothing. At the port he carried their bags to the loading point and tried one last time. He pulled Consuelo aside and said, "Please remember, people can change. I didn't know how deeply you felt about it."

"We'll see."

He moved to kiss her, but she offered her cheek. Then he stooped and picked Sammy up and hugged him and kissed him. "Don't eat too many mangos. Too much of a good thing can make you sick."

Hand in hand, Consuelo and Sammy walked the gangplank and stood at the railing. Sammy waved and she stood motionless as the ship disconnected from the dock and drifted out. Pablo could only think about the day she would walk down that gangplank and into his arms.

13 – CONSUELO - 1939

*

WPA Won't Add New Men To Florida Rolls

*

Britain Asks Japs' Intentions

*

Mobster Gets 18 Months On Lottery Charge

*

Churchill Warns Britons Of Invasion Threat

*

When Will Batista Become Cuban President?

*

"Ay, my baby," doña Inez said, looking down at Sammy. Then turning to Consuelo, "I heard you were in Matanzas. I was wondering if you would call."

"Samuelito wanted to see you."

Sammy reached up to his grandmother, but she did not pick him up. "I'm sorry, Samuelito, but my back has been hurting. Let's sit in the living room." Doña Inez was dressed as if she were going to a party with a slinky, black dress, a diamond necklace, and diamonds on several fingers of each hand. Her hair was pulled back severely into a tight bun. Unlike their last visit doña Inez's hair no longer showed streaks of gray.

"You're looking well and fit, Inez."

"Appearances deceive. Actually I'm not at all well. First it was a sinus attack and now my back. I've been quite miserable, but I prefer not to display my problems for the world. And Pablo? Why didn't he come?"

"He couldn't leave work."

"Poor Pablo. What is Christmas without his son?"

"The depression hasn't hurt his business."

"I'm glad to hear it. And how are you doing, Samuelito? Do you miss Papá?"

"*Si, Abuela.*"

Turning to Consuelo she said, "It's hard on a boy to be away from his father. Especially on the day we celebrate the birth of our Savior. Do you attend mass, Samuelito?"

"Not in Matanzas; at home we do."

"Why not?"

"It's been a little hectic," Consuelo said.

"It wouldn't be if his father were here. But to miss mass! Such a small sacrifice for our Savior and the Blessed Virgin, who gave everything for us."

"*Abuela,* could I have a batido?"

"Certainly; come with me, Samuelito." As doña Inez took Sammy's hand, Consuelo stayed in the living room, giving thanks for Sammy's diversion. She overheard doña Inez say, "It's not good to be away from your father, Samuelito. He should be here. Poor man must be very lonely. He needs you."

"We'll come back another day," Consuelo said, returning to the kitchen. Not wanting to make a scene she resolved never to leave Sammy alone with his grandmother.

While Sammy drank his milk shake the old woman turned to Consuelo and continued harping on the effect of keeping a boy away from his father. "He's at a very impressionable age. He needs his father."

"How is the business going?"

"Better. With God's help I've managed to retire most of his debts, and in a short time, I'll have the business profitable again."

"You're a good businesswoman."

"Does that surprise you? What did you expect me to do?"

"Women are much more capable than people think."

"Quite true," doña Inez said. "And you? How do you help Pablo's business?"

"I'm rearing his son."

"You have no other occupation?"

"I'm planning a piano recital."

"Pablo mentioned that."

In less than an hour Consuelo had endured all the subtle and not so subtle criticisms she could take. "My father is expecting us," she said. "One of my cousins is coming to see us this afternoon."

"I shall see my grandson again, won't I?"

"Of course."

*

Pablo soon discovered that being lonely in Brandon was not the same as being lonely in Ybor City. He wrote to Consuelo and separately to Sammy every day. Sammy answered every letter, but Consuelo answered none. Having more time to devote to his work Pablo was reaping rewards, but they brought little comfort.

Christmas was especially lonely, and with every passing day he considered going to Cuba and surprising her and Sammy, but he had thought better of it, for he did not want to give Consuelo an excuse to stay away. On Christmas day he telephoned and talked mostly to Sammy and his grandfather.

"Have you seen Abuela Inez?"

"Yes, Papá. Last week."

"And how is Mama?"

"Fine. Here she is."

After a few moments he heard a weak, "Hello."

"I miss you, Consuelo."

"We're fine. We saw your mother last week. She complained of a bad back, but she's fine. She's pulled your father's business almost out of debt. Are you well?"

"I miss you terribly."

"Sammy talks about you a lot. Here, my father wants to say something."

"Hello, Pablo. You have to straighten this out. Married people should be together."

"Thank you, Juan. How have you been?"

"Can't complain. The business keeps me busier than I need to be at my age."

"Tell Consuelo I'm sorry for everything."

"I will."

Consuelo's coldness was almost too much, so he ventured into Ybor City. It was late afternoon and cool when he drove up La Septima. After driving around a while, in and out of the side streets crossing and recrossing La Septima, he parked and went into the Café Cubano. El Rubio and Matilde were sitting over their coffee at the bar. Jacinto, El Chulo, Huesito, and Sarna were playing dominos at a table near the back. El Rubio and Domingo were discussing the war brewing in Europe. When they saw Pablo, they all stopped to greet him with loud hellos and Merry Christmases and slaps on the back."

"Have a beer, Pablo," El Chulo said.

"That's a good offer," Pablo said.

"What are you doing in Ybor City?" Huesito asked.

"My wife and son are visiting her parents in Matanzas."

"L-l-left you on Christmas?" El Rubio said.

"I couldn't leave; too much business." Then sitting beside Matilde at the bar, he said, "And you, *mi amigo?*"

"*Como siempre.*"

He sounded so down Pablo asked what he had been doing.

"Making cigars anytime and anywhere I can. Otherwise I work at the Cuban Club. How about you? I hear you're doing well."

"Not bad, considering the depression."

"I've been thinking about buying some land to farm where I could be more independent."

"It's a hard life, Matilde."

"With a few acres of good land I could grow enough to live on and sell the rest. It's the only thing I can think of. The cigar trade is dead, at least for me. Know of anything?"

"I haven't seen that kind of land lately. You wouldn't like the area. They're mostly backwoods Crackers, not very friendly to Latinos."

"You've done all right."

"Just lucky."

"Uh-huh. It was just a thought."

From the way he turned away Pablo knew he was hurt, but he did not feel he should take a chance of ruining his business by bringing a mulatto with a light-skinned wife into that community. He decided to let the topic drop and sat at the chair El Chulo had just vacated. "May I sit in?"

"Sure," Jacinto said. "Maybe you'll bring me luck."

"What about you, Jacinto?" Pablo asked.

"I'm living with Mario and his family. I help him out around the house."

"Not working?"

"Retired."

Pablo knew what that meant. With little of the usual banter and joking, the Café Cubano looked and felt as impoverished as its patrons. Sitting on his stool behind the bar, Domingo sipped his coffee silently. A fly buzzed around the empty, cold soup pot; breadcrumbs covered the sandwich board. Cigarette and cigar butts littered the floor. Oswaldo slept near the back door in a ray of sunlight.

Pablo recalled an evening when he was twelve: His parents had sat through supper without a word. Every time Pablo tried to start a conversation, don Ignacio would not look up from his plate and doña Inez would only smile at Pablo apologetically. When they had finished their dessert, don Ignacio stood, laid his napkin on the table, and said, "Time to get back to Matanzas," and walked out of the house.

Shaking the memory out of his head Pablo said, "I've got a long drive. See you, *caballeros.*"

They all returned to what they were doing: Jacinto, Huesito, and Sarna continued to play dominos; El Rubio asked Domingo what he thought the Germans meant to do now that they had taken Austria; Matilde continued to sit facing the wall behind the bar. On his way out Pablo felt he had never walked in.

*

Cynthia could not cure Pablo's desperation and loneliness. Oddly, he was spending less time with her than when Consuelo was home. When he did visit her, they would argue over inconsequential things.

During one afternoon when Pablo walked in feeling more depressed than usual she said, "You're free now, sugar. Why don't you come by more?"

"I don't feel good." He sat on the sofa.

"How about a shot?"

"No thanks."

"It's a real nice day. You need to feel good like me."

"Well I don't."

"You're no fun." She reached to the end table for a cigarette.

"I'm not in the mood for griping."

"What the hell are you in the mood for?"

"Some peace and quiet!"

"Come on, sugar. Don't get mad." She lit the cigarette and took a long drag.

"Just leave me alone," he said. "I don't need anything." He stood and walked out to his car and drove off. As he drove toward Brandon he realized he had behaved stupidly, but he did not turn back.

The silence at home had come crashing down on him. He ran his fingers down the piano keys and stared at the music she had left open. Large, Gothic letters spelled the words, *Liszt Sonata*. Pablo knew nothing about either Liszt or sonata and would have given anything to have her explain them. He sat in the kitchen to write her a letter. It was his fifteenth in the four weeks since they left. He began, "Dearest Consuelo," and then stopped and started to talk to himself: What can I say that I haven't already said fourteen times? She won't return until she's ready. Nothing I can say will convince her. It'll take action, but what? She shouldn't have taken Sammy away; it was cruel, unforgivable. But toughness won't work; at least not with her. I've never seen her so angry. How can I show remorse when I'm so far away? Action! Yes, action, and not action at a distance. Of course!

The next morning he drove to Marvin's house. When Marvin opened the front door, Pablo said, "I don't have much time, Marvin, but I want to talk. May I come in?"

Pablo could see Suzanne working in the kitchen. "I've done some thinking about our partnership. I cheated you. I sold the office at a good profit."

"I know."

"I'd like to get together again. Don't decide now. I'm going to Cuba for a few days. We can talk when I get back. I just want you to know I'm sorry. Whether you agree or not, here's a check for your half of the profit."

Looking at the thousand-dollar check, Marvin tried to speak, but Pablo stopped him. "Please," he said, raising his hand. "When I return."

Pablo stood and started to walk out the door.

"I'll think about it," Marvin said, shaking Pablo's hand.

*

Carrying concrete proof of his change of heart, Pablo felt optimistic for the first time in weeks as he walked the gangplank. He did not warn her, hoping the surprise would throw her off balance enough to give him the advantage. He hoped Sammy's happiness at seeing him would move her. If she wants more babies; all right, more babies, he thought. God, even the thought brings a knot to my stomach, but I'll manage it.

*

It was a cool, sunny January day in Havana. The city spread out before Pablo like a feast, white buildings and stone steeples and dominating all, the Morro Castle guarding the harbor as it had for centuries. He rented a taxi to drive him to Matanzas and stopped on the way to buy flowers and candy for Consuelo, cigars for her father and some games and trinkets for Sammy.

Anticipation had him trembling as the taxi stopped at the González house. Bearing flowers and candy and packages, he walked onto the porch and knocked on the door. Juan González opened the door, and his surprise immediately turned to a pleasant smile. "Good to see you, Pablo. Come in. Sit down."

Pablo handed him the cigars, then put down the other packages and returned to shake Juan's hand and embrace him. "Where are they?"

"In Havana with Consuelo's cousin. They won't be back for several hours."

"I'll rest a few minutes and then visit my mother."

"She'll be happy to see you."

"How is Consuelo?"

"Samuelito is having fun, but he misses you. Consuelo is … you know."

"I've come to take them home," Pablo said, trying to sound forceful and dramatic.

Juan warmed some leftover café con leche and brought out some pastries while they talked. Pablo did not want to open up to him until he knew what Consuelo had said about him. Juan only skirted around the topic, leaving out details and concentrating on the hope that they would soon get together. After about an hour of gentle sparring with fancy footwork but no punches, Pablo excused himself and called a taxi.

*

Doña Inez answered the door in a business outfit with tailored jacket and skirt.

"*Hola Mamá!*" he said, embracing her.

"What a surprise. I didn't expect to see you while Consuelo was here."

"Why not? I've come to take them home."

"Aren't you separated?"

"Why no. Where did you hear that?"

"I naturally assumed, seeing her and Samuelito here without you. Well, don't just stand there. Come in."

"How have you been, Mamá?"

"Not at all well. I've had a terrible sinus infection, and my back is still acting up. You know."

"You look younger."

"May I fix you something to eat? I don't have much, you know, with my problems, but I can fix something simple."

"I just had a snack at Juan's house."

"Oh, you went there first?"

"Of course. I wanted to see Consuelo and Samuelito."

"Why aren't they with you?"

"They went to Havana for the day."

"Pablito, this separation may be a blessing."

"It's certainly made me think."

"Think well, Pablito. This is your chance to correct a grave error. You should never have married her."

"For heaven sake, Mamá, she's my wife and the mother of my son. Yes, we've had a spat, and I'm here to atone for my faults."

"Your faults? Don't be stupid! Ask yourself why she is here. It is because she is not happy with you. You're a successful businessman and a good father, but that is not enough for her. She will always want more. Shake her off while you have the chance, before she drags you down to her level."

"Stop it, Mamá! I'm not leaving her. She hasn't demanded anything. Maybe if she had she wouldn't be so angry. I want to show her I'm worthy."

"She's angry? What a joke. That nonentity has nothing to be angry about."

"Enough, Mamá. I went through all this with Papá. I don't want to argue with you."

"See what a life she's giving you? You'd be better off alone. Remember, my son: our Savior has shown us the way. Follow him."

"This isn't what I came for. I'll try to see you again before I leave."

"You'll try? How sad that makes me. I only want what's best for you, Pablito. A mother's love is eternal; it never wavers. Remember that."

"Yes, Mamá. Goodbye."

*

Sammy ran to him and put his arms around his father's waist and screamed until Pablo picked him up and kissed him. "I brought you something."

"Oh boy! I missed you, Papa."

"Your father and I have to talk," Consuelo said. "Why don't you go with *Abuelo?*"

"Into the back yard, little man," Juan said.

When they had gone, she turned to Pablo with a scowl. "You knew I didn't want to see you."

"I couldn't stand it. I've come all this way. Please talk to me. That's all I ask."

"You're impossible."

"Is time so precious? Can't you waste even a little?"

Pablo knew she could not resist his logic. "Not around Sammy or my father."

"Fine. We'll go out for supper."

She smiled, but with little feeling. "All right. We can use my father's car."

*

Perched on the side of a hill overlooking the bay, what had been their favorite restaurant looked like a bird's nest. The place had run down, but Pablo didn't care. Leading her to the terrace, he found a table overlooking the city and the bay in the distance. The pink sky was slowly ebbing to the eternal blue of evening.

"I've done a lot of thinking these past few weeks," he said.

"So have I."

"You're completely right," he said. "I've been a spoiled child. I had no right to demand so much of you, and I've made some business deals I'm not proud of. I wanted to succeed so much for you that I did what I thought I had to." He paused a moment to get her reaction. Seeing none he resumed. "I gave Marvin half of the profit from the office. When he saw how sorry I was, he softened."

"I'm glad for Marvin, but it's sickening that you expect to get me back by paying your debts."

"Please, Consuelo. That's not it. You made me see it was right."

Consuelo looked out at the water and sipped her wine.

"I've thought about babies. That was wrong too. We'll have more babies. I want them too. I always have."

"You mean you'll swallow your fears?"

"I'll do anything to get you back."

Consuelo looked away again, anger building.

"Isn't that what you want?"

"You don't have what I want."

"What, for God sake?"

"I want you to want our children as they are. I carry a blemish you find abhorrent. Now you say you'll accept the awful truth. That's even worse. If I had a little dark girl, I would love her. You might accept her, but you'd be ashamed of her. You'd never love her completely. I can't live with that, Pablo. That fragment I carry that you find so loathsome would separate us even if we never had another."

"That's not true. Nothing about you is loathsome."

"I'm sorry, Pablo. Maybe some day you'll stop lying to yourself. That'll be a start."

He could not respond to such finality. They ate their meal with few words. Unspoken conversations flooded their brains. Only when they were through did he speak again.

"My mother's glad we're having troubles. She wants me to leave you."

"She's never hidden her feelings."

"I don't know what to say, except I don't care what she says or does. I know she's wrong. Please, tell me: what are you thinking."

"I've written to my old professor in Florida State College. Maybe they have an opening."

"Doing what?"

"Anything in music. Your mother's right about one thing: women should have their own work."

"Mamá just wants us to separate."

"I know, but she's right about having our own work."

The conversation dwindled, so Pablo paid the check and they drove home through the dark evening with the windows open, neither enjoying the cool Caribbean air or the sounds of the waves clawing the beach. As they approached her house, he said, "I'll make arrangements to leave on the next ship. May I stay here tonight?"

"My father expects you."

*

Though the weather was clear, sunny, and calm, inner turbulence churned Pablo more than the Florida Strait ever had. He walked the decks until he knew every door, window, and railing by heart. Sitting at the bar nursing a drink did not help, so he returned to the deck to walk some more. Finally he sat in a deck chair and slept more soundly than he had had since leaving Tampa.

When the ship docked in Tampa the next morning, he carried his bag to his car in the parking lot and drove home. The drive through Ybor City sparked feelings that he was, after all, still alive and well and in a place that felt like home. He was sure Consuelo would come around. I'll work through Juan and Sammy, he thought. In my letters I'll let her know what I'm doing and feeling. She'll realize I haven't given up and that I'm doing things she can be proud of.

Marvin's car was backing out of Pablo's driveway when Pablo pulled in. "Pablo, good! I was about to leave. I've been by several times to say thanks. I hate to admit it, but I had terrible thoughts about you."

"You were right."

Marvin looked puzzled.

Pablo invited him into the living room and they sat down. Pablo took out a cigarette and offered Marvin one.

When he had lighted them both, Pablo continued: "Looking back ... some of my deals ... well, I wish I hadn't ..."

"I wondered, but there's no need."

"Consuelo's left me."

"I'm sorry."

"Buying you out and then selling the office so soon afterward pushed her over the edge. She figured it out and got furious."

"She left for that?"

"There's more." Pablo put his head in his hands and stopped for a moment. "I need a drink. How about you?"

"It's kind of early, but ... sure. A beer."

Pablo handed Marvin the beer and took a long sip of brandy. "Marvin, you've been a good friend, and I was too wrapped up in myself to realize it. I wanted to make big money. I'm not sure why, maybe to show my father. This is personal, and I don't feel quite right telling you, but I can't stand it. I don't feel comfortable talking to my cousin; I know what he'd say, and it wouldn't help."

He reached for the glass and took a big gulp.

"Look, Pablo, if you're not sure about this ..."

"If I don't talk to somebody I'll blow up." He took another sip. "My parents were against our marriage. My mother didn't want me to marry anybody, but my father was the real problem. He learned Consuelo had a great-grandmother who was half black. When I told him I was going to marry her anyway, he disinherited me."

"Jesus!"

"Wait. That's not the worst. When Consuelo told me she was expecting, I almost went out of my mind with worry. I feel bad telling you, knowing how much you and Suzanne have wanted a baby, but I thought the baby might look ... you know. I couldn't stand it."

"That it would look like a Negro after that many generations? I hate to tell you, Pablo, but that's stupid"

Pablo held up his hand to make him stop as he looked down. "I know. I made her life miserable, but she never complained. I said I was worried about the strike and losing my job. She put up with my stupidity, so sweet and understanding she was. Of course, when I saw Sammy I felt great. But later I told her I didn't want any more babies. She didn't complain, but I knew it bothered her. It'd been gnawing at us for eight years. Well, a few weeks ago, when I told her about buying you out, she thought I was ungrateful. When I sold the office she went wild. Said terrible things. She'd known all along why I didn't want another baby; I don't know how the hell she figured it out. She'd had enough betrayal, I guess." He took another sip and lit a cigarette.

"I don't blame her."

"What do I do, Marvin?"

"I don't know. But she's a great girl and you're a sap if you lose her."

"I know. She wants to find a job in Tallahassee, at the college. I don't want her to, but I'll pay her expenses. I don't know what else to do."

"Sounds right."

"I'm serious about us getting together, Marvin."

"What do you have in mind?"

"I've done pretty well, but if we pool our resources, we could be sitting pretty in a few years. This depression's got to end. With things heating up in Europe, America will be producing all kinds of things, and that means money. I think we should buy all the land we can get."

"I hope you're right. You've shown a good instinct. Anyway, I'm glad we're getting together. At least we'll save on office expenses."

"Good. Talk it over with Suzanne. I'll write Consuelo right away."

14 – TALLAHASSEE - 1940

*

Eastern Airline Begins New York – Tampa Run

*

Roosevelt Opens U.S. Arms Market To Britain

*

Nazi Planes Ferry Fascist Troops To Front In Albania

*

Tampa Gets Second Rain In 3 Months
Drizzle Measured At One Hundredth Of An Inch

*

Looking back on her year in Tallahassee, Consuelo saw both liberation and loss. But she could not stop questioning herself. Refusing to give in to Pablo's selfishness felt right, she argued, or was she just being stubborn? And what about Sammy? Was it right to keep him away from his father? Never complaining, the boy seemed to know more than a child his age should know. After four cold months she could enjoy strolling to the music department without an overcoat. Dogwood trees hidden among the oaks lightened the sleeping, gray forest. Then there was the thrill of being a professional musician and living the life she loved. Accompanying vocal soloists and choruses kept her busy constantly learning new music.

She much preferred coaching piano students for the regular faculty, but as a teaching assistant, she could not make demands.

Sammy's school, their apartment, and the music department were all a short walk from one another. With her job flexibility, Consuelo could work while Sammy was in school. Though he excelled in his third grade class, he was no longer the lively charming child he had been. Finding few friends in Tallahassee he buried himself in his books. His mother knew he missed his father, but returning to him or divorcing him both seemed frighteningly irreversible. Consuelo's father had offered to help with her expenses, but Pablo insisted: she was his wife and it was his duty to support her. Though he wanted her back, he would not push her. Weighted down by his effusive kindness and generosity, Consuelo was weakening. Pablo seemed to have revived the man she had fallen in love with. In their regular letters Marvin and Suzanne testified that he had truly changed.

*

"How about supper?" Tony asked.

The young assistant professor in his late twenties dressed and acted like an academic with his glasses, tweed jacket and pipe. He fit the artistic mold even to having straight black hair that fell limp over his eyes as he played the piano. Behind his glasses, his light brown eyes seemed irrestistably to implore. Consuelo considered herself the better pianist and offered occasional advice, which he accepted graciously. Having been at Florida State College two years, he was not yet tenured. Their warm friendship had blossomed with four-hand music, which neither had played before they met.

"I'm sorry, Tony, but I have to cook for Sammy; besides, it's not a good idea."

"You've got to eat. Bring him."

"I don't think so, but thanks."

"You've been putting me off all semester. Why?"

Not wanting Sammy to sense finality in their tentative separation, Consuelo had told him she was there to study and work, and his father could not leave his business. She knew Sammy did not completely accept her explanation, but deception seemed better than unvarnished truth. Sammy did not want reasons; he wanted his father. But though he did not fully understand, he knew questions made his mother unhappy and rarely asked. His father visited them several times, but his visits were always short and he always stayed at a hotel.

"All right, Tony. Why don't you come to my apartment around seven this evening? I'll fix supper."

"Swell. What may I bring?"

"Just yourself. I'm nervous about this because of Sammy. I don't want him to worry."

"When does he go to sleep?"

"Around eight."

"Why don't I come at 8:30? I'll be quiet as a mouse."

"I don't like sneaking around."

"I won't sneak," he said, smiling.

After some complaining, Sammy went to bed early that evening. "I'm having a friend over tonight. It's one of the professors I work with. We're working on some music, but we'll try to be quiet. You can go to sleep in my bed."

"Tony?"

"Yes. Now go to sleep."

Tony arrived a little past 8:30, with flowers and a bottle of vintage wine. "Supposed to be a good year," he said, as he pulled the cork. "Also I brought another duet for you to look at."

Her efficiency apartment had one bedroom for her, a small living room with a couch that opened into a bed for Sammy, a bath, and a small kitchen.

After supper, Tony spread the duet music on the kitchen table. "This is a nice suite, Bizet's <u>Jeux d'Infants</u>. Look it over and we'll play it through at the studio tomorrow.

She sat next to him as they read the score. Tony put his arm around her shoulder; she did not move away.

"They look like fun," she said.

"That's what I thought. You know, Consuelo, I've really enjoyed working together. I've never enjoyed anybody as much."

"Me too," she said, turning to look at him. When he moved toward her and kissed her, she did not back away. When they broke away, he said, "I hope you don't mind."

"I don't, but I don't want to go any further. Pablo and I are still married."

"I noticed he always stays in a hotel when he comes up."

"I still love him, Tony. It wouldn't be fair to let you think otherwise."

"I understand, but I also know how I feel about you."

"I like you, Tony, but I can't think straight right now."

"How about helping with the dishes?" he asked.

"Sure. I'll wash and you dry."

Tony stood beside her. "This is a duet," he said, as she handed him a dish and he dried it and put it away.

She smiled. When they were through, he said, "Well, I guess it's time to go."

"It's still early. Stay a while."

They sat in the living room sofa and made small talk about the music department and about their upcoming recital. About an hour later, he stood and said, "It really is time." As they approached the door he kissed her again, more ardently this time. After a long moment, she pulled back. "Please, Tony."

He looked at her for a moment; then he said, "See you tomorrow."

*

Pablo seemed tobe leading an exemplary life in Brandon. He worked harder than ever, and, though still a tough businessman, he kept his dealings with Marvin and with his clients clean and ethical. He and Marvin had bought three large citrus groves at bargain prices and were holding them. Having invested most of their cash, they were at a standstill. They could not acquire more until they sold some, and Pablo held out saying, "It's got to go up."

Sitting at their desks one late afternoon over coffee and a newspaper, Marvin closed his paper and slammed it on the desk. "Now that the British are in it, we won't be far behind."

"Roosevelt says no, but you know when politicians deny something you have to wonder."

"How about coming to supper?" Marvin said. "Suzanne's making chicken and dumplings. Take my advice and come; it's pretty good."

"Sorry. Got to see a friend in Ybor City. Poor guy's bad off."

"Your loss."

*

"You think she's comin' back? How long's it been?" Cynthia was still lying in bed smoking a cigarette. Wrapped in a towel Pablo stood by the bed and lit a cigar. After several puffs he took the cigar out of his mouth and looked at the burning end. "She'll be back."

"I don't get you. You want her back, but you're here with me."

"I'm a man. Besides, I like you." He looked around the small, clean, airy house. "You like it here better than that other place, don't you?"

"Six Mile Creek ain't exactly Paris."

"You know I can't afford to be seen. This house is comfortable, and the Ford can take you anywhere you want to go."

"It's all right."

"Stop complaining, then."

"I ain't complaining, but if I loved somebody, I'd go after him. I wouldn't hang around screwing another guy."

"Well you're not me."

"I'm just lonely. I miss my friends."

"Go where you want as long as you don't screw around. You've got a good deal if you ask me."

"Why do men always wanna keep a woman all for themselves?"

"I'm not in the mood to argue and I especially don't feel like explanations." He walked to the chair near the door.

"Come on back, sugar," she said as she pulled the sheet back. Pablo drew on his cigar, then laid it down on the ashtray and slipped into bed. "You've got too much on," she said. Rising and straddling his knees she pulled away the towel. "I know what you like, sugar."

*

The next morning the mailman brought one of Consuelo's rare letters. Tearing it open he found an invitation to her recital. She included the program, which closed with some duets with Anthony Sekul. In her letter she said she hoped he could come and noted that Sammy wanted to see him. At the end she wrote, "I'd like you to share this important moment with me." Pablo immediately wrote back congratulating her on the recital and saying he would come.

It was still dark two weeks later when he finished loading the Packard and headed north, whistling as he drove through cattle country, the sun appearing to his right. He hoped he had not read too much in her letter, but the subtle ambiguity raised his optimism. The day before, he had filled a box with the last oranges and grapefruit of the season. He also took a new long-blade pocketknife, like his, for Sammy.

*

Carrying presents and oranges, Pablo arrived at Consuelo's apartment at six o'clock. She and Sammy had just brought in some things from the grocery store and were putting them away.

"I'm glad you came."

He laid the box of fruit on the kitchen table and embraced Consuelo. "I am too. And where is that big boy?"

"Papa!" Sammy shouted as he ran to his father.

"You're getting too big; I can't pick you up anymore. One of these days you'll be carrying me."

"I'll start supper," she said.

"Forget it. We're going out."

Consuelo talked nervously about her recital the following evening and how hard she had worked and how patient Sammy had been. As she practiced on campus several hours a day, Sammy would either sit with her or play on the grass. Sammy asked about Brandon and his friends and about the big grapefruit tree in the grove. Every few minutes Pablo would hug him.

*

The hotel restaurant was only half full. It was a typical old south plantation house with tall portico columns. Widely spaced tables with white tablecloths gave the dining room a formal look. The courteous Black waiters moved with perfect decorum and without haste. Consuelo greeted two couples at one of the tables and introduced Pablo. When they sat down at the far end of the dining room she told him the men were voice professors. "I accompany their students during their lessons. It's the part I like least, but it's interesting and it's helped my sight-reading."

"Who's Anthony Sekul?"

"A member of the piano faculty, very nice and a good musician."

Consuelo immediately saw Pablo's face cloud over.

"He's just a friend, Pablo. We practice together and I work with some of his students. I also work with three other professors."

Pablo smiled. "You seem to like your job."

"Very much, but it's only temporary."

"Why?"

"No credentials."

"What about getting an advanced degree?"

"All I ever wanted was a loving husband and a family. Music is recreation."

Pablo reached for her hand across the table; Sammy smiled.

*

Music faculty members and students and other university people as well as people from town formed a small but appreciative audience. Consuelo walked onstage with the assurance and authority of a seasoned performer. She wore a dark green, sleeveless gown and a gold necklace. Sitting at the piano motionless for several seconds before beginning, she resembled a porcelain figurine looking down at the keys with her milk-white arms in her lap and her short, brown hair hanging forward. The gentle first movement of the Beethoven <u>Sonata Opus 109</u>, seemed to rise from nowhere. The sublime movement increased and decreased cleanly and lovingly. This sonata had special meaning for Consuelo. In its gentle first movement she expressed the happiness of youth. The agitated chords of the short second movement shattered the delicately meditative spell of the first. Between the chords, rippling runs tossed her back and forth between excitement and anger. At the end of the brief movement her eyes had filled with tears and she seemed lost in the music. The leisurely third movement opened with a gentle theme that expanded almost imperceptibly into a series of variations that rose to dramatic highs and lows along a secluded path that evoked every emotion she had ever felt. After the long pause that followed the decaying final notes, the audience exploded and roused her from her reverie. After two curtain calls she returned to play four Chopin <u>Etudes from Opus 10</u> that displayed her virtuosity.

After a brief intermission, she returned with Debussy's <u>Children's Corner Suite</u> with its childlike treatment of difficult dances and children's games that ended with <u>Golliwog's Cake Walk</u>, a robust, carefree dance. For the finale, Tony Sekul joined her for Debussy's <u>Petite Suite for Four Hands</u>. Piano duets were rarely played in recital and the audience responded with smiles of anticipation. With Consuelo sitting at the high end and Tony at the low end of the piano, they sounded like one person playing the four miniatures of the Bizet suite.

For an encore, the pair returned to play a pair of Brahms's <u>Hungarian Dances</u>, which again raised the audience to their feet. They returned three times for curtain calls, holding hands as they bowed.

After the recital, people gathered around Consuelo, offering congratulations and adulation. The Music Department Head shook her hand vigorously and seemed truly impressed. Later, Pablo saw him talking excitedly to Tony Sekul. When the crowd dispersed, Pablo invited Tony to join them for supper at the hotel restaurant. Tony accepted.

Sammy sat between his parents, as if he could be the glue that would hold them together. Pablo ordered Apalachicola Bay oysters for appetizers and a bottle of white French wine. At first the talk twirled around music and the recital. Tony was pleased with his performance, but even more with Consuelo's.

"I've never heard the Beethoven done so beautifully," he said. "I heard Myra Hess play it in New York three or four years ago; you played it better. By the way, Dr. Smith was really impressed." Then turning to Pablo, "He's the department head."

"He said some nice things," she said.

"He talked my arm off about you," Tony said.

"I owe you a lot for arranging it, Tony." Then she turned to Pablo and Sammy. "What a glorious evening!" and hugged them both.

"Papa, Tony and I caught a big bass last week."

"I only scooped him up, Sammy."

"It was this big, Papa," Sammy said, marking the size with his hands.

Forcing an approving smile, Pablo said, "So you studied at Julliard."

"The Eastman School of Music, and after six cold winters in Rochester I'm delighted to be here."

"I know what you mean. I spent four years in South Bend."

"Consuelo's been a bonanza for the department. She does everything. What talent."

"I know," Pablo said.

"You're embarrassing me," she said.

"No kidding, I think you could work into a tenured position. You should have heard the old man."

"Thanks, but I'm not interested. I'm going back home at the end of this term," Consuelo said, glancing at Pablo.

Pablo lifted his glass: "To Consuelo, wife, pianist, mother, and friend."

They all lifted their glasses. As the waiter headed to their table, Pablo asked Consuelo and Tony if he could order a large roast snapper for them all. "They make it better than I've ever had before," he said.

They agreed and he ordered side dishes of potatoes, string beans, salad, and another bottle of wine. "I'd like this to be an evening we'll all remember."

Sammy was smiling, holding his mother's hand under the table.

Tony offered another toast: "To Consuelo and her talent. May she continue to share it with the world."

Pablo raised his glass.

Two hours later the evening wound down over coffee. Talk of music and the college eventually yielded to the war in Europe and what they might be confronting in the immediate future.

Tony drove home, and Pablo drove Consuelo and Sammy home. At her apartment she said, "Please come in. I feel bad having you stay in a hotel. Stay with us."

As Pablo parked the Packard, she stood at the door and made the sign of the cross.

15 - THE WAR - 1942

*

*Grim Congress Declares War
On Japan With One Dissenting Vote*

*

U.S. Will Grab 1000 Japanese Aliens

*

Six Tampa Officers In Thick Of Jap War

*

Costa Rica Declares War On Japan

*

In the spring of 1939 Washington announced that a new Army Base, to be called MacDill Field, would be constructed in Tampa on the bay. Reading the story in the morning newspaper, Pablo visualized hordes of military personnel demanding housing near the base. In the office Pablo found Marvin poring over the newspaper spread across his desk.

"Have you seen this?"

"Yes."

"Are you thinking what I'm thinking?"

Taking out his city maps Pablo spread them out on Marvin's desk and said, "I'm betting it'll be here," pointing to the southern tip of the Interbay Peninsula.

It was the only large undeveloped bayfront parcel. Marvin picked up the phone and called a banker friend. Turning to Pablo he said, "This guy ought to know if anybody does."

When he told Pablo that the man did not know, Pablo said, "Maybe he does and maybe he doesn't."

The second and third men he called gave Marvin the same opinion, which was confirmed by the fourth: that it would be at the southern tip of the peninsula.

Within half an hour scouting the area they found a mostly forested area south of Ballast Point with a large, relatively treeless area at the extreme south end of the peninsula.

"This has to be it," Marvin said, looking south across Tampa Bay at Bradenton and Sarasota rising in the mist. "It's perfect for an airbase, surrounded on three sides by water and isolated from the rest of the city by virgin land."

By the time they returned to the office they had organized a plan to determine who owned the land bordering what they assumed would be MacDill Field. Within three weeks they had several large plots under contract awaiting confirmation of the base's location.

*

On September 1, German troops marched into Poland as Americans sat by their radios enthralled and horrified by the outbreak of war. Two days later both Britain and France, respecting their pledge to Poland, declared war on Germany and thereby lit the fuse to World War II. Within a few months German troops marched into Paris, and the blitzkrieg began to batter England with day and night bombardments that would continue through most of the war. At first, Americans wondered whether they would enter the war; soon the question became when.

Through most of 1940 Pablo negotiated with landowners, trying to generate large tracts by stitching together all the small ones he could find. By mid-1941 Burke and Iglesias owned several large tracts near MacDill Field and were talking with developers.

*

The Burke's renovated Florida Cracker frame house on the lake was bursting with celebration that Sunday. With such a mild, calm, early December day, Suzanne had set up a table in their back yard, which sloped down a hundred yards to the vast lake. From where they ate, about half way down to the lake, Sammy saw, between giant cypress trees, a fish jump just beyond their boat dock.

"Did you see that?" Marvin said. "I've been after him for days."

"Relax," Pablo said. "He'll wait for you."

"Don't you like turkey?" Suzanne asked with a smile.

An occasional cloud cast its shadow on the festivities and then passed on to restore a grateful, dappled sunlight on their lunch.

Sammy gobbled his food and said, "I'm finished. May I go look at the lake?"

"That's my fish. Leave him alone," Marvin said, smiling.

"Go ahead, Sammy," Suzanne said.

Sammy ran down the hill and stood on the dock looking out over the lake. Soon he was lying on his stomach staring into the water.

Marvin and Pablo had just sold one of their largest MacDill properties to a Tampa developer, who planned to begin construction of small houses within weeks. It was all they could talk about. Returning from the kitchen where she and Consuelo had taken the dishes, Suzanne said, "I hope you didn't mind a belated Thanksgiving dinner."

"It's thanksgiving for us," Pablo said.

After lunch they reclined in the sun-speckled shade to recover from the copious lunch and wine. Sammy remained on the dock waiting for the fish to reappear. Soon, they were all yawning, except Sammy, who was up to his knees at the water's edge.

"I think it's time to go," Consuelo said.

"I guess so," Pablo said, making no move to get up. Nor did anyone else, for how could they lift themselves from that lovely, wooded lakefront? It took Consuelo half an hour to extract them from their repose. Sammy was drenched when he got into the car.

On their way home Pablo turned on the radio. Kate Smith was singing when they turned into their driveway. Suddenly a voice interrupted the music: "We interrupt this program to bring you an important announcement."

Pablo was about to turn off the ignition, but Consuelo held his hand. He left the car idling as the announcement continued: "At seven o'clock AM, Hawaii time, two hours ago, Japanese airplanes attacked Pearl Harbor, our naval base in Hawaii. Many casualties are reported, but exact figures are not available at this time. Several naval vessels have been destroyed along with those aircraft that could not get off the ground in time. The attack was unexpected because Japanese emissaries were at that very moment discussing peace with members of the administration in Washington."

"God help us," Consuelo said. She and Pablo spent the rest of the day by their living room radio, waiting for more news about casualties and what the government would do. Though his parents' concern and the excited radio voices frightened Sammy, he was also curious about war and what that meant.

The next day President Roosevelt addressed a joint session of Congress to ask for a declaration of war against Japan. With only one negative vote, the Congress took the United States into the war that had been raging in Asia for a decade between the Japanese and the Chinese. A few days later, Congress declared war on Germany and Italy, and World War II exploded into the largest conflict in the history of the world.

*

By early spring 1942 the cigar business was showing signs of revival. Old cigar makers who had not worked in years were working in small shops that had sprung up in Ybor City and West Tampa. Others survived on social security payments that barely kept them alive, though a sure check every month, however small, helped calm their fears.

Finding only occasional work as a cigar maker, Matilde Gómez still worked at the Cuban Club and at several stores on Seventh Avenue in the late afternoons. A cold rain was falling one late afternoon in February when he finished sweeping the sidewalk in front of the Ybor Men's Store. Finding shelter from the rain under store canopies when he could and covering himself with a newspaper across open spaces, he arrived home drenched. The door at the sidewalk was stuck shut, swollen with moisture. Cursing and tugging, he finally got it open. The light bulb at the top of the stairs had burned out, and the stairway was dark. Leaving a trail of water, he lumbered up the narrow wooden stairs, running his hand as he always did along the grooved wallboards. He hated the dull, gray paint that looked dirty even when it was fresh. Where it had peeled off, the wood showed gray. Opening the door at the top of the stairs he went directly to the bathroom leaving a trail of water. The small apartment was over a barbershop on Fourteenth Street facing the Cuban Club. With the building sandwiched between two other buildings, only the living room in front and the kitchen in back had windows. In the tiny kitchen Zoraida was preparing their supper over a two-burner gas stove that stood on a table. The only other item in the kitchen was a small, wooden icebox. She had barely room to move, and the small high window offered no view unless she stood on a chair. She mixed freshly cooked rice with black beans from the day before and was frying the mixture with a little grease.

Returning to the living room Matilde walked to the window and raised the shade as high as it would go, grasping for light. He plopped into the rocking chair next to the window with a loud exhalation and looked around at the gray, dank walls. In the center of the living room stood three straight-back chairs around a table. A smaller table and Matilde's rocker were the only other furniture. The only adornment on the walls was a small, framed Christ with a crown of thorns and his heart exposed over his chest. Under the window stood a cedar chest that Zoraida had brought from Cuba. It contained all her personal possessions including her sacred tureen, *caracoles*, and beads. On a little table beside the chest stood the image of Saint Barbara surrounded by three candles. The dining table was bare except for an unlighted kerosene lamp. At night it might give enough light to read by.

"*Que pasa?*" Zoraida asked as she came in and kissed him.

"Just tired. I finished at the Cuban Club and was sweeping the sidewalk in front of the Men's Shop when the rain started."

"Want some coffee?"

"Thanks."

When Zoraida brought his coffee his head was lying back on the cushion. Seeing his mouth wide open and his eyes closed, she quietly set the cup on the table next to his chair and walked back to the kitchen.

"I'm awake, Zoraida. How long can we go on like this?"

"We're well. We eat every day and have where to sleep. What more do we need?"

"There's a war on. Men are fighting or making money for the first time in years. Everybody but me."

"You cannot do more than your best, my love."

"Look at this dump. We're living like those poor wretches in the scrub; this is Ybor City, where other Cubans are making money."

"That is life, Matilde. Do you want to go back?"

"To Cuba?"

"Why not? At least we would be with our own."

"Things aren't any better there. No, the opportunity is still here. The problem is finding it."

"Come, you'll feel better when you've eaten." As he walked to the table she said, "With this storm I should play 99 on *bolita*."

"No you shouldn't. Aren't we poor enough without you gambling?"

"Only a nickel, *amor*."

"That's a loaf of bread."

With his eyes dripping bitterness Matilde turned to Zoraida and said, "You could have done better. As white as you are you could have married a white Cuban. Why do you accept this poverty?"

"Never call me white, Matilde. I am your *mulata* and do not forget it. It is all I have ever been and will ever be."

He shook his head and said, "I can't believe it."

Through clenched teeth she said, "I am as black as you. Never question me again. Now, are you going to eat or not?"

Seeing her standing defiantly, arms akimbo, he smiled and stood. "*Vamo', mi negra.*"

*

Only two domino tables were occupied in the Cuban Club cantina, four feet below ground level. The bartender was straightening the bar and washing last evening's glasses, occasionally looking out through the small, high windows at the legs of the people who passed on the sidewalk outside. Matilde began to mop at the far end of the cantina. When he approached one of the occupied tables, one of the domino players, a cigar maker, turned, holding his hand over his necktie, and spit on the floor next to him. When he looked up and saw Matilde standing near where he had spit, he said, "Pardon me, Matilde. I didn't see you."

Matilde said nothing. He walked to the closet, placed his mop in it, closed the closet door, and walked out.

*

"*Estás loco?* You're going to fight for people who have done all they can to keep you down?"

"It's my only chance, Zoraida. I'll become a citizen. We'll finally be a real part of this country."

"The country that treats us like animals? And what will I do while you're out killing Germans who have never harmed us?"

"I'll be earning money. If you get bored, you could go back to being a midwife. You're good at it and you like it. We'll save our money and, when the war's over, we'll start a business."

"You're trading the cow for a goat."

"I won't do it if you're not with me."

"I won't be with you in the army."

"I mean your support."

"Ah! I'll have to support you."

"*Coño!* You know what I mean. I want you to make me feel like I'm doing the right thing."

206

"Go ahead. Kill yourself! If it gets bad, I'll wait for you in Cuba."

The heat of the argument cooled gradually as Zoraida realized Matilde had his heart set. Even if she considered it madness she would send her man to war with blessings, not curses. As often happened, they ended their argument in bed making love.

When she got up, she said, "War – that's number 93." Before Matilde could react, she said, "Just kidding, *mi amor*."

*

The recruiting office was small and sparse with the sergeant's desk, a filing cabinet, and two chairs. Fluorescent lights hanging from the ceiling brightened the small room. Recruiting posters dramatizing some of the jobs soldiers do covered the brightly painted white walls. Prominently displayed was the well known, Uncle Sam Wants You poster on the inside wall and outside the large window facing the street. The recruiting sergeant was as big as Matilde and about the same age, but lean and rugged. With back and neck straight as a plank and muscular shoulders and arms straining the creases of his neatly pressed shirt, he sat erect in his chair with his arms relaxed on the desk in front of him. Looking down on him, Matilde could see his shiny, tan scalp through his blonde, GI-haircut. The sergeant looked up at Matilde with a broad, but menacing smile that cut across his tanned face as if he were waiting for Matilde to screw up so he could tear him to pieces. "You don't speak much English do you, boy," he said with a distinct southern drawl.

"I read and write it, but I haven't had much practice speaking."

"Well, let's see if you can fill out this here form." The sergeant handed him some papers on a clipboard.

Matilde sat with the clipboard on his lap and answered all the questions except one.

"That's pretty fast. Let's see how you did. Uh-huh, fine … fine … Uh! You didn't fill in your race," he said, and picked up a pencil.

"My father was white and my mother was Negro. I didn't know what to write."

The sergeant looked up at Matilde, smiled, and checked the box marked Colored. "Wait over there." Matilde resented his rudeness, but said nothing and returned to the chair.

Within thirty minutes Matilde had enlisted in the U.S. Army. "You'll report to the Army base in Tuskegee, Alabama," the sergeant said. "You'll board a bus with other Colored recruits at the Zack Street entrance to the Post office next Monday at 8:00 AM sharp. It's all on this sheet. You understand, boy?" the sergeant said, handing Matilde several sheets of instructions.

"Yes, Sir."

"You don't address a sergeant as Sir, boy," the sergeant said.

"Yes, Sergeant."

*

It was still dark that first morning, and the barrack was dark and silent with a row of double-bunk beds on either side of the long room. Each bed was aligned with a window. In the middle of the floor stood a large, pot-bellied stove that was not in use because spring had arrived early. Out of still, dark sleep erupted the loud whistle blast followed by banging on the metal beds. As he walked down the row of beds, banging, the platoon sergeant yelled, "All right. Everybody up. I want you all in formation on the street outside the barracks in four minutes. Now move it." The sergeant was a slight man, lean and sinewy and very erect. His head was shaved except for a small patch on top. His high-pitched voice rattled in Matilde's ears.

As Matilde ran out and stood at attention, he saw the sergeant facing where his men would assemble and looking down at his wristwatch. When the last straggler came to formation, the sergeant said, "Six and a half minutes. Now I'm going to dismiss you pansies, and I want you to go back in, undress, and tuck yourselves in bed again. When I call you out this time, you'd better be out here in four minutes. Dismissed!"

The men ran back in, pushing and scrambling to get their clothes off. A few of the slower ones got into bed fully dressed. When the sergeant entered, he walked down the aisle looking at each recruit. "You, there," he said, banging on a recruit's bed. Get the hell out of there and take your clothes off like I told you, and be quick about it."

The man uncovered and did as he was told. "OK, now get back in." Then he stepped into the middle of the barrack and said, "Anybody else in bed with his clothes on better get up now and undress or I'll have his ass." Four other men got up, undressed, and got back into bed. "You men are going to learn to follow orders. Then, blowing his whistle, he yelled, "Fall in!"

When the last man reached formation, the sergeant looked up. "Four and a half minutes. We'll repeat this if it takes all morning, breakfast or no breakfast. Dismissed!"

The third time, when the last man came to attention, the sergeant said, "Three minutes and fifty-five seconds. OK. Rest!"

208

Trying to relax, Matilde tried to extract a cigarette out of a package with one hand while holding his rifle with the other. Leaning his rifle against his leg, it slipped and fell to the ground with a loud slapping sound.

Seemingly out of nowhere came the piercing, high-pitched voice: "Pick up that rifle, soldier, and give me twenty pushups." Standing toe to toe with Matilde, he was nearly a foot shorter. "And don't let that piece touch the ground again unless you want another twenty."

"How, Sergeant?"

Inches from his face, the sergeant yelled, "Lay it on the backs of your hands, damn it. Now get your ass down!" Half way up in his fourth pushup, trembling, he fell on his face.

"You're pathetic, soldier. We'll fix you or you'll die trying."

Matilde spit out dirt as he stood and brushed the dirt off his uniform. The sergeant then called the platoon to attention. "Right face! Double time march!" The platoon jogged along the road to a turnoff and then up a steep hill. When they had gone half a mile up the hill, the sergeant barked, "Halt! About face! Double time march!" and they jogged back downhill to the road and on to the PT field, where a tall, well-built corporal standing on a raised platform led them through an hour of calisthenics. Then the platoon sergeant marched them to the mess hall where they filed in for a breakfast of pancakes, fried eggs, ham, grits, toast, and coffee. The sign above the servers read, "Take all you want, but eat all you take."

The next ten weeks was a series of marches, usually double-time, to and from various events: medical and dental exams, IQ and aptitude tests, and physical training and drill, mostly physical training and drill. The food was good and by the end of the training period Matilde had lost fifty pounds and looked like a different man. His six-foot frame now seemed taller, and his narrow waist and flat belly no longer served as refuge for his excess weight. For the first time in his life he looked like an athlete, a muscular, human machine.

The training was harder than Matilde had imagined. The drill instructors were tough, but they were black, and that made a difference. They did not call him boy, and they did not assume he was stupid. He would never march so much, so far, or so often as he did those next ten weeks.

During his last week of training each recruit was interviewed and his test scores evaluated to determine his next assignment. Matilde had scored so high in all his mental and aptitude tests as well as in physical coordination that his platoon sergeant gave him an application for Aviation Cadet Training School.

"Fill this out if you're interested. I think you can make it."

Being a pilot had never occurred to Matilde, and the thought sent a shiver through him. It felt good to be recognized, and after a few moments he began to like the idea. He submitted the application that day.

Two days later, Captain Oliver began the interview by asking him why he wanted to fly.

"I want to be an American, Sir, and I think I can be a good pilot."

"It's tough duty and dangerous. Takes steady nerves. Think you can handle it?"

"Yes, Sir," Matilde said with military crispness.

"Good. You'll begin with pre-flight training, then on to basic and then to advanced flight training. It'll be the hardest months you've ever spent. Good luck."

Matilde stood and saluted. "Thank you, Sir."

Captain Oliver saluted and then stuck out his hand. Matilde smiled and shook it. The following day he received orders for a one-week furlough, after which he was to report back to Tuskegee.

*

When Matilde inserted his key into the lock, Zoraida opened it and stared at him a moment before jumping up and hugging him. "*Ay*, Matilde. How good to see you." Then, after looking him over hungrily, she said, "I wouldn't have known you on the street. You look beautiful." She hugged him again.

Zoraida had prepared lunch for him, but could not tear herself away from him. Finally, after they had eaten, he spent the rest of the afternoon recounting every detail of basic training, even his first attempt at pushups and how embarrassed he was. "At the end I was doing twenty with no trouble."

"Where are they sending you?"

"Back to Alabama for more training. And then more until they make a pilot out of me."

She gasped. "You'll get killed."

"Not me. I won't take one up until I know what I'm doing. Don't worry. I'm older and wiser than the others. I'll be fine. Now what about you?"

Matilde could not calm her.

"Pretty good. I've made a few dollars delivering babies. You were right about keeping busy." Then she put her arms around him and said, "I'm glad you're back. I don't want you to go back."

*

No one recognized him when he walked into the Café Cubano. Domingo seemed confused and stared at Matilde when he asked for café solo. At the sound of his voice Jacinto turned. "Matilde!" he said and slapped him on the back. I didn't know you. You look like a real soldier with that short hair and uniform."

"I am, and I'm buying."

By that time every man in the place was standing around him poking at his muscles and laughing and joking with him. "I h-h-heard that you had en-en-en-enlisted," El Rubio said.

"That uniform looks good on you, Matilde," El Chulo said. "Maybe I'll get fitted for one."

"Bull," El Gordo said. "Not until they start making them out of silk."

His friends were as happy as they were startled to see Matilde looking so prosperous and healthy. Even his pace had quickened. With his higher energy level he moved easily, confidently.

"Where are they sending you?" Domingo asked.

"I have one week at home and then for the next few months I'll be back in Alabama training to become a pilot."

"You mean like in the picture shows?" Jacinto asked. The thought seemed unbelievable.

"That's right."

"Where will they send you?" Jacinto asked.

"Europe, I hope."

"You'll come back a hero, Matilde. Won't that be something?" El Gordo said.

After an hour Matilde stood to leave. "Where are you going?" Huesito asked. "I haven't bought the drinks yet."

"*Caballeros*, it's been two months since I saw my wife. You'll just have to wait until tomorrow. By the way, what about Pablo?"

"He comes by once in a while. He's doing well, I hear," Huesito said.

"I'm sure."

*

Besides the sale of a large tract near MacDill Field, Pablo and Marvin had sold several citrus groves they had been holding and bought others. Bargains could still be found even though demand had risen with the war.

The tiresome "I told you so" flying out of Pablo's mouth would have made Marvin angry if his profits had not been so good.

Sammy was in the fifth grade, startling his teachers with his mathematical talents. He had taught himself algebra and used it almost intuitively. His father had recently bought him an elementary calculus textbook, and the boy was studying it intensely. He spent three hours on it the first day before his mother made him put it down and come to supper. Within a week he was asking questions his father could not answer. It became an exciting challenge to learn something he could explain to his father.

Pablo came home one evening and found Sammy at the dining room table with his books and papers. "OK, Papa, work this one," he said, handing his father a word problem he had just solved. Pablo sat beside him with a blank sheet of paper and began while Sammy timed him on the kitchen clock."

When his father handed him the solution, Sammy looked it over. "Not bad, fifteen minutes. I did it in twelve." Then Pablo pretended to beat him up as they tussled on the floor until Pablo cried, "Uncle … uncle."

Having practiced the piano regularly since her year in Tallahassee, Consuelo arranged a recital at the Centro Asturiano to help sell war bonds. Admission would require the purchase of a twenty-five dollar war bond. It became a sell-out. She had also convinced Arthur Smith Music Company in downtown Tampa to provide a Steinway concert grand piano for the occasion. She hoped to repeat the performance at the Municipal Auditorium if the first went well.

But even during quiet times her home did not know tranquility. Ardor and intimacy had leaked out of their marriage. Pablo and Consuelo moved around each other quietly, as if under repulsive forces. Consuelo had lunch with Lizzie every Friday and telephoned Sara regularly, hoping to keep a semblance of normality. She enjoyed Sara's directness and honesty and confided in her as a sister. Pablo kept his cousin Benito at a distance, feeling he had outgrown him and had little in common with them. Marvin and Suzanne were their closest friends, and they often dined together.

Pablo stopped at the Café Cubano the evening Matilde returned from basic training. It was 10:30 and most of his friends had gone home. Only El Rubio was there, sitting in front of a beer. *"Hola Pablo.* Where have you b-been hi-hi-hiding?"

"Too much work. Where is everybody?"

"You missed Matilde. He left ju-u-ust a while ag-g-go."

"Coño! I'd sure like to see him."

"You should have be-e-en here earlier. What the h-h-h-hell are you doing here this late?"

"I had some business nearby and didn't want to go home without seeing my old friends."

"He'll b–b-b-be back tomorrow," El Rubio said. "He looks good. M-m-m-must have lost fifty p-p-pounds at least."

"What's he doing?"

"G-g-going to be a pi-pi-pi-ilot. Wants to see ac-ac-action."

"*Que cojones!*" Pablo said. After a few moments he said, "I'll see him tomorrow."

*

"Matilde's home," Pablo said.

"I know. Sara called. Did you see him?"

"No. I don't get it. An aviator! Must be crazy. What can he gain except getting killed?"

"Maybe he feels he owes it to his country."

"It's not his country."

"He probably sees it as an opportunity to do something worthwhile with his life."

"Maybe."

"Lots of men are joining."

"We have no business in Europe. Japan's different; they attacked us, but Germany didn't do anything to us," Pablo said.

"They want to take over the world."

"Propaganda."

"America's been good to us," she said.

"And ...?"

"Nothing." After a few moments she said, "Suzanne told me today that Marvin's thinking about joining. She's scared, but proud."

"They don't have kids. Look, Consuelo, I'm not a patriot; I'm a businessman and I'm going to make all I can now that things are better. Other guys want to fight ... fine. Lots of men say they want to join knowing they're too old. It's their way of claiming patriotism without actually joining. I'm beyond draft age and I know it."

"Don't you feel anything for your country? You're a citizen."

He just stared at her.

"Maybe I am falling for propaganda, Pablo. I don't really want you to go."

"Glad to hear it."

*

The following evening Pablo got to the Café Cubano early, hoping to catch Matilde. He drank a beer with El Rubio and Jacinto before Matilde arrived looking handsome and strong in his uniform. He held himself erect and moved with more agility than Pablo remembered. Pablo stuck out his hand; Matilde shook it vigorously and then embraced Pablo as if they were brothers. Matilde could not completely suppress the memory of Pablo's snubbing just months ago, but he talked with a great show of friendship and enjoyed regaling Pablo with his camp experiences. It was clear he had enjoyed the camaraderie of an army unit. Matilde did not mention that his unit was as segregated as the rest of American life. Besides, segregation did not bother him as it had earlier.

Matilde spent most of the evening describing Tuskeegee and what he would do during the next phase. "After that, I hope they send me to Europe where I can get some action and see the sights."

"That's swell, Matilde. You've got courage," Pablo said. "And when you get back, you'll have a good career."

"And I'll be an American citizen automatically."

"Terrific!" Pablo said. "Let's have a bottle of brandy, Domingo. We've got a lot to celebrate."

As he turned to find a chair at the table, Matilde heard a loud screeching under his foot. He had stepped on Osvaldo's tail. "*Pobrecito gato,*" he said, reaching down and picking up the cat. He sat at the table with Pablo, Jacinto, and El Rubio, holding and petting Osvaldo.

"Don't feel bad," Domingo said. "It isn't the first time his tail has found its way under a heavy foot. He's getting old. Reminds me of my grandfather. Lived to be ninety-nine. He could have bragged of living a century if he had died one year later, but he caught a cold, and it turned into pneumonia. We did all we could for him, gave him medicine and nursed him, but he died anyway. Actually, I didn't nurse him, my mother did. She was his daughter; you know how a girl loves her father. It's the same for a mother too, of course. Children always love their parents, don't they, Matilde?"

"I guess so. Anyway, I'm sorry for this poor cat."

Pablo was not listening; he was recalling an argument he had witnessed as a boy at supper. Don Ignacio was telling him how his father came to Cuba with the Spanish army, but later fought with the rebels. Don Ignacio

214

poured out the last of a bottle of brandy. 'Cuba is my country now,' Papá said, 'and Spain is in the wrong.' What a man!"

Doña Inez had interrupted: "I heard it differently: that he left Spain to escape military service, and later left the plantation to capture some escaped slaves, and on his way back he got into a fight with some Spanish soldiers who had captured a rebel village."

"That's not true. My father would not try to escape the army. He was hard to deal with, but very brave." Don Ignacio swigged down the last of the brandy. "And why shouldn't he go after excaped slaves? I would have done the same. I was there. I remember it."

"But he was a deserter who later refused not to take sides," doña Inez said.

"Yes, he helped some villagers whom the Spaniards were about to execute," Ignacio had said. "He was with the rebels."

"Only to get rid of Spanish taxes," doña Inez had said. "He was no patriot."

"You're mean and insensitive. I won't listen to another word against my father."

"You didn't like him too well when he was alive. Why do you defend him now?"

Pablo had trembled with fright wondering which was lying.

"You look stunned, Pablo. What's the matter?" Matilde asked.

"Poor defenseless creature."

"Never hurt nobody," Domingo said. "Catches mice when he can. He's getting pretty old. Has a hard time running after them, but he tries, poor thing."

As Domingo poured brandy for the four, Matilde said, "Don't forget, Pablo, you have a long drive home, amigo."

"I'm an adult. But you're right, I've got to be going. I'll see you again, Matilde."

*

The week blew past like a fresh breeze for Matilde until the day he had to leave for Alabama. Zoraida accompanied him to the train station, where they waited in the Colored waiting room, a large cavernous room separated from the White waiting room by a single door. The long, varnished benches along the walls and back-to back in the middle were moderately full of people waiting.

"Matilde, last night after you went to sleep, I threw the *caracoles*. I did not want to wake you, so I only turned on the kerosene lamp"

"You know how I feel about that."

"They never lie, *querido*."

"Uh-huh."

"Only one mouth faced up. That is *Okana Sode*: 'If there is nothing good, there is nothing bad.'"

"That's double-talk."

"Don't you see? It means you will return safely."

Just then a muffled voice over the loudspeaker announced the train to Jacksonville. At the boarding platform, hand in hand, they found Pablo and Consuelo.

"We couldn't let you go without saying goodbye," Pablo said, embracing Matilde. Consuelo embraced Zoraida, who asked about the little boy she had helped deliver. "He is very well and quite bright," Consuelo said. "He is in school already."

The train suddenly appeared with loud hissing and chugging. Within minutes the three were waving, tears streaming down Zoraida's cheeks, Matilde smiling through the coach window.

Matilde's situation fascinated Pablo, but not as much as Zoraida's. What will she do, he wondered ... a beautiful woman like her ... he had never understood why Matilde had enlisted, but he admired this cigar maker who had transformed himself into a warrior.

*

The base buzzed with excitement when Matilde reported for duty at the Tuskegee Army Air Field. Walking past a line of P-40 Warhawks he visualized himself inside the cockpit of the long-nosed fighting machine and shook his head wondering how such a heavy metallic object could get off the ground.

The Japanese had grasped the advantage in the Pacific, and things were not going well for American forces. The sergeant in charge of the orderly room seemed more serious than he had been the previous week. It was now early May and in the months since Pearl Harbor the Japanese had taken Wake Island, Guam, Hong Kong, Singapore, Indonesia, Burma, the Solomon Islands, and the Philippines. Their plan seemed to be to fortify a chain of islands from the Aleutians through Midway to Papua that would serve as a shield to protect their conquest of East Asia.

"You're assigned to Company B, Gomez. Stash your gear and report back immediately."

From there the training revved up. He sat through lectures and discussions about the theory of flight, the history of military aviation, and of the trainer aircraft he would be flying. Interspersing the lectures were physical training and more testing. Matilde drank in the information like a thirsty child on a hot afternoon. When he could find a free moment he would write to Zoraida about his latest adventures and accomplishments. Matilde had never worked so hard and had never been happier.

*

Consuelo felt as ready as she could be for her recital. Her program began with the Suite Espanol by the Cuban composer Ernesto Lecuona and ended with a medley of her own virtuoso arrangements of Columbia, The Gem of The Ocean and the Star Spangled Banner as a patriotic finale. Sammy listened to her practice sessions with admiration. Pablo especially liked her patriotic finale and had her play it for him over and over. Though he was not an enthusiastic classical music fan, he enjoyed watching her play. The way she hovered over the piano, undulating arms making long, curved movements, and then caressing the keys with delicate fingers or pounding out shattering chords, her back arching and straightening, her eyes moving to the ceiling and down to the keys, her hair swaying with each movement, all struck him as erotic. She seemed to be seducing the instrument, teasing out its voluptuous sounds. When she was finished and sat beside him on the sofa, he kissed her.

"You like it?"

"Very much, and you too. You're beautiful." After a few silent moments he said, "I wonder how Matilde's making out."

"I spoke with Sara; she saw Zoraida a few days ago. Says he is enthusiastic and happy."

"I just hope he comes home."

"The war seems to be going better since that battle in Midway," she said.

"We finally stopped them." He stopped a moment. "Consuelo, I've joined the Harbor Patrol."

"What's that?"

"A civilian outfit that patrols Tampa Bay at night. Looking for submarines, things like that."

"Full-time?"

"No, just twice a week. The problem is, it's all night."

"I'm glad. You'll feel better doing your part for the war effort."

"I think so."

16 – WAR TIME 1943

*

Soviet Pilots Fly American Planes
Against Nazi Horde

*

Civilians Want Unclean Tampa Cafés Posted

*

Job Freeze Hits All Tampans
No Worker May Change Jobs Without U.S. Permit

*

Greatest Air Offensive In Second Week
Blasts French Airfields in Daylight

*

Civilians To Get 16 Million More Pounds Of Butter

*

In March 1943 Matilde received his second lieutenant's commission. Instead of being shipped out immediately as the white squadrons were, the Tuskegee pilots were kept on base for continued training. Primed for action, these fresh pilots received no satisfactory answer when they asked why they were being kept there. Finally, after four months of waiting and training and flying simulated combat missions, the squadron was transferred to New York where they boarded a troop transport ship to North Africa. The ship, a converted luxury liner, carried so many soldiers that each was assigned one of three daily shifts for sleeping.

The Negro squadron's mission would be to escort convoys of allied ships transporting supplies and troops to Europe and North Africa. The Old World Matilde was so anxious to experience was vaporizing under the strategic Allied bombardment of Germany, France and Italy. In the meantime he was flying in and out of an airbase on the outskirts of a small town near Fez, Morocco. Until Matilde saw it, Africa had never occupied more than an incidental part of his consciousness and certainly not as his ancestral home.

On his first three-day pass he wandered into town. The sun-baked houses and buildings on the edge of the great desert evoked a dormant curiosity. The red-brown sand of the desert blended almost imperceptibly into the baked stone houses. Majestic date palms offered the only relief as they spread their fronds to the sky to cast grudging shade. But in spite of its burnt appearance, the town radiated serene beauty. He walked the dry streets recalling the green island of his childhood, where graceful rain was common. In the desert heat, he did not perspire. He knew it was because of the low humidity, but it might also be because the dry heat pacified him.

This was not the world of his black ancestors. That world was more than a thousand miles to the south, although a few Black Africans had drifted into the Arabic countries of North Africa. "So these are the Moors he had heard about, the people who conquered Spain and held it for centuries, the people who were the most enlightened in Europe at the time and who were now considered backward and ignorant."

He stopped for a beer at a terrace café tucked under a huge grape arbor that shaded half a dozen tables. One or two locals and a dozen American military men sat around small wooden tables enjoying their respite from the sun. The waiter, a thin, young, Black man of medium dark skin, spoke to him in English with sublime gentility. "I have heard much about America," he said. "That the streets are lined with gold, and water flows from springs in everyone's home, and people eat all they want."

"Not quite," Matilde said.

"It must be a glorious country where people are so rich and healthy."

"It's a good place, but you have to work hard to get rich," Matilde said. "And even then you don't always make it."

"I have always dreamed of visiting America. I would not want to live there because they say our people are not treated well. Is that true?"

"I'm afraid so."

The man took Matilde's order and walked to the bar. When he returned with the beer, Matilde stopped him.

"Are you from here?"

"I am Ethiopian. I came here to make my fortune. There is much more here. Also we are not treated well at home."

"What did you do in Ethiopia?"

"Worked on my father's farm. I left because it could not support so many. I have six brothers and two sisters. And you?"

"I made cigars in Florida."

"America is very beautiful, no?"

"Yes. Florida is flat and green and the winters are mild. Other parts of the country are mountainous and cold."

"Are there many Africans in America?"

"Yes, quite a few."

"I hope you win this war. The Italians have been bad. They invaded us and bombed and raped and took whatever they wanted. I am glad that you are pushing them out of Africa."

Matilde wondered what it must be like to have invaders in your country raping and stealing and disrupting your society. Then his thoughts went to the conflicts with Spaniards in Cuba. He was about to tell himself that that was different, but realized he could not say how exactly.

"Thank you," Matilde said. "We'll do our best."

After his beer and brief conversation with another American soldier at a nearby table, Matilde strolled through town looking at street vendors and their wares, not eating anything for fear of getting sick. He liked the people; they were much the same as people back home; only their appearance, clothes, and manners were different.

When he returned to the B.O.Q. and told his friends about the town and how much he liked it, one said, "Sure; it's home."

*

Back home, Americans huddled around their radios after supper for what had become a nightly ritual: listening to the evening news. The disembodied voices of H.V. Kaltenborn, Edward R. Murrow and Robert Trout invaded living rooms across the country with their characteristically taut deliveries. These home front celebrities introduced Americans to strange places: Bataan, Guadalcanal, Wake Island. And there were familiar ones too: Vichy and The Aleutian Islands. Also people at home were learning to live with rationing: gasoline, tires, and sugar. Because they used cars in their work, Pablo and Marvin qualified for C ration stickers on their windshields, which allowed them to buy all the gasoline they needed. Most people's cars carried <u>A</u> stickers, which limited them to three gallons per week.

But these were minor hardships that distracted people from more serious worries about sons and fathers whose lives were balanced on bayonet points on distant battlefields, and about brutal enemies who focused their destructive power from opposite poles of the earth. The war had gripped the soul of America. Overhead, bombers and smaller planes coming and leaving MacDill Field droned over Tampa, day and night, reminding all of the destructive power of war. Those sounds had worked their way among the customary sounds of nature. And through those sounds rose prayers of thanksgiving that the war was over there, not here.

But despite the worry, a feeling of exhilaration had swept across the land. After clinging onto the rim of the vast depression for a dozen years, people were slowly pulling themselves up onto firm ground. A spirit of national purpose and dedication had uprooted the dread of those terrible years. Unlike the faceless economic specter that had gripped the hearts and minds of Americans, the Nazis and Fascists were enemies they could see.

In their windows, mothers and wives hung small white banners framed in red with a blue star in the center for each son or husband in the service, a gold star if he had died. Front doors and windows all over America displayed these banners proudly. Of course, some, like Zoraida, feared such flags as bad omens. School children bought stamps they pasted into booklets to trade in for a twenty-five dollar war bond when they had accumulated $18.75 worth. They organized scrap metal drives, paper drives, and scrap rubber drives in neighborhoods all over the country. Boy Scout troops marched and drilled like soldiers in preparation for war.

Ybor City was no different. Most families could boast of at least one husband, son, cousin, or uncle in the armed forces. In spite of her feelings about America and her anger at her husband for volunteering, Zoraida admired his courage. As ardent a Marxist as ever, she knew the Axis menace had to be stopped.

Each Thursday Pablo and other volunteers would set off on their boats to cruise the port of Tampa Bay through the dark of night. He felt patriotic in his dark blue uniform, a revolver strapped to his side. Tuesdays nights were for Cynthia.

Spending hours each day on the road, his days had always been relatively free. The Harbor Patrol expanded that freedom into the night. His relationship with Cynthia cooled when Consuelo returned from Tallahassee, but Pablo would not end it. He felt he had invested too much in her house, her car, and her allowance to break it off before he was sure his marriage would work out. Consuelo's absence, after all, had driven him to Cynthia, the only woman with whom he could share his feelings. Consuelo had left without indicating when or even if she would return. Waiting with no end in sight was not the proper role for a man, he thought. Just thinking about Consuelo abandoning him was enough to drive him into a rage. Cynthia relieved those rages. He had not confided his affair to anyone, not even Marvin, having learned that ignorance was far simpler than explanation.

With Cynthia it was not love as it was with Consuelo, but Pablo enjoyed her company. Something about her crude, unfettered outlook excited him. With her he could talk, relax, be himself without pretense, for if she detected even a whiff of sham she would pounce mercilessly. She was a wall of reality on which he could lean. Being a realist, Cynthia understood Pablo better than he understood himself. She knew Consuelo was back, but that was not her problem.

*

When she had nothing to do, Zoraida watched the passing scene from a chair on the sidewalk outside the entrance to her apartment. It was just a few feet from Paco's barbershop where friends would stop to hear the latest news about Matilde. Whenever she received a letter she would take it down and read and reread it and show it to any friend who happened to pass. Matilde wrote often and at free moments, so his letters were often cryptic. She had one of his letters when Felipe, *el boletero*, stopped by.

"Want a number today?"

"I told you, I have promised Matilde no *bolita*, and I don't break my promises."

"I know, I know. How is our hero?"

She showed the letter. "It's short; here, I'll read it:

June 20, 1943

Dearest Zoraida,

We have just finished a long flight. (You know where.) It was a beautiful sight from 6,000 feet: ships of all sizes and types stretched out for miles like specks on the beautiful blue water. It was good to land though. I'm not where I wanted to be, but it is turning out better and more interesting. Will write more later.

My friends are terrific and dedicated to duty. I'm proud to serve with them. I'd trust my life to any of these men.

Got to report back now.
With all my love,
Lieutenant Matilde (ha, ha)

"*Que hombre!* You must worry."

"Yes, and if he gets killed, I'll never speak to him again." Zoraida laughed nervously. "He's a wonderful man, my Matilde."

"Flames are falling today," Felipe said, wiping his brow.

"I know; the temperature is 90, but no *bolita!*"

Felipe left laughing. Zoraida remained on her chair surveying the neighborhood: the Cuban Club across the street with its expansive terrace reminiscent of tropical Havana. Its Caribbean openness reminded her of home. Next to it, the two-story, red brick El Pasaje Hotel offered respite from the heat under its rounded, brick colonnade. It had served the famous and the common since the previous century. Across Ninth Avenue stood the magnificent Martinez-Ybor cigar factory, and across that, the *Bien Publico* Clinic. Between there and La Septima stood two restaurants, a Chinese laundry, and other stores and shops. Cars moved along Fourteenth Street in a never-ending parade, as did pedestrians. The odor of fried green plantains drifting from a vendor across the street lifted her mood on that sunny afternoon, as did the lively parade of people who stopped to chat. To the residents and patrons of the area, Zoraida soon became a fixture, sitting in that chair with her skirt pushed down between her knees and her legs spread, gasping for any breeze.

Zoraida deposited Matilde's allotment checks and what he sent home into a bank account that held more money than she had ever dreamed of. Seeing her sprouting fortune made her feel that she had already won the *bolita.* Soon she would be able to move back to their old neighborhood.

As she reread Matilde's letter, a man's voice interrupted her concentration: "*Hola, Linda.*"

Looking up, she saw El Chulo, young, handsome, and immaculately dressed. "*Hola. Como estás?*"

"How's my haircut?" he said, turning around.

"Paco's a good barber."

"You must be lonely after all these months."

"Not as lonely as Matilde."

"You can't tell about roaming soldiers." She looked at him squinting in disbelief. "Maybe you'd like a little comfort. A beautiful white woman like you so full of life shouldn't waste herself on this sidewalk."

"Why do you call me white?"

"*Mulata?* Even better."

"Your nickname fits you," she said.

"I appreciate a good looking woman, black or white, but especially the color of *café con leche*. And I know you need more from a man than words on a piece of paper."

Flashing a malicious smile, Zoraida stood and faced him. "I might do you the favor ..."

He moved toward her.

"... of not telling Matilde. But if you ever talk to me like that again, I will, and he'll smash you like the roach you are." Then she sat down and began to reread Matilde's letter.

As El Chulo walked away she heard him mumble, "<u>If</u> he comes back." Her heart pounded so hard she could not read.

*

Burke and Iglesias unloaded their MacDill Field property at an enormous profit. That brief investment had come from profits gained from the citrus land they had bought in the 1930s. Pablo's prediction had come true: their fortune was blooming. Now they began to look for large tracts northwest of Brandon, in the direction of Orlando. They worked together when they needed large amounts of cash for a big venture and independently at other times. Both of them succeeded beyond their expectations.

Pablo bought a house in Pas-A-Grille Beach at the southern tip of the Pinellas peninsula out-islands. It cost much more than any property he had ever bought, but he could well afford the luxury of a second home. On weekends and holidays he would take his family there to play in the sun and swim in the placid Gulf of Mexico. Consuelo loved the spacious house and its large screen porch. It was a typical beach house with large windows all around and a large patio in back with a brick barbecue. Typically, Sammy began begging at midweek, and by Friday morning his pleading was merciless.

Pablo considered taking Cynthia there, but too many Tampa people had houses nearby. When he could, under the pretense of a Harbor Patrol assignment or an overnight trip to scout out property, he would take her to one of the beaches farther north along the coast, St. Petersburg Beach or Treasure Island. They especially liked to go out in late afternoon when the beach was deserted, remove their swimsuits under water and cavort nude, usually ending in wild passion. In the evenings a local tavern provided drinks, dinner, and dancing. Pablo preferred dark taverns to the more upscale restaurants where he might be recognized, and Cynthia did not mind. They seemed more her element. He had never forgot his first embarrassing encounter in bed and delighted in holding out as long as he could to torment Cynthia. Sometimes they would bounce and tussle for over an hour, completely bathed in sweat with the gulf breeze caressing them. As enjoyable as those times were, they became feats of endurance that expressed little intimacy. Afterwards, to demonstrate his prowess, he would insist on a midnight stroll along the beach. On moonless nights, walking along the dark shoreline with only the sound of the waves to guide them, Cynthia would cling to him.

Never happy in the little house in Six Mile Creek, Cynthia filled these outings with complaints, as if the beach reminded her how much she was missing in her life of isolation. To Pablo her nagging expressed ingratitude. One afternoon, as they carried their bags into a motel, she began to complain. In a sudden rage he said, "OK, that's it. We're leaving."

"Why, Sugar?"

"I can't take this."

"Aw, come on, Sugar. We haven't spent the night yet and it's paid for."

"One more peep and we're gone."

"Don't get sore, Sugar. It's just a little boring out in the sticks."

"Not again?"

"Let's go for a swim. They ain't nobody in the water."

*

His family beach excursions were filled with swimming, fishing at the water's edge with Sammy or off the pier on the bay side and then cooking their catch over an outdoor fire in the patio. In the evening they read or listened to the radio. Like a little adult, Sammy stayed up late reading, so Pablo and Consuelo had little private time together. Pablo reveled in his dual life; he felt like two different people with different personalities, purposes, and goals. One indulged his hunger for thrills, danger and excitement, the other enjoyed calm family life. And with his business success, he could afford both. After all, he reasoned, I earn my money through astute planning and intelligent management, and I deserve to enjoy it.

With no hint of his duplicity, Consuelo was content if not thrilled with her home life. She, too, had organized a part of her life separate from her husband. Her successful recital at the Centro Asturiano had made people aware of her musical talent. And when she repeated the recital at the Municipal Auditorium, her fame spread. She had become an important fundraiser as an artist for the war effort.

*

It was mid-morning Thursday when Consuelo answered the telephone. "Tony! What a nice surprise! Where are you?"

"In Tampa. I left Tallahassee early this morning."

"How are you? What are you doing here?"

"I've been assigned to MacDill Field. May I come by and tell you in person?"

"Of course. Have lunch with us. Pablo was with the Harbor Patrol all night and he's still asleep. He'll be glad to see you too."

"OK. How do I get there? I'm on Florida and Buffalo Avenues."

When he had written down Consuelo's directions he said, "See you in an hour, I hope."

Consuelo immediately looked in her refrigerator to see what she had. "Ah, good, a chicken," she said aloud. "And baked potato and some okra. That should do it. Oh, and the makings for a salad."

About an hour later, she went into the bedroom and woke Pablo. "Get up. Tony Sekul will be here any minute."

"What does he want?" Pablo asked, rubbing his eyes.

"He's stationed at MacDill Field. Just wants to visit."

"Uh-huh." He rolled over and closed his eyes.

"Come on," tugging at his feet. "He'll be here soon."

"All right, all right." Throwing off the covers he sat on the side of the bed. "Don't expect me to be a perfect host after only four hours sleep."

"You'll be fine; now up."

*

Tony Sekul looked good in his army officer's uniform. Slightly over six feet tall and with a few thin streaks of gray in his thick black hair, he looked handsomer than she remembered.

"What a beautiful place, nestled in an orange grove. You can make music here," he said.

With large windows on two sides and comfortable wicker furniture, it was a typical Florida Cracker house. The view of orange trees through the windows and the vases of homegrown flowers scattered throughout the house gave the feeling of a tropical garden.

"Ah, the Chickering." He walked over to the piano and struck a few bass keys. "Play much?"

"Quite a bit. Two recitals this year. Nothing serious, just to sell war bonds. Did pretty well, too. Sit down; I'll call Pablo." She bumped into Pablo as he was walking out of the bedroom straightening his tie.

"Hi, Tony. Good to see you." They shook hands and stood facing one another for a few seconds. "So you've gone to war."

"Teaching got boring; the pay isn't bad and I get to stay in Florida, for a while anyway."

"Sit, both of you, while I put lunch on the table."

"I'm in the Harbor Patrol. We cruise around Tampa Bay at night in little boats. It's been boring so far, thank God," Pablo said, laughing.

"I hope I'm not putting you out, dropping in like this; just wanted to see how you two were getting along."

"Very well," Pablo said, suspecting a darker intent.

"How's Sammy?"

"Too bright for me. I can't keep up with him. He'll be home at 3:30."

"I have to report at four."

"That's too close," Pablo said.

"Come and get it," Consuelo said, obviously happy to see her old friend again. They sat down to fried chicken, mashed potatoes with gravy, string beans, steamed okra with tomatoes, and a salad. "My only concession to our ancestry is Cuban bread from the Segunda Central Bakery. We don't do without it."

"I haven't had food this good in a long time."

"When were you drafted, Tony?" Pablo asked.

"I wasn't."

"Enlisted! Wow!"

"I would've sooner, but tenure was too close."

"They're supposed to hire servicemen back," Pablo said.

"I didn't want to go through it again. How are you doing, Consuelo?"

"I'm thinking about taking on some students."

"When would you find the time?" Pablo asked. Then, turning to Tony, "I don't know how she does it all."

"We'll see," she said, frowning at Pablo.

"We miss you at FSCW. We haven't been able to find anybody to take your place. I'm glad you're going to teach."

Consuelo smiled and looked down at her plate.

"This is wonderful, Consuelo."

"She does everything well," Pablo said. "Sammy's her main preoccupation now."

227

"Does he still play?" Tony looked at Consuelo.

"Pop music mostly," Pablo said. "She has him on classical, but you know kids."

"That's normal; main thing is he's still interested. Consuelo's good with kids."

"Don't I know it?" Pablo said. "Do you have a music assignment?"

Tony laughed. "No such luck. I traded the piano for a bombardier's button. It's only one note, but it takes practice."

"Seen any action?"

"Not yet. Soon, I hope."

"What kind of plane will you be flying?" Pablo asked.

"B-17. I hope I can see some of Europe. I've never been interested in the East."

"We're hoping to visit Europe after the war," Pablo said.

"I'll tell you all about it when I get back."

"If you can see it from up there." Pablo smiled.

"How about some flan? Consuelo said.

"Sounds great!" Tony said. "You're wonderful, Consuelo."

"Yes she is," Pablo said.

"I'll bring some coffee." The way Tony's eyes drank her in made her blush.

"When do you ship out?" Pablo asked.

"Even if I knew I couldn't say."

"I hope this damn war ends soon."

Consuelo brought out the flan and served each a piece. Then she poured the coffee and milk. "You like it light, I believe."

"You remembered."

"I like it dark and hot," Pablo said.

A few minutes later when they had finished their dessert and coffee, Tony looked at his watch. "Holy cow! It's 2:35. Hate to run, but I'll keep in touch, Consuelo."

"Please do."

As the three walked to the front door, Pablo put out his hand and said, "The best of luck, Tony."

"You too, Pablo." Taking Consuelo by the shoulders, he kissed her on the cheek. "Take care, now."

"Goodbye, Tony," she said.

*

That Tuesday evening, as usual, Pablo left a little past seven wearing his uniform. "See you in the morning," he said. "Duty tonight."

"I hate these Harbor Patrol nights."

He brusquely pecked her cheek and left. Within minutes he and Cynthia were having a rum and coke in her small living room.

"What's the matter, Sugar?"

"Nothing, why?"

"The way you plopped on the sofa, like you're mad."

After he told her about Tony's visit, she took a drag on her cigarette and said, "So she likes the guy. What's so terrible about that?"

"I just don't like it."

"You kinda like me, don't you?"

"Damn it, don't make fun of this."

"Why not? What's good for the gander oughta be good for the goose. OK to keep a woman on the side, but you can't stand your wife even enjoying another man's visit. It's not like he was having her, for Christ sake."

"I've told you I'm tired of your arguing and nagging; just drop it."

"You know what I'm tired of? The double standard you macho men carry around." How do you think it makes me feel?"

"What do you have to do with it?"

Smashing her cigarette into the ashtray beside her, she said, "I'm stuck in this shithouse, all alone, out here in the sticks with no friends just so's you can come around whenever you wanna screw. This is worse than whorin'. At least back then I had friends."

"Nobody dragged you here."

"You're a real hard-ass, aren't you," she said, reaching for another cigarette.

"That does it. I've had enough of your insults."

"Insensitive bastard," she said as she held a match under the tip of the cigarette and sucked.

"What the hell do you want from me?"

"A little respect wouldn't hurt none."

"Respect? You cheap ..."

"Say it, you bastard! A cheap whore, just the kind of woman you need. Well this one ain't yours no more."

"I didn't mean it. The only reason you make me so mad is that I ... I guess ... I kind of love you."

"Up yours! The only thing you love's your dick. Now get out of my house."

"Your house?"

"Tomorrow it'll be yours again, but while I'm here, it's mine. Now get out!" She was yelling and crying. Pablo moved toward her to comfort her. When she felt his hands on her arms, she turned and hit him in the face as hard as she could and almost knocked him down. He thought something had broken. When he recovered, he said, "All right, but be out by tomorrow night."

Not wanting to face Consuelo after such a scene, Pablo drove to the Café Cubano. The sun had set and a light drizzle blurred his windshield, so he turned on the wiper. On the horizon he heard the rumble of thunder. As he drove down Seventh Avenue, the image of Cynthia yelling at him was chiseling into his brain. His conversation with himself pushed all else out of his mind: Ungrateful whore. It didn't involve her. Must've been brewing. She might have broken my jaw. He rubbed his face. Matilde said she was a whore, but what's wrong with it? All men do it. My father, everybody I know. Some don't admit it, like Matilde, but I'll bet he does too."

It was nine o'clock when he walked into the Café Cubano. With the rain, only El Gordo and Domingo were there, talking across the bar. Domingo seemed sad.

"What's the matter?" Pablo asked.

"Osvaldo's dead," he said, with profound sadness.

"The cat?" Pablo asked, smiling. "I thought it was somebody."

"Osvaldo was somebody. He was part of our family. He respected my wife and me as if we were cats too. He was human. Sometimes when I got too busy he would rub against my leg as if to say, 'take it easy.' Cats have their own way of talking. I knew what he meant. He treated me better than some of my own family. Like my cousin Machito: when I see him coming I know he wants something. Last month he came for some Cuban bread. I said, 'Why don't you go to the bakery?' You know what he said? Without any embarrassment he said, 'They charge too much. Besides, with my false teeth, I can't eat fresh bread. I have to eat stale bread.' When I told him they sell day old bread for one cent a loaf, he said, 'You have no heart.' That's nerve. Osvaldo never treated me like that. He always earned his keep. Just the day before he died he caught a mouse right here behind the counter and brought it to show me. I was sitting at a table in back with some customers that I don't know too well. He wanted me to know he could still work."

"Come now," El Gordo said. "You'll get another."

"There will never be another Osvaldo."

"How did he die?" Pablo asked.

"A car ran over him. Poor thing was thirteen years old. He was deaf and walked across La Septima without looking both ways. A car came down the street like a bullet and hit him. The *cabrón* didn't even stop. A man like that should be in jail."

"Three cognacs, Domingo," Pablo said, "We'll drink a toast to his memory."

"That's very good of you, Pablo," Domingo said. He reached for the bottle and three glasses.

"To Osvaldo, the most valiant cat in Ybor City," Pablo said, raising his glass.

When he had put down his glass, El Gordo said, "Did you hear about Matilde?"

"What?" Pablo said.

"Shot down a German bomber. Zoraida told me when I got my haircut this morning. He's flying a P-40, I think. She was scared and excited at the same time, poor thing."

"Then we'll drink a toast to Matilde," Pablo said. "I never figured him for a war hero. That takes real *cojones*."

At 11:30 Domingo said, through numb lips, "If I don't close up soon, Rosa will come down and kick you both out."

"It's early," Pablo said.

"He's right, Pablo," El Gordo said. "I'm glad I don't have to drive home."

"I don't mind," Pablo said.

"Nonsense," Domingo said. "You've had too much, and it's a terrible night. You can use the spare bed."

Remembering that Consuelo did not expect him until morning, Pablo said, "Sure Rosa won't mind?"

"Absolutely not. Call your wife," Domingo said, pointing to the telephone.

"No need. She'll figure it out."

*

The next morning Pablo stopped at Six Mile Creek to try to calm Cynthia. The car was there, but the house was locked, so he took out his key and went in. He found the dresser drawers partly open and empty. Everything that was his was still there. A scribbled note on the kitchen table under a saltshaker read:

Go to hell.
Cynthia

Pablo went through the house looking for anything of hers he could throw out, but she had left nothing. Finally he picked up the phone and called a locksmith in Ybor City. "I want the locks changed on my house in Six Mile Creek, front and back doors right away," he said.

"It'll take an hour."

"Get started and bill me as usual. I'll leave the key under the pot on the porch."

"OK to leave the new ones there?"

"No. I'll pick them up later."

Let's see the bitch try to get back in, he thought, as he got into his car.

It was nine-thirty when he got home, later than normal for a Harbor Patrol night. The sounds of clanging pots drew him to the kitchen, where Consuelo had laid them all on the table and was placing them in the cabinets. She seemed to be working furiously, angrily.

"It was miserable, rained all night," he said and sat down at the kitchen table.

When she turned to him her face told him she had not slept. Her hair was in disarray, and she was trembling visibly and in constant motion. "Major Knapp called last night after you left to tell you not to come Thursday." She was barely able to control herself.

"I don't know what happened. I arrived and one was there. Finally, I gave up and went to the Café Cubano. I had a few too many, and Domingo invited me to spend the night upstairs."

"Major Knapp also said you have no duty on Tuesdays."

"He must have me confused with someone else."

"A little later I got another call."

No response.

"It was a woman who said her name was Cynthia." Pablo started to speak, but Consuelo continued, "She said some things I couldn't believe at first until I started thinking." By this time she could barely keep her voice from cracking. "She said I should know where you are Tuesday nights and on those overnight trips."

Pablo sat frozen in his chair.

"I don't have to ask if it's true. Your face says it all."

"When you went to Tallahassee I couldn't stand the loneliness. I know it was wrong. I just needed someone."

Consuelo exploded. She swung a pan at him, he backed away, and it missed him. Throwing herself at him she pounded his face and chest and kicked his legs. "Get out of here. I don't ever want to see you again."

Pushing her back and holding her arms he said, "Please, Consuelo, I love you. She doesn't mean anything to me. You've got to believe me."

Her mouth filled with venom, she spit on him. "Get out! I'm sick of your lies and I'm sick of you."

Wiping his cheek with the palm of his hand, he said, "She's just trying to make trouble because I broke off with her."

"The poor, stupid woman loves you, you ... bastard!" Then running into the kitchen she screamed, "Get out! ... Out! ... Out!"

Pablo knew there would be no use talking to her in that state. Through the kitchen window, Consuelo watched his car disappear among the trees, not believing he had left without arguing. "What'll I do now?" she said aloud. "Maybe I shouldn't have been so angry."

She went outside and strode around the house shaking her head, looking for something, not knowing what. Entering through the back door, she sat in the kitchen with her cheeks in her fists. Her married life had been shaky from the start, but she never expected this. She knew Pablo loved her once. The whole episode felt incomprehensible, nightmarish. Walking to the bedroom she picked up her bible, but could not bring herself to open it. She fell back into bed and lay with her arm over her eyes. When the phone rang she realized she had slept. Running to the living room she picked up the receiver and heard a man's voice.

"Hello ... who?"

"I'm leaving in a few minutes; I wanted to say goodbye."

Trying desperately to comprehend, she said, "Oh ... Tony. Where?"

"I can't say and I don't have much time."

"I'm sorry. I'm terribly upset."

"What is it?"

"I wish we could talk. Please write."

"You bet I will. Say hello to Pablo and Sammy, and take care of yourself."

17 – WAR HEATS UP - 1944

*

Gestapo Starts New Wave Of French Terror

*

Romans Hear Guns As Allies Close In

*

De Valera Wins Irish Election

*

Nazi Sub Stops Refugee Liner;
Takes Two Yanks

*

It did not take long for Pablo to realize that Cynthia was right: Six Mile Creek was an outhouse. There was no place to relax in the claustrophobic living room. The kitchen reeked of rancid food. Every time he got into bed he felt the walls would smother him. It usually took four or five drinks to make him fall asleep. Then there was the constant blowing of the electric fan on the bedside table. It felt worse than the heat. But worst of all, everything reminded him of Cynthia. He avoided the place in the evenings, even if it meant eating a greasy hamburger at Frenchy's and going back to the office until he could no longer think clearly. When the thought of a hamburger was too revolting, he drove to the Café Cubano for a sandwich or soup and a few drinks. When they closed, he drove home if he could; otherwise, he spent the night with Domingo. Rosa didn't seem to mind; in fact, she enjoyed hosting a prosperous young man.

Pablo hated the house and Cynthia and everything about his life. Every time he stopped in on Sammy, Consuelo would leave them alone together, usually in the living room, but she always stayed where she could listen. She knew how much Pablo loved him and how well they got along, but, recalling doña Inez's badgering of Sammy, she could not trust Pablo with the boy.

During his last visit Pablo had taken Sammy for a walk in the grove. Consuelo followed close enough to see and hear them, pretending to tend the plants. As much as he resented her distrust, he never complained, but knew she felt no forgiveness. On the way home his mind churned with viscous imaginings: She's not the woman I knew. How could I have been so stupid, outsmarting myself like that? She can't really be worried about Sammy. Just wants to show me she doesn't trust me even with him. She probably wants me to stop seeing him, but I won't.

As soon as his father had driven off, Sammy sat beside his mother in the living room. She had an open book in her lap. "Why did Papa move?" he asked.

One can never be sure how much a child knows, especially one as smart as Sammy. She did not want to explain too much, but felt she had to be truthful. "We've had a disagreement, Sammy, and it's become too uncomfortable to be together."

"Can't you talk to him?"

"No, Sammy."

"What's the disagreement about?"

"That's private, Sammy."

"Is it about me?"

"Absolutely not. We both love you very much; we've never disagreed about anything concerning you."

"Does he have a girlfriend?"

"Please, Sammy. Don't ask any more questions. It has nothing to do with you." Consuelo looked down at her book to conceal her watery eyes.

"Don't cry, Mama. He'll come back."

*

Looking over his draft registration form, the clerk looked up. "You're not a U.S. citizen. You aren't required to register."

In his loose fitting, silk shirt and pleated trousers, his long black hair curled over his collar, El Chulo bent down and looked her in the eyes, flashed his charming smile, and said, "I know, but I'd like to anyway."

Blushing, she finished processing his application. He said nothing to his friends at work or at the Café Cubano.

Two months later at the Café Cubano he announced dramatically, "I've been drafted."

Huesito looked up from his coffee and said, "They can't do that. You're not a citizen."

After explaining, El Chulo said, "I'm going to look up that big mulatto and see what the hell he's really doing over there. I don't believe all his crap about flying. I bet he's just a grease monkey."

The following morning El Chulo left for Camp Blanding to take his induction physical. It was June 1943, but the heat and humidity felt like August. From Camp Blanding he went to Camp Campbell, Kentucky. No one heard from him until he came home at the end of basic training. On the last evening of his two-week furlough, he threw a party in the Café Cubano that lasted into the early morning. Jacinto had phoned Pablo about the party, and he showed up. El Chulo was the first to get drunk and the last to leave. Pablo left before midnight. He would have stayed on, but he had telephoned Consuelo to let her know where he was in case she needed him. His real reason was to show he was responsible.

"Go where you please," she had said.

Over the din Rosa's voice could be heard yelling at her husband about keeping the café open so late. Domingo smiled and, loudly enough for all to hear, said, "It's a special day when a friend leaves to fight in the war. I remember when my cousin Pedro went to fight in 1917. You remember, Rosa; Hortensia's son, the handsome one. You should see him now; he's bald and fat and looks like an old man. He was barely nineteen then. He had never been out of Tampa until the day he left for the Army. What a party they threw!"

As he spoke Rosa raised her arms in desperation and walked away, but he followed. "All his friends and relatives came to his house to see him off, and everybody brought whiskey. Of course, his mother never allowed liquor in her house. Well, that night there was enough to float the house away. She was mad, mad, but couldn't stop it. Every time she poured out a bottle through the kitchen window, someone would bring in another. They must have brought a dozen bottles. Anyway, Pedro got blind drunk. Hortensia was so embarrassed she didn't speak to him that whole evening. Of course, he was too drunk to notice. At seven in the morning the party ended when his friends drove him to the train station, carried him into the

train, and propped him up in his seat. They pinned his ticket to his lapel
so the conductor could see it. I wish I could have seen him when he woke
up trying to remember getting in the train. "

"*Mierda* is all that ever comes out of your mouth," Rosa said, and
continued to clean up and tend the bar, checking on the size of the drinks
and keeping track of how much they were consuming. Domingo smiled
and poured himself another.

El Chulo was assigned to an armored outfit, but would not say where
they were sending him. When everyone guessed Europe, he flashed his
noncommittal smile. The following Friday his outfit left for New York,
where they boarded an ocean liner that had been converted into a troop
ship. His destination, North Africa

*

El Café Cubano, still dingy and dark, had a surge of business when
both MacDill Field and Drew Field brought the Army Air Corps to Tampa.
However, the khaki flood stopped abruptly when the commanding officer
of MacDill Field declared Ybor City off-limits to military personnel.
A week later the police closed the whorehouses on Fifth Avenue and
elsewhere in Ybor City. When they disappeared, MacDill rescinded
the order, and suddenly La Septima overflowed with soldiers, many of
whom soon discovered the dingy charm of El Café Cubano. In addition to
soldiers and old regulars, shipyard workers on their way to and from their
shifts sought respite from war worries in a place where they could relax
and chat over a five-cent cup of coffee.

The place was usually too crowded for the old men to tie up a table
playing dominoes, though Domingo never complained. Domingo had
found a new cat, a white female called Esperanza. He fed her only enough
to keep her alive, hoping she would supplement her diet in a way useful
to him. Instead, she preferred to curl up under a chair and hiss and claw
at customer's trouser cuffs. Whenever he saw her doing this, Domingo
would chase her away with a broom to peals of laughter. It became one
of the rituals that fed the Café's popularity. During the busy hours Rosa
would come down to help. The large, gruff, Spanish-born woman had
little patience with men who dawdled their lives away drinking coffee and
telling stories.

Cigar makers always gathered at a table near the back of the Café to
trade gossip and news about the war and sometimes, to reminisce about
the old cigar strikes and depression days. Time and prosperity had gilded
the memories of those anxious days. In the world of pure memory the
Great Depression had become days of strength and idealism. They spoke

of the Depression like proud veterans of a virtuous war. Rosa had clearer memories. When anyone from that table called for a drink, she would invariably slam it down on the table, usually spilling some. She never apologized or cleaned up, apparently having forgotten that they had kept her in business through those times.

It was past ten o'clock when Jacinto rose to leave. "Don't you have a home, Pablo?" he asked, his hand on Pablo's shoulder.

"A man comes and goes as he pleases," Pablo said, calling for another beer. That night after everyone else had left, Domingo helped Pablo up the stairs. The small apartment was neat and clean with scrubbed pine floors and sparse, simple furniture and beige drapes over the windows. The living room opened to a broad balcony that overlooked La Septima.

"Hold him a minute while I fix his bed," she said.

"I'm sorry, Rosa, but I couldn't let him drive home."

"It's all right. I don't mind helping a man of his nobility." She passed her hand over his hair to straighten it. "Such a melancholy face."

"He seems pretty happy to me."

"That's because you're a stupid man. Men never see the feelings in other men's faces."

The following morning, after breaking his fast with buttered Cuban bread and dark café con leche, Pablo walked out on the balcony to look at the calm street in its morning yawn with cars honking and people walking to work. As usual he thanked Rosa and left two dollars on the living room table.

*

The August heat was smearing its face into the evening when Pablo skidded his Ford into Consuelo's driveway and stopped with a loud screech. He had left the Packard for Consuelo to use. Leaving the car door open he stumbled twice on a potted plant, and had to hold on to the railing to pull himself up the three steps to the porch. Since moving out he never used his house key and never entered unannounced. When Consuelo came to the door he was crouching, trying to poke the doorbell with his finger and missing.

"You're drunk."

"You're right. I want to see Sammy."

She stepped out and shut the door behind her, holding the screen door ajar. "I don't want him to see you like this."

"I won't hurt him."

"If you were sober, you'd understand."

"I'm going crazy, Consuelo."

"That's <u>her</u> problem."

"I haven't seen her, and I'm not looking. I need you." He was swaying.

"Go home." Before he could answer, she went in, and shut the door behind her.

"I won't go. It's my house and my money that's keeping you." He kept yelling and pounding on the door until it opened.

"Please, Pablo."

"Is that Papa?" Sammy asked, running to her.

She closed the door again and in a minute opened it. "All right, Pablo. She was holding the boy's hand, still standing behind the screen door.

"*Hola, Sammy.* How's school?"

"Fine, Papa. What's the matter? You all right?"

"I just wanted to say I'm proud of you, son." Then seeing the worry etching Sammy's face, he stepped back. "I'm sorry. I'll come back." Turning, he stumbled down the steps and into his car. He sat in the driver's seat a few seconds before starting the engine. Visually unanchored to the vertical, he saw the house and trees rotating; he was on a merry-go-round. When he looked out, Consuelo was standing by the car telling Sammy to stay in the house until she returned. Opening the window with great effort, Pablo looked at her and smiled.

"Move over."

"I can drive."

"Move over." She opened the door.

Awkwardly, he slid to the passenger's side and let his head fall back. Consuelo drove the old Ford sedan to Six Mile Creek and helped him out of the car and to his front door. Walking back out to the car she said, "Call me when you want the car."

"You were right, Consuelo," he said, as he stumbled and fell into the sofa, asleep.

The next morning he phoned at nine o'clock. "I'm sorry about yesterday."

"I'll be right over." He was standing on the porch when she drove the Packard into the long, rutted driveway. By the time she stopped, he was standing in the sun, dressed in a suit and tie, opening the door on the passenger side. "Was Sammy upset?"

She was at the street turning east onto Seventh Avenue before she answered. "Don't ever do that again. You can see him anytime you want, but not when you're like that."

"Consuelo, I've done a lot of thinking these past few days. I've screwed up my life pretty badly; I need a new start ..."

"Forget it," she said looking straight ahead.

"That's not what I was going to say. I've talked to Marvin about putting all my holdings in our names jointly, yours and mine."

"Not interested."

"Please let me finish. I'm enlisting in the Navy. That's why I came over yesterday, to tell you and Sammy. I made the mistake of stopping at the Café Cubano first."

"Very commendable. Good luck."

"Thanks. I have to report for my preliminary physical day after tomorrow and I'd like to see Sammy before I leave."

"Anytime. I hope you're doing it for the right reason."

"I don't blame you for doubting."

Relenting, she said, "I hope it works out, Pablo. With your talent you could do great things."

Pablo looked at her as citrus trees rushed past on the narrow road. He tried to remember if anyone had ever told him that. He had an urge to put his arm around her, but he knew it would revolt her. Instead, he smiled. "Thanks. I'd like to live up to that opinion."

As they turned into the driveway, Consuelo faced him. "Sammy's in school. If you want to see him today, come after 3:30. And stay for supper."

"I'll see Sammy, but supper would be too uncomfortable for you."

"I know how you love him and how good you've been with him. It's for him, not for you or me. Be here by four." She handed him the keys to the Ford.

*

Pablo could not remember a hotter August. Even the two large, electric fans did not help. The cavernous room in the Hillsborough County Health Department was full of young men in various states of undress waiting in several lines. He had done it all before just days ago for his Navy physical. Two doctors and three nurses were leading them through their dawdling routine, their first step in the Army enlistment process. Someone had told him that no one ever failed the Army exam. He spent most of the morning in the low-ceilinged room where acrid perspiration permeated the smoke-filled air. Some of the men were talking and joking; others were silent and grim. When Pablo dressed and reached the head of the last line, he sat opposite the doctor. The doctor looked up from Pablo's open file and uttered the same words the Navy doctor had used three days ago: "You have a heart murmur, young man. You're unfit for military service. Sorry."

"What about a noncombatant job?"

"Sorry. You'll just have to do your part as a civilian."

This was the last straw, Pablo thought, as he walked out of the large building onto Tampa Street in the noon sun. Down the street was the Marine recruiting station, but he knew they would not take him. She'll never believe me, he said to himself. Never aware of a heart problem he doubted the doctors. He had never been athletic or done heavy work, but he felt fine. A heart murmur? he said aloud. Remembering how he had ridiculed Matilde for enlisting, he shook his head as he opened his car door. His natural inclination was to say to hell with it and go on with his life, but his empty life was what he wanted to escape. He was not sure why he wanted it so badly. As he drove he wondered: am I escaping, or is it to prove something to Consuelo? I can't say it's to save the world from a tyrant. I'm not a patriot. It's not my fight.

It was strange that Marvin had also been rejected; perhaps it was an omen that their business was important after all, and that he could do his part that way.

*

Sitting on her front porch, Zoraida smiled thinking of that dingy apartment, though she missed the activity of 14th Street. With Matilde's most recent letter on her lap she reread it and imagined his voice:

August 6, 1943
Dearest Zoraida,

North Africa is beautiful and dramatic. From the air the desert seems to cover the entire earth. Villages look like dots on a massive blanket at high altitudes. The locals are very friendly. I still haven't found anyone who speaks Spanish, though.

I'm writing this from the cockpit of my P-40. We're on alert and have to stay in our planes in case we're called out on short notice. It's a little cramped, but I have nothing else to do except think of you.

We've got the best pilots in the Air Force. And the ground crews broke down and rebuilt those old P-40 engines so many times back in Tuskegee that we never have engine failures. It was disgusting the way the Air Force kept us so long out of combat. We should have been here months ago. My buddies think they were afraid we would look too good and the white generals would see that black men can do everything whites can. The military is as segregated as the rest of America, but we're showing them. We might win two wars at the same time.

We're escorting bombers now. We keep the German fighters off
during bombing runs. We haven't seen much action. I guess the Germans
are losing and don't want to take risks defending the Italians. We haven't
lost any men or planes.

On one run some of our men got a bomber out of big trouble with some
Kraut fighters. When the bomber crew got back to the base, they looked
up the fighter pilots to thank them. When they saw our guys were black,
they just turned and walked away. Didn't even say thanks. Nice guys!

Don't worry, we're having a blast. Keep writing.
Love,
Matilde

P.S. When I think of you on the porch reading my letters, I want to fly
to you and cover your entire body with kisses.

Zoraida still enjoyed sharing his letters with her neighbors. She wanted
them to know the kind of man he was. Many of the Cubans she knew in
Ybor City were serving, but none were officers much less fighter pilots.
"He's an officer in the Army Air Force," she would say, pronouncing the
words clearly, and with feeling. She did not talk about the discrimination,
only about Matilde's heroism.

Matilde's unit helped escort bombers and ships, but he and his fellow
pilots also strafed ground targets in Italy. In one of those strafing runs
their target was a train carrying troops and provisions. In the briefing the
captain had said, "It's essential to keep those troops and munitions from
reaching their base in northern Italy." It was their first ground mission, and
the men were ready to show what they could do. The crowded briefing
room shook with cheering when they heard the order.

Matilde was the first to spot the train. "Target at two o'clock," he
yelled into the radio. The formation made a slight right turn and headed
down. Fixing the rear of the train in their sights, he and the other four P-40
pilots let go their volleys and watched with fascination as the hits moved
up along the train to the engine. In a blinding flash the engine exploded
and deafening cheers came through the earphones as he pulled out of his
dive and climbed into the blue. Looking back they saw the derailed cars
piled into stacks with flames leaping through the smoke. At the debriefing,
the squadron cheered when they saw the film of the action.

Later, he and a few friends went for a drink at the officers club. After
a long silence, Matilde said, "I've never felt so much in control. I felt like
God up there."

"True, Mat. But the Krauts have a different idea."

"That's their problem."

They sat at a table apart from the rest, but after a while two white captains walked to their table. When Matilde and his friends looked up, one of the white officers said, "Congratulations, gentlemen. You Tuskegee men are real marksmen."

"Thanks, captain," Matilde said. "Buy you a drink?"

They pulled out chairs and sat. "Sorry, men," the captain said. "But the drinks are on us."

*

It was a little past noon in late September when Consuelo jogged into the living room to answer the phone. "This is Marvin. I haven't seen Pablo all week."

"Me neither."

"May I come by?"

"Sure."

A few minutes later Marvin drove into her driveway and hopped up the steps to the porch. Consuelo escorted him into the living room. "Something wrong?"

"I'm worried about Pablo."

"He moved out two months ago," she said, anger welling in her eyes.

"I know. He told me about it when I asked why he was driving that old Ford."

"He left me the Packard."

"You must be lonely out here."

"I've always been a city girl, but I fill my days. It's only bad in the evenings, after supper, when Sammy goes to bed and the silence takes over. Sometimes, when I'm trying to sleep, I pray for the crickets to fill the stillness." She started to cry; Marvin sat quiet. After a few moments she continued: "My father spent four weeks with me, trying to talk me into take him back, but ... Then he tried to convince me to return to Cuba. I won't do that to Sammy. He's better off here. He's doing well in school, and his teachers like him."

"You have good instincts, Consuelo. I wish I could say the same for Pablo."

"There's no point in secrecy," she said, standing. "Come into the kitchen." Even with all the windows open there was not the slightest breeze. The mass of air hung heavy around them. The table was in the center of the nearly square kitchen. She cut three lemons in half and squeezed them into a pitcher. As she opened the refrigerator to take out ice cubes, she spat out some of Pablo's lies, his sleazy financial deals, and finally his latest scene. As she filled the pitcher with water from the faucet and added ice cubes, she told about the morning Cynthia and Major Knapp called. By now she was seething with rage. After stirring the mixture, she poured Marvin a glass of lemonade and pushed the sugar bowl toward him. Then she filled her glass and sat across from him, completely drained.

"No more. Maybe in Cuba in another generation, but not me, not here, not now."

Marvin knew about Pablo's business deals and knew he and Consuelo had separated. Now he knew more than he wanted to know. "Want me to talk to him?"

"Do what you like; I don't want him back."

"Is he still with the Harbor Patrol?"

"Apparently not. Major Knapp has called several times."

"Is he with the other woman?"

"Who knows?"

*

Less than an hour later Marvin drove down the ruts that led to Pablo's house in Six Mile Creek. The sudden afternoon shower was so heavy he could barely see through the windshield. Parking in the driveway close to the porch, he waited a few minutes for the rain to slack off and finally decided to go in. He opened the car door, held out the umbrella, and opened it. Then he crouched under it and hopped to the porch where he stopped to shake out the umbrella. Pushing the doorbell, he waited, knowing Pablo was home because his Ford was sticking out of the barn. He pushed the button again and waited. Finally he pounded on the door and waited and pounded again. Hearing nothing he turned the doorknob and found it unlocked. He took a tentative step and called again. Hearing nothing, he walked in to find the living room littered with clothes, dishes, two unmatched shoes, and a sock. Two empty brandy bottles lay on their sides on the floor next to one of the shoes. One of the bottles was lying in a puddle on the linoleum. In the kitchen he found the same chaos: four bottles on the table, two empty and two partially full and an almost empty glass with a cigarette butt floating in it. Five or six roaches scampered around the dirty dishes in the sink and among the crumbs and pieces of ham and cheese on the countertop. In the bedroom he found Pablo on his stomach with his head under a pillow and one bare foot sticking out from under the sheet. The rain made such a racket on the metal roof that Pablo could not have heard Marvin's knocking.

Marvin shook Pablo's shoulder, "Wake up."

Without opening his eyes Pablo moved out from under the pillow and turned to the opposite direction.

"It's Marvin. Wake up."

"No," Pablo said without opening his eyes.

"Come on. Wake up," he said, tugging at his shoulder.

Pablo looked up and said, "What do you want?"

"Where the hell have you been? Nobody's seen you in days."

"Nowhere. I don't feel good."

"No wonder. Come on; let's have some coffee."

"I don't want any. Leave me alone."

Marvin pulled him by the arm to a sitting position and moved his legs so they hung over the side of the bed. "Let's go." As he raised Pablo to his feet, he realized how dark the room was even with the window shade rolled up. The heavy raindrops were pelting the windows and the roof like bullets. Marvin felt as if he were under enemy attack. The scene out the window looked like a hurricane. Kicking aside the stray clothes on the floor, they walked out of the bedroom.

As Pablo walked barefoot toward the kitchen in his shorts, Marvin could see that his legs were wobbly. "Sit down. I'll fix the coffee. Have you eaten?"

"I don't know; yesterday or the day before. I don't know."

"You're crazy."

"Pipe down!"

"All right. Let's see what's in the refrigerator." Pulling out some ham, a half tomato, and some stale bread, he put them on the counter and moved a pot of cold coffee to the burner. Then he put two slices of bread in the toaster. "You look like hell."

"I feel like hell."

"I saw Consuelo this morning. I'm really sorry, but I must admit, I don't blame her."

"So now you know," Pablo said, holding his head in his hands at the kitchen table.

"Enough to understand some things. Do you know what a jerk you are, losing her ... and Sammy?"

"Doesn't involve him."

"Like hell it doesn't."

"I see him almost every day."

"It's been over a week."

"Damn! I didn't realize ..."

As they talked, Marvin put together the sandwich and poured coffee into two cups. "Here," he said, pushing the sandwich toward Pablo.

"Come to the point."

"This drama has played long enough. I want you back. We have business to tend to."

"You don't need me."

"I hate to admit it, Pablo, but I do."

"Well, I don't care."

"You'd better start caring before you lose it all."

"I already have."

"If you'll just can the self-pity, you might figure out how to get it back."

"Too late."

"Not necessarily. Consuelo's mad, but I sensed something."

Pablo pushed the sandwich aside. "I don't want this," he said, reaching for the almost empty brandy bottle.

"If you pour that drink, I'm leaving."

Grasping the neck of the bottle, Pablo looked into Marvin's eyes and put the bottle down. "I know you're trying to help, but it's too late." He picked up the sandwich and took a bite.

"We can talk after you wake up. Now go shower and shave. After work, you're going to see Sammy, so try to look human."

For the next hour Marvin led Pablo around his house like a pawn on a chessboard. When they emerged, Pablo had removed a five-day beard and was wearing a white dress shirt, dark tie, black trousers, and a gray plaid jacket. The rain had let up, so he followed Marvin's car east on Seventh Avenue toward Brandon.

*

Zoraida jumped when she heard the mailman at the front door. Dropping what she was doing, she ran to the porch. The letter was from Matilde:

September 30, 1943

Dearest Zoraida,

We are finally in Europe. We flew into Licata, Sicily day before yesterday. The weather is cool and dry. We haven't seen much of the country from the ground yet, but it looks beautiful from the air. Its green fields and mountains are a relief after the African desert. We're still strafing and escorting bombers. The Germans don't seem anxious to defend this part of Italy, so we haven't seen much action. It's cool and very beautiful. Our BOQ is big and the boys are friendly.

I have to attend a briefing in a few minutes and want to get this letter off, so I'll sign off with all my love,

Matilde

Zoraida sat in the rocker and reread the letter. Seeing Mrs. Puglisi walk by, Zoraida called her and talked nearly an hour about Matilde and Sicily and his bravery and how he loves flying. She then handed Mrs. Puglisi his letter.

That evening she walked to the Café Cubano to share her letter with Matilde's friends. The sight of such a stunning woman in that male institution brought silence as heads turned. Spotting Jacinto, she walked to his table and asked if she could sit down.

Jacinto stood and held a chair for her.

Hearing her story told in deep, mellow, dramatic tones, others moved to her table, men enthralled by her voluptuous presence and the drama she unfolded. When she finished her story and answered questions, she rose as dramatically as she had entered. Seeming to float out the café like an apparition, she opened the door without looking back and disappeared.

Domingo walked to their table and said, "I didn't even offer her something to drink. I feel terrible."

"That's because you were drooling so much your brain was out of gear," Jacinto said, laughing.

"The wife of such a good friend, and I ignored her like that," Domingo said. "I did that to my mother's cousin once and she never let me forget it. It was her cousin Osvaldo; we named our cat after him. I hadn't seen him for a long time because he was living in Havana at the time. He walked in here and asked for a drink. I served it to him and before I could talk with him I got busy with other customers. Soon I forgot he was there. It was a very busy time of day, lunchtime, I think. Anyway, he sat at a table in back by himself and I forgot about him. Well ..."

"*Vamos*, Domingo. We've all heard it," Jacinto said. Bring me a *café solo*."

"Me, too," El Gordo said, still thinking about the apparition who had just vanished. "How did that big mulatto get such a woman?"

Almost speechless, Huesito said, "She's beautiful!"

"Matilde will c-c-come out of this b-b-b-better than he went in," El Rubio said. "He's be a ve-ve-veteran, a ci-ci-ci-citizen, and he'll have that woman to co-co-come home to."

"If he comes back," Jacinto said.

*

With Marvin's support Pablo was working every day and seemed to be trying to stifle his problems with work, searching out properties, scouring want ads, calling prospective bankers and other investors who might be looking for attractive deals. Nearly every afternoon, on his way home, he would stop in to see Sammy. Those visits were the highlight of Pablo's days.

By early November the heat had finally dissipated. Pablo drove off with Sammy, but did not tell him what they were going to do. At the edge of a large lake, Pablo took a shovel and a coffee can out of the car and walked, shovel across his shoulder, to a dark, damp spot under a sprawling oak. With his foot he drove the shovel into the ground and turned over a chunk of black sod. Sammy looked with wide eyes at the wiggling worms, trying to burrow back into the dirt.

"Wow, worms!" Sammy said.

"Right!" Pablo scooped them up and dropped them into the empty coffee can. With a full can of worms he led Sammy to a boat at the dock, lifted him in, and pushed off.

"Here's your pole," he said, lifting two bamboo poles from the bottom of the boat. "We're going to catch supper."

Pablo rowed out to a bank across the lake where the plant life was thick along the water's edge, and a large live oak hung over the water.

"This is the spot," he said with authority.

Dropping their lines into the water, they waited. Sammy stared into the depths where the line disappeared. Suddenly his line jerked his pole down. He looked to his father, who nodded to play the fish himself. Soon Sammy had it alongside. Pablo dipped a net in and plucked the fish out. The small bream looked gigantic to Sammy. Before long Sammy hooked a medium size bass.

It had turned dark when they got home. Sammy held up his fishes for his mother to see.

"That's wonderful, Sammy. Are you going to clean them?" his mother asked.

"I'll show him how," Pablo said, taking the fishes into the kitchen. "Watch carefully. You're going to be doing this from now on," scraping the scales off with a knife until the skin was smooth. He cut off the head and cut a slit from head to tail along the bottom to remove the innards. Sammy's face was contorted when his father lifted out the guts, but he never took his eyes off the operation. "Understand?"

"Yes, Papa."

Consuelo stayed in the background. She avoided Pablo as much as she could without making Sammy feel uncomfortable. By December the routine was so set and stable, that she began to relax and invited Pablo to supper. Sammy could not stop smiling all evening. The conversation was friendly and noncommittal. Sammy did much of the talking about school and how much his teachers liked him and how much he liked math. His parents were delighted, each realizing that Sammy was the glue that held them together.

At the end of the evening, Pablo kissed Sammy and said, "See you tomorrow," and smiled his thanks to Consuelo.

Soon he was eating supper with Consuelo and Sammy several evenings each week.

Christmas Eve Consuelo invited Marvin and Suzanne for a typical Cuban, *Noche Buena* supper, with a small pig baked in La Segunda Central Bakery, as was the custom in Ybor City. The bakery cooked thirty-eight pigs for their customers that Christmas Eve.

January 15, 1944
Dearest Zoraida,

Things are going well. Our squadron has moved to this base near Naples where we have joined a White fighter group. Last month when the new Black fighter squadron came to Sicily, they told horror stories about discrimination in Detroit. In the city as well as the base. They were not allowed in the Officers' Club, the PX, or anywhere the white officers went. There were some protests and even some fighting on the base, but the base commander would not change the rules. We're good enough to fight, but not to eat or drink with. What bastards! It's different here in our new base. We fly missions together, have briefings together, go to the Officers' Club and the movies and everywhere else we want. The new guys can't believe it after what they went through back home. Who can understand?

Somebody found posters all over town warning Italian women not to associate with Negro soldiers because Negroes are inferior human beings who live in America among their own. The posters threatened that machine guns would cut down the prostitute who sells the honor of her race, and that there will be revenge upon her and her black son when this crime has been brought to light. The Italian government denied responsibility. The Chief of Staff of the Mediterranean Theater ordered an investigation and found that an American colonel and two enlisted men had put up the signs in Italian. Anyway, we don't go into town anymore. It's not worth it. You can never tell what will happen.

Besides these stupidities, things are good for me. On one day last November our squadron flew nine missions! Not bad.

Will write again soon.

Love,
Matilde

P.S. I'm glad you went to the Café Cubano.

*

The BOQ was a large room for two with lavatory, closets, desks, and large windows with a view of the mountains beyond the landing field. The austere, temporary buildings were set up in days and could be taken down as quickly. The men of the Negro squadron shared the officers club with white officers but not living quarters, but that seemed normal and certainly better than any Air Force base they had seen.

The morning sun cut through the cool February air and Naples beckoned.

"Come on, Mat. We're wasting time," Edwin Pitt said. Lieutenant Pitt had joined the squadron one month after having his wings pinned on at Tuskegee. The twenty-two-year-old was lean, bright, and still excited about flying combat missions. Except for a brief visit with relatives in Florida and his training in Tuskegee, Edwin had never been out of Washington, D.C. Now, after a dozen dog fights, he was a combat veteran.

"I can't get over that skirmish. Five German planes in five minutes!"

"It was great!" Matilde said. "Tough about Bruce, though."

"Yeah. Wish I had gotten to know him better," Edwin said. "Anyway, we've got three day passes. Let's go."

"I want to write some letters and relax."

"It's a sin to stay on base with a pass in your pocket."

"There's nothing in town except sexy women, liquor, sidewalk cafes, beautiful scenery, and wonderful weather. Nothing to get excited about," Matilde said.

"How did I end up with such a sad sack for a roommate?"

"Have fun." Matilde picked up his copy of Stars And Stripes and stretched out in his sack.

"What's the matter, Mat?"

"Nothing. I like it here."

"It felt great to knock out those Krauts; now it's time to celebrate. This is not my idea of high living. Italian girls don't care what color we are. All they see is our uniforms and the color of our money."

"Sounds great, Ed. Have fun."

"How come the crap at Selfridge Field didn't piss you off?"

"It did, but there's no problem here."

"We're fighting two wars, Mat."

250

"What was the name of that college you attended?"

"Howard University. What's that got to do with anything?"

"You enlisted a year after you graduated?"

"Right."

"And what did you do that year?"

"I told you; I helped my father in his hardware store," Edwin was losing patience.

"I fought my own war for ten years before I enlisted. You may have read about the depression. And the bigotry you talk about pushed me deeper into poverty. I could barely support my wife."

"I'm sorry, Mat, but we can't just take whatever they hand us."

"I send home most of my salary so we'll have something to start with when I get home. My wife is back in a house like the one we left before we hit bottom. She doesn't have to live in the roach-infested hole anymore like she did when I was the nigger janitor in the Cuban Club. Now we're both living well and my only gripe is she's there and I'm here. Aside from that, I feel like I've died and gone to heaven."

"I know I had it easy, but times are changing. What should we do?"

"Show what we're made of. We're flying with the best of them. Things are bound to change when they see that. We'll go home to a different country, Ed. What we do here will show we're men and not invisible flunkies. Raising hell won't get us a damn thing but clubs on the head."

"All right, all right. I give up. Sure you won't go into town?"

"Give me a minute."

*

After an hour walking through narrow streets, browsing store windows, visiting wine stores, and commenting on every Italian girl that passed, Edwin and Matilde finally came to rest at a sidewalk café opposite a church whose piazza teemed with people. With glasses of brandy before them they summed up the morning's work: the enticing Italian women, the sights, the local wines.

Suddenly Edwin stopped and stared into the distance. "What will you do when you get home, Mat?"

"I'm not sure. I've been thinking about learning a new trade, but I'm not sure what."

"Congress is talking of paying veterans to go to college. I read it in Stars And Stripes."

"I was thirteen when I left school."

"That's no problem, Mat; not with your brains."

"It would be nice. What about you?"

"I've got a girl waiting. We're going to get married."

"Pretty, huh?"

"Pearl's a beauty," Edwin said. "Puts these Italian lovelies to shame."

"Then what are you looking for?"

"Not looking for, just looking."

Matilde dropped some change on the table and said, "Come on, let's see Naples."

Returning to their BOQ that evening at eleven o'clock, they were surprised to see so many men out.

"What's going on?" Edwin asked one of the ground crew men outside their BOQ.

"The major's called a briefing for 0600. Sounds like something big."

At 0559 the pilots were waiting in the briefing room when the major walked in.

"Gentlemen, we are about to embark on the most concentrated bombing raid yet," he said.

A cheer went up.

When he quieted the men down, he continued: "Our target is Monte Cassino, but this time we're going to level it. Nothing is to be left standing, including the Blessed Monastery, which up to now has been out of bounds."

A murmur spread around the room.

"According to intelligence, the Germans are using it as a storage facility."

Within half an hour they were in their planes and revving their engines.

*

February 21, 1944

Querida Zoraida,

This has been quite a week! We just returned from a bombing raid on Monte Cassino. They told us it was the most concentrated bombing of a limited area in history. We even bombed the monastery. The Germans and Italians had it full of explosives. You should have seen the fireworks when we hit it.

I'm so tired I can hardly move, but it was great. Edwin, my new roommate, is a good pilot and has *cojones*.

I'll write again after I get some sleep. If I'm lucky I'll dream of you and that mysterious smile that drives me crazy. I can't wait to hold you.

All my love,
Matilde

P.S. I just woke up and feel much better. Did I tell you Edwin is from Washington, D.C? He told me his parents were raised in the Scrub in Tampa. They moved north before Edwin was born. They said anything was better than the Scrub. His father started a hardware business and has done well. Edwin graduated from Howard University. He's a very intelligent and educated young man. You'd like him, Zoraida. He thinks I should go to college when I get home. Stars And Stripes had a story about Congress helping veterans go to school. Nutty idea, isn't it?

March 1, 1944
Querido Matilde,
Sounds like they're working you hard. Be careful, my love, not to get so tired that you don't function well. I shouldn't lecture you, but I worry. You understand.

Dearest, I think college would be wonderful. With your intelligence you could have a good career. It never occurred to me before, but yes. There's a Negro college in Tallahassee called, I believe, Florida A and M. Consuelo Iglesias went to college in the same town. I'll ask her about it. Anyway, I know you will do well, and with government help and our savings we'll have no trouble. What an opportunity! There's nothing nutty about it.

All my love,
Zoraida

*

Marvin was not sure he was doing the right thing and almost changed his mind at the last minute, but he was already in her driveway. It was a cold, clear, sunny, March morning as he shut off the engine and sat a minute thinking. Shivering in his old Notre Dame parka, he knocked on her door and kept hopping around on the porch. Consuelo was surprised to see him and wondered if anything had happened to Pablo. Marvin's demeanor did not communicate an emergency, however, and she asked him in.

"I've never been so cold," she said. "Must be in the twenties. I've been trying to practice, but my fingers won't cooperate. How about some coffee?"

"Thanks."

"If you're looking for Pablo I don't know where he is," she said.

"I know. He left the office a while ago. Driving to Lakeland to look at some property."

She looked at him passively, as if waiting for a revelation.

"We've been working pretty close the past few months. He's changed, Consuelo. I don't know what did it, but something's happened."

"Uh-huh."

"He's working harder than ever."

"What do you want, Marvin?"

"Darn it, Consuelo, I'd like to see you together again."

"It wouldn't work. I don't trust him, and I won't follow him around, spying on him."

"I could be wrong, but I don't think it would be like that."

"People don't change."

"He's not ruthless the way he used to be. It's hard to put my finger on it; he's just different."

"Was this his idea?"

"No. I've talked with him though. He says there's no way he could convince you."

"He's right."

"You two have a lot going; and there's Sammy."

"Sammy's why I have him to supper. It's important for a boy to be with his father. It's not for Pablo."

Marvin felt the hardness in her voice. It was an edge of Consuelo he had not felt. "Want me to leave?"

"No. I appreciate what you're trying to do, but you don't know the whole story and I don't want to go into it. There are things he can't change." Tears filled her eyes and she turned away.

"I've probably meddled enough," he said, but after a few moments he continued. "Marriage is never easy. We've have had our problems. Suzanne wanted children right away. I wanted to wait. Finally, when we began to try, nothing happened. She thought she'd waited too long, that she'd had a short fertility period. She blamed me, and there was nothing I could do. It still hangs over us."

"That's an act of God, Marvin. What separates Pablo and me is an act of stupidity at best and utter egoism at worst."

"I guess what I'm trying to say is that sometimes you have to live with a bitter memory. It might even be an unforgivable one, but it may be better than living apart. For what it's worth, I think he truly regrets what he did."

"Why?"

"I don't know. I just think things are possible now that weren't possible a year ago. Maybe waking out of that five-day binge opened his eyes."

"Thanks, Marvin. It means a lot to have friends like you and Suzanne. If it's meant to be … we'll see."

After saying her nightly prayer before the figure of the Virgin Mary, Consuelo sat before the mirror of her vanity dresser and stared at her features in the glass. Grey had begun to invade her brown hair, and the tracks of tiny wrinkles had formed at the edges of her eyes. Moving down to her nose and lips, examining every detail, she tried to imagine the face of her slave ancestor and wondered how much she had passed down into that visage in the mirror. I always thought I was pretty, she thought. But I'm ugly. She turned off the lamp and went to bed.

*

It was too hot to fish, but Pablo took Sammy out anyway. They had been bobbing in the lazy heat for nearly two hours when Pablo suggested they give up for the day.

"I've got it," he said as he rowed back to the dock. "We'll buy one at the fish camp on the way home and tell Mama we caught it."

"Yeah! It would be fun to fool her."

His answer stabbed Pablo as he realized it was another deception. "On second thought, it's not good to lie, Sammy."

"OK." Sammy was obviously disappointed. "I never told you, Papa, but it really made me mad that you and Mama lied to me about Santa Claus."

"All parents do that."

"I figured it was a joke on me."

"I'm sorry you saw it that way, Sammy. It wasn't a joke; it was a little lie that seemed worth telling when we saw how happy you got, waiting for the fat old man to come down the chimney. We thought you enjoyed it."

After a few moments Sammy said, "Maybe it wasn't such a bad lie." Then he put his arm on his father's shoulder as they drove home on the country road. With the windows open and the wind blowing their hair in all directions, they were both smiling as the car turned into the driveway.

During supper Sammy told his mother about their plan to buy a fish. She smiled at Pablo, but he could see that the story made her uneasy. After supper she asked Sammy to go to his room and finish his homework. When he left, she asked Pablo to come with her to the back porch. Though it was dark and the invisible mosquitoes were making their aerial runs, she sat in one of the rockers and he sat in the other. "I visited Sara and Benito yesterday evening after supper."

"How are they?"

"Fine. The wholesale grocery business is booming."

Pablo wondered why she took him outside, but he had something he wanted to say. "I saw somebody yesterday evening too."

"Who?"

"Cynthia. I was on my way to El Café Cubano. I wasn't looking for her and tried to avoid her, but she stopped me on the sidewalk."

Obviously angry, Consuelo said, "I was driving down La Septima and saw you. I thought it might be her." Trying to control herself, she added, "You're still together, I suppose."

"No. She wanted to apologize for calling you that day. She said it was very mean."

"What did you say?"

"I thanked her for doing me a great favor."

"Am I supposed to understand that?"

"For doing what I should have done. I was too much of a coward to break it off and tell you about it. I was too used to lying. I always tried to avoid the truth. Any lie was better. The truth is I had an affair with her and let her use that house, and lent her a car, and gave her money. I thought it was what a man was supposed to do. I was wrong."

"Thanks."

After a few moments he said, "Did you want to talk about something?"

"I enjoyed hearing Sammy tell about buying the fish and about Santa Claus. You handled it well."

Pablo smiled and looked out into the darkness.

"You'll come for supper tomorrow, won't you?"

"I'd love to."

18 – THE WAR'S OVER - 1944-1945

*

Yanks And Brits Enter Rome

*

Big Federal Tax Cut Predicted

*

County Taxes Up 25 Percent

*

Allies Parade Military Might Through Berlin

*

The white frame church stood about a quarter mile from the Iglesias home along the narrow road that led to Route 60. Sammy walked along a trail near the road. With socks pulled high over laced-up riding pants and a World War I-vintage, wide-brimmed felt hat, Sammy had barely swallowed his supper when he ran out of the house. Carrying the Boy Scout Handbook he had carefully read, he dreamed of exploring and of making a fire without matches and surviving in the woods by eating rattlesnake meat. Huge live oaks sprawled generously over the church's front yard with a large, open area in back. With pews for about forty and tall, clear windows along both sides, the church presented a homey, inviting place for Sunday worshipers. On cold or rainy evenings the Boy Scouts met in a back room that had several chairs and a small table for the scoutmaster. In good weather they met outside on the ground. The meeting would usually end with the older boys telling ghost stories about their haunted camp.

On this late April afternoon Mr. Lawrence, in his mid-thirties and wearing his scoutmaster uniform, introduced Mr. Smith to the troop. This rugged-looking, fiftyish man wearing a crew cut, khaki shirt, tie, and trousers, and fatigue jacket could have walked out of a movie set. Back straight and emitting confidence, he immediately drew their respect. Mr. Lawrence introduced Mr. Smith as a World War I veteran.

The sun had dropped into the oaks behind the open area, and cool dampness pushed away the dying daylight, but weather would not stop the old veteran. When Mr. Lawrence turned on the outside floodlights, Mr. Smith began: "Ten-hut! Now stretch out your left arm and touch the man's shoulder beside you and push away to the left until he's at arm's length. Like this. Keep your head and eyes right and make the line straight." When the shoving and straightening and stifled giggles ended, Mr. Smith said, "For--ward, Harch!" and they all started walking. From the side, their legs looked like flailing rubber appendages.

"No, no!" he yelled. "Halt! When I give the order to march, step out with your left foot and stay in step. I'll count."

The sun had set and the boys were perspiring an hour later, when Mr. Smith dismissed them and they all ran into the church. "What do you think, Mr. Smith?" Lawrence asked, as they walked back in.

"You can't expect a miracle the first time. They'll get the hang of it."

"I think they had a good time," Lawrence said.

"They won't when they have to do it for real."

*

Sammy burst in: "I'm home, Mama. Guess what: Mr. Lawrence invited a war veteran to drill us. We marched, did about face, to the rear march, and all that stuff. Look, I'll show you." After going through his motions, Sammy went on. "Alfred couldn't get it; couldn't keep in step for anything. The other boys did good; like me."

Consuelo smiled through Sammy's litany, but thought of friends and acquaintances in the military. "That's fine, Sammy. How about your homework?"

"Did it all at school, and Mrs. Graham didn't give me any extra. I want to finish that library book, though."

"OK. Into the shower and then to bed." While Sammy was showering, she called Pablo in Six Mile Creek. Lying in bed reading the Wall Street Journal, he picked up the phone on the third ring.

"Glad I caught you. It's the Boy Scouts. They've got them drilling like soldiers."

"What's wrong with that?"

"I don't like it. He's a child."

"How did he like it?"

"Loved it, but ..."

"That's what boys do, Consuelo. Don't worry. The war can't last much longer."

"You don't know that."

"Let him enjoy it. It'll make him feel like he's doing his part."

"I guess you're right. Hope I didn't bother you."

"Not at all."

"And thanks."

"Thanks for asking. By the way, great supper last night."

Pablo had been working hard, making lots of money, having supper with Sammy and Consuelo most evenings, and staying home nights. Maybe ... maybe, he thought. And she called for advice; good. Glad I was home.

The next afternoon, after Consuelo had picked up the supper dishes and Sammy had left to shower, Pablo asked her why they had not used their beach house.

"I don't want to interfere with your social life."

"I'm not using it."

"It's silly, just Sammy and me. Or were you thinking of going too?"

"I wasn't thinking of anything, but there's plenty of room. I'd stay out of your way. I'd love to take Sammy fishing." Then after a few moments, "Just a thought."

"He'd like that."

"Good. How's next weekend?"

"Why not?"

"OK. Well, I ought to get going."

"Why don't you stay a while and tell me what you and Marvin have been up to. Any new projects?"

"You sure?"

Consuelo nodded, put on the coffee, and began washing the dishes. Pablo remained at the table, bringing her up to date on his business and chatting, all the while aroused, as she picked up each plate, bent over, scraped it into the garbage can, and then, with rhythmic motions, scrubbed it. He loved the voluptuous dance. They soon carried their demitasses to the living room, both feeling they did not want to destroy the mood.

259

Two hours later he had exhausted the pretense for staying, he kissed Sammy goodnight and put him to bed. "It really is time to go now. Thanks for everything. It's been a long time."

"I enjoyed it too. Good night."

*

Edwin had finished shaving and dressing before Matilde opened his eyes. It was Matilde's first uninterrupted sleep in a week.

"Aren't you going for breakfast?" Edwin asked.

"In a while," Matilde said, reaching for some paper and an Italian travel book to write on. As always, his first words were, "Dearest Zoraida." Looking at his watch he realized he had an hour to get breakfast and report for duty. He had been through some hair-raising dogfights during his bomber escort runs, and his squadron had not lost any men or planes. Even excitement becomes routine, he thought.

The sun shone brightly into his BOQ, and the ancient city of Cerola sparkled in the distance. Lying in bed in his skivvies with a pillow propping his head up, he wrote:

May 2, 1944
Querida Zoraida,

We've had some real excitement this week. We have been reassigned to a bigger Fighter Group in Cerola, Italy. Two weeks ago one of the top officers said we had made a magnificent showing during our flights in the past month. Our next assignment will be to support ground troops and knock out enemy supply lines. They want to destroy the German war machine, including industries, energy reserves, and transportation systems. It sounds tough, but we have a very good safety record.

I have counted the days since I saw you last and wish for the day when we can dance again and end up in each other's arms.
With all my love,
Matilde

The letter threw Zoraida into a panic. Even after praying fervently to Saint Barbara, she could not sleep that night thinking about Matilde's plane being shot down or blown up in mid-air. The war seemed more intense the closer the Allies got to Germany. The thought of Matilde being the last casualty of that terrible war was too much to bear. She immediately wrote to warn him of her fears and that he should do whatever he could to avoid those terribly close combat situations. "Don't be a hero," she pleaded. But when she had finished the letter and read it over, she crumpled it and threw it into the trash. He shouldn't worry about me, she thought. He might get jittery and have an accident.

The next morning, sitting at her kitchen table, she wrote another letter:

May 13, 1944
Querido Matilde,
Your letter frightened me, but I know you are doing what you must and with your usual care. I can't wait for this terrible war to end and for you to come back to me.

Please know that I love you more than I am able to say, so listen only to my heart. Be careful. I cannot wait to see you again.
With all my love,
Zoraida

A day passed before she could tell her friends. Soon, however, when she had come to terms with the danger he faced every day, she wanted to talk about it and walked to El Café Cubano again. It was a warm May evening, and she felt good strolling past neighbors and familiar stores, greeting everyone she knew. With all the service men lined up along the bar and most tables occupied, she stood at the door for a moment looking for a familiar face. Domingo hurried to her and led her to a back table.

"None of the regulars are here," he said. "Only soldiers."

"I just wanted to tell Matilde's friends the latest news."

"Please sit here. I'll call Rosa. We want to hear everything."

He hurried to the rear of the café and yelled up the stairs, "Rosa, come down." Then he returned. "What may I bring you?"

"Nothing. I can't stay long."

"Nonsense. You can't come here without eating something. I'll bring you some *café con leche* and a guava turnover."

Before she could object he had scampered behind the bar. The soldiers had all turned to admire the shapely woman who lit up the dreary café. Wearing a clinging dress and low-heeled shoes with no stockings, her loose, easy stride drew every eye. Only Rosa's acerbic presence deterred anyone from approaching her table. When Domingo returned with the coffee and guava pastry, he sat down. "How is our hero?"

"His squadron got a commendation for their work and bravery. They have seen much action."

"I knew it," Domingo said as he stood. "Attention, everybody," he shouted in his crumpled English. "A good friend of this café, Lieutenant

Matilde Gómez, is a fighter pilot and a war hero. I am treating everybody to whatever they are drinking."

"*Este hombre está loco!*" Rosa said, slapping her hand on the table. "There must be thirty soldiers here."

"Matilde's lucky to have friends like you and Domingo," Zoraida said.

Finishing her coffee and pastry, she stood to leave, but Domingo would not let her go. "Please stay. I'd like to hear more about Matilde. What will he do when he comes home?"

Leading her back to the table he asked Rosa to finish pouring the drinks for the rest of the customers at the bar. "I'll gladly pour out our day's profit," she grumbled.

When Zoraida told him Matilde was thinking about college, he said, "Can a grown man do that?"

"I'm not sure, but he thinks so."

"No one deserves it more. He could learn a good trade in college; better than making cigars. The industry is dying. The only big factory left is Hav-A-Tampa, and they hire mostly women and no Latinos. Jacinto and a few other old timers work at small, two or three-man shops, but it's not like the old days. Matilde is very intelligent. He will do well."

"Thank you, Domingo. I'll tell him I spoke with you. He likes me to keep his friends informed. By the way, how is that other friend who enlisted? The one they call El Chulo?"

"Nobody hasn't heard nothing. His whole family is in Cuba. One of these days he'll surprise us."

"I really must be going. Thank you for all your kind attentions." As she passed by the bar, she said, "*Adiós, Rosa.*"

"*Adiós, guapa.*"

As she walked through the door, a very fat man entered and nearly ran into her. "I'm sorry, Zoraida. I didn't see you.

"No harm done, Felipe. How have you been?"

"Fine. The *bolita* business is booming now that people have money. Still not playing?"

"Not until Matilde comes home."

*

The weather was warm in mid May, but the gulf water was still cold. Even Sammy would not venture in, so they fished off the pier. The pelicans fascinated Sammy as they dived for fish. They would climb and then head straight down into the water like a Kamikazi dive-bomber. He wished he could spot fish as well as they could, noticing that the pelicans always emerged from the water facing the opposite direction: they had turned 180 degrees under water. He asked his father why they did that, but Pablo did not know. Sammy pondered that question every time he saw a pelican dive.

Early mornings and late afternoons would find Sammy and his father at the pier. And nearly always they brought fish home. When it was time for bed, each person went to one of the three bedrooms. The arrangement was awkward for everyone, but no one would raise the issue, least of all, Pablo.

On their last evening, Consuelo prepared the beautiful sea trout Sammy had caught that afternoon. "This is wonderful," Pablo said. "I don't know if it's because Sammy caught it or because his mother baked it."

"Thanks," she said.

"Thank you, Papa."

When they had finished their supper and the wine, Sammy said, "I brought some homework that's due tomorrow. Why don't you all go for a walk on the beach?"

"How about it, Consuelo?"

"OK. I'll do the dishes later or tomorrow."

"I'll help," Pablo said.

*

The water felt invigorating on their bare feet. Though the sun had long disappeared below the horizon, the beach was bright with the full moon sprinkling its silver over the restless water. With the deep sky above them and sand shifting beneath their bare feet with every step, they walked slowly, comforted by the sound of slapping waves. They did not speak, but memories and thoughts bounced around like prickly balls in each one's head, each conversing with the person who used to be, for in many ways they were not the same people that had walked Varadero beach fourteen years earlier. They were now suspended in a universe that echoed with all the words and songs that human beings had ever spoken and sung since the beginning of time. They walked as if they had walked forever, stumbling occasionally, but striving to move elegantly, slowly, splashing when a wave lapped their feet. Pablo, being taller, walked on the water's edge. Climbing in the sky, the moon's glow made the sand silvery.

"I love this place," Pablo said.

"Yes, but it's chilly." Consuelo bundled her arms around her sides.

"May I?" he said, moving closer and putting his arm around her shoulder. She neither answered nor pulled away.

"It's been a long time," she said, snuggling into his warmth.

263

"I wish I could change that."

"I always believed people don't change," she said.

"I like to think I am who I was meant to be. That other person was living a nightmare, a fool trying to be something he wasn't."

"I'd love to believe that."

"You've made me believe it. We've been in love all our lives. You could not have loved the person I was. You might think I'm playing with words, but I believe I'm the man you knew long ago. That other person was lost, but he's found his way back."

Consuelo came closer and put her head on his chest, still walking. "God help me, but I love you, Pablo. I have never loved anyone else."

He stopped and turned to her. "Nor have I, *querida*." When his lips came near hers, he paused. After their lips met and they kissed for the first time in months, they turned and continued walking side by side as if they would walk to the end of the earth.

The next morning at breakfast, Consuelo said, "Sammy, when we get home Papa's going to move back with us if that's all right with you."

Sammy ran to his father and hugged him. Then he hugged his mother.

*

On June 6, 1944 the Allies launched upon the shores of Normandy in northern France the largest invasion force ever assembled. The invasion had been planned for over a year and was launched from England with American, British, and Canadian troops. The mind staggers under the thought of 1,200 fighting ships, 10,000 airplanes, 4,000 landing craft, 800 transport ships, and hundreds of amphibious and other special purpose tanks, all intent on putting 156,000 troops on the shores of Normandy. About one of every six men in the invasion force was airborne, either parachuting in or conveyed by gliders; the rest came by ship and landing craft. The invasion began before dawn, and by nightfall large beachheads had been secured on all five landing areas. The curtain had risen on the final act of the war in Europe. The Normandy Invasion was also the bloodiest battle of the war. Men died by the thousands, some before they could leave their landing crafts, some in the bloody water trying to reach shore, and many on blood-soaked soil. Those who made it alive were ready to begin the long march to Berlin.

June 27, 1944
Dearest Zoraida,

We are moving fast these days. We're back on the west coast for a while at least. At our rest camp we have a beautiful view of Mount Vesuvius. After the war I want to bring you here to feel its glory and its history. There is a small hotel I have passed many times. It's on the beach. You will love it. By now you probably know more about the big invasion than we do. All we hear is that it was the biggest in history and that many died, but we have the Germans on the run. I'm fine. We are still escorting bombers into Germany. We've seen plenty of action, but we haven't lost a single bomber. We're also bombing targets in northern Italy. We'll soon be flying P-51s. They're faster and have a longer range than the P-40s. Our fighter squadron has lost very few men.

Let me know if you've heard anything about the racial unrest in Selfridge Field near Detroit. Some black officers are being court marshaled for protesting the segregation of the officers club. I have no details, but it sounds ridiculous. My friends here think the public doesn't know.

My life has never been so exciting, but I miss you very much. Keep writing.
All my love,
Matilde

Zoraida had not heard about the racial disturbance or about a court marshal. Nor had any of her friends. Angry at the suppression of news about an important incident, she walked to *La Tradución*, a Spanish language newspaper in Ybor City. After being passed from person to person, she finally found a reporter named Juan Font who sounded interested. It was a small room with other reporters and workers walking around and talking. She sat across from Font at his desk.

"My husband is in Italy. He wrote me about racial problems at an Air Force base in Detroit, but I haven't seen anything about it."

"It's news to me, *Señora* Gómez. Fill me in: what happened, when, and who was involved." Juan Font took out a writing pad and pencil.

"All I know is that Negro officers protested when they were not allowed in an officers club. Now they're facing a court marshal."

When he had finished writing, he said, "*Muchas gracias*. I will investigate. Leave me your phone number, and I will get back."

A week passed and she saw nothing in the paper. The radio carried nothing about the incident. She began to wonder if Matilde had been misinformed. After two weeks she called Juan Font. "I still haven't seen anything in the paper."

"The American newspapers don't know anything. I called the commanding officer at Selfridge Field, and they were not helpful. His adjutant told me we should concentrate on defeating our enemies and not on stirring up trouble in the military. He said there was a problem, but they're handling it. They don't want to agitate the troops or the public. Frankly, I agree."

"But if it happened, it's news, and it's important. Negroes are being denied their rights while they're fighting for their country."

"Thanks for your concern, *Señora* Gómez. If anything we can print comes out, I promise you'll see it."

Zoraida did not know whether to tell Matilde or just forget it. But unable to convince herself, she mentioned it in her next letter, saying that since she had no details she could not insist. "After all," she said, "maybe it was exaggerated." She could not put it out of her mind, however. Through her Marxist lens, it had become another example of exploitation, and of the worst kind: They're being excluded from the white world that put them into the line of fire. One day, she thought, will come retribution.

*

Following the Normandy invasion, the Allies moved with speed and determination across Northern France and into Belgium. By late autumn, however, they had lost momentum. On December 16, 1944, with bad weather hampering Allied aircraft, the German 5th and 6th Panzer Armies attacked the Allied forces in the hilly, mountainous Ardennes region of southern Belgium, apparently intent on retaking the port of Antwerp.

During the late fall and early winter months, Matilde's squadron was out almost every day escorting bombers to German oil production targets. They targeted oil fields in Romania, Austria, Czechoslovakia, and Germany itself with success and few losses.

The BOQ was littered with pilots lounging after days of flying, strafing, and dive-bombing. For the first time in weeks they had some time to themselves. Matilde was taking an afternoon siesta when Edwin burst in. "Have you heard? The Germans have broken through the Allied lines."

"What? Where?" Matilde was trying to understand the shouting in the middle of his dream.

"Belgium. Everybody's supposed to report to the squadron. All leaves are cancelled."

Matilde's squadron attended a briefing that afternoon. Their assignment was to continue to pound at German war production. "We'll be hitting targets as far away as Poland and into Germany itself," the major said.

By early January they were striking installations in France and southern Germany almost daily. The Battle of the Bulge, as the German offensive was called, continued with intense fighting for nearly a month. But trying to maintain an inadequate supply line in the face of Allied determination, the Germans were running out of steam. On January 3 the American 1st Army launched its counteroffensive and by January 16, had pushed the enemy back. The Germans had lost more than the battle; they had depleted their dwindling resources in a last desperate attempt to drive the Allies off the European continent.

In March 1945 the Germans unveiled their new jet fighters, the Messerschmitt 262. By that time the Allison engine of P-51s had been replaced by Rolls Royce Merlin engines. Still, with a speed 100 miles per hour faster than the modified P-51s and more devastating gun and bomb capability, the German jet fighters posed a serious threat. After a few encounters, however, the American pilots discovered that, in spite of their advantages, the jet fighter was not as maneuverable as the American planes and had a range of only forty-five minutes. Our pilots worked out a plan to use the jet's disadvantages to overcome their speed advantage. They would use deflection shots, catching the jet fighters as they climbed vertically through the bomber formation.

On March 24 the squadron embarked on one of its most dangerous missions to date, a bombing mission to Berlin with P-51 escorts for a round trip of 1,600 miles. They encountered little resistance on the way, but when they arrived over Berlin the German jet fighters appeared. Within minutes and employing their new strategy the escort P-51s they had shot down three jets and disabled two and had lost no bombers. On the way back, Matilde noticed that Edwin's plane had some bullet holes near the cockpit. He radioed Edwin. "Are you OK?"

"I've been hit."

"Can you make it back?"

"I think so. Stay close."

Matilde stayed on Edwin's wing the entire trip home and radioed ahead for help. When they landed at their base in Italy, Matilde ran to Edwin's plane and found him slumped over in the cockpit with blood on his left sleeve. The waiting medics rushed him to the hospital.

After waiting an hour outside the operating room, Matilde stood when the doctor came out.

"He's fine, Lieutenant. We had to do a little reconstruction. That's what took so long."

"Is he going home?"

"Oh no. He'll be flying again in a few weeks."

Matilde was both happy and sorry. He returned to his room and showered, then sat down to write to Zoraida.

March 25, 1945
Querida Zoraida,

We just returned from our longest mission to date. We bombed the hell out of Berlin. You've probably heard about it on the news. It was spectacular. We shot down several German jets and lost none of ours. A German fighter got on Edwin's tail before Edwin could see him. By the time I got there the German had fired shots into his plane. Edwin was wounded in one arm, but he was able to fly back and he'll be back in the cockpit in a week or two. Before the German could fire again, I nailed him. He made a beautiful fireball when he hit the ground. Don't worry about me. I can see in all directions at once.

I just wanted to alert you to this strike. Listen to the news; I think it was important.

With all my love,
Matilde

P.S. I'll write when I can. Have to go to a briefing.

She had always worried about Matilde, but now, with Edwin's combat-inflicted wound, she was frantic. Not wanting to write when she was so worried, she waited and prayed to Saint Barbara. That evening she went to the Café Cubano hoping Matilde's friends would cheer her up.

A sea of khaki churned La Septima. Soldiers sloshed in and out of stores and cafés and restaurants and bars like massive waves. The news of the Nazis on the run had pushed spirits to a new high.

Zoraida had to push her way into the Café Cubano. Both Domingo and Rosa were working the bar and waiting tables. With no unoccupied tables, she walked to the bar and asked for *café con leche*.

"*Hola, Zoraida. Como estás?*" Rosa asked.

"Very well. I just had a letter from Matilde and had to see you. It seems I picked a bad time, though."

"Nonsense. Jacinto's back there with El Rubio. They'll be glad to see you," Domingo said.

He pointed them out and Zoraida made her way to their table.

"Please sit down, Zoraida," Jacinto said, holding a chair for her. "What do you hear from your famous husband?"

"Matilde's fine. He wrote to say they just returned from bombing Berlin. It must have been a big operation. He seemed happy. One of his friends was hurt, but not seriously. Matilde shot down the German who shot his friend."

"*Coño!*" El Rubio said. "Oh, excuse me, Zoraida,"

"The street is jumping," Zoraida said. "What's happened?"

"Maybe the news about the bombing of Berlin," Jacinto said. "People are excited."

"Too b-bad ab-about . . ." El Rubio stopped abruptly when Jacinto kicked him under the table.

"What?" Zoraida said.

"Nothing. El Rubio was just about to say that it's too bad Matilde isn't here to enjoy the good times. We were just talking about him."

"Please tell me. If you don't, I won't sleep."

After staring angrily at El Rubio, Jacinto spoke. "Domingo got a letter from El Chulo's father in Cuba. He was killed during the Battle of the Bulge."

Maintaining her poise, tears began to run down Zoraida's cheeks. "Please go on."

"It's so ironic. He made it through the Normandy Invasion, ran onto the beach, dug in, and went on during the bloodiest day of the war without a scratch. Then he marched a hundred miles into the heart of Europe, only to die of a minor wound, a bullet in the calf. He and his friend, a Puerto Rican, were separated from their platoon for several days and couldn't get help. El Chulo couldn't walk, so the Puerto Rican stayed with him. On the third day, some Germans found them and shot and killed his friend. El Chulo pretended to be dead, so the Germans left him there. When help finally came three days later, it was too late. Gangrene had spread; he died the day after they got him to the hospital." Jacinto could barely speak when he finished. El Rubio was weeping. He had heard the letter read an hour ago, but only now, seeing the tragedy reflected in Zoraida's eyes, did he cry, as if seeing it in the face of a woman finally made it real.

Zoraida sat silent. She barely knew El Chulo and did not like him, but he was Matilde's friend and a Cuban who, she thought, should not have been there. Booming in her mind was the thought that he should have been with his family in Cuba working their farm or whatever they did, not on some battlefield fighting another country's enemy.

"Thank you," she said, finally. "I'll tell Matilde when I write him tonight. He will want to know. I'm sure he has lost friends he hasn't told me about." She stood and walked out of the Café Cubano and home through the cheerful crowd.

A week passed before she could find the words:

April 4, 1945
Querido Matilde,

Tell Edwin that I hope he is better by now and that I pray for him. It is good that you were able to help him with the German. You saved his life! You must feel good about that. I try not to worry knowing how good you are at everything you do, but come home soon. I can't stand to live without you.

I heard the other night at the Café Cubano that El Chulo died during the Battle of the Bulge. He was shot in the leg and developed gangrene. Poor man. Jacinto, El Rubio, and Domingo and Rosa send regards. I send every drop of my love.

Until tomorrow.

Zoraida

On March 31 Matilde's squadron undertook another long strafing mission, this time to Linz, Germany. During the strafing, his squadron encountered jet fighters and shot down thirteen of them. On the following day, the squadron escorted a bombing run to St. Polten. When the jets appeared the Americans were ready. Before the jets withdrew, the men flying the inferior P-51s had destroyed twelve of the superior jet fighters. By this time in the war, Germany had lost most of her experienced pilots and had been reduced to using young, inexperienced boys.

*

The war had begun to take a devastating toll on President Roosevelt. In movie news reports he had begun to look haggard and old. The once handsome, burly man with the cigarette holder and the embracing smile had shriveled and grayed. He now wore a shawl over his shoulders, which made him look even frailer. The country wondered if he could successfully carry out his unprecedented fourth presidential campaign in the closing months of 1944. However, in a spurt of energy near election day, 1944, he managed to overcome Thomas E. Dewey. After an unprecedented third term, many worried that a fourth term might lead to permanent presidency. The majority, however, recalling the man who led them out of the Great Depression, preferred the Democrats' popular slogan, "Don't change horses in mid-stream." After two terms with John Nance Garner as his vice president and one term with Henry Wallace, in 1944 he turned to Harry Truman, a relatively unknown senator from Missouri for his vice president.

At his "Little White House" at Warm Springs, Georgia President Roosevelt could swim, relax, and work his paralyzed leg muscles in the hot waters of the natural spring. At 2 o'clock PM on April 12, 1945, in the third month of his fourth term as president, Mr. Roosevelt sat before a fireplace in the Little White House to relax. Moments later a massive cerebral hemorrhage struck. The President's African-American valet, Arthur Prettyman, and a Filipino mess boy carried the unconscious President to his bedroom. By 4:35 he was dead. Ten years earlier, Harry Truman had been an obscure county judge in Missouri. At 7:09 PM April 12, 1945, the solemn-faced Missourian accepted the honor and the burden of President of the United States.

A stunned stillness covered the nation. Tampa scheduled a parade for all the troops at the various bases for 10 o'clock the following morning, and all military flags on the posts were set at half-mast for the next thirty days. On Saturday, April 14th, downtown Tampa and Ybor City stores closed at four o'clock in the afternoon and remained closed the rest of the day. Drug stores closed from two to four o'clock; grocery stores remained open except for five minutes in the afternoon during President Roosevelt's funeral. Theaters closed until six o'clock. All government offices except post offices closed; cigar factories closed all day. Churches conducted memorial services on Sunday, and a citywide memorial service was held at the municipal auditorium on Sunday at three o'clock.

Worried, Consuelo asked Pablo to stay with her after Sammy walked to school that Monday morning. In less than an hour Sammy reappeared with a serious face. "The principal sent us home. Because of President Roosevelt. All the teachers and the kids met at the flagpole out front. The principal made a speech, something about the wonderful man who brought us out of the depression, who did not live to see the end of the war he worked so hard to end. He said some things about our brave fighting men and then he said a prayer. That's when he told us we should go home for the day to mourn our dead president with our families."

"Pablo, I'd like us to go to church this evening."

"Sure, Consuelo."

President Roosevelt's sudden death and the ascendance of the relatively unknown and untested Harry Truman disturbed the troops as well as people back home. Everyone wondered who was this man? But in keeping with the spirit of the time, Americans would support their new president during their greatest national emergency in nearly a century. In Tampa the newspaper ran a cartoon on its front page that showed Truman as a farmer driving his tractor in a field with perfectly straight rows. The caption read, "He plows a straight furrow." The print and radio news carried details of the new president's life and his reputation as a straight talker and straight shooter, a man with the slogan, "The buck stops here," prominently displayed on his desk in the Oval Office.

*

Only the continual bombing runs could take the president's death off their minds. Matilde's squadron had little time in those remaining days of April to think about the terrible news. But by the end of that month it had become evident that their work was paying off. Rumors spread like flames in a dry field during the early days of May. On May 7 the squadron commander called a briefing to announce that a European cease-fire was in effect following the German surrender, and it would become official on the following day. The cheering and slapping and jumping went on as the major tried to dismiss the assembly. He finally gave up and joined the ruckus.

The following month the men who had enough points were rotated back to U.S. bases. With more than enough points, Matilde was happy to be going home, where bombs were not dropped and he did not have to kill anymore. He felt he had earned his rest. Within two weeks he was on his way.

In the Pacific the Allies had invaded the Philippines in October 1944. The naval battle in Leyte Gulf soon after practically destroyed the remainder of the Japanese navy. When the Allies captured Iwo Jima and Okinawa after terrible fighting, they were finally poised to begin heavy strategic bombing of Japan. Now they could make plans to invade the Japanese islands.

*

On July 17, on his way to a meeting with the president of the First National Bank in downtown Tampa, Pablo stopped a boy who was running down Franklin Street yelling, "Extra, extra!" The headline read, "New Bomb Exploded in New Mexico." Stopping on the sidewalk, he read about a devastating new bomb that had been detonated in a desert testing area near Alamogordo, New Mexico. It had delivered an explosive force equivalent to more than 15,000 tons of TNT! The United States had been secretly developing the bomb for several years. The report told of a new kind of energy that was released when atoms split apart. The winds and heat could be felt twenty miles away in the desert, and windows had shattered at even greater distances. When Pablo walked into the banker's conference room, he held up the newspaper and said, "Have you seen this? It could end the war tomorrow."

Standing, he met Pablo with a handshake. "I've just seen it," the banker said. "You think one bomb can do what millions of men haven't?"

"I don't know; it sure sounds impressive."

"I hope so. Now to business."

"This is business," Pablo said. "When the war ends millions of soldiers will be coming home. I, for one, want to be ready."

"I'm listening, Iglesias."

"I want to build houses for them, small, inexpensive, two- and three-bedroom houses, and a supermarket and other stores. I envision a complete neighborhood. There's some land in St. Petersburg just a little north of town that can be had cheap. If we can talk a builder into coming in with us we can build hundreds of modest homes for ex-G.I.s that will help them and make us a lot of money."

"What makes you think they'll come to Florida?"

"Not counting the men from here, think of the number of men from the cold, snowy north who have been stationed in MacDill Field. I'm betting a lot of them will move down.

"Do you have time for a brief tour?" the banker said.

"Let's go. We'll pick up my partner on the way."

*

Three weeks later, on August 6, another spectacular announcement burst out of radios and onto the pages of newspapers. A specially equipped B-29, taking off from Tinian Island in the Marianas, had dropped an atomic bomb on Hiroshima. The heat and blast pulverized the area surrounding the explosion. Spontaneous fires burned everything in an area of almost four and a half square miles, killed between 70,000 and 80,000 people and injured another 70,000. The world was dumbstruck. The story went on to say that the U.S. Army had warned the citizens of Hiroshima for several days that a new, devastating weapon would be used against them and that they should flee.

On August 9 a second atomic bomb exploded on Nagasaki. Between 35,000 and 40,000 people died and a comparable number were injured. An area of nearly two square miles was devastated. It was only after the second bomb that the Japanese government conceded the power of the new weapon. On August 8, the U.S.S.R. declared war on Japan. Japan was on the ropes. The Japanese people were shaken. The next week's news focused on negotiations over the Allies' demand for unconditional surrender and Japan's insistence on terms. On August 14, Emperor Hirohito accepted the terms of unconditional surrender. It took almost two weeks for the Japanese government to convince their people to accept the surrender, which they had considered unthinkable. By late August the Japanese government had come to terms with the inevitable.

It was a windy September 2 on the deck of the Battleship Missouri in Tokyo Bay that General Douglas MacArthur stood to read the surrender papers into a microphone. President Truman had designated him as the Allied powers' supreme commander to accept Japan's formal surrender. It was an emotional moment in history, set in the harbor of the defeated nation's capital, in full view of the enemy, on a ship bearing the name of the home state of the new American president. As he stood in front of the microphone, General MacArthur had trouble keeping the papers still against the wind and his trembling hands as he read the surrender terms. Following his dramatic presentation, the Japanese foreign minister, Shigemitsu Mamoru, dressed in formal attire, solemnized the surrender by signing the document on behalf of the Emperor and his government. Then General Umezu Yoshijiro signed on behalf of the Imperial General Headquarters. Following them, General MacArthur, Admiral Chester Nimitz, and representatives of the other Allied governments signed for their respective governments.

*

When he heard the news late that August afternoon, Pablo drove home to tell Consuelo. She and Sammy already knew. "Let's go," he said.

"Where?"

"Ybor City, to celebrate."

By the time they approached the city, the streetlights of La Septima were coming on and the traffic had slowed. At 22nd Street cars had lined up in both direction with their horns blowing. With no destination in mind they only wanted to celebrate. Sammy joined the festivities by leaning out the window and yelling to people as they passed. On the overflowing sidewalks people shouted and danced. It seemed everyone wanted to raise his voice in thanks. After driving around for twenty minutes trying to find a place to park, Pablo finally found one on Fifth Avenue, near the long-closed brothel, and the three of them walked to the Café Cubano. Most of Pablo's old friends were buying each other drinks and talking and singing. When he saw Pablo, Jacinto ran to him and put his arms around him. Then he saw Consuelo and held out his hand to her. She embraced him. "If only Matilde were here to enjoy this day with us," she said.

"He's back and training pilots for the Pacific war," Jacinto said. "Zoraida was just here." Jacinto turned away with sad eyes and said, "but not El Chulo." Turning back, he said, "This has to be Sammy. What a big boy." He shook the boy's hand with vigor.

"Zoraida doesn't know when Matilde will come home."

"For the moment I'm buying," Pablo said. "Domingo, bring a bottle of Fundador and a grape soda for my son." He introduced Sammy to the rest of his friends, El Rubio, El Gordo, Huesito, and Sarna, most of whom he had not seen in months. Consuelo could not repress a feeling of sadness standing where her husband had spent so much of their life. The noise, activity and people speaking Spanish rattled Sammy, but he enjoyed it.

It was ten o'clock when Pablo and Consuelo remembered that Sammy had school the next day. They quickly said goodbye, reminding Jacinto to call when Matilde arrived.

"Your friends are fun, Papa. Especially Jacinto. He's a good story-teller."

"He's lived a long time and seen a lot. I've known these men since we came from Cuba, Sammy."

For the next few days after V-J Day people around the world were glued to their radios. Within days they would stream to movie theaters, where newsreels would etch that great moment in their memories. For Pablo and his family, the memory would include those hours in the Café Cubano.

19 – POST-WAR TRAUMA

*

Teacher Group Forms AFL Union

*

Government Urges Flour Rationing

*

Draft Extended Nine Months

*

Strike Called In Seven Sugar Refineries

*

Office of Price Administration Increases Orange Price 15 Cents A Box

*

Experimental Atomic Electric Plant Planned

*

People had filled the station when the train lumbered through the thick slum area and past the city gas tank. A few minutes later, holding two suitcases, Matilde looked around as he stepped down onto the platform.

Spotting Zoraida running to him, he dropped both bags, ran to her and lifted her with a bear hug. She was crying and laughing at the same time.

"I telephoned some of your friends from the Café. Only Jacinto could come," she said, as the old man walked to them slowly, obviously hurrying.

Matilde held her out at arm's length to take her in completely in her new blue outfit. "You're more beautiful than I remembered."

"*Hola Matilde!*" Jacinto said, puffing. The weight loss made him look older in his loose, threadbare pinstriped wool suit. Matilde remembered him as sturdy and handsome. Now unhappiness seeped through his smile. Matilde shook his hand and then embraced him. "You're looking good, my friend," Matilde said.

"El Rubio wanted to come, but he wasn't feeling well. He sends regards. The old goat still lives on La Septima. I called several others. El Gordo's in bed with a cold. Sarna's doing well; still making cigars at a small *chinchal* on Eighth Avenue. They all send regards. Oh, and Huesito died."

"I'm sorry to hear that. I'll look up the rest when I get settled. And you, my love, you look wonderful."

"I wanted to have a party at the Café, but we'll do it later, when everybody can make it," she said, and hugged him again. "I can't believe you're finally home."

*

Matilde soon learned that a war hero had to find his way in a changing world, like everyone else, with little help. Even if the industry were not dying, he could not imagine making cigars again. But he would not worry yet. He had looked forward to a vacation, even if only to loaf at home. Then, and only then, would he think of the future. In the meantime he would read, see his friends, and take long drives with Zoraida to the sights that bring tourists to Florida. Because Zoraida did not drive, he had sold his Model A Ford when he left for Tuskegee. One of the first things he did his first week back was to buy a 1942 Chevrolet with only 3,000 miles on the speedometer. The royal blue coupe was almost new, and he loved it.

That evening he walked to the Café Cubano. He wore his first lieutenant's uniform because his old clothes no longer fit; besides, he wanted his friends to appreciate where he had been and what he had done. As he walked along 17th Street toward La Septima, he saw only strangers on the front porches of the little houses, and many were English-speaking Negroes. He was glad to see them moving up, but missed his factory friends.

He stopped in front of the Café Cubano and read the notices on the windows: a dance Saturday night at the Cuban Club, a Miss Ybor City pageant to he held in two weeks, a roughly written menu. The window itself was as dusty and opaque as ever. When he opened the door and stood in the doorway Domingo ran to him and shook his hand. "Matilde! I heard you were back. Welcome! Anything you want, Matilde, on the house!"

Three men and three women were drinking at the bar. At two of the tables, men talked animatedly in English. They all stopped to look at the mulatto soldier as he made his way to the back of the bar. One man sneered when Matilde sat at the bar.

El Rubio walked in, looked around, and sat at an empty table near the back. Matilde had been talking with Domingo and did not notice him. Spotting him, El Rubio got up and went to Matilde and slapped his back. "Jacinto told me y-y-y-you were back. Come, sit with me."

Matilde shook El Rubio's hand and took his coffee to his table, where Domingo joined them.

"Some of the old timers show up once in a while," Domingo said, "but when the factories closed, most of them moved in with their children. El Rubio is our only regular. He still lives at the same place upstairs on the next block."

"They'll need an a-a-at-t-t-omic bomb to get me out," El Rubio said. "I hear you are a w-w-war hero."

"Jacinto's wife died a few months ago. He hasn't worked in a while. The poor man was so melancholy," Domingo said. "His son took him in. They live in Tampa Heights."

"He didn't tell me that."

"El Gordo lives with his daughter in West Tampa. You probably know Huesito died. Not long after you left. He was pretty old; eighty-something, I believe."

"Jacinto told me. Well, I'm looking forward to seeing the rest."

"You'll see them, do-o-on't worry. When they hear you're b-b-back, they'll come," El Rubio said. "Now tell us about the w-w-war."

"I was in a good squadron. They were all Negroes and what fighters!" He described their bomber escort missions and how they were able to shoot down German jets that were faster then their P-51s. After half an hour, Matilde could see El Rubio's eyelids drooping. "Getting sleepy?" he asked.

"I don't slee-eep well," El Rubio said.

"I've bored you long enough, amigo."

"No, no. I wa-a-ant to hear every detail, but I am a li-li-little tired. It's good to see you again, Matilde. Ma-a-aybe we can talk again tomorrow."

*

"How did you find your friends, *querido*?" Zoraida asked, as he walked up the porch steps. She had been rocking and talking with any friends that passed.

"I saw El Rubio and Domingo. The rest were strangers, most of them Crackers," Matilde said, sitting in the other rocker.

"Did you have a good time?"

"Even the neighborhood's changed."

"But people have money now," she said.

"The ones I saw don't look any richer."

"The ones who made money moved to Davis Islands or Hyde Park."

"Maybe we'll move too," he said. "Now come here. We've got a lot of catching up to do."

*

Matilde and Zoraida spent much of the next few weeks at home, Matilde reading, Zoraida puttering and talking to neighbors. She knew he needed solitude at times and accommodated him. With little to do, Matilde found that time hung heavy. Most of his friends deserted Ybor City when the factories closed, and Blacks had filled the void. Matilde had conflicting feelings about the change.

Rocking on the front porch alone one afternoon Matilde looked around when he heard Zoraida at the door. "Come on out, Zoraida. Let's talk a while."

She kissed him on the forehead and sat beside him on the rocker.

"Something has changed, Zoraida."

"Much has changed, *mi amor.* Tampa is a different city."

"I mean me. I've learned to see myself as a Negro instead of a Cuban.

That is good, *querido*".

"I've fought with them and listened to their problems. I've seen how they survive and how they die. My white Cuban friends haven't changed their attitude. They still see Negroes as inferior. Something about their tolerance toward me feels patronizing."

She looked at him as if he were a child who had discovered the simplest truth.

"I know it's sounds silly. I've always known the truth. The war pulled it out of the dark recesses of my mind. I see it clearly now in the light of

279

day. In the factory I felt insulated from white opinions. People looked up to me. But deep inside they still saw me as a Negro. No matter how hard I tried to prove my equality I failed. It's probably why I joined the Army."

"Don't be so hard on yourself, my love."

"I knew it back then, but couldn't think it. Like at the Café Cubano: I always stayed on the edge, where I felt more comfortable, watching and listening from a distance. I only spoke when I could say something significant. I wanted to see myself as the son of my Spanish father, but I was really my Negro mother's son. She's the one who nursed me and taught me."

"Reality is frightening, but it is good, Matilde. You cannot hide from it."

He looked into her intense dark eyes, smiled, and said, "Enough of this introspection. Tomorrow we drive to the beach. To see what the tourists come for."

"I would love that, *querido*."

The ensuing week turned out to be a time of fun and disappointment. They enjoyed the beach and then two days inland visiting Silver Springs, the Everglades, and finally Miami. But to take the edge off new sights and delicious fun were barriers that made it difficult to find accommodations. On the first night they stopped at a modest motel on the outskirts of Lake Wales. Matilde walked to the clerk, but before he could ask for a room, the clerk looked at him suspiciously.

"The Negro motel isn't far. Just follow the road across the railroad tracks. On the left."

Seeing Matilde's reaction Zoraida took his arm and led him out. "Come, Matilde. We are on vacation. We must not let this person ruin our enjoyment."

When they got outside she said, "I always expect the worst, and I am never disappointed."

Even with his new outlook on Negro life, Matilde could not accept the reality so easily.

"You must not take offense, Matilde. It is not personal."

He smiled trying vainly to submerge his anger.

*

"It'll take months, no years to catch up with all we missed," he said, on their way back to Tampa.

"We will keep trying," she said and snuggled up to him.

"Let's take a drive through the Scrub."

"That's a bad neighborhood."

"I want to see how they live. Edwin Pitt's parents came from there. He never said much about it. Said he was there only once. In all my years in Tampa I've never seen it."

Not knowing why, she said, "Why don't we go home first? I need a bath."

"We're here now," he said, turning off Nebraska Avenue and heading west toward Central Avenue. Turning onto Central Avenue, they found a surprising number of stores and bars.

"Looks like La Septima before the war," he said, "except it's seedier."

The Scrub seemed to be thriving. People stood on street corners and sat on storefront window ledges. In the twilight the streetlights had just come on.

"Let's take a walk," he said.

She did not like the idea, but said nothing. She knew she was safe with Matilde.

They parked along an unpaved side street just off Central Avenue. The row of identical houses, all worn gray, had few intact screens, and the front yards were hard-packed dirt. An enormously fat woman sat on a porch rocking a baby. An elderly man in a work shirt and overalls sat by her, whittling a piece of wood. In the front yard stood a derelict Model T Ford. Around the house next door, four small children played hide and seek. Nearly every porch was alive with people talking. Matilde and Zoraida walked to Central Avenue and passed a poolroom radiating the boisterous sounds of men laughing and arguing. The cracking sounds of colliding balls punctuated the uproar. Zoraida did not like those sounds. A crude bar on one side was lined with men, each with one foot on the rail. They walked on past a grocery store whose window was covered with signs advertising catfish, fatback, pole beans, chitlins, and many foods they did not know. The unfamiliar smells emanating from the grocery store and the poolroom repelled both Matilde and Zoraida.

In front of a drug store, two men surrounded by teenage boys sat in chairs leaned against the wall. The older men, apparently veterans, were telling war stories. Across the street a brightly lit movie theater was showing *Air Force* and *The Battle of Bataan*. The next street was also unpaved and looked much the same as the one where they parked. Matilde decided to walk down that street and around the block to their car. The scene was like the other street, except that on one side stood an empty building, half a block long, with most of the windows broken. Even in that cool January evening, most of the children running around and yelling were barefoot.

"My Army friends told me, but I couldn't believe it."

"How can they keep their homes clean on a street like this?" she said.

"Look around. People seem happy," he said. "Kids are playing the way kids play everywhere. People are entertaining themselves. Either they don't they know how other people live, or they've accepted their lives."

"Let's go. A bath."

*

The next night Matilde went to the Café Cubano again. Jacinto was at a back table. Matilde sat with him. "How are your son and his family?"

"They're fine. Mario still works at the shipyard. His wife works in a department store downtown. Between them they bring in good money. I don't do a damn thing but watch the kids when they come home from school. You know how teenagers are; can't tell them a damn thing. You heard about Angelina?"

"Yes. El Rubio told me. I'm sorry."

"I have only my grandchildren now. My children are too busy."

"I remember my grandparents with affection; your grandchildren will too. Say, what happened to your moustache."

"I caught a bad cold. It got to be a problem. It's only one of the many things I've lost. When I walk down La Septima, I have to stop every block to get my breath. It's hell getting old."

"I know lots of young men who would give anything to be as well off as you."

Jacinto looked slightly embarrassed. "Still thinking about college?"

"I don't know. At first I thought I'd try flying, but too many aviators are trying to do the same."

"I've never flown, and I never learned to drive a car." Jacinto smiled. "I was born too soon, I guess."

Matilde looked around the old café. Its walls were dirtier than ever. He expected Domingo would have painted them with all the new business, but he was getting old too, and didn't want to bother. Business was good enough without a paint job. He still had the white cat that liked to sit under customers and hiss and claw their pants; Domingo no longer chased her. He had long ago decided to let his customers defend themselves. Rosa helped him more now by making sandwiches and serving tables. She was still strong and energetic. The old pot of Spanish bean soup was simmering as it had for years. Matilde smiled imagining that some of those beans might have been in that pot since before the war. The tile floor with its intricate, three-dimensional pattern still fascinated him, but it needed scrubbing. The place smelled of old cigar butts and stagnant urine from the toilet in back. Domingo's only concession to increased business was to put in three more tables, and now finding your way through the room involved pushing chairs out of the way or asking people to move. The atmosphere was oppressive. Matilde had expected to find friends playing dominoes and talking about problems in the factories or about the union or politics. Having fragmented into small, unrelated groups of shipyard workers and local shopkeepers, the small café now resembled more a bus station than a friendly neighborhood bar.

After running out of topics to discuss with Jacinto, and watching the other patrons come and go, Matilde said, "I guess it's time to go."

"Stay a while. Mario won't pick me up for another half hour."

"I'll see you another time."

On his way home he walked through a familiar neighborhood. Negroes occupied every house. A small group of boys played baseball under the streetlight. As Matilde approached them, a fly ball came to him and he caught it. The boys all stopped and looked at him. "That's a home run," yelled one boy.

"It ain't," another said. "The soldier, he done caught it. He's out."

Matilde walked to the boys and handed one the ball. "What do you say, mister?" the same boy asked.

"I'm as tall as a fence; I think it's a homer."

"See, see. I told you," the other said.

"It's pretty late, boys. You have school tomorrow."

"I ain't."

"Why not?"

"My momma's sick."

"School's too important to miss," Matilde said.

"That's what my momma always say, but she don't mind."

"I think school's the most important thing in your lives right now. You shouldn't miss a single day. Do you think we could have won the war if our soldiers had been dummies who skipped school?"

"Sure. School ain't got nothin' to do with shootin,'"

"It's got everything to do with it, young man. We won the war because our soldiers were trained to think. Germans and Japs were trained to do what they were told without thinking. They were the dummies. American soldiers could figure out ways to get out of tough spots. Believe me, I know what I'm talking about."

There was general mumbling among the boys at Matilde's discourse. "Did you go to school, Lieutenant?"

"Not enough, but I'm going to start college."

"Wow!" one boy said. "I ain't never heard of no grown man goin' to college."

"Things are changing," Matilde said. "You should all aim at college."

"We goin' in soon, Lieutenant," a boy said. He saluted and the others followed. Matilde gave them his sharpest military salute.

"Carry on, men," he said, and walked on.

*

"The Café Cubano stinks," Matilde said.

"True, but people are better off," Zoraida said.

"Some of them maybe." He thought a while and said, "Goofing off is fine, Zoraida, but I think it's time."

"For what?"

"College."

"Good."

"What do you think about driving to Tallahassee tomorrow?" he asked.

"Should I pack?"

"Just for a couple of days."

*

The drive up US 19 that bright January day took longer than he expected with all the traffic and the towns that dotted the path. The road was narrow and every little town had stop signs and speed limits posted. Matilde knew it would be inviting trouble for a Negro to speed through any of those speed traps. It was dark when they stopped at a small motel whose sign, "Serving Fla. A & M Since 1935," suggested that they took in Negroes. It was on the edge of the college. Tired, they ate supper and returned to their room to relax and fantasize about their future and what an education would mean.

"Imagine me in a classroom with teenage college students?"

"Don't you think there'll be other veterans?"

"I hope so."

It was cold even for January when they drove onto campus. The tall, spreading oaks reminded Matilde of Alabama. He liked the hilly, red clay terrain and especially the activity on campus. This was the farthest north Zoraida had ever been, and she was enjoying the change. "Strange," she said. "Doesn't look like Florida."

Classes had just let out, and students had poured out into the sidewalks and streets. Dodging people made driving difficult. Matilde stopped twice to ask where the admissions office was before he found the red brick building. Not in the least intimidated, he walked down the hall until he found a door letter, Director of Admissions."

"My name is Gómez," he said to the receptionist. "I'm interested in applying."

"Please sit down. Mr. Smith won't be long."

The austere room had beige plaster walls, dark, heavy wood trim, and comfortable office chairs. On one side of the room, near a large window that overlooked a shaded part of the campus, stood a conference table with six chairs around it. The receptionist, an attractive, well-dressed, woman in her fifties, took several phone calls while they waited. Matilde's army years had taught him the ways of administrators, so he picked up a magazine and began flipping through the pages, smiling. Zoraida kept looking around as if she was seeing things for the first time. Only the fact that everyone was Black made the situation tolerable for her. Sitting erect, she held Matilde's hand and tried to appear nonchalant.

Finally the receptionist said to Matilde, "You may go in now. You too, Mrs. Gómez."

Zoraida was bursting with curiosity and glad not to wait alone.

After shaking his hand and Zoraida's the small thin light-skinned Negro man asked them to sit down. "What may I do for you?"

"I'd like to enroll, but I didn't finish school. In fact, I didn't go past the eighth grade in Cuba. Is there anything I can do to qualify?"

"That's not necessarily a problem. We sometimes accept people without a high school diploma if they can demonstrate an equivalent background."

When Matilde told him he had been a fighter pilot in Africa and Europe and had finished first in his class of cadets in Officer Candidate School and in pilot training, the director smiled. "Impressive. I know you've come a long way, and I don't want to waste your time. Fill out these forms. You can use the conference table in the outer office." Leading Matilde out he said, "Take your time. Return them to me when you've finished and we'll talk some more."

Matilde liked the man's efficiency and openness. In half an hour he was back in the director's office with the forms completed in a clear script. The director looked over the forms and asked Matilde what he wanted to study.

"I'm not sure. I don't know what's available, but I think I would like to be a teacher. I'd like to help young people become what they want to be."

Mr. Smith looked at Matilde with genuine admiration. "With your background and that attitude, you'd make a dandy teacher. Demand for teachers has to improve now that opportunities are opening up for Negroes. Our department of education was the original mission of Florida A & M. We've trained most of the Negro teachers in Florida. Perhaps one day, when segregation is abolished, jobs for Negroes will really open up."

"What next?"

"When I've processed your application I'll write to you. It should be no more than a week or two. Will Mrs. Gómez be coming with you?"

"Of course. We've been apart too long already."

"Good. When the time comes I'll send information on housing for married students and jobs available for wives, if you're interested."

Zoraida nodded.

"With the G.I. Bill, we're expecting a flood of veterans this fall. By then we'll have housing for married student. We're converting surplus army barracks that will have one- and two-bedroom apartments with a small kitchen, bath, and living room. I'll send information on that too. While you're here you might want to drive by and see how they're coming." Mr. Smith gave Matilde a map of the campus and pointed out the married housing area on a campus map. Try our cafeteria. I think you'll like it.

"Thank you," Matilde said. As they walked out, Matilde picked up his pace. "Wait for me," Zoraida said.

"I'm sorry. Isn't this great? Looks like they're going to take me."

Zoraida put her arm around him and they walked into the bright day. They spent an hour walking around the campus and ate lunch in the cafeteria. It was good Southern cooking: fried chicken, lima beans, rice, salad, and lots of desserts.

After lunch they drove to the new married students' buildings that looked like all the army installations Matilde had known in Alabama and later in Africa and Italy.

"They'll have laundry rooms and everything," Zoraida said.

"You're terrific, Zoraida. I thought I was through with barracks life, but I guess I can take it with you as my roommate."

*

Pablo's development in St. Petersburg went well. With the bank's financing and a good contractor, he and Marvin spent days inundated with blueprints, contracts, and estimates. The project was for two hundred houses that would sell for four to six thousand dollars each. With only a handful built and much of the land still to be cleared, they already had orders for forty houses.

In the fall of 1945 Pablo asked Consuelo if she would like to move to Tampa, knowing she would be thrilled. Though she rarely complained, she left no doubt about the loneliness and isolation she had felt in Brandon. Sammy was not as happy. He loved the grove and his friends and the school and the scouts. "Why can't we stay?" he asked.

"We can, Sammy. We don't have to move. The thing is that Mama has never liked it here. She agreed to move here because of my job. Now most of my work is in town. I'm sure, after a week or two, you'll love it."

"Gee, Papa, I don't know." Sammy's thoughts went to the large grapefruit tree in the grove. He would not admit how much he would miss that tree and the feeling of freedom he had climbing it with his friends. "What about school? Can't we wait until graduation?"

"Mama and I want you to go to Jesuit High School. It's a very good school. You could finish here in Brandon and start Jesuit in the fall if you like. But if you don't mind, and to avoid the daily drive to Brandon, you could finish ninth grade at Wilson Junior High School, which is just a couple of blocks away."

Wilson's a good school, Sammy," his mother said.

Feeling he had some choice in the matter, Sammy said no more.

"I've located a nice house if you and Mama like it. I haven't bought it, of course. It's in Hyde Park and it's really nice, close to your friend Lizzie. We can take a look at it tomorrow."

"That's a lovely area."

*

They moved in January 1946. Because Sammy's grades were so high, Jesuit High School accepted him into their ninth grade class. He was not happy in a new school with no friends. But the wily Principal had arranged for several of the new ninth graders to take him around the first few days. These were bright boys like Sammy. By the end of that week, he was telling stories at home about the fun he was having there. He especially liked coming and going on the streetcar with some of his new friends.

Along with the new house, Pablo bought Consuelo a new Steinway grand piano. He wanted to surprise her with it, but did not because she had often said choosing a piano was very personal. Now, with the piano and Sammy in Jesuit High School and Burke and Iglesias in their new offices in downtown Tampa, they were again settled.

After his first week in school Sammy said, "Jesuit has all the sports. I'm going to play football."

"You'll get hurt," his mother said.

"The ninth graders play touch, Mama. And they have a band. I may play in the band too."

*

It was mid-afternoon in early April, and Pablo was looking out his tenth story window at the overcast day. The lead sky seemed too heavy to hold up. It looked as if it would rupture at any moment. The ringing telephone woke him from his wool gathering. "Hello," he said.

After a brief silence he heard a woman's voice. "Hello. This is Cynthia. How are you?"

"What do you want?" He was shaken.

"Don't get mad. I gotta see you. It's important."

"I don't want to see you and I don't want you to call me anymore," he said, and hung up. He tried to return to his work, but could not. He hesitated when the phone rang again. Finally he picked up the receiver. "Yes?"

"Please don't hang up. This really is important. Please."

"What do you want?" He felt more anger than curiosity.

"I gotta see you. Something we need to discuss."

"What?"

"If I tell you, you won't come."

"Then forget it." He listened a moment to make out the sounds he was hearing. She was crying. "All right, but only for a minute. I'm very busy."

"Thanks. There's a little tavern in Sulfur Springs, the Hole-In-The-Wall, on Nebraska Avenue. Nobody won't know you there."

"When?"

"Ten minutes?"

"It'll take me half an hour, and I won't have much time."

Twenty-five minutes later he walked into the Hole-In-The-Wall Tavern and looked around for a moment before he recognized her. Her cheeks were sunken; she looked emaciated. Her once beautiful, red, wavy hair was gray-streaked brown, short and stringy. Wearing a loose-fitting shift, she looked more like a hobo than a seductress. Pablo's anger turned to pity as he approached her table, where a cup of black coffee stood before her. She had waited for him to recognize her.

She looked down into her coffee. "Thanks for coming."

Assuming she was broke, he said, "May I order you something to eat?"

"I'm not hungry. I know you're busy, so I'll make it short. I have a little girl. She's two and pretty as a button. I been takin' care of her myself, but I cain't no more." She began to cry.

"Do you want money?"

"She's yours," she said, bracing herself.

"Bullshit!"

"She is. I swear it."

"Well that's your problem. You're a professional. You should have been more careful."

"She was born a few days before I saw you in Ybor City that day. I was gonna tell you 'bout her then, but I couldn't. I wanted to handle it alone. I figured you wouldn't give a damn anyway. I'd given it a lot of thought, but when I finally faced you, knowing men, all I could think of was apologizing for hurting your wife."

"Nice try, but you're wasting your time and mine."

"I wouldn't have said nothin' now or never if they was any other way."

"That baby could belong to any of a hundred men." He pushed his chair back making a loud scraping noise and walked out. The owner, standing by the cash register, looked at him with contempt. Pablo stood beside his car in the bright sun with the key in his hand, but didn't open the door. Instead he returned inside. She was sitting with her face in her hands, crying.

"What do you mean, 'if there was any other way?'"

"I cain't keep her no more."

"You want me to take her?"

"For the love of Pete, you know I wasn't with nobody else. She's yours."

"It'll take more than your word."

"Look at this then." She reached into her purse and pulled out a snapshot of the little girl standing by a palm tree at the beach. Pablo looked at the V-shaped smile he was known for, and her yellow-colored hair. He stared almost a minute, entranced by the thought that she was his. She could, indeed, be Sammy's sister, he thought.

"I was pregnant when we split up."

"I don't know any such thing."

When she started to cry again, he softened. She looked so worn and sick, yet it had not occurred to him to ask an important question. "Why can't you keep her anymore?"

"I don't wanna talk about that. It don't matter."

"You want me to take her, but won't tell me why? Hurting business?"

"You must be blind. Do I look like …?"

"Why, then?"

"I was hoping you'd do it for the right reason."

"Right reason?"

"I thought you would love your daughter."

"I still want an answer."

She looked down at the floor. "I have a cancer, that's why. The doctor says I'm gonna die in a month or two. Goddamn it, I cain't leave her in the street, and I cain't stand the thought of her in a orphanage like me."

He put his hand out to hers, but she withdrew.

"Don't get mushy. All I care about is our daughter. Will you do it?"

"Can I call you?"

"I ain't got no phone. I'll call you. Tell me when."

"Call me in my office day after tomorrow. Are you in pain?"

"Just think about your daughter."

"What's her name?"

"Sally. Keep the picture. I gotta go now." She rose and slowly walked out of the Hole-In-The-Wall Tavern. Her once shapely legs looked like dowels holding up the bony body under her loose dress. Even her face had lost its charm; it was as pale gray as the sky and her freckles were darker gray. Still in her thirties, she was a hag. Pablo sat frozen in that rundown tavern wondering what to do. Then he wondered what he wanted to do. He could not answer either question.

*

Their new home had changed Consuelo's life. She believed Pablo had finally changed. In that spacious house she could spread out. Pale green stucco made the house appear to have sprouted from the earth. The broad front porch faced the side street, which pleased her. Better than opening onto Swann Avenue with all its traffic, she thought.

Taking Pablo at his word, she bought expensive, solid maple dining room furniture that looked quite modern. The kitchen and breakfast nook were large enough for all their meals, but Consuelo liked a more formal supper in the dining room. She did not like rooms for show and insisted on using it all. A screened back porch overlooked a small, beautifully landscaped garden. Consuelo bought rockers for the back porch like the ones she had in their old house. At the back of the house, beside the back porch, a bedroom with bath would serve Consuelo as sewing room. It was connected to the dining room. Stairs led from the living room to a wide hall on the second floor, which opened to three ample bedrooms and two large bathrooms. The master bedroom sat over the porch and extended the entire width of the house. Indirect lighting throughout the house conjured a warm inviting glow in the evenings.

The living room was Pablo's favorite with comfortable plush chairs and two sofas. The piano sat at one end and the sofa and chairs at the opposite. Pablo loved the wide fireplace especially when chilly weather gave him an excuse to light it. He also liked the large white bookcases at each end of the room. They remind him of his father's study in Matanzas. Consuelo suspected they make him feel intellectual. He rarely read, but enjoyed looking at the books and occasionally pulled one out to flip the pages. Sammy could not resist the banister and always slid down it. Consuelo scolded him dutifully, but didn't insist

After Sammy had gone upstairs to finish his homework and Consuelo had finished the dishes, Pablo and she sat in the dining room, sipping coffee and chatting about Sammy and his schoolwork, and other mundane things.

"Anything wrong?" Consuelo asked after a while. "You seem distracted."

"Let's go outside. Something's come up."

The tone of his voice worried her. She followed him out

The small garden outside the screened-in porch was Consuelo's favorite place. She had removed much of the overgrowth planted by the previous owners and planted azaleas around the property line and flowering annuals in front of the azaleas. The porch opened directly into the yard with three steps down to a stone path that led to two benches and a picnic table beneath a spreading avocado tree. With no moon, most of the garden lay wrapped in darkness. With only the living room lights they could make out only the table in the middle of the porch and the three oak rockers with wicker seats and backs. As their eyes adjusted to the darkness, the garden came to life. Looking into her face, Pablo began to swing gently. "I saw Cynthia today."

Consuelo threw up her hands and stood.

"Let me tell you about it before you jump to conclusion."

"I thought that door was closed."

"Please. Just listen. OK?"

In weak tones he told her, in detail, the story that sent her heart racing. He described the phone calls, what they said to each other, his feelings of anger and then of pity when he saw her at the tavern, wondering whether it was his child, the photograph, his fear of getting involved, of wanting to help but not knowing how. Her glare froze him. He knew how much she always wanted another child, especially a girl, but her reaction was so silent and so strong and so frigid that he could not go on.

Unable to restrain herself she exploded, "It never ends, you bastard!" and she walked back in the house.

Pablo stayed on the swing. After a few minutes he came in and found Consuelo sitting in the living room sofa, breathing fast and pounding her fists into her lap. "Don't say another word. I want you out of here, now!"

"This is my home."

"I don't care. Go to her … to hell." Then she ran up the stairs and closed the bedroom door behind her.

After sitting in the back porch for at least an hour, Pablo went into the living room. Upstairs, Consuelo tossed back and forth in bed and rose several times to go to the bathroom, not really wanting anything. Then she sat in the rocker by the bed until after three o'clock. The rocker crunching against the wood floor seemed to be crunching her calm orderly life to dust.

That night Pablo slept on the living room sofa. In the morning, he was up before her. She heard him moving around and the back porch door opening and closing. When she finally went down to the kitchen, he came in.

"I told you to get out."

"I'll leave, but I'll return to talk when Sammy goes to school."

"Just get out!"

Pablo went to the front porch and walked down the street toward Bayshore Boulevard. The day was cool and breezy. Consuelo watched until he disappeared along the broad promenade.

An hour later, he reappeared. Consuelo was still in the kitchen working furiously, on her knees, cleaning the oven.

He knocked gently on the kitchen door and said, "I'm back."

She kept working without looking up.

"Consuelo, I don't blame you for hating me. I hate what I did and how it hurt you, and I've tried to make it up to you. I'm truly sorry. I had no idea there was a child until yesterday. I'll tell Cynthia to put the baby in a home. It won't be the end of the world. Lots of children are raised that way."

"You don't know it's yours. She's a whore, isn't she? The father could be anyone."

"Look at the picture," he said, taking it out and putting it on the table.

"I don't want to see it."

"I never had any reason to suspect that she went with anybody else."

"A true-blue whore. How wonderful." She looked away.

"She was a whore and knew a lot of men. I know that, but that baby is not to blame for her parents' stupidity."

As Pablo talked her eyes fell on the photograph. The little girl in the photo transported her to a schoolyard long ago, where she first saw that face through the fence. Then she remembered her grandmother and the woman who took her in.

After a long silence, she said, "I guess she's pitiful. We only spoke once, but I could hear through her terrible anger how much she loved you." Then she pushed the photo toward him. "Keep it."

"What do you want me to do?"

"I don't care."

"It's not that easy, Consuelo. You know that's all over. I don't want to lose you. This is part of the past you forgave."

"You've always been good with words, Pablo. But it won't work this time."

"I mean it. Please tell me, what should I do?"

"I couldn't sleep last night, thinking about that poor woman and the innocent child and your arrogance and complete disregard for Sammy and me. I feel only revulsion. But you're right about one thing. This isn't something new. It was a terrible thing you did back then, and I forgave you. But I couldn't forget. And now you want to do another terrible thing. "How could you put that child in an orphanage?"

"I don't want to; I just meant I would do it rather than lose you."

"If you didn't have to worry about me, what would you do?"

"You're my only concern."

"Put my feelings aside. You've never had trouble doing that, have you?"

"If only she were yours. We've wanted another for so long." Then after a pause, "It wouldn't be fair to you, but I would take her."

"I wanted one so badly, and I think you did too."

"We have to think it over carefully. Anything we do will affect us all."

"I couldn't live knowing she was in an orphanage," she said.

"Then you believe she's mine?"

"The picture ..."

"Maybe we could find her a good home with people who want a child, like the Burkes."

Consuelo frowned and shook her head.

"Why not? Let's think about it."

"We have to take her."

Pablo reached for her hand and they sat in the sofa.

"Pablo, I don't know how I feel … this girl is the living proof of your disloyalty ... I wanted a girl so … it's so confusing … it'll change my life … I'd be tied up again for years … and Sammy? How will he take it? How do we tell him? And the girl? How have they raised her? She could be a problem child coming from …"

"Let's go out to the porch," He said.

They sat in the brilliant morning, talking about the problems a baby would cause and all the trouble and the loss of independence.

"If you're serious, we would adopt her legally. I know a lawyer who could handle it."

"Have you talked to him?" she asked.

"Of course not."

Within an hour the discussion had turned to clothes and which room to fix for her and the changes they would make. The leaves of the avocado tree sparkled in the breezy sunlight. The flowers were in their glory.

As the sun approached its zenith, Pablo turned to her. "Why don't we have lunch out for a change?"

"The refrigerator's full."

"Come on."

He ran upstairs, shaved, showered, and dressed and came downstairs where she was waiting. They got into the Packard and drove to the Valencia Gardens restaurant. Pablo went past the headwaiter, directly to the owner and asked if he could have a private table.

"Of course, Pablo," Manuel Beiro said, and led them to a small room with four tables. "I won't put anyone else in here."

As she spread her napkin on her lap, Consuelo said, "We haven't talked about Cynthia."

"What about her?"

"Are we going to take her baby and leave her to die?

"We don't owe her anything," he said.

"It's not a matter of owing. It's a matter of right and wrong. It's obvious she can't support herself. Soon she won't even be able to care for herself."

"She said she would call tomorrow," he said. "We'll meet some place with her and the child. I want to know how she's living and with whom. We don't really know enough to decide. I want to know what we're getting into."

It was a nervous day for both of them. Consuelo could barely wait to see her new daughter, for that was how she had begun to think of Sally. She had pushed aside all thoughts of Pablo's transgressions to make room for what she considered a gift from God.

Her grandmother had intruded into her thoughts to the point that Consuelo had begun to feel a duty to the child. That woman long ago, she thought, took Clarita in so willingly. But there's a difference: I know Pablo's the father. Will that matter? The woman long ago could have known it too. Women always know. But only Sally matters. Pablo would love her more because I accepted her. Pablo's pragmatic. He wants to know the child's environment. He's right. She could be living with a bum for all we know. Pablo thinks of Sally as an emotional investment that could easily snag on the rough edges of doubt. He won't be satisfied until he meets Sally and talks with Cynthia. I don't need to. I'd take her now. But … will Pablo love Sally more because her mother's white? And why do I assume she's not part Negro just because she's a Cracker?

Pablo also thought of little else that afternoon. They spoke again that evening but nothing new came up. Consuelo was still ready to take Sally, but respected Pablo's businesslike approach and said little.

The next morning Pablo reached his office in the First National Bank Building early. He took the elevator to the tenth floor and opened his door. His hands trembled. He had bought a newspaper on his way in and sat down to read it, but he could not concentrate. The phone rang three times. Each time he picked it up on the first ring. One call was from Marvin, another was from a developer, and the third was from Consuelo wondering if Cynthia had called. It was about ten o'clock when Cynthia finally called.

"Hello. I've talked with Consuelo; we'd like to see you today."

"Where?"

"The Columbia Restaurant Café for lunch."

"I won't eat nothin', but it don't matter."

"Twelve o'clock, then, and you'll bring Sally?"

"Sure."

Pablo immediately called Consuelo, told her, and said, "I'll pick you up at 11:30."

Consuelo spent the next hour at Sacred Heart Church praying and then talking with the pastor. Father O'Brien, a thin, Jesuit in his fifties, smiled as she related the situation.

"What you are doing is the greatest act of kindness I can imagine," he said. "I can imagine no greater love."

*

The Columbia Restaurant Coffee Shop was loud and busy when Pablo and Consuelo walked in. Pablo greeted one of the waiters and led Consuelo to a table by a window as he looked around the room for Cynthia. "Would you like to order something?" the waiter asked.

"Not yet," she said.

"We're expecting two more," Pablo said. "We'll wait."

Within a few minutes Cynthia walked in leading a little girl by the hand. Cynthia was wearing a white blouse and a blue skirt and jacket, and her hair was neatly combed. She still looked drawn and gray and very thin, but she was well groomed. Pablo stood and approached her. "Over here," he said. "Consuelo, this is Cynthia. And this must be Sally?"

"Yes," Cynthia said, moving the little girl toward Pablo and Consuelo. Sally wore a pink dress with a bonnet and white socks and white patent leather shoes.

"I'm happy to meet you, Cynthia," Consuelo said, extending her hand. "And I'm very glad to know this beautiful little girl too."

Consuelo reached for Sally, but she turned and put her arms around her mother's legs. Sally had straight, blonde hair and blue eyes and was big for her age.

"She don't take to strangers."

"Can we talk?" Pablo asked, motioning to Sally.

"Sure."

The waiter reappeared, and Pablo asked what everyone wanted.

"How about some chicken, Sally?" Cynthia said.

Sally nodded, and when she smiled, Consuelo saw Pablo's smile across her face.

"I don't want nothin'," Cynthia said.

"You've got to eat," Consuelo said. "I'm having yellow rice and chicken. We'll share it."

"Maybe a little. I cain't eat much."

"I'll have chicken and yellow rice too," Pablo said. "And fried chicken and some vegetables and a glass of milk for the little girl." When the waiter left, Pablo turned to Cynthia again. "Where do you live?"

"Sulfur Springs. I got a little house there. It ain't much, but it's clean and comfy."

"Is it just you and Sally?"

The anger in Cynthia's face came through, but before she could answer, Consuelo spoke: "It must be difficult bringing up a child all alone."

"It ain't been easy, but nothin' ever is." Then turning to Pablo, "Just me and Sally. I've brought her up decent; she's a good girl."

"That's easy to see," Pablo said. "I don't want to pry, but how do you support yourself and Sally?"

"I saved all I could soon's I knew I was expecting. By the time she was born I had a fair nest egg." Looking at Consuelo, she smiled and looked down in embarrassment.

"What would you think about us taking her?" Pablo asked.

Cynthia's eyes overflowed and she looked down again. Consuelo thought she was praying. "You'll love her. She's a great kid. She don't wet the bed no more nor nothin', and she eats everything. She ain't no trouble at all."

"Going to a new home with strangers and not seeing you again will be frightening," Consuelo said. "Would you mind coming with us?"

"I'll take her, but I cain't stay more'n a few minutes. I got to take my medicines."

"Stay with us for a while, so Sally can get used to us and her new surroundings," Consuelo said. "We'll stop by your house and pick up your medicines."

"No ... no, I couldn't do that."

Pablo looked at Consuelo with disbelief. They had never discussed inviting Cynthia. "Here comes our lunch," he said.

When the waiter placed the plate before Sally, she picked up a drumstick and bit into it energetically. Cynthia was embarrassed. Consuelo smiled and asked if she would like some yellow rice too. Sally nodded and sat back as Consuelo put two spoonfuls of rice on her plate. "How about some rice and a little chicken for you, Cynthia?" Consuelo asked.

"It looks good and smells good too. Maybe a little."

Consuelo watched as Cynthia took a tiny bit on her fork and chewed it as if it were a mouthful, then sat and rested as if she had performed hard labor.

"Please come with us," Consuelo said. "For Sally. Stay as long as you like or as long as it takes to make her comfortable."

"All I care about is Sally. I can manage."

Pablo frowned through the exchange. But calmly and persistently Consuelo continued to press the invitation. Putting her hand on Cynthia's she said, "Please. For Sally."

"If you're sure ... I could pick up a few things for a day or two."

"Good. Isn't that wonderful, Pablo. Cynthia will help us with Sally."

Pablo struggled to force a smile.

*

When Sammy walked in the house he saw the strange woman in the guest room off the dining room and the little girl sitting on the floor. Carrying his books he went to the kitchen and said, "Who's the kid?"

"It's a long story, Sammy. The lady is very sick and needs help. The girl is her daughter, and her name is Sally."

"Who are they?"

"Her mother is an old friend. We want to adopt Sally. How would you like a little sister?"

"Why is the lady letting you adopt her daughter?"

"She asked us to. She's too sick to take care of her."

"So we're going to have a brat running around?"

"Please, Sammy. Go comfort her. She must be worried about her mother."

"Not now, Mama. There's a football game down the block."

"Later then. It'll mean a lot to all of us."

Cynthia did not leave her room that day except to go to the adjacent bathroom. When Consuelo called her for supper, Cynthia said, "Honest, I cain't eat. I'll be all right."

"I can bring it to you."

"It ain't that. I just cain't."

Sally spent most of the day with her mother. Consuelo had to plead to get Sally away from her mother's room. When she did Sammy ignored her.

Consuelo had not yet rearranged the spare upstairs room for Sally, but she fixed the single bed for her and brought out one of her own stuffed dolls for her. She put Sally to bed with a beautiful recounting of Little Red Riding Hood. To her surprise Sally dropped off within minutes. Sammy was reading in the living room when Consuelo came down. "What do you think of your little sister?"

"She's not my sister."

"Please, Sammy. If we adopt her, she'll be our daughter. That'll make her your sister. She's not related to us the way you are, but won't you try to accept her?"

"She's a pain."

"We won't keep her if you don't want us to. The adoption won't be final for a while; you can help us decide." Consuelo felt a tinge of guilt making such a radical promise, but it was a chance she would take. She hoped he would accept Sally once he understood the situation.

"Could you have gotten rid of me that way?"

"Of course not. You're our real son. When I call her our daughter, I mean we want to treat her as a daughter. It doesn't mean there's no difference between you and her."

"Why is her mother here?"

"It's only fair to tell you: she's dying, Sammy." Consuelo tried to hold back tears.

"Gee. I guess I'll have to think it over."

"Sure, Sammy," she said and pulled him to her and hugged him and kissed him.

When Sammy came home from school the following day, he found Sally sitting in the hall outside her mother's room.

"Want to help me build something?" he asked.

Sally got up and followed Sammy to his room where he found an old cardboard box full of building blocks and cabin logs.

"Come on," he said, leading her down to the living room rug. He poured out the blocks and logs. "What do you want to build?"

Sally shrugged.

Selecting the letters of her name, he said, "See, that says SALLY." Then he made his own name and said, "See, my name is almost the same."

Before long, Sally was stacking blocks into walls and houses. Hearing the sounds, Consuelo stopped at the door and smiled. Sammy smiled back and shrugged.

Later, Consuelo heard Sally screaming and found Sammy flying a paper airplane from the top of the stairs and Sally chasing it below. When he got tired of that, he made tiny paper helicopters and dropped them from the stairwell. She waited downstairs and tried to catch them as they slowly twirled down. After a while, Sally dropped the helicopter and walked upstairs to look for her mother.

After supper that evening, Sammy told his parents to go ahead and adopt Sally. "She's all right, I guess."

*

Cynthia had given them Sally's birth certificate, so Pablo took it to Bob Whitaker, a lawyer in his building, and explained the situation. "Can you arrange an adoption?"

"Sure. I'll draw up the papers; you get her to sign them, and I'll take care of recording it."

That afternoon Pablo brought the papers home for Consuelo's and Cynthia's signatures. Bob Whitaker came to notarize the signatures.

"There it is," Consuelo said as she signed the paper. "All we need now is Cynthia's signature."

"Would you mind taking it?" Pablo asked.

"I understand," she said, "Sure. Come, Mr. Whitaker."

"I can see her sign from the door," Whitaker said.

In bed, Cynthia was looking out the window at the dry, barren oak, feeling she would not live to see new leaves. "How are you doing?" Consuelo asked.

"Fine."

"Pablo brought the adoption papers for you to sign."

Eagerly, Cynthia moved to sit up, but Consuelo stopped her. "Read it over first," she said. "When you've finished, I'll hold it for you so you don't have to sit up."

"I don't need to read nothin'." She signed with great effort and sank back into her pillow.

It was clear that Cynthia was growing weaker with each passing day, and Consuelo wondered what to do. Though she did not complain, Cynthia could barely walk and seemed to be in continual pain. Consuelo stayed with her as much as she could and read or tried to comfort her with conversation, but Cynthia usually wanted to be left alone. Pablo kept his distance and only saw her when she ate with them

One afternoon when she was feeling relatively good and Consuelo was reading to her, Cynthia took Consuelo's hand. The thick rays of sun coming through the windows reminded her how beautiful was life. The sheer window curtains and off-white furniture created a cheerful atmosphere. It was the kind of room she had always dreamed of.

"I guess Pablo told you what I did for a living," she said, smiling.

"I'm sure you did what you had to."

"Aw, I didn't have to; I liked it."

"Did you really? With strangers?"

"Sure. Oh, once in a while there'd be some bastard who liked to hurt women, but they was rare. I learned to spot 'em fast." Then smiling, she said, "I had to kick one guy in the nuts once. That sure stopped him."

"How awful."

"Most guys were fun, though. All they wanted was a good time with no strings attached, and that was fine by me."

"Did you ever want to marry and have a family?"

"Once, but it didn't work out."

"Pablo?" Consuelo bit her lip when his name slipped out, but her curiosity had boiled over.

"Naw," she drawled, turning away.

"Why do married men go to prostitutes?"

"Who knows? They like a little strange stuff, I guess. It mostly ain't the wife's fault. Pablo and I had fun, but he never cared nothin' about me. It was always you. Men never love my kind. I ain't complainin'. That's just the way it is."

"I wish I could do something to help you, Cynthia."

"Cynthia's not my real name. My first madam gave me that. I'm Edna. She thought Edna wasn't sexy enough."

"It's a good, American name. I like it."

"I was born and raised in Jasper, Florida. My mother abandoned me. I'd never do that to my baby."

Consuelo put her hand on Cynthia's. "Where's Jasper?"

"Just a little ways from the Georgia line on US 41. Jasper's the shits. That's how come I left."

"The next time we get up that way, we'll stop and show it to Sally."

When Cynthia seemed about to cry, Consuelo bent over and hugged her.

"Pablo's lucky."

"I'm glad we met, Edna."

"I'm glad Sally's gonna have you." Her eyes were closing.

"Rest now. You've talked too much already." Consuelo stood to leave.

"I'll have time to rest soon. Don't go."

Consuelo sat by the bed and Cynthia reached out for her hand.

*

Since the day Cynthia moved in, Consuelo had tried to get a doctor to see her, but she would not have it. Eventually, Consuelo realized that Cynthia desperately needed immediate medical help. "Who's your doctor?" she asked.

"I ain't got one. The one I saw didn't do nothin'. No need wastin' money."

"You can't go on like this. You're going to the hospital." Despite Cynthia's protests, Consuelo called their family doctor. "Get her to the emergency room; I'll meet you there," Dr. Winton said.

Pablo and Consuelo gathered her up carefully, and Pablo drove to Tampa Municipal Hospital. Consuelo stayed home with Sally. Cynthia was immediately admitted and taken to a room where she soon had glucose solution and other nutrients dripping into her vein. Consuelo left Sally with a neighbor woman and came to the hospital. When the doctor emerged, he walked them down the hall. "She doesn't have much time," he said.

"How long?" Consuelo asked.

"It could be any time."

Consuelo told Pablo to go home and stay with Sally. "Sammy will be home soon. I want to stay here a while."

"There's nothing you can do."

"Please, Pablo, I want to." Reluctantly, he walked down the hall and out; Consuelo returned to sit by Cynthia's bed.

"You don't need to stay," Cynthia said.

"I'd like to keep you company for a while."

"I feel pretty bad, but it's OK. Sally's in good hands." Cynthia's voice had dropped to a whisper.

"Would you like me to read to you?"

"OK."

Consuelo opened her purse and took out the romance novel, opened it to where she had left off, and began softly.

"Would you mind reading somethin' from the Bible? There's one in the drawer. The Book of Ruth."

"Of course." She opened the Bible to the place, and began: "Now it came to pass in the days when the judges ruled, that there was a famine in the land." Every few minutes she would glance at Cynthia's face etched with pain. "And a certain man of Bethlehem-Judah went to sojourn in the country of Moab, ..." Seeing Cynthia's face calm and relaxed, Consuelo stopped and ran to call the nurse.

Consuelo was composed during those few minutes that the nurse worked over Cynthia's still body. When Pablo answered the phone a few minutes later, her voice trembled and she was barely able to talk.

"I'll be right over."

"At the hospital entrance."

*

Pablo could not completely comprehend Consuelo's grief, nor could Consuelo. She acted as if she had lost an old friend or a sister. Reaching their driveway, she managed to compose herself enough to face Sammy and Sally and found Sally crying in the kitchen. Sammy was standing over her eating a tangerine.

"What's the matter?" Consuelo asked.

Sally just cried harder.

"What happened, Sammy?" Pablo asked.

302

"She started to eat my tangerine, and I took it back," he said, taking another piece.

Pablo tore the tangerine out of Sammy's hand and gave it to Sally. Then he took another one out of a bowl on the table and broke it open. Holding Sammy's head in one hand, he said, "With all this fruit, you have to take one from a baby? Here, take this one!" he said as he smashed the fruit into his face.

Sammy was crying when he wiped the juice off his face with his sleeve and went into the back yard.

"Pablo, there was no need to be so rough. He's only a child."

"He's got to learn to share. I can't stand a bully."

Consuelo found Sammy under the large tree. "Forgive him, Sammy. We're both very upset."

"I never saw him like that."

"Sally's mother just died. I think he's feeling bad for Sally."

Sammy returned to the kitchen and saw Sally trying to peel the tangerine. His father had gone upstairs. "Come on, Sis. I'll help you peel it out on the swing."

20 – MATILDE 1950

*

Truman Charges Red North Koreans With Unprovoked Attack

*

Scientist Arrested For Hiding Red Party Membership

*

U.S. Action Eases Threat Of Reds In Indochina

*

U.S. Plane Shoots Russian-Made Plane Over Seoul

*

Truman Orders U.S. To Attack Communists

*

Matilde emerged from the bathroom with his head shaved clean.
"What have you done?"
"Looks tough and military, don't you think?"
"But you look so … different."
"I must set a good example for the kids." When he smiled at her, Zoraida put an arm around his waist, rubbed his head with the other, and said, "I like the way it feels—smooth and virile."

Their apartment was in a modified army barrack. Far from luxurious, it was better than the tiny apartment they had rented during the war. As Matilde had said that morning, "The only luxury we know exists in magazines." Their two-bedroom apartment on the second floor was large and simply furnished, and it included an electric range and refrigerator. The walk to class would provide a pleasant time to collect his thoughts, so the car stood cold much of the time.

Zoraida's strong accent embarrassed her, though Matilde had told her she would never lose it and shouldn't worry about it. "Language is for communicating," he said, "and you do that very well."

That first day in the university a neighbor came to their door. "I'm Sarah Brown, your next-door neighbor," she said. "Anything you need, just holler."

"Thank you. I am called Zoraida Gómez. I don't speak English good, but I'm content to know you."

"You speak it fine, honey. I love that accent. Where you all from?"

"Cuba, but we have lived in Tampa for years."

"You a veteran?" Sarah asked Matilde.

"Air Force," he said.

"Wow! Charlie was Infantry, and we're glad to be here."

"Zor . . . what was that name again?"

Zoraida spelled it for her and pronounced it, Zor-ay-da."

"OK if I call you Ida? That's a whole lot easier."

"OK," Zoraida said. Then she turned to Matilde. "You call me Ida too, OK?"

Zoraida soon realized that her looks and exotic culture fascinated her new friends. She lacked no friends to help her shop and find her way around Tallahassee. By December she had become the star of their building and enjoyed the attention her accent brought.

*

The four years passed quickly and without hitches. At the end of Matilde's final week he received a note from the Dean inviting him to his office. Matilde knew Dean Brooke only through two interviews, and he suspected it was good news. His grades were good, and his professors had judged his student teaching high.

"Mr. Gómez, I've got your final semester grades," Dean Brooke said. "Straight <u>A</u>'s for the whole four years."

"I didn't know they were out yet."

Dean Brooke was short, fat, and nearly bald except for a ring of closely trimmed hair. Though he smiled much of the time, he was never familiar with students.

"You already knew you're valedictorian. What you may not know is that you're the first student ever to achieve a perfect grade record in the history of our college. I wanted to congratulate you in person."

"Thank you, sir."

"Shows what hard work can accomplish. Don't be surprised if I mention it during commencement."

"I hate to admit it, Dean Brooke, but it wasn't that difficult. I enjoyed it. I have to laugh when I hear the younger students gripe about the work."

"Easy compared to flying combat missions?" the Dean said with a chuckle.

"Well, if I didn't get an A up there, I wouldn't get back. This is a great place; I'm lucky."

"Mr. Gómez, you're going to be a superb teacher. Your students are the lucky ones."

"Thank you, sir."

"I'm looking forward to your speech at commencement," Dean Brooke said. Then he stood and shook his hand.

Matilde ran home and burst open the door to their apartment with a loud, "Zoraida!"

She dropped the book she was reading and stood.

"Keep reading like that and they'll give you the degree," he said, picking her up with a bear hug.

"*Que paso?*"

"We knew I was going to be valedictorian, but now ..." he dragged out the details of his interview until she was staring at him with a broad smile and sparkling eyes. "The dean told me I have the best grades in the history of the college."

"I won't be able to touch you," she said, embracing him.

"You'd better," he said, pulling her close. "We're going out to supper tonight."

"*Que bueno!*"

*

Matilde could see Zoraida fidgeting in the audience, listening to President Gore drag through the long, boring introduction of guests on the speaker's stand. The visitors sat in the grandstand of the football field that June afternoon, surrounding the graduating seniors. President Gore, a thin, distinguished-looking man in his fifties, wore a thin moustache. With his doctoral robes rippling in the breeze, he finally introduced Matilde as Valedictorian. As President Gore summarized Matilde's career at Florida A & M, Zoraida sat up in her chair to watch him march across the cinder track from the student section to the podium. Matilde held his head high and maintained his best military bearing.

The speaker's platform stood on the infield just inside the track at the fifty-yard-line. A light breeze lifted from time to time, forcing the ladies to hold onto their hats. The sun was still high enough to warm the proceedings, but no one seemed to mind. Zoraida's light green, satin dress seemed to be wrapped around her like a sarong with a darker green waistband. A broad-brimmed summer hat of the same color with a similar dark green band accentuated her exotic features as if to frame them in jungle green. Matilde thought she was so beautiful he fantasized picking her up and running into the woods. Still sitting on the edge of her seat, she watched Matilde approach the podium. Looking down at the President and shaking his hand, he felt a confidence he had rarely known.

After thanking President Gore he began: "I'm the luckiest man in the world. With an eighth grade education and a knack for rolling cigars, I came to the United States to broaden my opportunities. As the cigar industry declined, my opportunities declined with it until the war interrupted my freefall. Desperate to find a way to support my wife and myself, I joined the Air Corps, where I found a totally unexpected opportunity. I was selected for fighter pilot school. Flying was not a career I had chosen or one that I wanted for the long term, but it was the most exciting work I had ever done. I met the best people I have ever met, and I enjoyed those two and a half years that seemed, at the time, like a century. The people I met along the way taught me things about myself that one can only learn in war. Every day we confronted the distinction between the important and the trivial. When I graduated from the Army (for it was an education), I returned to Tampa, where I floundered, wondering what I would do next. One thing I knew was that cigars were no longer an option.

"The G.I Bill is the greatest thing the government has ever done for our people. It opened a door for us that led to an education we could not otherwise have dreamed of. It would have been inconceivable ten years ago that I would attend college, and I expect the same could be said for many of you.

"In my homeland most people's lives are prescribed at birth. The children of cigar makers become cigar makers. Those of bankers may have wider possibilities, but they rarely become cigar makers. Most of them, rich or poor, have but one life. I've been fortunate. I've had three lives, and each has lifted me to new fulfillment. God only knows how many more lives I'll have before it's over.

"I hope you will all be as lucky and that you will all have the right life from the start or, if not, that you will have the opportunity to find it. I'm convinced now that any of us can reach our goal if we put our hearts and muscles into the task.

"It would be arrogant to pretend that I have carved out my lives alone. I must thank my wife, Zoraida, who was the catalyst for all the good I have ever done. She offers encouragement when I need it and a kick in the pants when I need that. I also thank Dean Smith who helped me into this wonderful college, Dean Brooke, who helped me when I needed it, and all the dedicated professors who took their time and energy to help all of us through the greatest four years of our lives.

"Thank you all. Now the work begins."

The applause made him jump. As he walked down the podium, everybody was smiling at him and applauding. The entire audience stood as he walked back to his seat.

After all the diplomas had been handed out, the crowd broke into groups and milled around. No one wanted to leave. Zoraida embraced him and held his hand as other students showered him with congratulations. When most of his friends had dispersed, President Gore appeared, still in his academic robe.

"You've set the bar pretty high, Mr. Gómez."

"Thank you, President Gore. It's been one of the best experiences of my life."

"Lives!" the President said with a chuckle. "I understand you have a job waiting."

"Yes, sir. I'll be teaching at Booker T. Washington High School in Tampa."

"You'll do well. Helping young people is the highest calling a man can have. Good times lie ahead for Negroes. It'll take men like you to help our children attain full citizenship."

Impressed at how the president spoke to Matilde, Zoraida smiled throughout the conversation.

*

They rented a house on Sixth Avenue just east of Nebraska Avenue, a spotty neighborhood between Ybor City and the Scrub. Near the busy intersection with Nebraska Avenue, the houses were small and poor with few amenities. Two blocks east, where Matilde and Zoraida lived, the houses were better. Theirs was gray frame with white trim and short, brick columns on the front porch. The porch opened into a living room with lots of windows, and beyond that, two bedrooms, an ample bathroom, and a modern kitchen.

Matilde liked the three-block stroll to school every morning, greeting people as he passed their houses. It was the neighborhood where most of his students lived, and he wanted to get to know them.

His first school day was wild with students trying to find their classes and faculty trying to keep order. Matilde had moved into his classroom the previous week and had attended orientation sessions for new teachers. His classroom held twenty-eight student desks and a large desk for him. The door opened to the hall, and on the opposite wall, three windows looked north. Matilde liked the north side because the sun wouldn't shine directly in, but he worried that the playing field outside might be a distraction. A blackboard lined the front of the room and part of the wall on the hall side. During the previous week he had hung a map of the Western Hemisphere and one of Europe. He requested a map of Africa, but the school didn't have one. After two days of shopping in the various bookshops in town, he found a large, second hand world atlas that had a full-page map of Africa. He cut it out and hung it beside the others.

His first period was a fifteen-minute homeroom. He introduced himself, relayed announcements from the principal's office, and tried to keep order, which was not easy without a subject to discuss. Eventually he gave up and let them talk. His first real class that morning was American History. After writing his name on the blackboard and pronouncing it for them, he abruptly asked who could name all four of their grandparents.

"Don't tell me their names; just raise your hand if you know their names," he said.

About half the class raised their hands.

"OK, now how many of you can name all eight of your great grandparents?"

No hands went up.

"All right. How many can name at least one of your great grandparents?"

Three hands went up.

Matilde pointed at the girl who was waving her hand and said, "First tell me your name and whether you knew that person."

"I'm Louise. She died before I was born, but my grandma told me about her," she said. Tall and thin, Louise sat forward in her desk. Her wide eyes made her look frightened. She was wearing a white pinafore and had her hair in two pigtails.

"Can you tell me anything about her?"

"She was real nice. That what my momma say."

"Fine. Now what about the other two? Did you know their names?"

Both of the boys shook their heads.

"OK, now suppose you wanted to learn about them. How would you do it? Judging from your faces, you're all wondering what this has to do with history."

About half of the class nodded.

When he asked how many had heard of Abraham Lincoln, every hand went up.

"So you know about a man who lived long before your great grandparents, but not about your own relatives, without whom you wouldn't be here."

"Well, Lincoln was a great man," Louise said. "He done freed the slaves."

"Right. And why do you suppose so few of you know anything about your great grandparents?"

One boy on the front row raised his hand. "I'm Richard. They was just regular folks, I guess." Richard was a stocky boy with short hair. His muscles bulged through his tight shirt.

"Right again! If one of them had invented the electric light or discovered a continent, or emancipated slaves, you'd darn well know about them."

The students nodded and started talking and laughing. Matilde smiled too. When the noise died down, he continued. "What do you think history's all about?"

"Dates and kings and wars and stuff like that," Louise said.

"That's part of it. We're all part of history. Some of you may end up in history books someday." They looked at each other, pointing and laughing. "But most people live out their lives with little fanfare. They don't do anything notable enough to end up in history books. Anybody heard of Socrates?" About a third of the class raised their hands. "When did he live?"

A short, thin light-skinned girl raised her hand and said, "I'm Louella. Last century?"

"Twenty-five centuries ago, Louella. Five hundred years before Jesus."

"Man!" a boy said, grinning. That brought a ripple of giggling.

"Just imagine how important he was if we remember him two thousand five hundred years later."

The class again erupted. "What he done, Mr. Gómez? Oh, my name's May." With a wide smile, the fat girl was sitting back in her desk twirling her hair in her fingers.

"Socrates was a philosopher. In case you don't know what that is, philosophers think about the meaning of life and of knowledge and other complicated ideas. In fact, Plato, one of Socrates' students, invented the word, idea. But getting back to history, the trouble with history is that it records only the lives and works of people who did something important enough to affect us all. The vast majority of us work, raise families and live sixty or seventy years. After three or four generations, even our descendants won't remember us. Most won't even know our names, much less what we did."

"Our ancestors they came from Africa," Richard said. His comment brought a few raised eyebrows from the rest of the class.

"That's right. Half of mine did too."

"What about the other half?" Richard asked.

"My father came from Spain, but I never met him. That's all I know about him."

The class became serious. Richard again raised his hand.

"Yes, Richard?"

"Is that why you talk funny?" Most of the students expressed interest in Richard's question and looked at Matilde.

"No. The reason I speak with an accent is that I was born and raised in Cuba, where everybody, white and black, speaks Spanish. I learned English when I came to Tampa as a young man."

"Would you tell us about yourself, Mr. Gómez?" Louise said.

"Well, I was raised by my mother and her parents and became a cigar maker in Havana. I came to Tampa to find better opportunities and worked in a factory in Ybor City for a few years until a big strike cost a lot of us our jobs."

"What about the white workers?" Richard asked.

"Most workers, white and black, kept their jobs. I was one of the lucky ones. I thought it was bad luck at the time, and it was tough during the Depression, supporting my wife and myself. When the war started I joined the Army."

"What you do?" another boy asked.

"I flew fighter planes." The students were sitting with their chins on their hands and their eyes wide open. "After the war, I wanted something better than cigars, so I went to college. I graduated last June, and here I am."

311

"You shoot down many planes?" the handsome boy with the big eyes asked with his chin in his hands.

"Your name, please."

"Andrew."

"Thank you, Andrew. Yes, I got a few, and one big German bomber. The period is almost over. For tomorrow I'd like you to ask your parents about their grandparents. Tomorrow, anyone who wants to can tell us what you found out that you didn't know before. I'd also like you to write a short paper on what you've learned about them. It's not mandatory, and I won't ask you to hand it in if you don't want to. This assignment is just for you to learn something about your own family history."

When the bell rang, and the students got up, Richard, Andrew, Louise and three others stayed around his desk. "This gonna be a great class," Richard said. The others nodded.

"Thanks, but soon we'll have to get to the book."

Watching them walk out, he thought, This is as exciting as flying. I touched them ... sparked their curiosity. Every single one of them is an intellectual at heart, and I tapped into that part of them.

The next morning before the first class, the principal dropped into his classroom. "Why hello, Mr. Jones."

"Good morning, Mr. Gómez. How was your first day?"

"Very well. I had a lot of fun making them think about things."

"That's good. It's not a big thing, but the mother of one of your American History students called yesterday to complain about your assignment."

"Complain?"

"She wanted to know why you asked about her daughter's grandparents. I believe her words were, 'It's none of his business.'"

"I told them it was voluntary; they didn't have to hand it in. It was just to get them thinking about history and how difficult it is to get information about the past."

"It's an interesting approach, Mat. That mother's not married. She may not even know who the father is. She's probably embarrassed."

"I'll call her."

"That's not necessary. I calmed her down," Jones said. "Besides, she was calling from a pay phone and complained about having to spend a nickel."

"I'd still like to talk with her. My mother was in the same boat. She might like to know that."

"I don't know, but if you wish, it's Carmen Davenport. I'll get her address for you."

"Oh, Louise's mother."
"You know your students' names already?"
"A few."

*

Carmen Davenport was sitting on her front porch at 4:30 when Matilde walked up. There was no curb along that part of Scott Street, only dirt with a sprinkling of weeds between the blacktop street and the unpainted frame houses. The entire neighborhood was gray, even the trees. Carmen Davenport was stout and in her mid-thirties; her legs were rippled with veins, her eyes webbed in red. Wearing a faded housedress and slippers and sitting on a straight back chair next to an old icebox, she was rocking back and forth on the back legs of her chair.

"Mrs. Davenport?"
"Uh-huh," she said, still rocking.
"I'm Mr. Gómez, your daughter's history teacher."
Carmen Davenport came down on all four chair legs, ready for a fight. "Mr. Jones said you called, and I wanted to see you. May I come up?"
"Don't like nobody pryin' into my family."
"I came to apologize, Mrs. Davenport. Most people don't know much about their ancestors. I only wanted them to realize how difficult it is to learn about the past. I know absolutely nothing about my own father."
"Well, I knows too much 'bout Louise's daddy. He ain't no good, a drunken bum, and I don't want her frettin' about him. He gone, and good riddance!" Her entire body was coiled into a scowl.
"Didn't she tell you the assignment was optional?"
"She done tol' me, but that don't make no difference. She drivin' me crazy, wantin' to know about him, an' I don't want her thinkin' about that no-good. I got enough to worry about, makin' enough to live on without havin' to explain him."
"What do you do, Mrs. Davenport?"
"I wash clothes for people. Ain't dignified, but we's eatin'."
"I admire you, Mrs. Davenport. What you're doing is very dignified. Your daughter's very bright; I'm going to enjoy teaching her. Well, I've got to be going. I'm truly sorry for the trouble I caused. This is my first teaching job, and it seemed like a good way to get students interested in history. Other parents are probably put out too. I'm glad you called. I won't trouble you anymore, Mrs. Davenport. Goodbye."

*

313

Mr. Jones was smiling when he walked into Matilde's classroom a few minutes before the bell the next morning. "You sure impressed Mrs. Davenport, Mat. She called to say she hoped she hadn't got you in trouble. She said you were just trying to do a good job, and she appreciated it. We'll have to get you a job in Washington. Keep up the good work. And stick to your ideas."

Won my first battle, he thought.

His class went smoothly that day. Several students reported on their ancestors. Matilde could see discomfort in Louise's face and a few others, but their ancestry was a reality they would have to deal with. When the oral reports were finished Matilde congratulated them on their efforts and posed a new question. How do you know World War II happened?"

They looked at each other as if he had asked the most stupid question imaginable.

Richard spoke up. "From the radio and the newspapers. And my uncle was in the Navy; he told me all about it."

"Does anyone have any doubt that it happened?"

The students all shook their heads, still wondering what he wanted.

"How about World War I? And let's hear from someone else this time." He smiled and winked at Richard.

"I seen it in our history book last year," a petite, bright-eyed girl said. Oh, my name is Ruth."

"Is that proof, Ruth?"

"It's in the book," she said, confused.

"Do you all read Superman?" After watching the class laugh and nod, he said, "Do you believe what you read in Superman comics?"

"That's different," Richard said. "Everybody knows that stuff ain't true."

"Mr. Gómez, I don't know what you're getting' at," Louise said.

"What do you know about Moses parting the Red Sea?"

The faces became serious. "The Bible say so," Louise said.

"Is that proof?"

"Sure," she said.

"What about the people of India, China and Japan? They're not Christians and don't know our Bible. Do you think they'd believe it because it's in our Bible?"

The blank, staring faces worried Matilde. Perhaps he had pushed too far. "Let's back up a little. What about the Civil War? Let's ask the question a little more precisely. What evidence do you have that the Civil War happened? Let's assume that there aren't any eyewitnesses left alive. There are a few, but let's pretend."

"We could read about it in old newspapers if we could find 'em," Andrew said.

"That's right. Libraries keep old papers. Sure, that would be evidence. Listen, I'm not trying to convince you all that these things didn't happen. The purpose of my questions is to get you to think about where the facts you read in history books come from and how reliable are they. For example, if a wreck occurs out in the street and a dozen people see it. Do you think they'll all describe it the same way?"

"I seen a wreck last week on Central Avenue. The police come and asked a buncha questions. Everybody told it different," Richard said. "Started a big argument."

"That's normal. So how do the police determine the facts in a case like that?" The faces were covered with question marks. "I don't hear any answers ... because it's a tough question. It's the same with history. Everybody knows the Second World War happened because most of us had family members in the service, but what about historical events that occurred centuries ago. It's not easy to get the facts about those. That's probably why history concentrates on important people who left a trail of accomplishments."

"Tomorrow we'll start on the discovery of America. That's the usual starting place of American history, and it's where our textbook starts. I want each of you to read the first four pages of the chapter and keep in mind what we've said about how we know things."

*

"How was school?" Zoraida asked.

"Good. I didn't know I'd enjoy it so much. Bright kids."

He sat on the porch with Zoraida and told her about Mr. Jones's reaction to his visit with Mrs. Davenport.

"Poor woman," Zoraida said. "So valiant trying to support her small family all alone."

"Yeah. You wouldn't believe how uneducated they are. They're intelligent, but many have never been past the first few grades. I hope I can help them."

He stopped when he saw Mr. Jones walking toward them. "Well, nice to see you, Mr. Jones," Matilde said.

"I wanted to have a little chat, Mr. Gómez, and meet your beautiful wife," Jones said.

After he introduced Zoraida and asked Mr. Jones to sit Matilde asked him what brought him this way?"

"I don't want you to think I'm criticizing your work. You have a very original approach to history, but there have been more complaints." Zoraida rose and went inside.

"Two days on the job, and complaints both days? What was it this time?"

"Well ... I know it's unfounded, but one parent called to say you were teaching that the Bible isn't true."

Matilde explained his questions and why he had asked them. "I should have used a different example. I told them not to assume that I think the Bible isn't true, only that it's difficult to know facts about the past."

"I figured it was something like that. Mrs. Warren mentioned it too."

"The other history teacher?"

"She believes you're going off on a tangent that has little to do with the material."

"Why didn't she talk to me about it?"

"You've got to understand, Mat; she's been teaching twenty years. She has her own routine. Your creativity probably feels threatening."

Matilde shook his head. "In all the jobs I've had, workers stuck together, especially in the Air Force. We depended on each other for our lives. A colleague complaining to the boss, I don't get it."

"Please don't take it that way. She means well. Why don't you talk to her, ask her opinion. It'll make her feel better. Just a suggestion, of course."

Zoraida opened the door carrying a tray with three cups and saucers and a pitcher of hot coffee and one of boiled milk. "You'll have some coffee, won't you Mr. Jones?"

"Thank you, Mrs. Gómez; I love Cuban coffee."

Matilde smiled at Zoraida as she poured from both pitchers into Mr. Jones's cup.

"Make it light, please," he said.

"I'll see Mrs. Warren tomorrow," Matilde said.

As they drank their coffee, the conversation turned to Korea.

"What do you think about this Korea police action? It looks like a war to me," Jones said.

"I'm afraid so."

"I'm not even sure where Korea is," Mr. Jones said.

"I looked it up," Matilde said. "It's adjacent to China, a bad place to fight a war."

*

Mrs. Warren was surprised to see Matilde walk into her classroom. She was sitting at her desk arranging her notes for the day's lesson.

"Why, hello, Mr. Gómez."

"Hi, Mrs. Warren. My friends call me Mat."

"Thank you, Mat; I'm Helen. How can I help you?"

"Mr. Jones said you were concerned about my class."

"You told your students to question their backgrounds. Some parents won't like that. But the reason I went to Mr. Jones was your questioning the Bible. He told me what you were trying to do, but I'm afraid it'll cause trouble."

"I know. Some parents have already complained. I may have gone where I shouldn't, but it seemed like a good way to get the kids to think about history in a way that's concrete and makes them part of it."

"Another thing, it sounded as if you're questioning the truth of our textbook."

"Not at all. I just think it's healthy to question."

"Frankly, Mat, not being an American, you may not understand our culture well enough to teach this course."

"Does that mean you're not competent to teach European History because you weren't raised in Europe?"

"Don't be rude. You're new here; I'm just trying to help."

"I don't mean to be rude, but I wish you had come to me instead of going to the principal. I think I understand American History as well as anyone here."

"I'm not suggesting otherwise. Look, I'm quite busy. I have to prepare my classes."

"I'm sorry. Now I have been rude. You were right to offer help, and I guess I can use some. How do you start your American History classes?"

"I stay away from slavery and anything that makes the children feel like outsiders. It's easy for these kids to feel like they don't belong; I don't want to hurt their chances to succeed. Of course, when it comes up, I cover it, but I don't dwell on it. Otherwise, I just try to point out the people and events that have changed the course of history and what it means to us today."

"Did you know that Negroes fought in World War II?"

"Everybody knows that."

"And that we were kept out of the real fighting because they considered us to be cowardly and inept? That wasn't the real reason, of course. They knew if we did the job well, they'd have trouble keeping us segregated."

"What are you getting at?"

"Only that maybe our young people need to know what they're up against." Matilde was showing more anger than he wanted.

"That's a dangerous point of view, but I really don't have time to discuss it now. Perhaps later."

*

When Mr. Jones came to see him that afternoon, Matilde said, "I know; Mrs. Warren's been to see you."

"Why no. Did you talk with her?"

"Yes, this morning."

"How did it go?"

"Not too well. We got into a discussion of Negro assertiveness."

"That's a very touchy subject, Mat."

"So I found out. It wasn't that way at A & M or the Air Force."

"Well, I don't like to give unsolicited advice, but I'd steer away from that topic."

"It's inconceivable that the head of a school would tell a teacher to avoid the most important issue in our students' lives. I put my life on the line for this country; that gives me the right to question."

"Don't get excited, Mat. I agree it's important, but don't push too hard. I know what you Tuskegee Airmen faced, and you showed what you could do. That's the only way we'll get equality, by showing them. We don't want to drive our youth to violence; as a minority, we'd lose everything."

"It's funny, Mr. Jones; I argued against demonstrations in the service. I thought we should do the job the white power structure thought we couldn't do, and we showed them. Your advice is to do nothing. That will say we approve of what they're doing. We can't just wait for the majority to liberate us. It'll never happen."

"Don't give up hope, Mat, and don't curb your creativity and energy. You're going to be our brightest teacher."

"Thanks."

"And by the way, call me Henry."

21 – CONSUELO, 1950

*

Americans Gamble $30 Billion A Year

*

Former Soldier Who Worked On A-Bomb Arrested As Spy

*

U.N. Orders An End To Korean Hostilities

*

Temperature Hits 98 In Tampa For New Record

*

U.N. Observers Report Reds May Win South Korea Soon

*

Greater Tampa Area Population Tops 200,000

*

Pablo and Consuelo rehearsed the story they would tell: "A poor woman, who was dying of cancer, left her two-year-old with the sisters at The Academy of The Holy Names. We learned about the child from Father O'Brien at Sacred Heart Church and visited Sister Agnes at the Academy. 'We've been wanting another child for so long,' Consuelo told her, 'especially a girl.' When we saw Sally we fell in love with her and begged to adopt her."

After clearing the story with Father O'Brien and getting his blessing, they approached Sister Agnes at the Girls' Academy. "I see more of these cases than you might imagine," she said. "The life of a child is far more important than the indiscretion of a foolish man or the feelings of a loyal wife." Then, turning to Consuelo she said, "I can't tell you, my dear, how much I admire your kindness and generosity. You won't regret it. You will be truly blessed." Then turning to Pablo, "I have no problem with an untruth that assures the life of an innocent child."

*

After the hectic weeks that followed the adoption, Cynthia's funeral, and talking with the sisters at the Academy, this was their first quiet evening. They had put Sally to bed and had relaxed over supper and a bottle of wine that Pablo had bought for the occasion. Only Sammy did not approve of the lie and said so at supper.

"We don't want people to know who her real parents are," Consuelo said.

"Why not?"

"Her mother had a bad reputation," Pablo said.

"She seemed nice."

"She was, Sammy," his mother said.

"Well then?"

"You don't have to know every detail," his father said.

"Who's her father?"

Pablo looked at Consuelo, who put down her fork and gazed back fiercely. "We don't know." Then, seeing Consuelo's grim face Pablo added, "No, that's not true. Look, Sammy, we just don't want to get into it."

"I'm part of the family."

"He deserves to know."

"Oh, God," Pablo said. "Shouldn't you and I talk it over first?"

"Tell him. I'm tired of made up stories." She stood and walked into the kitchen.

After a long pause he said, "Sammy, people do stupid things sometimes, and I'm no exception. I knew Sally's mother a long time ago and, well ... I'm Sally's father."

"That's what I figured."

"What do you mean?"

"She looks like you, Papa. Why didn't you just admit it in the first place?"

"I didn't want to hurt your mother and Sally. As part of the family you should know, and so should Sally, when she's old enough to understand, but no one else."

"OK."

Hearing the exchange in the kitchen Consuelo could barely contain her anger. Thoughts ground her as she scrubbed the large frying pan: He needs to know the kind of man his father is. And Pablo needs to face his son's judgment. Suddenly Sara's words erupted: "he's just demonstrating his *cojones*." She put away the frying pan and returned to the dining room to move plates into the kitchen, as Pablo walked into the living room, his arm around Sammy's shoulder, man to man. She shook with fury.

*

The next four years were packed with work for both Consuelo and Pablo. Consuelo took to her new daughter with love and enthusiasm, feeding, and dressing her in bright, new outfits and teaching her Spanish. She kept a baby book filled with every milestone as she had done for Sammy. Sally was a lovely, calm child who made few demands. At first, when she asked about her mother, Consuelo told her that she had gone on a long trip. The same question always followed:

"Why?"

"She loves you very much, but she had to go away."

It was not easy to tell a three-year-old that her mother had died. What could it mean to her? As Consuelo saw it, she was not lying; Cynthia had gone away. Before long Sally stopped asking. Responding to a question four years later, Consuelo told her how good and loving her mother had been, and that she died when Sally was two. Sally was quieter than usual the rest of that day, but eventually came out of it.

Coming home after work, tired and impatient, Pablo would play with his daughter a few minutes and then find someplace to rest. It had been the same with Sammy when he was that age. He enjoyed her in short bursts, and talked about sending her to the Academy of The Holy Names so she could have the same advantage as her brother in Jesuit, but his interest remained at a distance. He rarely took time to talk or read to her.

But as the years passed, the problem became Consuelo, whose life had filled with static. Hours and days of monotony had swollen into months and years of the same. Sammy's departure to college had increased her anxiety and loneliness. With little to lift her spirits, the monotony had melted into dreary obligations, her mind unbearably noisy. She did not like the person she had become as her fortieth birthday stared back at her. That sparkling, fun-loving young woman had become a detached, middle-aged drudge whose daily wish was for a restful night's sleep. Monotony had paralyzed every spontaneous flight of her soul. She felt that someone else had moved into her body, someone hardened and angry who found little joy in the tiny surprises that had thrilled the young Consuelo. Her head filled with cacophonous echoes of whispered lies and excuses, disloyal sounds of self-gratification. Those noises had driven out the magical resonance of harmonious longing, leaving dry, static dullness.

During those months a simple, childhood memory kept returning to haunt her: building a sandcastle on Varadero Beach when she was five. Imagining the classic walls and turrets, her fantasy begins to take form. The memory is vivid. Wearing her pink swimsuit and bonnet, she fills a bucket with sand and packs it down in the blazing sun. Then she inverts the bucket and lifts it to leave a neat tower of hard-packed sand on top of hard-packed walls. She fights against time as the tide closes in like an army. Then, a little boy, a stranger, happy, singing, not caring, follows a boyish whim and runs through the sandcastle, kicking it into the sky and laughs as sand rains down on both of them. She watches, trying not to cry, and decides not to build another because the fun has been lost in the air. It is too late for crying.

Then she relives her recent, last minute rush to Matanzas after Inez's massive heart attack: She doesn't know whether to bother Sammy, but she finally calls him.

"Don't feel you have to come," his father says. "She'll understand."

Sammy hesitates, and then agrees to stay in College, saying, "Give her my love, and tell her I'd love to have one of her *batidos*."

The sailing across the Florida Strait upset her less than the thought of visiting a mother-in-law who could not stand her. It was a hot, rainy day when they walked up the stairs to the old woman's room. They found her on her deathbed with a Black nurse hovering around her like a slave tending a royal mistress. Doña Inez called Sally to her and looked into her eyes and smiled. For a moment Consuelo thought, Finally the old woman will be kind. Instead she heard, "She's yours, Pablito." Consuelo looked at Pablo and he blushed. Consuelo could not believe he had told her. Stroking Sally's light hair, the old woman said, "You are your father's daughter."

Sally's eyes turned to Consuelo with confusion. Consuelo tried to read Pablo's mind for the millionth time and wondered why the old woman had not asked about her other grandchild, her son, but nothing made sense. She hated that mausoleum of a house and could not see the beauty of her homeland. Instead she sat in the decaying living room sipping Cuba libres laced with rage and looked through the window at the rain and the smothering overgrowth that was waiting for the old woman to die so it could swallow up the house and its inhabitants.

*

Doña Inez died six days after they arrived, adamantly refusing to speak to Consuelo and insisting that Sally was Pablo's, but not Consuelo's. Every visit had been more traumatic and darker than the last. Now, with the old woman gone, she hoped things might improve, but nothing had changed, especially the monotony. Unlike Pablo's father, doña Inez carried her burning hatred into her coffin.

Two days before they left Matanzas, Inez's attorney read her will to Pablo, Sally, and Consuelo in his office in Matanzas. The attorney, middle-aged, short, chubby, and bald, escorted them into his conference room. Sally wished she had known her grandmother longer.

Pablo sat and turned to Consuelo and whispered, "Why do I feel so anxious?" Repulsed by the thought of having things that had belonged to the old woman, Consuelo barely listened to the attorney's monotonous, droning recitation: "I wish my estate to be divided as follows: ten percent to my son, Pablo, and fifteen percent to my granddaughter, Sally. I bequeath the remainder of my estate, including what I inherited from my deceased husband, to the church, to be administered by Father Valdés. My instruction to Father Valdés is that he use it to aid the poor orphans of Cuba."

Pablo rose, said goodbye to the attorney, and walked toward the door.

"We should discuss the details," the attorney said.

"Just send me the money through the bank."

"But much of the estate is in properties."

On his way out the door Pablo said, "Have it appraised and send our inheritance to my bank."

Out in the sunlight he said, "I don't know why I'm surprised."

Consuelo smiled sardonically, knowingly. Then, sensing Pablo pain, she said, "We don't need the money."

"It doesn't matter. I've been cheated, and I don't like it. First Papá and now her."

After a long afternoon of sulking alone in the overgrown garden, he returned saying, "She's absolved me of any filial obligation."

Back in Tampa he plunged into his work with renewed ambition and vigor. He had bought controlling interest in a new bank shortly after the war. With vivid memories of the depression and bank failures still hanging in the air, he bought in at a good price. He never told Consuelo how much he paid, and she did not ask. Like most of his ventures, the bank flourished and made Pablo and his fellow stockholders wealthy. Consuelo was glad for him, but she could not bask in his happiness. A ferocious anger was gnawing her insides.

At the end of Sammy's freshman year at MIT, Pablo decided to fly there and bring him home. He said he wanted to see how Sammy was living and to meet his friends.

"It'll be fun, Consuelo. We'll fly and be back in a few days. It won't hurt Sally to miss a few days of school," he said, as they were finishing breakfast.

"Please, Mama, can we go, please?"

"It's not right to miss school like that," Consuelo said. "You go. Sammy will enjoy showing you around."

"I don't want to go without you."

"It'll do you good to get away."

"Sammy will be disappointed."

"I'll see him when he gets home," she said, and went into the living room. Pablo looked at Sally and shrugged. Something about the ease with which he could leave everything and do whatever he wanted irritated Consuelo. I could go, she thought, but I have obligations. Can't take Sally out of school for such a frivolous trip. The more she thought, the angrier she got and the worse her head ached.

*

It was late afternoon, and cool air was pushing out the sun as Pablo's taxi pulled up in front of the dormitory. Standing three inches taller than his father and wearing a sport jacket and tie, Sammy looked lean and muscular, and wore his light brown hair in a crew cut.

"You sure look collegiate, Sammy."

Sammy talked nonstop about the semester and his friends and how well he had done. "Four point average for the year."

"Fantastic. Come on; I want to see your room."

"Sure." They walked to the second floor, where Sammy shared a room with a young man from New York.

When Sammy had made introductions, Pablo asked Sammy's roommate, "What's your major?"

"Engineering, I guess. No point coming to MIT and not majoring in engineering." Morris Feldman was as tall as Sammy, but with piercing brown eyes, black hair in a crew cut, broad shoulders, square jaw and bulging muscles.

"Sam says you're quite an athlete."

"I like to wrestle."

"That's a tough sport."

"It's great. I can beat up my buddies and we're still friends."

"I'm not one of those buddies," Sammy said. "I enjoyed intramural rugby, but it's only a diversion to me, a way to get the cobwebs out of my head."

"I guess you're proud of Sam, Mr. Iglesias. I can't believe he aced every course."

"I certainly am. Still planning on math, Sammy?"

"I really enjoyed chemistry. Professor Smith, my advisor, said I could get a double major."

"Won't that take longer?"

"Not really, just a few extra courses. But it'll be worth it."

"I was always a little thick in science. Let's see: I know chemists work in stinky labs, but I have no idea what mathematicians do. I always leaned toward money. It's so much softer, cuddlier and rewarding." He rubbed his fingers and smiled.

"Come on, Dad. You told me you liked philosophy. Talk about useless careers."

"Your memory's too good, boy."

"Anyway, I want to go on for a Ph.D. and teach in a university and do research."

"How's the pay?"

"My professors seem well fed."

"I don't know what I would've done as a philosopher. I'm sure it would have been fun, but I'm having fun now. I'll fill you in this evening."

At supper he told Sammy about the bank and how it had led to new business ventures. "We're building federally sponsored housing for poor people, some whites, but mainly Negroes. It's going to be a big project."

"If the government is paying the bills, how do you make money?"

"We provide banking service. We handle everything that involves a transfer of money and charge a fee. And individually, those of us who have the resources invest in surrounding land and buildings. It's great business now that Tampa is growing."

"Do you still own our farm in Brandon?"

"Sure. I couldn't sell it; it means too much to me."

"Me too. If I ever live in Tampa, which is pretty far fetched in my field, I'd like to live there."

"Consider it yours."

*

The next morning Sammy took his father on a tour of the campus beginning with the library and the chemistry labs. "I remember the smell," Pablo said. "Takes me back to those awful years of freshman chemistry."

"Years? How many times did you take it?"

"Only once, but it seemed like years."

Sammy stopped at Professor Smith's office. "I'd like you to meet him, Dad."

Professor Smith invited them to sit down. The two large windows overlooked a beautifully restful quadrangle. The professor was sitting at his desk. Beside the large desk a bookcase covered the entire wall; to his left were the windows. He also had two comfortable chairs in front of the desk and a couch behind them at the far wall. "Sam will be doing research before long. He's our best chemistry freshman. The way he's going, he'll graduate ahead of schedule, even with a double major."

As Smith spoke, Pablo sized up the surroundings, visualizing what he could do to modify his office at the bank. More books, he thought.

"Thank you, Professor. His mother and I are very proud."

They chatted for several minutes more and Sammy, seeing the pile of papers on Professor Smith's desk, said they had to leave.

On their departure Pablo helped Sammy pack his clothes and books for the summer, and they took a taxi to Logan Airport where they waited for their Tampa flight.

*

Consuelo welcomed her son with a warm embrace and kisses. "I've made your favorite, yellow rice and chicken, Ybor City style, with fried plantains."

"Great, Mom. I haven't had a decent meal since Christmas."

Just then Sally stormed down the stairs. Her reddish-blonde hair bounced and her blue eyes flashed as she hopped down as fast as she could, yelling, "Sammy, Sammy!" and ran and threw her arms around his waist.

Sammy picked her up under the arms and held her high. "You're almost too big for this."

"I'm starting school this year."

"I heard."

"Aw, I wanted to surprise you. Academy of The Holy Names."

"That's a long name."

"Everybody calls it the Girls' Academy," Sally said.

Sammy smiled at his mother. He had dated girls from the Girls' Academy in high school.

Then she said something that neither Pablo nor Consuelo understood. Sammy laughed and said several words that meant nothing to their parents. It sounded like Spanish, but was a mixture of mispronounced English and Spanish words.

"I see you haven't forgotten your private language," Consuelo said, smiling.

By this time Sally had dragged Sammy to the living room and was straddling his lap on the living room sofa as they engaged in their undecipherable chit-chat.

"You don't fool me; you're not saying anything," Pablo said. "It's just a plot to drive us crazy."

Sally turned to her brother and said some more syllables and Sammy turned to his parents. "She said she and Mom had fried fish and potatoes for supper last night."

"Not bad," Consuelo said. "Come on, supper's almost ready. Sammy, take your bags upstairs and wash up."

After supper, Sammy left to meet some high school buddies at the Colonnade Drive-In. "I'll be back early."

"Before eleven," his father said.

"You don't know when I come home in Cambridge."

"This is Tampa. Eleven o'clock."

*

Sitting in her easy chair near the fireplace facing them on the sofa, Consuelo was quietly fuming. Sally was cuddled up beside her father, and he stroked her hair. Imagining what was going through his mind, Consuelo's mind raced: Sure, he favors his daughter because she's all white. The thought had bored into her brain, planted itself, and germinated. He does all the right things, she thought, but watching him run his fingers through Sally's reddish hair he … must have stroked Cynthia's hair. Then they would go into the bedroom. Her brain continued to churn: It doesn't matter that other men do it. He didn't have to. With all the dirt he's handed me I always come back for more. I'm a nonentity. I can't function around him. My face is etched into a hard frown. Intimacy has dried up. I love Sally so much more than I expected to, but she's driving the wedge deeper. Nights are unbearable. I can't sleep thinking about Pablo and Cynthia and <u>their</u> baby. I can't quiet the noise. I know Pablo worries about me, but how can I tell him? I treat Sally better than my carnal son to show I don't favor him. Sammy doesn't notice; he babies her too. Pablo thinks I've got the girl I'd always wanted. So stupid, I have, but ...

*

"Want me to drive Sally to school?" Sammy asked.

"No need," Consuelo said.

"OK, I'm going to Chuck's house. His folks invited me to lunch. May I use your car, Mom?"

"Sure, Sammy."

"I'll take her," Pablo said.

"Good. I have a lot to do."

"Come with us," he said.

"Why?"

"I'll tell you in the car."

On the trip down Bayshore Boulevard, Pablo and Sally talked about school and her friends. When they left her off, returning along the same route, past the palatial homes on the curving boulevard, Pablo turned to Consuelo. "How about stopping at Las Novedades."

"I've got laundry and then grocery shopping."

"They can wait. Come on."

"I really don't feel like it."

"We need to talk."

"I'd rather not."

"What's wrong? Is it because Sammy's gone so much?"

"Nothing's wrong."

Consuelo kept her gaze straight ahead. The long, curving drive was lined with palm trees and beautiful houses, but she focused on the street's broken lane line, its pattern like a monotonous Morse code message. She barely noticed the morning sun rising over the bay or the bright, warm day that was opening like a flower. Only the broken lane line tapped into her brain. She looked at the electric wires hanging over the trolley tracks in the grassy median for a while and then the choppy bay.

"I really want to go home."

"OK," Pablo said, "but I know how much you like their pastries."

She looked at him with revulsion.

When they reached Orleans Avenue, he turned the Cadillac toward town and drove the rest of the way silently. As he pulled into the driveway he stopped and turned to her.

"I'm going to stay home this morning. We really have to talk."

Consuelo did not look at him, but opened the car door and got out and walked onto the porch and into the house.

Inside he walked up behind her and grabbed her arms and turned her around to face him. She did not respond except to scowl.

"What have I done?"

"It's too much." She was sobbing.

She tried to pull away, but he held her. She struggled, turned her head, but he held her so tightly she finally looked into his eyes and then looked down and stopped struggling.

"Please tell me."

She put her head into his chest and sobbed violently. Her whole body shook. He held her as she cried. After a few minutes she backed away, looked at him, and said, "I can't go on like this."

Sitting her down on the living room sofa he said, "Please talk to me."

"I feel terrible all the time. I've prayed and prayed, but it hasn't helped. I love Sally more than I can tell you, but she's brought so much pain. Her past, no ... your past ... it haunts me."

"Will it ever end? You know I've never loved anyone but you. Cynthia was a mistake I regret, except for bringing us Sally. One thing's sure: I never loved Cynthia."

"Why did you tell your mother about Sally?"

"I didn't."

"Somebody told her."

"While you were unpacking I took Sally to meet her. I thought Sally would want to know her grandmother. She was in bed, waxen looking. Took great effort for her to turn her head toward Sally. Then she said, 'She's your daughter.' In front of Sally, I repeated our story of how we got her. Then she told me to ask Sally to leave. When she had gone, Mamá said, 'She's your flesh and blood, but not Consuelo's.' When I asked her why she would say such a thing, she said, 'I'm your mother; I know.' Her next words made me hate her. She said, 'I don't blame you for having another woman.' I told her she was hateful, that I have always loved only you. She scoffed, and I saw hatred in her eyes that I had never seen before. My mother has always been a hard woman, but what she told me years ago about her life with Papá, and now this ... I guess I never knew her before that moment. She was vain, hard and mean. I hate to say it, but it's true." At that, he looked down.

"Your mother said terrible things when I took Sammy there after your father died. She had always treated me like poison, but that time she sank to a new cruelty, probably because you weren't there. Your father surprised me with his kindness at the end. It was late, but I loved him for it. Your mother was cruel to the end. I wish I could pity her, but I can't."

"The way I got when we were expecting Sammy; you haven't forgiven me, have you?"

"I can't forget it."

Pablo looked at her for a long time then said, "Just like my mother."

"Maybe you deserve a wife like your mother."

"Probably, but that's not you."

"Always the right words." She turned away.

"I've changed more than you want to admit, and you're the one who changed me. I worshipped my father. I could have turned out like him. I'm so glad I saw him before he died. I was able to love him again. Isn't it a shame how some people have to face death to become human? It didn't happen to her. She died with her hatred intact. You have always been warm and human; I hope you can get over this desperate hatred because I won't live with hatred like my father did. I've done all I can to convince you. If you can't accept my mistakes, well, then …" He could not finish the sentence. The words would not form in his mouth.

"Is that an ultimatum?"

"It's a fact. You can call it an ultimatum if you're looking for an excuse."

She turned away. Still on the sofa, she was quiet for a while. "I've got to think," she said, and got up and walked out the front door.

"Where are you going?"

"For a walk."

As she opened the door Pablo laid his head back on the sofa. Consuelo imagined he was praying.

She walked toward Bayshore Boulevard and turned south with no destination in mind and crossed the boulevard to the sidewalk by the water. The breeze was blowing warm out of the east where a menacing darkness had poured itself across the sky. Rain would come in minutes, but she did not notice or care. The sounds in her head had drowned out all else.

Why now, she wondered, when nothing's happened? It's not like when I took Sammy to Cuba alone, or that devastating night of Major Knapp's and Cynthia's calls. But no matter what, I always came back like a stray dog to lap his hand. I'm ashamed. I forgave him and took in his whore's child. What a waste I am. Cynthia was a good woman after all. She had guts. Maybe Pablo's changed and maybe he's just gotten better at keeping secrets. He may still have a woman somewhere.

As she stopped to look down at the water, her frantic thoughts began to overtake her: All these thoughts … a wild energy is driving me to horrible, unthinkable … no, I won't solve my problem that way. I'm not to blame.

The wind was blowing her hair, her heart beat furiously, she tried to think clearly: I know he's not deceiving me. Maybe I'm only torturing myself over nothing. He's given no grounds ... lately! I'd like to punish him, but I can't when he's trying. He loves his children, and he's given us a better life than I ever expected. Imagine living like his parents, with nothing but cold hatred. How could they? Two people can live together without love, but with such hatred ...

She stepped onto the porch dripping from walking three blocks in a driving rain. At first the rain annoyed her and she tried to hurry, but then she began to enjoy the refreshing downpour: a cleansing to wash away anger, a baptism.

The rain did not wash away her doubts, but her thoughts had clarified. She visualized his mother snarling and thought, have I become like her? I believe Pablo won't tolerate a marriage like his parents'.

Reflected in the oval glass pane of the front door appeared another image—calm, sweet, smiling Tony Sekul.

That wispy image filled her with joy and a slight terror. She knew he loved her, but that was long ago.

Pablo was asleep on the sofa, his head back, mouth open. She went upstairs, dried off, changed clothes, and returned to the living room. She sat in a chair across from him. Slumped as he was, his middle-age belly seemed more prominent and the etching of his face deeper. She felt sorry for the young Pablo, so full of life, now growing fat and solemn. She remembered the dances and picnics at the Cuban Club and strolling along La Septima. Then the image of Tony returned, playing four-hand music together, sitting close on a piano bench with entwined arms, making music, and then his kisses; then feeling guilt. She looked again at Pablo and thought, I had loved him desperately once. Could I again? Have I ever stopped? Did I love Tony? What's he doing now?

Questions came at her like darts. She was not sure how she felt, but in the last hour the noise had eased.

"I'm sorry," he said, straightening up. "I must have fallen asleep. Have you been there long?"

"A few minutes. Perhaps I haven't been fair. I've been imagining the worst about your feelings for Sally and Sammy and me. I guess that's a mistake, especially when I'm so angry and confused."

"You've never been unfair. I love you, Consuelo. I've said it many times, and I'll say it as long as I live. I just wish I could convince you."

She stood, walked to the sofa, sat beside him, but did not look at him. "I need time."

*

Sammy had just left with his friends. Consuelo stood at Sally's door as the girl scampered around her room gathering her books, notebooks, and pencils. Pablo was enjoying watching the little girl so seriously moving around her room.

"Come on, Sally," Consuelo said. "You don't want to be late."

"There's plenty of time," Pablo said. He stood smiling.

"If she's late, the sisters will embarrass her."

"Don't worry," he said.

Finally Sally emerged with her belongings under her arms and said, "I'm ready, Daddy," and took his hand as they walked to the front door.

Consuelo watched them get in the car. When the car pulled out and turned onto the street, Consuelo ran in, sat by the telephone, and dialed the number of the Florida State University in Tallahassee. Yes, Tony Sekul was still there. Nervously she wrote down his studio phone number. She hesitated a while and finally dialed it. When she heard his voice she considered hanging up. After a pause he repeated, "Hello."

"Tony?"

"Consuelo? What a wonderful surprise."

"How've you been? I know you must think I'm crazy calling like this, but I just wanted to talk."

"No such thing. Hearing your voice is like the echo of a beautiful song. You won't believe it, but I'm just leaving for a music teachers' meeting in St. Petersburg. I was planning to call you this evening."

"Wonderful! I'd like very much to see you." She immediately regretted her frankness.

"Great. I'll call when I get to St. Pete and we can get together."

"Tell me where you're staying. I'd rather call you."

"The Vinoy. I'll be there by six tonight. Call me before seven. I have a meeting then."

"I will ... goodbye."

When Consuelo called that evening, Tony had just checked in and sounded even happier than before. "I'm tied up all evening," he said. "How about lunch tomorrow?"

"Noon?"

"Perfect. I'll wait in the lobby. Pablo too?"

"No."

*

All evening she planned her tryst with Tony as if she were on the threshold of committing a grave sin. During supper she told Pablo that she wanted to attend the music society meeting in St. Petersburg. He accepted it without question.

When everyone left she went upstairs to dress. Though not sure why she felt such a sudden urge or even what she would say, seeing Tony had become momentous. She put on a light summer dress with a floral pattern that she thought would make her look younger, and then she sat in front of the mirror combing her shoulder length hair. Not too bad, she thought.

The traffic over the Gandy Bridge was light and she arrived at 11: 30. Not wanting to appear anxious, she drove around St. Petersburg for a while. Tony was sitting in a lounge chair in the lobby when she walked in at 11:50. Wearing a sport jacket and open collar shirt, he looked as if he would embrace her when he walked toward her. Holding out his hands he said, "You look terrific. As if I'd seen you yesterday."

"You, too. It was nice of you to see me."

"I couldn't miss last night's meeting; I was the speaker. Hungry? The dining room here is pretty good."

"Not very, but let's go."

They sat at a table by a large window overlooking a sculptured garden. The dining room was light in color and mood with two elaborate glass chandeliers hanging majestically from the sculptured ceiling. Each table had a candle in a glass chimney and a vase of fresh roses.

"I've never been here," she said. "It's beautiful."

"Why don't I fill you in on what I've been doing?" When the waiter came to take their order Tony said, "We need a few minutes to get reacquainted." Then he turned to Consuelo, "I got out of the Army in '45 and returned to FSU. I was lucky, got back whole. That year I married. We had known each other since soon after you left."

"Do I know her?"

"No. We've been divorced almost two years."

"I'm sorry."

"What about you?"

"We're fine." Then after pausing a moment, "No we're not. I was desperate yesterday when I called. I had to talk to you, and now I don't know where to begin."

"I've got all afternoon."

"You must have noticed the tension in the air when you came to Brandon that day during the war."

"It was hard to miss."

"Well, I didn't know it, but Pablo had been having an affair. I learned about it the night before your last phone call. I must have sounded terrible that morning; I was devastated."

She described Pablo's affair with Cynthia, his contrite behavior, Sally, Cynthia's death, and how much she had come to love Sally. She spared no details including her ancestry and Pablo's anxiety over their pregnancy. When she got to her latest confrontation with Pablo she said, "I think it's been building for years, and now I'm ..." When tears blurred her vision she stopped to look for a handkerchief in her purse.

"You've always been so kind; I felt I could turn to you. I don't know what I'm trying to say, but I felt you were the only one who could help."

Tony listened intently until she had finished. After a long silence he said, "I'm sorry, Consuelo. You've been through hell. No wonder you're upset. It wasn't the same with my wife and me. There was no infidelity; I just didn't love her. I'd been looking for you. You know I've always loved you; I still do."

Consuelo looked away, trying to avoid his eyes. "I know."

"How about you?"

"I don't know. My life has always revolved around Pablo. I don't know."

"From what you say, he's sorry, and he's true to you now. His actions sound convincing. I remember the first day I saw you in the music building. You were dazzling and still are. I'd marry you any time you gave the word, but I'd have to be your choice, not your escape hatch."

His clarity and candor frightened and embarrassed Consuelo. "I wish I could say what you want to hear."

"I care too much for you to let you to make the same mistake I made."

Neither spoke for several minutes. When the waiter saw them sitting quietly, he returned and asked if they were ready to order. Tony gave Consuelo a questioning look.

"I think so," she said.

*

As he walked her to the parking lot an hour later, he turned. "What about restarting your music career?"

"With only a B.A.?"

"Your talent doesn't need a degree. You should have something for yourself. Sammy's gone, Sally's in school, and Pablo has his bank." Seeing her surprised look he continued, "The University of Tampa had a position a few weeks ago. Why don't you call? I know where you can get good letters."

"Tony, you're wonderful." Embracing him, she said. "I'm glad I came."

"Keep me posted."

22 - CONSUELO, 1951

*

Eighty Movie Actors Face House Red Probe

*

49 Nations Sign Jap Peace Treaty

*

2 Hurricanes May Collide; Bermuda Braces For Big Blow

*

MacDill To Be Nations's First Strategic Air Command Base To Receive B-47 Stratojets

*

"Glad you called, Consuelo; it's been a long time."

Lizzie seemed genuinely glad to see Consuelo walk toward their favorite table. As Consuelo saw her, Lizzie became part of the large painting behind her, a Spanish village in which farmers and artisans worked at their tasks with Santiago de Compostela in the distance. Consuelo had often said that the young woman carrying a load of grapes on her head resembled Lizzie.

"Sorry I'm late," Consuelo said. Then after sitting, "and for waiting so long to call."

"How's Sally? She must be pretty big."

"Pretty and big. She loves the Girl's Academy." Unfolding the napkin and placing it on her lap, she looked at her friend. "It's good to see you, Lizzie."

The waiter asked if they were ready to order.

"I'll have the salad and baked grouper," Consuelo said.

Lizzie ordered the same. It was their usual order. Then with a dubious grin Lizzie said, "OK, what's going on? I could smell something was cooking when you called."

"I'm not sure; I've been angry and humiliated so long I can't remember what it's like to feel happy."

"Pablo?"

"He's been fine for the past four years, but it still haunts me. Until a few days ago, I couldn't sleep or think about anything else."

"A few days ago …?" Lizzie said, waiting.

Looking into her friend's eyes, Consuelo hesitated. Recalling her ambiguous meeting with Tony and how good it felt to see him again, she still wasn't sure telling Lizzie was a good idea. But she started, feeling foolish and embarrassed to talk about Tony. Soon her courage mounted and, as she continued, she relaxed. Somehow her problem shrank as she heard it pass her lips.

"Did you tell Pablo?"

"That evening, after the children were out of the away."

"How did he take it?"

The waiter appeared, and Consuelo waited for him to serve the salads.

"Better than I expected. I was nervous as a cat, but it felt good letting him know how it feels for me to see another man. I didn't do anything, but I felt guilty just the same. It's funny; I think he was glad. He knew I hadn't betrayed him. Oh, Lizzie, why is it so different with men? They have an affair and brag about it. If a woman does it she's a whore."

"Did you tell him what Tony said about being in love with you and about marriage?"

"The whole thing."

"Wow! You've got guts."

Consuelo could not help smiling. "In Spanish, they say *cojones*." Until that moment, watching Lizzie's reaction, Consuelo had not thought in those terms.

"What about Tampa U.?"

"I don't think he liked the idea. He wondered if I could manage a job with Sally and the house. I told him I could and that I'd hire a maid. I wasn't asking for permission, just letting him know I was considering it."

"Good for you."

"Anyway, after a while he said it might be a good idea. I don't know if he was competing with Tony for the understanding man's prize or what."

"Does it matter?"

"Lizzie, this is new territory for me."

"Every day you step into new territory, pal. Some people call it do-do, but it's life."

"Sometimes I envy you, Lizzie, not having to live around another person."

"It's not that great. There's nobody to share the good things with. I know one thing: life isn't all happy-happy. It's trying to find little chips of happiness among all the manure that's thrown at you."

Consuelo had to laugh at Lizzie's cynicism, knowing she was right. "We all want happiness."

"Sure, but who gets it?" Lizzie said. "Life is making good choices and living with them. If it gets unbearable, take action. I guess the trick is deciding when it's unbearable. Well listen to me, will you. I'm an expert."

"Sounds good to me."

"It's not that easy. From what you say, your marriage isn't over. Of course, only you know that."

"I called the university yesterday. The job is still open; they scheduled me an interview. It's just an instructorship and doesn't earn tenure, but I don't care. My livelihood won't depend on it."

"When?"

"Monday. Keep your fingers crossed."

When the waiter appeared, he asked if they wanted to keep their salads, which were untouched as he held the two plates of fish. "We'll keep them," Consuelo said, pushing hers aside to make room.

When he left, Lizzie said, "What can I do?"

"You've done it."

"Well, you're smiling, anyway. You know, roomie, with your head tilted like that and your hair hanging down on one side, you look right cute."

"This fish is always good," was all Consuelo could say.

*

Dean Wilson's office was on the main hall in the old Plant Hotel, which had been converted into the University of Tampa in the early 1930s. It was a spacious office with several leather-bound easy chairs and a large desk. The outer office was smaller, with a desk for his secretary and several leather chairs. Dean Wilson's old, barrister bookcases were stacked up to about six feet. A rotating fan on a table near his desk provided some relief from the heat. A large window overlooked the wide, curving porch that opened onto the grassy park that sloped down to the river. Across the river were a series of ugly warehouses; beyond them rose the buildings of downtown Tampa, topped by the Floridan and Tampa Terrace Hotels. Enormous live oaks stretched a canopy across the park.

"We'd like to fill the vacancy soon, Mrs. Iglesias; we have more piano students than our faculty can handle," Dean Wilson said, "so I took the liberty of calling your references."

She nodded noncommittally.

"Dr. Sekul raved about your musical knowledge and natural talent. Said you were very musical and a good teacher. Professor Smith also raved. Said he tried to keep you at FSU."

"That's good to hear. I enjoyed teaching there. I'm sure it's changed since becoming Florida State University and coed."

"Professor Smith said he would hire you today if you were available. But returning to the here and now, the music faculty have asked to speak with you and listen to you play. Would that be all right?"

"I haven't practiced as much as I should, but ... sure."

Dean Wilson walked her down the hall to the music department and left her with Dr. Williams and Mr. Starke, both piano professors. After chatting a few minutes about her work at Florida State and her repertoire and asking about her recitals, Mr. Starke asked her to play something. Without hesitating, she sat at the old Steinway and played a few chords and ran a few scales, and then turned and asked if they wanted anything special.

"Whatever you wish," Starke said.

Consuelo began with Debussy's Claire de Lune because it was an easy piece to warm up with. She played it with subtlety and ended with a diminuendo that left her pleased with herself. Without turning to see their reaction, she began Chopin's Fantasy Impromptu, her favorite recital piece. The runs glistened under her fingers leaving clear the counterpoint of the two hands' melodies arguing with each other in the first section. In the calm middle section, she began to feel she was dreaming, floating along on Chopin's beautiful sonorities. When she returned to the first theme she awoke and finished with all the drama she could muster. Again without pausing more than a second, she charged into the first chord of the Bach Prelude and Fugue in A Flat Major. With straight back and haughty pose she followed the first chord with conviction that frightened her a little at first. Like most of the Preludes, this one takes only a little over a minute if played at normal speed. She did not rush it. She wanted it to build in drama, not speed. Without pause she went into the beautiful four-part Fugue, marching through it, enjoying each time the theme reentered in a surprising key. When she finished the Fugue she turned to see their reaction. Williams and Starke were staring, and Consuelo was not sure what that meant.

"That was beautiful, Mrs. Iglesias," Dr. Williams said. "You seem comfortable with all periods and styles."

"I love the piano."

"That's obvious. You'll be hearing from us very soon."

"I think you'll like it here," Mr. Starke said.

Saying little more, they escorted her to the dean's office. "Please wait," Dr. Williams said, and went in to talk with Dean Wilson as Consuelo sat in the outer office. In a few minutes they came out and shook her hand with congratulations on her fine performance.

Dean Wilson said, "I should have stayed to listen. You have the job, Mrs. Iglesias. May I call you Consuelo?"

"Of course, and thank you. This is so fast. When would I start?"

"Tomorrow OK?"

"Fine."

"Dr. Williams will show you your studio. It has a better piano than the one you played on. Any questions?"

"It's so sudden; I can't think."

"If you do, call me or either of these gentlemen. See you tomorrow."

*

Consuelo wanted to call Lizzie or Tony because they had been so supportive, but her sense of duty and fairness stopped her. She picked up the phone and dialed Pablo's office.

"How did it go?"

"I'm hired."

"Wonderful. Get Sammy to baby sit with Sally tonight; we're celebrating."

"Shouldn't we include them?"

"Nothing doing. It's time we celebrated something alone. By the way, what's the pay? Just to decide who's buying."

"I didn't ask."

"Typical artist. OK, my treat."

23 - MATILDE, 1953

*

*Cuban Rebels Stopped in Santiago.
Many Dead. Rebel Leader Fidel Castro Arrested*

*

Retired Admiral Now Grade School Teacher

*

Outlook Bright For June College Graduates

*

*Medics Want To Know What Makes One Soldier A Hero
And Another A Coward*

*

Texas Women Call Social Security Tax Law 'Slavery'

*

France May Get Out Of Indochina

*

Einstein Tells Witness Not To Answer McCarthy

*

Tenure was automatic after three years, but Matilde worried. In two years several of his colleagues had criticized his teaching. Even Mr. Jones, his most ardent supporter and mentor, had questioned his unorthodox style. Matilde believed his mission was to teach students to think critically, and that meant posing difficult questions. He was always careful not to suggest answers, but to some parents and colleagues, merely posing a question implied an answer. He carefully avoided favoring one point of view over another, but some suspected he had an agenda. He had supporters, of course, parents and colleagues who understood what he was trying to do, but they kept their silence for fear of finding themselves in his shadow as followers. Many parents saw him as a powerful man who would provoke their children to make trouble that would bring pain and disappointment. Having been a fighter pilot gave him an aura of knowing and strength. Students enjoyed his classes; some even idolized him. He preferred to focus on issues that affected them, knowing they would think most when the subject touched them directly. He told one of his classes about the Tuskegee Airmen who were court marshaled trying to integrate the Selfridge Officers' Club and other incidents from his years in the Air Force. Students responded angrily, especially the boys, and they took the stories home where they usually met hostility.

"What are you afraid of?" Richard asked his father. "It's true. It really happened."

"I ain't afraid of nothin'. But talk like that scares white people."

"So what?"

"They can do bad things and get away with it."

"But that's wrong." Richard's anger was rising.

"Drop it, boy. I don't want to hear no more about it."

In Early October of his third year at Booker T, a small group of students approached Matilde about starting a club and asked him to be their advisor.

"What kind of club?"

"A debate club. We want to meet and discuss things that affect Negroes," Andrew said. Andrew was a senior now.

"Why?"

"Nothin', just to talk about them."

"Yeah, Mr. Gómez. We wanna know what's going on," Joseph said. Joseph was the leader. With thick glasses and a thin build he looked studious. And he read hungrily.

"You need the Principal's permission to start a club," Matilde said.

"Why can't we just meet?" Joseph asked. "It's our constitutional right."

"You can meet with your friends anytime, but a club sanctioned by the school must be approved.

"Would you talk with Mr. Jones?" Joseph asked.

"Sure."

Mr. Jones frowned when Matilde walked into his office that afternoon. It had been a tense day and Matilde's presence meant problems.

Matilde explained the students' request as Henry Jones sat stroking his chin. "Mat, you know this sort of thing worries people. We can't have one of our teachers stirring up the student body."

"They're good kids, Henry. They just want to participate in self-government. How else can they learn about citizenship? By the way, it was entirely their idea."

"You know how many complaints I've had? I tell people you're one of our best teachers, but that only goes so far. Some of the other teachers are complaining too."

"I don't understand it. I try to get along with everybody."

"The way students look up to you, well, some teachers feel powerless."

"Threatened, you mean."

"I hate to say it, but you alienate people. You're too … I guess the word is effective. I admire your originality and energy, but you have to play the game to get anywhere. We have a responsibility to make good citizens out of our kids. If it gets around that we're encouraging political activity, the school board will come down on us like a sledge hammer."

"So what do I tell them?"

"To fill out the proper forms and we'll look them over."

"You'll make them go to the trouble before you turn them down?"

"Come on, Mat, I've always been straight with you."

"I'm sorry, Henry, but I can see it coming. We've got to trust them or they'll never learn to be responsible. If you turn them down they'll feel powerless; it could be worse than letting them have their club."

"I'm not opposed to a club as long as it's under control, and I certainly want to treat them like responsible citizens."

"They've asked me to be their advisor. I'll control them."

"I know you mean it, Mat, but if we approve their club, they'll have to have another advisor."

Matilde stepped back as if on his guard. "Why?"

"You're too controversial."

Hesitating, Matilde said, "Fine."

*

The sun had impaled itself on the treetops and the light had refracted into the sad purple that falls as waning day yields grudgingly to night. After the long summer, the cool snap promised a perfect October evening. The colors of the banana plant outside the kitchen window enthralled Zoraida. It reminded her how long she had been away from Cuba. They had almost finished their silent supper when Zoraida put her hand on Matilde's. "Why don't you tell me, my love?"

"Tell you what?"

"Something is bothering you."

"It's easy to see why whites have had the advantage so long."

"Trouble at school?"

"They're so worried about making trouble. It's discouraging. The Tuskegee men didn't eat that crap."

"That's the capitalist system: keep the workers under control so the bosses can scoop up all the goodies."

"I don't think it has anything to do with capitalism. It's been engrained into us not to question, even when we're right."

"And who engrained it? Poor whites blame Negroes for their troubles. Why? Because they're afraid to blame the bosses. People soon learn to love their abusers. And the Negroes have learned to blame themselves. It's all neat and efficient, and the real *cabrones* rub their full bellies."

"That's too simple, Zoraida, but no matter. The true solution is education. Problems don't go away if you hide from them."

"Why do you always find life so complicated?"

With downcast eyes, Matilde told her about the students and the club and Henry Jones' reaction. He had accepted Jones' decision to choose another advisor, but he had not realized how angry it had made him.

"I see. Your analysis is right, Matilde, but a little twisted. The capitalists have designed the education of the lower classes to keep Negroes in their place."

"And you call me pessimistic!" Matilde threw up his hands.

"Why else do they separate the races if not to indoctrinate them separately? They teach Negroes not to make trouble, and they teach whites that Negroes are the problem."

"OK, but Communism isn't the solution. It's worse tyranny. If everybody owns the means of production, nobody owns it, and the guys who run it become the owners by default."

"Is this any better?"

"I'm tired of arguing. Let's talk about something else." He got up, walked to the cupboard and picked a cigar out of a box. "I'll be on the porch," he said, as he held a flaming match under the end and drew a long breath.

When Zoraida was finished in the kitchen, she came out. "Mind if I sit with you, Mr. *Capitalista?*"

"How about a stroll down La Septima?" he said.

"Fine. A little movement will do us both good. Maybe we'll see Felipe. I want to play a number."

"You're the biggest capitalist of all, trying to get rich on the money of the poor."

Zoraida snuggled close to him and smiled.

*

Students promptly submitted the completed forms to Mr. Jones. A week later, Mr. Jones sent a message to Joseph through his homeroom teacher that he had approved the club, and that he had appointed Mr. Ryan, the physical education teacher and coach as their faculty advisor. When Joseph read the note, he went immediately to Matilde's room to complain.

"Mr. Ryan will be easy to work with, Joseph. The kids all like him."

"I know, Mr. Gómez, but we wanted you. You understand us. Mr. Ryan's OK, but he's a coach. He never talks about any of this stuff."

"You got your club, now go celebrate. I'm kind of busy."

"Maybe Mr. Jones doesn't like your ideas," Joseph said.

Matilde smiled. "It's easy to speculate, Joseph, but speculations are nearly always self-serving and often wrong. Now get your club going, and good luck. Let me know if I can help."

"Don't you want to be our advisor?"

"You've got an advisor. Don't worry. Mr. Ryan will be fine."

As soon as he got a free hour, Matilde stopped in on Henry Jones. "Just dropped by to thank you for approving the students' discussion club."

"Thanks for understanding, Mat."

*

The club's fifteen members met two afternoons a week after school in one of the classrooms. Mr. Ryan was there for the first two meetings to make sure they got organized and to help them set an agenda. After that, the football team kept him too busy to attend regularly. The club started well enough, but with little supervision the members began to argue among themselves about issues and then about points of view. The group quickly became polarized. The first issue was school segregation. Joseph and most of the members held the view that segregation was wrong even if the schools were equal, arguing that it was wrong to separate people by race. The opponents argued that segregation was good because it allowed Negro children a place where they did not have to compete with better-educated whites. Joseph was quick to point out that if whites are better educated, it's because the schools are not equal.

These arguments, in themselves, were not serious; students enjoyed the competition. Discussion of important issues was the objective of the club. The problem arose when they prepared a brief questionnaire and delivered copies to each classroom with a note asking each teacher to administer the poll and collect the papers for the club to evaluate. When they were tallied they would report the results to the teachers.

Mr. Jones' office was filled with irate teachers most of the day.

"They can't do this," Helen Warren said. "How dare they tell us how to run our classes?"

"It's dangerous to rile the students," Miss Haverty said. Miss Haverty was a pretty, young, math teacher hired the year after Matilde.

"What's the point of the questionnaire?" Mrs. Smith, the English teacher, said. "Segregation is the law."

"Was Ryan involved?" asked Mr. Tollens, the science teacher.

"No. I asked him," Henry Jones said. "He didn't know anything about it until he found it on his desk this morning."

"Sounds like the work of Mat Gómez, Helen Warren said. "I knew he'd make trouble."

"Take it easy," Henry Jones said. "Just hold on to the questionnaires until I can look into the matter."

When Henry got the teachers out of his office, he went to Matilde's room, where he found him eating a sandwich. "What do you know about this, Mat?"

"Nothing. I haven't been involved with the club since you told me to stay out of it."

"I guess they dreamed it up themselves."

"Probably. I don't think Ryan had anything to do with it either. One of the boys was talking about a big discussion they'd had a few days ago. If you want my opinion, let it go. What harm can it do? So we'll find out students don't like segregation? What's new about that?"

"Sounds reasonable, Mat, but some of the teachers are upset. Imagine how the parents will take it."

"I can imagine."

"I guess I'll be busy the next few days."

When Henry Jones walked out, Matilde sat back in his desk looking out the window. With no clouds, the blue of the sky seemed cleansed of doubting vapors. The boys at football practice were making hard, happy, striving sounds, learning to play the game to win. They were also learning to work together toward a goal and if they lost, to do it gallantly. There's a lot that's good out there, Matilde thought, but much that's bad. It's good to fight and not settle for scraps, he thought. A poll. How innocent.

*

The poll turned out as Joseph expected. Over ninety percent of the students were against segregation. What surprised Matilde was that some students were not.

The faculty met, as usual, in one of the classrooms after school. Mrs. Warren was horrified. "I knew this would happen."

"Nothing's happened," Mr. Jones said. "Let's keep our heads. So students don't like segregation. Neither do we. I don't think they plan to do anything about it."

"They damn well won't," Mr. Ryan said. "I'll see to that."

"We've got to be careful not to push them into something they never planned in the first place," Jones said.

"We've got to put a stop to this rabble-rousing before it goes too far," Mrs. Warren said, looking at Matilde.

"Mr. Ryan, exactly what are the students planning?" Mr. Jones asked.

"I haven't been to their meetings for a while, but I'll find out."

"Mr. Gómez, you've been closest to this group, what do you think?" Jones asked.

"I was close to them when they formed the club, but I haven't been to any of their meetings; I've kept out of their business."

"Are you sure about that?" Mrs. Warren asked.

"I'm positive, Mrs. Warren. I'm also sure we should not overreact. In their immature, stumbling way, these kids are trying to understand the world they live in. As far as I know, they aren't interested in taking action. Perhaps they just want to know the answers to questions that nag us all."

"They don't nag me," Mrs. Warren said.

"Well they should," Matilde said.

"Please, let's remain professional," Jones said. "We're not here to air personal grievances. Mr. Gómez is right. We mustn't overreact. Let's see what they do; we'll have plenty of time to act if necessary. In the meantime, let's go easy with the students; if we pounce on them before they've responded, they might do something stupid."

As the meeting dispersed with discussion spilling out into the hall, Mr. Jones called Matilde into his office. They walked down the hall to the first floor and into the Principal's office. "What do you think?" Jones asked.

348

"What I said before. I really don't think they're planning anything."

"How would you feel about talking with some of the leaders?" Jones asked.

"Is that wise? People don't want me involved. Some think I've been involved all along."

"I'm afraid Ryan might stir them up."

"I'll talk with Joseph and one or two others, but I won't do it under cover."

"What do you mean?"

"I mean I won't sneak around. In fact, I insist you tell the faculty."

"Right."

Matilde left the Principal's office planning his approach. He wouldn't see Joseph until third period American History the next morning, just before lunchtime.

The next day passed slowly for Matilde until third period, when he resumed the previous day's discussion. About half way through the period, he handed out a brief questionnaire. "This is not a quiz. It's a questionnaire on the topic, 'Taxation without representation.' I want your anonymous opinions. Don't put your names on the questionnaire. Then he turned and wrote on the blackboard: Is it legal for an appointed government agency (one that is not elected by the people) to levy a tax on citizens?

"Please mark 'yes' or 'no' and hand it back."

The students marked their answers in a few seconds, and Matilde soon had them in his hands. Handing Joseph the stack of papers he asked him to read out the responses as Matilde tallied the results on the blackboard. The results were nineteen no's and one yes.

"How would you interpret this result?" he asked the class.

Several hands went up. Matilde called on Joseph. "People think taxation without representation's wrong."

"The question was, whether it's legal, not whether it's wrong. I hope your votes reflect that distinction. We can all see the results on the board; you think it's illegal. Does that make it illegal?"

"I don't get it," Joseph said.

"Does a majority opinion make it illegal?"

"Sure," Joseph said. Most of the class nodded.

"Maybe I should ask what legal means."

Several hands went up. "OK, Lurleen."

"It means it's the law."

"OK, then what does your opinion have to do with that? If most of you think the humidity is high today, does that make it high?"

349

"Come on, Mr. Gómez. We ain't got nothin' to do with humidity," Morris said. Morris was a large, very dark, taciturn boy who always appeared bored or angry.

"That's right, Morris. And you don't have anything to do with whether something is legal or not. You can influence the laws by voting for the people who write them. For example, if you know a certain candidate is opposed to taxation without representation, and you think such taxation is bad, you can vote for that person and hope he votes against it when it comes up."

Silence.

"What country did the questionnaire refer to?" Matilde asked.

"The United States?" Lurleen said.

"How do you know?"

Silence again.

"Suppose it was the Spanish government of the sixteenth century?"

"It wouldn't matter," Joseph said. "It's wrong."

"The government of Spain was a monarchy with no legislature to represent the people. All state agencies were appointed."

"That don't make it right," Lurleen said.

"I agree with your sentiment, but, though it may not be right or good, the question is, is it legal. My point is that public opinion does not make something true or false, right or wrong, legal or illegal. It's simply the people's opinion."

"Is all this because of our poll?" Joseph asked.

"That gave me the idea. I thought it would be a perfect opportunity to get you to think about what such a poll means and what it doesn't mean. And since you brought it up, what do you think about the poll that went around the other day?"

"Shows most of the students of Booker T. are against segregation," Joseph said with a smile.

"Does that prove segregation is wrong?" Matilde asked.

"Sure," Lurleen said.

"How?"

"It's just wrong!" Morris said, visibly angry.

"Don't confuse the two questions, Morris. One is whether segregation is wrong. The other is whether the poll *proves* it's wrong. It may seem like quibbling, but there's a significant difference."

"It's wrong, and that's all there is to it," Morris said, mumbling something to a nearby student.

Matilde was glad to hear the bell; the debate was on the verge of abandoning rationality and falling into the seductive lure of emotion.

"We'll continue with the American Revolution tomorrow," Matilde said, as the class broke into small groups, sliding chairs, talking, and slamming books together.

After the final bell rang students began to congregate near the flagpole in front of the school. It was a cool, early December afternoon, overcast and windy. Normally they would have walked home or to the playing fields, but not today. Word had spread through the school that the new club was holding a meeting to discuss their poll. Standing on a concrete bench looking over the crowd, Joseph was speaking. By the time Mr. Jones realized what was happening and went out to see, students were yelling and chanting, "End segregation, end it now! End segregation, end it now!"

Trying to talk with Joseph across students' heads, Matilde yelled, "Not like this, Joseph. Call it off and let's talk."

"No, Sir. We want to talk about it now. We don't like segregation. If you like it, that's your business, but don't try to stop us. You had your chance." Then, yelling to the crowd, "We're right." That brought a roar of approval. Matilde tried to push his way to the bench to disperse the crowd, but he could not. He would have had to push harder than he thought prudent. Mr. Jones also failed to make his way to the bench where Joseph was talking. "See what you've started, Mat?" he yelled at Matilde.

Completely dumbfounded by the students' violent reaction and even more by Henry's accusation, he stood speechless.

Within minutes a police car pulled up in front of the school and four uniformed officers stepped out with nightsticks in their hands. When the students saw them, their immediate response was to prepare to fight, but Matilde ran to the police. "Please, go easy. They'll break up once they see you," he yelled as he ran.

When the cops saw him running toward them yelling, they grabbed him. Two of them held his arms behind his back while another stood in front of him yelling, "Shut up, boy, or I'll bash your goddamn head in." The policeman was very large and powerful.

Matilde stopped resisting. "That's better," the big cop said. "Now, what the hell's going on?"

"Please let me go. I've been trying to stop them. Don't hurt them. They don't mean any harm. They're just expressing their feelings," Matilde said.

"Let him go, men," the officer said. "OK, what are theyexpressing?"

Matilde explained briefly about the club and the poll. When he mentioned the word, segregation, the police braced up. "We'll put a stop to that," the big officer said. "Come on, men."

With deliberate steps, the officers marched through the students, who now stood silent. Mr. Jones walked toward the police with his hands raised, trying to stop them. "I'm Henry Jones, the Principal. These students are just holding a rally. There's nothing to worry about. They're breaking up."

"We got a call there was a riot," the officer said.

"Who called? There's no riot here," Mr. Jones said.

"I called them," Helen Warren said. "I knew this would happen. It's that big man over there," she said, pointing to Matilde. "He started it."

"No, no, Helen! Mat's been trying to stop them."

"He should've known better than to stir them up in the first place."

The large officer in charge of the detail walked to the bench. "All right, everybody go home, and there won't be any more trouble," he said, slapping his palm rhythmically with his nightstick. Standing on the bench like a statue, the six-foot-four-inch-tall policeman was in complete control. His blue eyes bore into everyone he locked on. Within minutes the students had drifted away. The other policemen stood at regular distances from one another as if in formation. When the crowd began to disperse, Mr. Jones turned to the large policeman and said in rapid, high-pitched tones, "They'll be all right now. It's over. She shouldn't have called. There was no riot. She's a disgruntled teacher."

"Best keep them under control, or we'll close you down."

Matilde was still shaken when he got home. Sitting on the front porch, Zoraida saw it immediately.

"We nearly had a riot. That Warren woman called the police."

"You're not making sense. Slow down."

Trying to calm himself, he sat down and told her about the crowd in front of the school. "The kids are mad because I didn't help them with their club."

"You should have told them why."

"Passing the buck to the Principal would've made it worse."

"Did they know you were trying to help them?"

"I don't think so. Then that Warren woman called the police. Can you imagine? It was the word, segregation, that really got the cops going. If the Principal and I hadn't stopped them, they might have cracked heads."

"Well, it ended all right."

"Depends. The students now know what it means to protest. They've seen the force of the law, not with words from the constitution, but with clubs and pistols, the *real* law."

"*Pobrecito.* How about a glass of cognac?"

"What? ... yes."

*

No one spoke about the incident to Matilde the next day or the day following. It was as if nothing had happened. Students were calm and respectful, but Matilde sensed a new anxiety. He conducted his classes as usual without incident.

The week before Christmas vacation, Mr. Jones called him to his office after the last bell. Matilde did not know what to expect. Nothing had come of the protest as far as he knew.

"Come in, Mat," Henry said. "As you know, we've been in the midst of tenure considerations. I wanted to tell you myself before you heard it elsewhere. Your tenure has been denied. I'm sorry."

Matilde was stunned.

"I know how you must feel, Mat."

"Was it your decision?"

"Yes."

"I thought you liked my work."

"You could be our best teacher. Your ability to identify with kids is good, maybe too good. It may have been your ability to make them question that led to our recent trouble."

"I see. It's not good for them to question."

"This is very delicate, Mat. Of course they must, but there's a thin line between thinking and acting. Their actions could bring horrible problems to us all, especially the kids."

"I didn't expect this hypocrisy from you, Henry. I understand Warren; she's protecting her little empire. But what you want is teachers who will tell kids to follow white man's rules without question. Is that what education means in America?"

"Please, Mat, don't be so hard. I agreed to the decision in the end, but only after I'd failed to talk them out of it."

"Them? The faculty?"

"No, the school board. When they heard about the fracas, they demanded your immediate removal. They wouldn't listen to me. Branded you a troublemaker; the discussion ended before it started."

"Will I be allowed to finish the year?"

"The semester. We'll have to find a replacement for January. I can't tell you how sorry I am."

"Nothing left to say then." Matilde, who had stood throughout the exchange, walked out.

*

It was dark when he pirouetted as a small boy whizzed past him on a bicycle. Zoraida was sitting on the porch, looking visibly worried. Matilde stopped at the second step, seeming to lose his balance then took the next.

"It's late. Where have you been?" she asked, standing to help him.

"I stopped at a little bar on the way home. I haven't done that in a long time. I met some nice people there, all Cuban Negroes. There aren't many of us left anymore. Where have they gone?"

"Matilde, tell me, what happened?"

"Nothing much. I met some old friends that I never knew before."

"You must be hungry. Supper's ready."

"I'm not hungry yet. For food, that is." He was smiling at her with droopy eyes. "You're still as beautiful as ever. Do you know that?"

"*Vamo' a comer*," she said, getting up.

"You're going to make me eat whether I want to or not. I want another glass of cognac first."

"After supper. First we eat."

"Yes, sir," he said, saluting.

Zoraida led him into the kitchen where he fell into a chair and put his chin on his fists. "How would you like to take a little trip to Cuba?"

She looked at him quizzically. "I'll answer you when you tell me what happened."

"Don't be so quick to turn down my invitation. I'm inviting you to go to Cuba, the land of our fathers, of Spanish domination, of darkness and light, the land of tropical evenings and green waters and warm breezes and love under the palms."

"Are you going to tell me or not?"

"Not!" he said, and began to laugh.

Zoraida had ladled *caldo gallego* soup into two bowls and set them on the table. "Then I'll tell you, my love," she said. "There was trouble in school."

"That is a matter of opinion. One man's trouble is another man's liberation."

"My God! They fired you."

"Let's eat. I'm too weak to tell lies."

As they ate, Matilde continued to talk about unrelated things. Zoraida ignored his attempts at humor, but she did not know how to take his sudden urge to go to Cuba. She tried to find out what he had in mind, how long they would stay, but his chatter was too cryptic to decipher. He stayed at the table after supper, drinking cognac, and soon, his eyes closing, he said, "I don't think I can stay awake any longer," just before his head dropped into his folded hands on the table.

"Maybe it's best," she thought, helping him to bed. "At least you won't have to think about it for a while."

*

The next morning he rose, showing little effect of the previous night's binge. Sitting down to breakfast, Zoraida demanded details of the previous day. When he related his conversation with Henry Jones she could not believe it.

"I'm surprised to hear you say that. Isn't it exactly what you always say about suppression of the under classes."

"This is no time to joke, Matilde."

"I'm not joking."

"And all that talk about going to Cuba? Was that just the cognac talking?"

"No."

"What's churning that brilliant mind?"

"Nothing precise except to visit my homeland. It's been almost twenty-five years. You've always wanted to go back."

"But I don't want you to do it for me."

"Doing things for you is my fondest desire. You are my life, Zoraida."

"I know, Matilde, but I don't want you to ruin your career."

"Don't you see? The school board fired me. They run the schools, *all* of them."

"What about going somewhere else?"

"That's what I have in mind."

*

Matilde walked into Mr. Jones' office ten minutes before the first class bell. "I'll be leaving right after the Christmas break starts, Henry. You'll have to get my replacement to finish the last two weeks of the semester in January. Here are my final exam questions."

"There's no need to rush away, Mat."

"Actually there is."

"What will you do?"

"Thanks for everything, Henry."

355

24 – ONE WEEK LATER

*

Naturalized American Refuses To Betray U.S.
In Deal To Save 2 Sons In Red Romania

*

Russians Execute Four Americans Accused of Spying

*

Adlai Stevenson Sees Fears Of Depression

*

Defense Dept. Ousts 118 As 'Risks'

*

Senate Candidates's Views On Teacher Raises Differ

*

Two State Dept. Aides Fired As Espionage Suspects

*

Like most cigar makers, Matilde was used to moving frequently in his early days in Ybor City. With such mobility they were accustomed to owning little: mainly their clothes, personal items, and minimal pieces of furniture. But even those few possessions took that entire week to pack.

Besides two boxes of books, Matilde had one suit, a sport jacket, two pairs of trousers, three shirts, two pairs of shoes, and some underwear. In a small box he kept important papers, such as his Florida A & M diploma, his citizenship document, an old union membership card, a few letters, some friends' addresses, mostly army buddies, and a couple dozen photographs. Riffling through the photos he found one of himself and Edwin Pitt standing at the nose of Matilde's P-51 in Naples. They were smiling with their arms around each other's shoulders. Examining every detail he knew those had been his happiest days. Returning the photo to the box he closed it and stretched a rubber band around it. He would write to Edwin when they got settled.

Zoraida had only three dresses, underclothes, small items of jewelry, knick-knacks, her Santería tureen and other religious objects, and her most cherished treasure, a set of silver flat wear and dishes that had belonged to her grandmother. Caressing each piece as she wrapped and laid it in the chest, she remembered all the times she had packed and unpacked them. We go home; this will be the last time, she thought.

Matilde expected to see her excited that week, packing and making arrangements for the trip. She was not unhappy, but quiet, hesitant, uncertain.

"What is wrong," Matilde asked finally. "Don't you want to go?"

"Of course. It is what I have always wanted, but I worry about you. Is it what you want?"

In moments like that Matilde wanted to hold her close. He pulled her to him and said, "Knowing how much you wanted to return, I should have done it sooner. Will you forgive me?"

She kissed him and then looked into his eyes. "It has been an adventure, Matilde. I mean my life with you, and I love adventure. Now let's finish."

After he sealed the second box of books he said, "While you finish up, I'll go to the bank and close our account."

Matilde had driven to the Tampa National Bank every payday since arriving at Booker T. He didn't like writing checks, so he always withdrew whatever cash they would need and deposited the rest in his savings account. To Matilde being a professional meant saving for a house, a new car, things that had always been beyond imagining.

Driving down Nebraska Avenue on that cool, crisp morning and turning onto Cass Street, angry memories of being kept out of the factories and of mopping floors at the Cuban Club taunted him. His life had followed an elliptical route from janitor to fighter pilot to college student to teacher to unemployed, probably unemployable, except as a janitor. He could not even consider trying to teach in another county or state. Cuba beckoned from beyond the horizon like ethereal salvation, a sweet place to lay his bones.

He parked on Franklin Street and walked half a block to the corner entrance of the bank. It no longer angered him that the doorman looked away as Matilde opened the heavy glass door, knowing that the man had inherited his bigotry as Matilde had inherited his skin. At one of the high tables he filled out a withdrawal slip and endorsed his check. Fridays were always crowded, and every teller's window had a long tail of people behind it. But Matilde did not care. There was no hurry.

The hand on his shoulder made him turn angrily. Before him stood a familiar, middle-aged man, portly, with thinning, sandy hair, dressed in a dark gray pinstripe double-breasted suit and blue and white polka dot bow tie.

"Matilde! Almost I didn't recognize you."

"Pablo. What a surprise running into you here."

"*Tienes tiempo para un amigo?*" he asked silently. Matilde nodded and Pablo said, "*Bien*," and motioned for him to follow."

Pablo led Matilde through a low swinging door in a balustrade behind the row of tellers' windows, past several desks to an elevator that took them to the third floor. When he opened his office door, Matilde saw the word, "President."

"I didn't know you ran this bank. I've been coming here for three years."

Pablo smiled and led him past his secretary. He handed her Matilde's deposit slip and said, "Take care of this, please, Mrs. Justin, and hold all calls except my wife's."

He opened the door to his spacious office and led Matilde to a plush chair away from his desk and sat in an identical one next to him. They faced a large window that looked west, across the river to Plant Park and the University of Tampa.

"I bought controlling interest in it when it opened in 1946. We've done pretty well. Now, what about you? I heard you went to college. Fill me in."

Matilde looked around at the bookcase that covered the entire south wall next to the large window. The opposite wall had several large photographs of Tampa scenes and two of citrus groves. Matilde hesitated to relate his failures to this obviously successful man.

Finally he said, "I've been teaching history at Booker T. Washington for three years. I loved it. The principal and students liked me, but some of the students made trouble. The police came and almost caused a riot. I got the blame and the boot." Matilde tried to smile.

"That's horrible. What kind of trouble?"

"Students were talking about segregation. I guess it scared the school board."

"It's unbelievable they would fire a man like you."

Matilde tried to be nonchalant. "Maybe it's for the best. The army was my only success. I probably should have stayed in, but I couldn't see it for the long run. Oh, it was exciting and fun, but a peacetime army would get boring. I didn't foresee another war so soon."

"What now?"

"Zoraida and I are going to Cuba."

"To stay?"

"Who knows? If we like it, maybe. It can't be any worse than this."

"Don't be too sure, Matilde. Batista's killing people, and he's sold out to American gambling interests. He's running the country solely for his benefit."

"There are bad people everywhere."

"I don't blame you for saying that, but you'll find something. With your talent and your war record you're bound to find a good post. You've got the stuff."

"Thanks, Pablo, but it can't happen here. My own people turned me out."

"That's odd. I always think of you as a Cuban. I've never been conscious of your race."

Matilde recalled the night years ago in the Café Cubano when he asked about property near Brandon, and Pablo's less than diplomatic refusal. He then remembered how elated Pablo was because his son was blonde and white. "I used to think of myself as a Cuban first and a mulatto second. Living in the America of white and black, where no gray exists, I came to see myself more and more as a Negro first and an American second. Now it's Negro first and second."

"But everybody respects you. Color has nothing to do with anything." Pablo started to say something then stopped, knowing he could not say anything meaningful.

"What is it?"

"Nothing. I'd sure like to help you, Matilde. What can I do?

Matilde smiled, "I'll be fine."

Walking to his desk, Pablo opened his humidor and offered Matilde a cigar. "Clear Havana."

"Thanks."

Matilde dug in his jacket pocket, but Pablo had a lighter flame blazing before his friend could find the match he was groping for. Leaning forward, he drew the flame into the end of the cigar a few times and then sat back again. In the meantime, Pablo lit one, and they sat facing each other exhaling clouds of opaque smoke into the space between them.

"Your shaved head lends an air of strength and authority that complements your tremendous, intellectual presence, Matilde. In fact, I have to say you look quite handsome in your tweed sport jacket. There must be all kinds of jobs for a man like you."

"I would have thought so, Pablo, but that's life."

"I've been wanting to get together. I'm glad I bumped into you."

"Where could we get together, Pablo, outside the privacy of your office?" He took another draw on his cigar.

"I never thought about that, my friend. We met in the Café Cubano. It never occurred to me what a rare place that was. This must be awful for you."

"What's worse is I've gotten used to it."

"There must be something I can do."

"Cuba's not perfect, but at least we'd be able to sit in a restaurant together. Who knows, maybe there I'll be able to assume my human form again."

"How's Zoraida?"

"She's always wanted to return. She put up with America all these years for me. If it hadn't been for her, I'd be crazy or in jail … And Consuelo?"

"She's teaching piano at the University of Tampa and loves it. Our son just graduated from MIT. He's in graduate school in California; our daughter's at the Girls' Academy. She's nine. We're all well."

"I'm glad, Pablo. I always knew you would succeed. You have success in your genes." Matilde looked at his wristwatch and said, "I've wasted enough of your time."

"When are you leaving?" Pablo asked.

"Flying out tomorrow morning at ten."

"We'll try to see you off."

"That's nice of you, but thanks."

When Matilde stood and shook Pablo's hand, Pablo took out three more cigars and put them in Matilde's jacket pocket and said, "See you tomorrow."

To Matilde the divide that separated them had grown immense. He knew their separation couldn't be greater if they lived in different centuries.

*

"Poor people," Consuelo said, when Pablo related his visit with Matilde. "Isn't there anything we could do?"

"Like what?"

"How about a job at the bank? As smart as he is, he'd be a great asset."

Pablo looked at Consuelo sheepishly. "I considered that as we talked. He would make a great manager, but can you imagine how the customers and stockholders would react? Negroes work only as doormen or janitors."

"That's awful, after all he did for his country. Did he talk about Zoraida?"

"She wants to go back too. I think he's desperate."

"When are they leaving?"

"Tomorrow morning at ten. I'd like to see them off. How about it?"

"Definitely. I'll get her a nice memento; we'll take the children."

*

The crowd was small. Matilde and Zoraida came with Joe Simmons, a friend from Booker T, who drove Matilde's car. Joe helped them carry their bags and boxes to the baggage check-in counter. A short, thin man with light brown skin, short hair and a thin moustache, Joe moved fast and efficiently. Matilde enjoyed watching his quick, darting moves and gestures. What a nice guy, he thought; so eager to help.

"Take good care of the Ford," Matilde said.

"I will. If you return, I'll sell it back for just a small profit," he said, laughing.

"Thanks, Joe. Just enjoy it and don't expect us."

Matilde turned to the check-in clerk to make sure the bags were correctly marked.

"I'd better go," Joe said. "I have to get back before school's over."

Matilde turned and shook his hand. "Thanks for everything, Joe. You've meant a lot."

"Booker T. has lost its best teacher, and I'm losing my best friend," Joe said. Turning to Zoraida, he shook her hand and wished them both a good trip. They walked him to the car, Joe got in, waved, and drove off.

As he drove off, a Cadillac pulled into the parking area and Pablo, Consuelo, Sammy, and Sally got out.

"Well I'll be damned," Matilde said.

"We couldn't let you go without saying goodbye," Pablo said, jogging to them. Consuelo walked to Zoraida and held out her hand. Then she handed Zoraida a gift-wrapped box. "Just a little something to remember us by."

"Thank you. It was good of you to come," Zoraida said. Then to Sammy, "I was one of the people you saw the first time you opened your eyes."

"I'll always remember that wonderful day," Consuelo said. "I've thought about your generosity and kindness many times, Zoraida." Then she turned to Sammy. "Mrs. Gómez helped deliver you."

Looking uncomfortable, Sammy said, "Thank you, Mrs. Gómez. My mother has told me about you."

"It was a good day for me too. Matilde had told me about your father, and I wanted to be part of their friendship."

Then pushing Sally toward them Consuelo said, "This is Sally, our daughter. She's nine years old."

"What a beautiful child," Zoraida said, stroking Sally's hair. As she squatted and looked into Sally's eyes, Zoraida's smile changed to melancholy, her eyes welled up and she remained motionless.

"What is it, Zoraida?" Consuelo asked, surprised by the woman's reaction.

"My back; sometimes it bothers me. I can tell Sally is a good and generous person."

Sally seemed taken with Zoraida and couldn't stop staring at her. Matilde noticed Zoraida's reaction and knew she had seen something. He said nothing.

As they walked into the terminal, Pablo pulled Matilde aside. "I want your word that you'll write and let me know how you're doing. Promise?"

"Sure, Pablo. I feel a lot better than I did yesterday. Cuba's where I belong. The 'American Dream,' as you *Americanos* call it, dazzled me for a time, but the dream resides in the heart, not in geography. Coming here was a good move for you. Today I'm making the right move at last."

"Don't forget: write," Pablo said. When Matilde held out his hand, Pablo instead grabbed him by the shoulders and embraced him for a long time and kissed his cheek.

Sammy seemed shocked. Consuelo took Pablo's hand. Then she turned to Zoraida, hugged her and kissed her cheek and wished her a good trip. "We haven't been to Cuba since my father died," she said. "But we want to go soon; we'll look you up."

"Please do," Zoraida said.

Showing their tickets to the attendant, they walked out onto the tarmac toward the plane. At the top of the steps Matilde asked Zoraida what happened with Sally.

She looked at him sadly.

"I saw how you reacted," he said. "You saw something."

"Please don't ask."

Seeing tears in her eyes he said no more.

25 – MATILDE, A YEAR LATER

*

Soldier Objects To Paying Tax On Pay While In Red Prison

*

McCarthy Charges 'Devilishly Clever Plans' Being Laid To Sabotage His Hunt For Reds

*

U.S. Charges Latin Reds Stepping Up Activity

*

Britain May Aid France In Indochina Struggle

*

School Board Superintendent Says Ending Segregation Will Take Time

*

Negro Group Maps Plans For Integration Battle

*

January 6, 1954
Dear Edwin,

I'm back in Cuba to stay. While packing a couple of weeks ago, I found a picture of us in Naples. It was a great time, wasn't it? That photo is why I'm writing now. To bring you up to date, I took your advice and got a teaching degree from Florida A & M College. Everything went well until I rubbed the school board wrong. They blamed me for a student demonstration against segregation. I had nothing to do with it, but they fired me anyway because the kids liked me. To think that my own people are afraid to question the laws that hold them down, well, it was too much. I'd had enough. I loved teaching and did it well. My principal thought I was too good. That's what the son of a bitch said when he fired me.

So we're back where we were twenty-five years ago, again trying to find our way in a strange country. Cuba has changed as much as the U.S., but at least segregation here is not as rigid as it is up there. I'm looking for a teaching job in English or American History; they need both here. We'll see. With every year that passes I look back at our flying days and our buddies with even greater respect and fondness. They saw injustice and fought it. Too bad people in Tampa won't.

We've rented an apartment in an old, but decent, neighborhood. Our parents died years ago, and we're trying to find cousins and friends. If you answer this letter, I'll keep you informed. It's not expensive to fly down. I hope you'll think about visiting us. I know you'll love our beautiful country.

I'm mailing this letter to your parents' home address hoping you will get it. Let me know what you're doing and if you married that pretty girl you talked about in Naples. I believe her name was Pearl.
Your flying buddy,
Mat.

*

January 20, 1954
Dear Mat,

It was terrific hearing from you! Your letter felt like a warm fireplace on a cold night. Yes, I married Pearl, and she's still pretty. You have a good memory. We have two sons, Marcus 7 and Harold 2. We have a nice apartment off 16th Street in Washington, a pretty nice area near some embassies, not far from Howard University. When I got back, I looked for a flying job, but there weren't any. Pearl didn't like the idea anyway, so I applied to the government. With a degree in engineering and my flying experience I landed a job with the Air Force as a civilian engineer. Pearl stays home with the boys and loves it (so she says). You'd like Pearl; she's fun and can tell a joke as well as the next guy. The boys are fun, especially Marcus. He's old enough to understand who's boss, and he can play ball and things I like. Harold still pisses his pants and has only two interests: eating and making trouble.

I've always had Potomac fever, I guess. If you come up we'll show you the sights. It's a great town; I hope you're not too alienated from the U.S. Pearl and I would like you and Zoraida to stay with us. She got all excited when I told her about visiting Cuba. You never can tell. Of course, we'll let you know.

I'm sorry teaching didn't work out. It probably wouldn't be much different here. People sometimes kill themselves avoiding trouble. Truman desegregated the military. We'll see what difference it makes. I'm sorry you left. Our country needs good Americans like you.

Let me know how you make out.

Your flying buddy, Edwin

*

March 12, 1954

Dear Edwin,

I've waited to answer your letter because we really aren't settled yet. I can't find a teaching job anywhere. As much as I love Havana, we may have to leave. I've found some of the family I was looking for. They were glad to see me, but things are not good for them either. There's a big gap between rich and poor. I guess there always was, but I never saw it as a youngster.

Sounds like you have a beautiful family. Zoraida and I would love to meet Pearl and the boys. Right now, I can't even think about a pleasure trip. We may move to eastern Cuba if I don't find something here soon. The other end of the island is where Zoraida was born. She's my constant support. It's a job she's always had and she does it well. If it weren't for her, I don't know who or what I'd be.

There was an uprising in eastern Cuba last year. Guerillas attacked the army barracks in Santiago de Cuba. Most of the guerrillas were killed. The army captured some of the leaders and sentenced them to long prison terms. You may have read about it. The leader was a man named Fidel Castro. They sound like a bunch of crazies.

Other than that, the island is calm and beautiful. Write when you can and please visit us when we get settled.

Your friend,

Mat

*

July 4, 1954
Dear Mat,

I have the day off and decided to do something useful. I hate parades, so here I am with pen in hand, hoping this finds you. I haven't heard from you in months. Have you moved? We're in a recession. I don't think it's like the thirties, but lots of folks are looking for work. I'm pretty lucky to have a government job.

For a while last month Pearl thought she was expecting, but it turned out to be a false alarm. We didn't plan it, but I was disappointed. The boys are well. Now that it's summer, they're around the apartment a lot. Pearl gets pretty tired, but she's fine.

Give our best to Zoraida and don't give up on us. We'll fly down there one of these days.
Your friend, Edwin

*

January 3, 1956
Dear Edwin,

I'm writing from our village in Oriente Province. We moved here last July right after your letter arrived. I didn't write sooner because I didn't know where we would end up. If you've written since then, I didn't receive it.

It's a small village, but they have a good school and they were looking for an English teacher. I'm happy to be working again, and Zoraida loves it. With her feet finally planted in the soil of her birth she's bloomed. It's a beautiful land with beaches and mountains and lots of farmland. Cuba's a natural wonder. It has everything. They say when God created Cuba He did everything to make it perfect, beautiful, temperate climate, lots of water, mountains, beaches, every kind of fruit and plant. Then He sat back and looked on what He had done. "This place is too perfect," He said. "It will only make the rest of the world envious." So he sprinkled Cubans all over the place. There's truth in that. We have a nearly perfect patch of earth, yet we argue endlessly about who will run things. Batista's a clumsy dictator. He released that crazy Castro from jail in a political amnesty last year. Instead of turning to what he could do here, Castro and his brother left for Mexico where they've organized other Cuban exiles against the Batista government. We get all their propaganda. They call themselves the 26th of July Movement. That was the date of their failed attempt to take over the barracks in Santiago de Cuba. Every president has been a failure, either ineffectual or simply crooked. That's one thing you have on us, Edwin. With all its faults, the U.S. government has continuity. You don't have coups. No one takes over from anyone else except through legal elections.

Sorry for the politics lecture. Zoraida and I are fine and my students are good and interested; they're perfect victims.

Regards to Pearl and the boys.

Your friend,

Mat

*

April 1, 1956

Dear Mat,

I enjoyed the politics lesson. It sounds like you've found your niche. Since your letter, I've been alert for news about Cuba and the insurgents. I think Castro's right. Batista sounds awful. Our newspapers say he's tied in with the American Mafia. There's not too much in the news, just dribbles. Our papers like Castro.

Marcus just celebrated his tenth birthday. Harold enjoyed it almost as much as Marcus. He's almost five and thinks he's fifteen, a real smart-ass, but, as his mother says, he's cute.

Keep writing. Pearl and the boys send their love.

Edwin

26 – ORIENTE PROVINCE, 1958

*

U.S.S.R Satellite Circles Globe At 18,000 M.P.H.
Tracked In 4 Crossings Over U.S.

*

Senators Attack Missile Fund Cut

*

Little Rock Prays For Peace In Integration Crisis

*

Rock 'n' Roll Ban Spreads Over Nation

*

Colombian Cavalry With Drawn Sabers Break Up Anti-
Nixon Demonstration

*

Integration Left Up To Schools
U.S. Judge Refuses To Order It In Florida

*

Cuban Rebels Said Gaining; Batista Forces Lack Arms

Government Warns Civilians Of Plans To Bomb
Insurgent Areas

*

Ike Watches Football Game On Quiet Sunday

*

February 12, 1957
Dear Edwin,

This place has become too exciting. I don't know if it's hit the newspapers up there, but last December Fidel Castro and an armed group of 81 men landed on the coast of Oriente Province near here. Most were killed or captured, but Castro, his brother Raul, an Argentine revolutionary they call Che Guevara, and nine others escaped into the Mountains. It's amazing how many volunteers have joined them. You remember about the schools in Tampa not wanting to make trouble? Well it's the opposite here. Almost everybody supports the rebels. They want Batista out, but sympathy with the rebels is dangerous. When anyone deserts to join the insurgents, he's immediately marked for execution. The army hasn't caught any of them yet, but we hear rumors. One thing certain is that the military is all over this region. The other day I heard the army used napalm bombs on the rebels in the mountains. Unbelievable!

My work at school is hard. Parents preach education as the only road out of poverty, but the government has cut off help to rebel areas. Children come to school barefoot and hungry, some from long distances. The area has few schools. And when their fathers need them on the farm, the boys disappear for weeks at a time. My pay is pitiful and unreliable, but I don't mind as long as I can help the kids.

Zoraida's happy. I believe if she were a man she would go into the mountains and fight with the rebels. I've never seen her so excited.

Regards to Pearl and the boys.
Your friend,
Mat

*

October 24, 1957
Dear Mat,

I would have written sooner, but Sputnik has turned my department into a nut house. It's as if the Russians had won the war or something. I've been as busy as we ever were in Italy. It's great for our missile

370

program. We're finally getting everything we need. I'm taking a break to write this.

I've been reading quite a bit lately about Castro and his insurgents. He seems to be winning some important victories, and the army seems scared to fight back. Dictators usually treat their soldiers well; Batista must be slipping. People must be sick of him.

I'm glad you're enjoying your work. You're a natural teacher with a way of explaining things that goes to the heart. Those kids are lucky. I'm sorry they lost you in Tampa.

Let me know how it's going for you. Pearl and I send best regards to you and Zoraida.

Your old buddy, Edwin

*

The way pupils were disappearing Matilde knew the school was doomed. With the government battering the area, most of the villagers had left for Santiago or Havana, and Matilde was again unemployed. Zoraida and he discussed possibilities, but the discussion turned into a four-day argument. At the end Matilde finally agreed to join the rebels. When he expressed doubts, she said only that they had little choice. When he was convinced there would be no future as long as Batista is in power they went to see Dr. Reyes, the village rebel contact.

Doctor Reyes knew them well.

Matilde said, "With the school closed, there's nothing I can do. I can't take this any longer; we want to join Fidel."

Reyes was serious and scratched his head and said nothing at first. Finally he asked why we had come to him.

"A very close friend told us," Zoraida said. "Don't worry, Doctor, we're with you."

"Fidel knows all about you, Matilde, and was hoping you would join him."

"I go too," Zoraida said.

"I must tell you that prospects for the revolution are not good. You will be in constant danger with little to rely on."

"I've been to war before."

"I don't know about you, Zoraida, but I will ask. Most important of all, do not talk of this to anyone, not even your friend who sent you. I will take care of everything. Come back here in the morning. And remember that the soldiers will be watching you. Take this medicine, Zoraida, in case they question you on your way home. That will be your excuse for returning tomorrow.

On their way home Matilde and Zoraida watched for soldiers and tried not to act suspicious. They saw several, but none paid them any attention. Crossing the village square they greeted the mother of one of Matilde's students, chatted a few moments, and continued. Throughout the exchange and watching the woman's smile and demeanor, Matilde had the feeling she knew. He knew it was impossible, but he had gained respect for way information seeps through the villages.

Zoraida fixed lunch as Matilde sat on the porch and read. Feeling that the walls had ears, neither spoke any unnecessary words. Zoraida imagined soldiers crouched under every window to eavesdrop. As usual before lunch Matilde sat on the porch to read.

After lunch Matilde walked to the café on the edge of the square for some dominoes. Everyone acted normal, complaining about the poverty that was creeping across the area. Matilde had a beer and bought two for friends and spent a relatively relaxed afternoon before returning home. When he got back Zoraida was waiting.

"Where have you been? Why so late? What happened?"

"If you don't calm down they'll know we're up to something," he said.

After supper they spent the rest of the evening reading and listening to government propaganda on the radio expanding on how the army was routing rebels from their hideouts in the mountains.

Zoraida and Matilde were awake before daylight. Don't turn on the light, Matilde said."

"Good idea. But what if they won't accept me?"

"We'll deal with that if and when we have to. The Americans have a good saying, 'Don't borrow trouble.'"

Matilde had parted from her before, but he knew this would be different. She'd be in danger whether she went or stayed. And if the rebels lost, they would be shot as traitors.

After a nervous breakfast of bread and café con leche, they strolled to the doctor's office at nine o'clock. Again they saw soldiers on every street corner, but they paid no attention.

Doctor Reyes was glad to see them. "I was afraid you might have changed your mind."

His broad smile told them what they were anxious to know. "When you leave here, go back home and continue as always. Sometime after midnight, a man named Alfonso Maduro will come for you. Take only what you can carry in your pockets. No bags, no guns. And don't turn on any lights when he comes. Now go and good luck."

*

With no moon, they easily found their way out of the village unobserved. They wore peasant's clothes and straw hats as if they were going to work in the fields. They were already on the mountain trail when the moon rose.

Matilde asked Zoraida why she stopped.

"Saint Barbara has brought out the moon to guide us. Now I'm sure we're doing right."

The trail was not new to them; they had walked it during the day for the scenery. Their more urgent purpose did not, however, diminish the beauty. They passed a banana farm and, higher up, a large coffee plantation before finally entering a wild forest that almost blacked out the moon.

Reaching a relatively flat part of the trail moving east, the sun's first light appeared like the opening flick of a lady's fan. Even Alfonso Maduro stopped.

"What a paradise this could be," he said. "Maybe soon ..."

It was mid-afternoon when they found the camp. It looked small at first, but its tentacles stretched deep into the forest. The smell of coffee drew them to the fire where Alfonso introduced them. *"Donde está El Jefe?"* Alfonso asked.

Someone nodded toward a hut where Fidel appeared and walked toward them. *"Comandante,* I present Matilde Gómez and his wife, Zoraida."

They all wore fatigues and beards. Fidel stood a head taller than the rest. It was not his stature that attracted Matilde, however, but his bearing and cool gentility. He radiated nobility, confidence, and the serenity of a man in complete command. Alfonso introduced them, and his companions made way for Fidel as he shook Matilde's hand warmly but with restraint.

"Encantado," he said in a quiet, gentle voice. "Your fame as a pilot reached me some time ago."

Then he introduced them to the men beside him, Camilo Cienfuegos, Che Guevara, and Fidel's brother Raúl. "We've just ended a strategy session; they'll return to their posts tomorrow morning."

Matilde stood silent taking in the group that surrounded him. He had seen fighting men before, but these were crude, dirty farmers. He could not imagine them in control of a popular revolution that would take the country in a new direction. Most had killed at close range, some with their bare hands. Camilo Cienfuegos was a fascinating presence. Thin and not tall, but with a ferocious black beard and long hair, he resembled an emaciated lion. Che Guevara was short and calm; his smile looked almost docile. He had joined the rebellion as their doctor, but seeing his courage in several skirmishes, Fidel elevated him to *comandante*. Having no appreciable beard, Raul's childlike, oriental features made him look weak and defenseless.

"Come, Matilde," Fidel said. "Alfonso, show Zoraida her quarters. Evelio, come with us." He offered Evelio and Matilde cigars and they spent the next hour sitting and talking about Jose Martí, the Ten Years' War, the American Civil War, and Batista's tyranny. Evelio said little, but his eyes never left Matilde throughout the conversation. Matilde soon began to wonder why he was there. He was too small and puny to be a bodyguard. A confidant, perhaps or simply a witness. Fidel didn't explain and Matilde did not ask.

Castro spoke with profound knowledge, understanding, and intelligence, but his most captivating feature was his calm, gentle manner. He never raised his voice in passion or anger. His kindly demeanor seemed to belie his reputation for savage bravery in battle. When Matilde let him know how much he wanted to expel Batista and his murderous crowd, Castro smiled. When he raised the subject of Marxism, Fidel took a long draw on his cigar, exhaled and said, "Marx was a brilliant analyst, but too much the intellectual missionary, too fanatical. He failed to understand human nature."

Matilde looked perplexed, so Fidel continued: "Marx taught that human beings are fundamentally good, but that they have been corrupted by capitalism. When they are reeducated to the truth, he teaches, during a temporary dictatorship, they will be able to govern themselves. That's bunk. Humans are vain, ambitious, envious, vindictive, and greedy. You know the seven deadly sins."

"That's how I see it," Matilde said. "His view of history is good, but the plan he outlined in <u>Das Kapital</u> is almost juvenile."

"No doubt about it: a communist revolution must be maintained in perpetuity. Of course, that would preclude democracy, so I oppose it."

"My wife Zoraida is a staunch Marxist. She wanted to join the movement even more than I did in hopes that it would eventually turn that way."

"That's not my plan, but how would you feel if it did?"

"I must be honest, Fidel. I don't know. I don't believe the theory, but in practice, it may become necessary."

"Please elaborate, and, by the way, I'd appreciate your honest opinion. Without honesty, we have nothing."

Not knowing how to take the man, Matilde decided to take him at his word. "Fidel, I don't like the dictatorship communism requires. But we have a capricious dictator now. Communism, at least, focuses on helping the people and developing the nation's resources."

"Do you prefer American democracy?"

"Yes and no. That democracy is selective. It favors the rich and powerful. Their treatment of Negroes is horrible. Negroes enjoy little democracy."

"Less than here under Batista?"

"Truthfully yes. Cubans, Latins in general, accept us better, but not because of Batista, but because that's how we are as a people."

"Talking with you is a pleasure, Matilde. I like your intellectual independence. We're going to get along well. *Verdad, Evelio?* And what about your wife?"

"She's passionate about the revolution. I hope you'll be able to use her. She's a remarkable woman."

"And amazingly beautiful for her age, possibly enough to cause problems." As he spoke he glanced at Matilde through his smoke, obviously studying his reaction. Then Fidel smiled and said, "Don't worry, Matilde. We have women fighters, almost enough to form a platoon, and there are no problems. From what I've seen, women can do everything we can, and some things better."

Matilde did not comment.

Standing, Fidel said, "Evelio and I have some things to do now. Tonight you can tell me about your Air Force experience."

He left Evelio in his hut and walked Matilde to his. A radio in the hut next door was blaring out dance music, and when Matilde opened the curtain, Zoraida was dancing in the middle of the floor, her back to him. Not seeing him, she swayed with the music, her hips swiveling and undulating like an animal and her shiny black hair swaying as she moved. Matilde stood spellbound. It had been years since he had seen her in that state. This was the Zoraida he had met in Havana, the supple teenage animal who had excited him and who could still make him ache. Her face radiated exultation. Without missing a beat, she danced toward him until her breasts and thighs met him, where she continued to move and gyrate. He found himself moving with her and sliding his arms around her and holding her as they moved around the small room. Rubbing his back she danced him into the back room, where, holding his neck, she wrapped her legs around his and they fell into bed.

"We are in heaven," she whispered, "in this mountain jungle like other savage animals. It's heaven, heaven."

Matilde was exhausted after a ten-hour, uphill climb, but the ordeal had energized Zoraida. What a woman, an unfettered animal, uninhibited and burning with desire, he thought. On the other hand perhaps only with such discipline can she put away inhibitions so completely.

Her face told him what words could not. Zoraida seemed to revel in her wild nature, and in the mountains, away from civilization and restraint, she had become an animal unchained.

Matilde told her about his conversation with Fidel.

"Who is Evelio?"

"I'm not sure. He said nothing."

"What do you think they will do with you? Did he say anything about me? I feel I'm finally going to do something important; the caracoles told me so while you were gone." She turned to put her arms around him. "And that we'd stay together."

Matilde did not like her mystical beliefs, but it made her happy, so he said nothing. Besides, he told himself, she seemed to have an uncanny ability to see what others can't. Who knows? Maybe she has special powers.

Excited as the rebel cause appeared, something about Castro bothered him. He admired the leader, especially his intelligence and power. But their conversation had left him wondering. This man could defend any position, whether he believed it or not. And there was the man's unpredictability. He had read about Castro's poorly planned attack on the Moncada Barracks years before and his exile in Mexico and then his return on an overloaded wreck of a boat. This man seemed capable of acting on his vision with no concern for consequences. Castro seemed to want Matilde to feel trusted, but why? Why did he want Matilde in his movement? Why? These questions would haunt him.

Matilde's doubts were based on scant facts. However, there would be time to gather more facts. For the moment, Zoraida's happiness was enough, after all she had put up with for him. Things feel right, he thought. I must learn to trust her instincts.

Matilde and Zoraida spent the rest of the day meeting the others and learning the area. Evelio explained the boundaries they could not cross without exposing themselves. He spoke slowly and tentatively, but apparently with understanding. Zoraida met the women, wives of rebels, others unattached, nearly all of them with fighting experience. In all, there were slightly under a hundred persons in the camp. Matilde decided that day to start a journal. One day, he thought, I'll look back on these momentous days with either calm pleasure or anxious pain. He knew that doubts about the future added spice to life. He mused as he wrote his first entry: "Even the most wonderful and unusual quest would lose its excitement if we knew the outcome beforehand. With that said, I shall philosophize no further in this journal."

*

Near sundown Fidel found Matilde talking with some other men near the camp's center and invited him for a walk in the woods. "So as not to be disturbed," he said. Evelio joined them and, again remained mute. They came to a lookout point hidden from view by thick trees and bushes. Below them, government soldiers milled around their camp apparently unaware of the rebel' presence.

"We'll kill them all when the time comes," Fidel said, then resumed his tour. "It would only bring reprisals now."

During their stroll Matilde described his flying experience, his African and European assignments, the aircraft, and some of the missions. Fidel asked brief questions, but mostly he listened. Evelio remained virtually invisible.

"We desperately need someone who understands air combat," Fidel said. "I want you to be a consultant to *Comandantes* Raul, Camilo, and Che. When the time comes to engage the enemy in the air, you will move into a direct role."

"Do we have planes?"

"No, but we will when we take over."

"Who will we be fighting then?"

"There are always enemies, Matilde; we must remain prepared."

"I want to join the fighting now."

"I can't afford to lose you. I want you to understand my commanders' roles and our resources and requirements. Most important, I want you to feel completely free to tell me what you think at all times. Frankness in my close advisors is essential if I am to make sound decisions. For now, I want you to prepare reports for *Radio Rebelde*. We're scheduled to start broadcasting next week."

Matilde guessed he was being tested, and he knew the main rule of war is to follow orders. It was late February before they made their first broadcast announcing their victory at the second battle of Pino del Agua. That battle expanded the rebels' operations enormously. The following week, Raul Castro and Juan Almeida led columns out from the Sierra Maestra to establish new rebel fronts in Oriente Province. Their goal was to encircle Santiago de Cuba. The troops were elated finally to leave their mountain retreat. The march to Havana had begun! Zoraida wanted to march with them, but Fidel said no.

377

"We'll have our women's platoon organized soon," he said.

"But other women are fighting."

"You need more training."

*

March 10, 1958

Dear Edwin,

As you may have read, the revolution is growing. Castro attacks Batista's men at will. I can see victory peering over the horizon. Writing this letter posed a small problem. I joined the rebels last September. I have to smuggle this letter to a nearby village to mail it. Zoraida's with me. Batista is devastating this province. I've given up trying to understand all sides of every issue. There's one right side, and I'm on it. I don't know where I'll end up, but I feel useful for the first time since Italy.

We live in the woods like guerrillas. It's rough, but exciting; I feel alive. Zoraida is in her element. Fidel has taken me into his inner circle, I guess because of my flying experience. Whatever the reason, I love it.

Fidel is fearless and intelligent and, as a lawyer, rarely loses an argument. Even in the Air Force I never met such a commanding leader. People will follow him to hell if he decides to go there. I know I would. He'll give our country back to the people. Wish us luck.

I don't know how often I'll write, and I can't give you an address, but I'll do my best to keep you posted.

Your good friend,

Mat

*

In April the July 26 Movement National Directorate decided to shift the national leadership from Havana to the Sierra Maestra and chose Fidel Castro as general secretary. It was a formality, for he had led the movement since the beginning.

During supper that evening, Castro basked in glory. He spoke floridly about land reform and education reform and other popular plans. His lack of specifics disappointed Matilde, but he knew they would come when the fighting ended.

Later, in his hut with Evelio and Matilde, Fidel offered a toast in rum and told Matilde to broadcast the news of his supreme leadership over *Radio Rebelde.*

"Make it big. Play it up to its full importance. I want the people to know I'm now in complete charge of the revolution."

"Why so big?" Matilde asked.

Fidel squinted defensively. "Why not?"

"Everybody knows you're our leader, but what about all the others who have fought at your side? Shouldn't they share the attention?" Seeing suspicion in Fidel's eyes, Matilde said, "You wanted frank opinions."

A strange look crept over Fidel's face. At first Matilde thought he would fly into a rage as he had done several times with others, but he did not. Instead, he put down his glass and walked around the room. Finally, he said, "You make a good point, Matilde, for my lieutenants deserve much credit for their bravery and loyalty. But people cannot maintain loyalty to a group or an idea or any other abstraction. People hunger to be loyal to a human person, one they can see and recognize and idolize. In their eyes that person soon assumes god-like stature, grand, illustrious, leading them from above. Every successful movement has had an individual to focus on. We had Martí; the American Civil War had Lincoln, the Soviets have Marx and Lenin, Christians have Jesus. The Germans couldn't have done what they did if they had not worshipped Hitler."

Matilde hated his allusion that Hitler had been good, but he had to admit Fidel was right about the people needing someone to admire. But he also knew that idolatry could easily lead to absolute power and the weakening of the people's power. Historical leaders popped into Matilde's thoughts—Caesar, El Cid, Charlemagne, Martin Luther, Queen Isabel, Washington. He also knew that devotion to a leader could leach out their devotion to principle. Matilde decided not to pursue the argument, though Fidel's uncanny insight into the human heart surprised him. "You are right," Matilde said. "It takes a good leader to drive people into battle in the face of death. You're right. I'm embarrassed I didn't see it."

Then a different tinge of embarrassment crept over him, for capitulating too easily. But Fidel's face and his defiant stance left no doubt that he disapproved of Matilde's opinion. Sensing he could easily drop out of Fidel's inner circle, Matilde said no more hoping his opinion would carry more weight when he had proved himself.

*

In late May, the Rebel Army held its first peasant assembly in the mountains. Farm workers came from all over the region. Fidel spoke for hours and laid out his vision of land reform that would give them farms and tools to cultivate them, and about educating all children. The farmers listened with mouths slack open, accepting, admiring this charismatic leader who promised salvation from poverty, ignorance and oppression. They might have been listening to the Savior himself. No leader had ever spoken to them so directly and so passionately.

The next day, President Batista launched a new offensive called "Encircle And Annihilate." He was determined to stop the rebel forces in the Sierra Maestra before they could spread to the rest of the island. The fighting was fierce and the rebels suffered heavy losses, but Batista's losses were greater. In that offensive Batista lost what no leader could afford to lose: his men's confidence. By mid-July near El Jigüe, the rebels inflicted over 1,000 casualties and captured hundreds of weapons and a hundred thousand rounds of ammunition.

During the next few months rebel columns moved like ants, each toward its goal—northwest to Las Villas, west to Pinar del Río, and eventually over the entire island.

By September, Zoraida was a better marksman than many of the battle-seasoned men. Matilde was on the range when she demonstrated her skill for Fidel, who called her aside.

"I think you're ready, Zoraida, but the real test will come when you have to fire at a live person. I'll give you a choice: the new Mariana Grajales platoon, part of the First Rebel Front, which I will lead, or with Camilo Cienfuegos."

"With you, Fidel." The expression on her face stung Matilde as betrayal.

"You haven't understood the second choice," Castro said. "Matilde will be with Camilo."

"Oh." She looked at Matilde. "That is the only thing that could deter me from following you."

On their way to their hut Matilde said, "Thank you, Zoraida. My only worry is your safety. I'm not sure I approve of women warriors."

"Fidel approves. That's good enough for me."

Later that morning Fidel dropped by Matilde's hut and found him cleaning his rifle.

"How do you feel about going with Camilo?"

"You're my leader, Fidel."

Fidel smiled. "It's better if you and Zoraida do not fight together."

Matilde said nothing.

*

November 1, 1958
Dear Edwin,

I don't have much time. We're beginning our move. Batista's army is demoralized and all but evaporated. We don't expect opposition, but we'll see. Zoraida cannot contain her excitement. She's been working like any man. I feel like I did in Italy. In the next few weeks we'll make history.

Give our best to Pearl, Marcus, and Harold and keep your eyes and ears on the news.

Your pal,

Mat

27 – VICTORY AND DEFEAT, 1959

*

Batista Throws His Full Strength Into Fight For Key City
Civilians Flee As Rebels Battle Army In Streets Of Santa
Clara

*

Stocks Hit New All-Time Peak

*

Ike Proclaims Alaskan Statehood

*

Two Missiles Blown Up After Separate Launchings At
Cape Canaveral

*

U.S. Denies Intervention Planned In Cuba Revolt

*

Schools Get More Time To Answer Negro Suit

*

Batista Flees; Havana Looted; Castro Man Of Hour

*

Even before Sammy had his coat off, Pablo was telling him about the fun they would have in Cuba.

"I'm only home for ten days, Dad."

"Plenty of time. It's our homeland, Sammy, your mother's and mine. You haven't been since your were a kid."

"But I had plans with my friends."

"Just four days. Then you can see everybody."

"I know how much it means to you, Dad, but ... what about the revolution? It sounds serious."

"Just some loonies in the mountains. It's all talk."

Sammy looked to his mother for help.

"Your father has been planning this trip for a long time, Sammy. It'll be Sally's first time." Seeing Sammy's forlorn face she put her hand on his shoulder and said, "Really, you'll like it."

New Year's morning was clear and cool. Sammy went to the broad front porch to enjoy the scene. He looked at the large live oaks drooped over with Spanish moss and recalled childhood romps up and down that sidewalk. From the steps he could see the bay two blocks away. When his father saw him smiling he asked what he was thinking.

"That big grapefruit tree in our Brandon grove," Sammy said. "If I saw it now, it would probably look like a shrub."

"It was big all right. That tree symbolized the place for me."

Knowing his father was determined, Sammy steered the subject onto his post-doctoral research fellowship: "Dalton's being a jerk. He's got me on the grant project I told you about at graduation. Well, nothing worked, so I tried something new and it took off. I thought he'd be upset, but he got so excited he put a new graduate student on it to help. Now he's pushing us day and night."

"What's wrong with that?"

"Nothing, Dad, but he's telling all his friends about *his* new idea. Last week he sent it to the journal as a communication, you know, just enough details to keep us from getting scooped, and he put himself as senior author. When he showed me the draft, I asked why he didn't put my name first. He said, 'Rules of the game,' and walked out of the lab."

"If it's as big as you say, it may need his name to convince people."

"I didn't mean my name alone."

"What happens if he doesn't get results?"

"His money dries up, I guess."

"Sounds like pretty big pressure."

"But he's a heavy hitter. He should be used to it"

"Let him have it, Sammy. You'll get plenty of ideas. He needs it, and it won't hurt one bit to have your name on an important paper with a big shot."

Sammy looked at his father blankly.

"He's paying you to produce, so produce; give him your best. He knows it's your idea. You don't have to rub his nose in it. One of these days he'll be in a position to help you get your own grants."

Sheepishly Sammy said, "But he didn't even say thanks."

"Some people have a hard time with thanks. It takes a big ego to get where he is. Don't expect humility."

"You know academics better than I do."

"Not academics, Sammy; people."

"Boys, come look!" Consuelo said. "The Cubans are fighting!"

The television screen bulged with crowds spilling into a Havana street and bands playing and people chanting and yelling. Over the sounds of jubilation, the narrator's voice was loud and high-pitched:

"We have just received a report that President Batista and his wife boarded a plane during the night, leaving this island nation in the hands of a military junta. But from where I stand it looks more like anarchy. The army is in disarray as Fidel Castro and his guerrilla forces have moved through the island gathering supporters. Instead of resistance, they have encountered cheers and flowers in every town and city. Few shots have been fired in anger. The shots you hear are in celebration."

They sat in the living room facing the TV. Sally lay on the sofa. "Look for Matilde and Zoraida" Pablo said. "It would be fun to spot them in the crowd."

"Who're they?" Sally asked.

"Matilde was one of my first Tampa friends. We saw them off at the airport five years ago. Don't you remember the beautiful lady?" Pablo asked.

"Oh, her? Sure."

"He promised to write, but never did," Pablo said. "I figured he didn't make out. It would be nice to know what's become of him."

The television scene shifted to the presidential palace where a throng had filled the square.

"The mood is definitely festive. The sounds you hear are fireworks exploding, church bells ringing; it's a fiesta! Fidel Castro, broadcasting from Santa Clara, has called for a general strike in opposition to the military junta left in place by President Batista. (Pause) We take you now to our correspondent at the edge of the city, where the rebel army is making its way toward the center."

A new voice begins: "People are dancing and singing all along the parade route, throwing flowers to the rebel soldiers. The city is erupting. Women are leaving their homes and holding their children so they may remember this day in years to come. It may be the greatest demonstration of popular enthusiasm Cubans have ever seen. Knowing the victory parade route, people have come to see their bearded liberators. Every balcony, attic, and tree is serving anyone who wants to catch every detail.

"Here they come now, a file of trucks packed with soldiers, many, but not all, of them wearing army fatigue uniforms. At their head are three Jeeps carrying their leaders. Rag-tag as this army looks, it is well trained. They're smiling, waving, and throwing kisses to everyone along the route. Camilo Cienfuegos is standing in the first jeep with a large man at his side, both wearing fatigues and waving triumphantly, long cigars in their teeth.

"That's Matilde with Cienfuegos," Consuelo said.

Pablo was already standing. "By God, it is!"

Matilde was standing in the open jeep with his massive arm over Cienfuegos's shoulder; both smiling, waving and yelling at the crowds.

"Are you sure it's him?" Consuelo asked.

"Even with the beard, there's no doubt about it. He's lost some weight. You remember him, Sam?"

"Sure. At the airport. Isn't that his wife in the next jeep?"

In the second jeep Zoraida was standing next to a man. Both were dressed in military clothes; she had a khaki bandana over her hair and waved a rifle over her head as she laughed and talked with the man next to her.

"That's her!" Sally said.

"Camilo Cienfuegos is one of Fidel Castro's closest commanders and is leading one of his main columns into Havana. We have been told that he is here to forestall the installation of Batista's military junta. The man standing beside Cienfuegos must be another of Castro's lieutenants. We don't have his name."

Pablo shouted at the television set, "Matilde Gómez!"

"In the next jeep are two other lieutenants, we're told, but we don't yet know who they are. The woman ... Wait. (Pause) I've just been informed that the woman is the wife of the man with Cienfuegos, and that his name is Matilde Gómez, one of Castro's advisors. We don't know anything about him, but I'm sure we'll be hearing more before long."

"He was one of the brightest men I have ever known," Pablo said. "A Cuban cigar maker, an ace World War II pilot. And after the war he went to college and became a teacher.

"In Tampa?" Sally asked.

"Yes, but when he lost his job, he was so frustrated and angry that he went back to Cuba. I'd sure like to know how he ended up with that bunch."

The television scene switched to Ybor City, where hundreds of people had gathered in front of the Cuban Club.

"Why don't we join the fun?" Consuelo said. When she saw Sally so quiet, lying on the sofa, she asked how she felt.

"A little pukey."

"We'll stay home then," Consuelo said.

"No. I want to see what's going on," Sally said.

In the car Sally sat next to Sammy with her head on his arm. As they turned into Seventh Avenue, the traffic thickened, and soon they were creeping along, bumper-to-bumper. Finally Pablo found a parking space two blocks from the Cuban Club, and they walked the rest of the way. Hundreds of people had come to celebrate Batista's ouster. A three-mile race along the streets of Ybor City had just begun with over a hundred high school and college boys and others of all ages joining in. A band played on the back of a truck half a block down, and people danced in the street.

"Like the old days in Ybor City when I was a kid," Sammy said.

The four of them stood on the curb across the street from the Cuban Club to watch, while people lined up to make speeches predicting the beginning of a new era of Cuban freedom and prosperity. They spoke of Castro in tones that resounded with religious fervor. A bystander who didn't know better would have thought they had witnessed the Second Coming.

Sally held on to Sammy's arm.

"Pablo you'd better take Sally and me home," Consuelo said. "You and Sammy can come back."

But they had seen enough and spent the rest of the morning in front of the television set as scenes changed from one locale to another. Before long, the reportage ground down into experts giving their opinions and prognostications. Pablo couldn't stop talking about Matilde.

"I never knew you respected him so much," Sammy said.

"I figured he had fallen into another low-paying job," Pablo said. "Cuba's not exactly the land of opportunity, Sam. But I just can't imagine the path that could have led him into that jeep. He's brilliant, no doubt about it. But with all his brainpower, he could never make anything of himself."

"A war ace and then college sounds like he did pretty well," Sammy said.

Because Sally was not feeling well, Consuelo decided to cook lunch, and they ate over the TV's droning. Sally picked at her food. After a few minutes she said she wasn't hungry and went to her room.

"What's the matter, Sal?" Sammy said. "Why aren't you driving your big brother crazy like always."

"I don't know."

He tried to make conversation, but she didn't respond, so he left her to sleep.

Pablo moved into the living room to watch TV, while Consuelo finished in the kitchen. When she came into the living room, she sat looking up the stairs.

"What's wrong?" Pablo asked.

"Sally."

"Kids get sick. It's normal."

"She likes attention," Sammy said.

When Consuelo went upstairs, Sammy followed. Lying in bed with her eyes closed, Sally said, "I don't feel good."

Consuelo took a thermometer out of her medicine cabinet and returned to take Sally's temperature. It was slightly above normal.

"If you're not better tomorrow, we'll call the doctor," she said.

The next morning Sally still had a temperature, so Sammy drove his mother and sister to their family doctor. While they waited, Sally sprawled out on a lounge chair. After about an hour the nurse called her in.

After the examination, Dr. Winton said, "It looks like an upset stomach; probably an infection of some kind." Writing on a pad, he said, "Give her this. She should be all right in a few days." He tore the prescription off and handed it to Consuelo and smiled at Sally, who was still on his sofa. Consuelo felt better, but not Sally.

Three days later Consuelo, Pablo, and Sally drove Sammy to the airport. Sally felt slightly better, but she was still tired and weak. When the plane was ready to board, the three walked Sammy to the plane. Sally leaned on Consuelo. They said goodbye at the airplane; Sammy kissed Sally and Consuelo, shook his father's hand, and walked in.

*

On their way home, Consuelo could not sit still. Her fingers tapped and her heart raced. "We've got to take her back to Dr. Winton," she said.

"But Consuelo, he said it was just an upset stomach."

"I'm taking her."

After calling, Consuelo drove Sally to the doctor's office. He felt her abdomen, listened with his stethoscope, took her temperature and then sat looking at her for a long moment. "Let's get some blood tests," he told the nurse. Then to Consuelo, "It won't take long."

When they had finished, he said he would call in a few days when he received the test results.

"What is it, Doctor?"

"We'll see when we get the results. Until then we'll have to wait. Just let her rest and keep her comfortable."

That Friday Dr. Winton called. "Mrs. Iglesias, Could you come to the office?"

"You want to see Sally again?"

"No, just you."

"What about my husband?"

"Bring him."

Consuelo dropped the flowers she had been arranging in a new vase, washed up, called Pablo, and told him to meet her at Doctor Willard's office. Then she went upstairs and told Sally she would be back soon.

Pablo was already there when Consuelo arrived. Seeing him she started to cry, "I can't control myself. I feel so stupid."

"Come on, now. He hasn't said anything yet." He put his arm around her.

In a few minutes the doctor came out, shook their hands, and ushered them into his office.

He hesitated and Consuelo could stand it no longer. "Please, Doctor, what is it?"

"There's no easy way to say it. I'm afraid Sally has acute leukemia."

As the air in the room turned yellow, Consuelo felt herself falling. When she opened her eyes she was lying on the sofa, and Pablo and the doctor were standing over her.

"Lucky your husband caught you, or you would have hit the floor," Doctor Winton said as he checked her pulse and blood pressure. She tried to stand, but felt dizzy and almost fell again. Recalling the doctor's words, she began to cry. The only words that came out were, "God, God, what'll I do?"

"I can ease her discomfort, but I'm afraid that's all we can do. This is one of those diseases that leave us powerless. I'm so sorry."

"What about taking her to one of the big medical centers up north, Johns Hopkins or The Mayo Clinic?" Pablo said. "Maybe they can do something."

"You can, but I assure you there is no cure."

"Are you sure that's what it is?" Consuelo asked.

"Yes," Winton said. "I don't mind in the least if you want another opinion. I just wish there were something I could do. I know how it hurts, but you had to know."

"I can't believe it," Consuelo said. "Her mother died of cancer."

"I remember," Dr. Willard said, visibly shaken.

"How long does she have?" Pablo asked.

"Hard to tell. Weeks, a month perhaps."

"You mean it could be less?" Consuelo said.

"There's really no way to tell. Here are two prescriptions. I'm sorry. Times like these make me hate my profession."

*

Later, Consuelo could not recall leaving the office. The next thing she recalled was Pablo turning on the ignition, and then beginning to sob. When he was able to talk again, he said, "This is payment for my sins."

"Your sins? You think God would strike down an innocent child to pay you back. How can you be so self-centered?"

"Please, Consuelo, don't. I can't ..."

Consuelo opened the door and got out. "I'll drive my car home."

Pablo sat paralyzed as she drove off.

Arriving behind her, Pablo opened the front door and called her, but she did not answer. He found her on the back porch.

"We'll have to tell Sammy," he said.

"I know, and Sally too. I feel like I'm drowning."

When Pablo bent down and put his head on her shoulder she could not pull away. They sat sobbing for almost an hour unable to speak.

*

"Why did you wait so long to tell me?" Sammy said. "It's been a week."

Pablo could hardly talk with the choking and sobbing. When Sammy hung up, he went to Doctor Dalton's office and told him. "My sister's dying. She's only fourteen. I have to go."

Doctor Dalton could hardly refuse.

"I'll keep in touch. I'll just be a few days; she's my first priority now."

"I understand. I'm Sorry, Sam. Hope it goes well."

*

Sammy spent most of that week with Sally on the porch and in her room talking when she was up to it, and sitting by her side when she slept or didn't want to talk. Windows on two sides brightened her room. Consuelo kept the room filled with flowers. Day by day Sally sank deeper and deeper into a calm resignation that was almost as hard for the family to take as the disease. It was bad enough to face death, but to face it willingly, almost longingly, they thought, was too much. In the late afternoon of Sammy's last day home, with the sun filling the room, Sally woke up. He was sitting by her bed.

"Sorry we won't be able to go on together," she whispered.

Sammy began to cry. When he composed himself he said, "I'm staying a few more days."

"No. You've got a long way to go, and I can't go with you. It's my time."

Sammy was astonished. "You're phenomenal."

"You too. I'm glad you're my brother."

He bent over and hugged her, and then got in bed beside her and held her hand until she dropped off to sleep.

28 – Spring, 1959

*

Mother Of 2-Week-Old Quads Arrested In Bar

*

Batista In Exile Says Castro Had Superior Arms

*

Rockefeller Inaugurated As Governor Of New York

*

Cuban Refugees Swamp Airports

*

Cuban Envoy In Paris Jumps On Bandwagon

*

Consuelo's grief was unbearable, and Pablo was too shaken to offer comfort. Occupying the same house, they rarely touched, avoiding each other like insulated, repellent planets in silent space. He had seen her distraught before, but never like this. She spent whole days in bed. When she was too tired to cry, she would stare out the window. Nothing could penetrate the grief that enshrouded her. Pablo tried to work, but would find himself staring into the vast sky that insulated the bustling city from endless space. At home, Consuelo would neither talk nor eat. Pablo brought food to her bed and helped her get it down. Witnessing this, Sam could not bring himself to leave, even though he knew he had to.

One late afternoon a week later his father sat him down and said, "Sam, we've all got to get on with our lives. Your mother has taken it very hard, but she'll find her way out."

Sam left the following morning. Two weeks had passed since the funeral. Pablo and Consuelo drove him to the airport. They did not stay to watch the plane take off. Consuelo seemed to long only for the silence of her bedroom.

*

That evening the Harvard campus was neatly tucked under a soft blanket of snow. Wispy flakes flecked Sam's hair and Navy P-coat as he made his way across the Yard enjoying the brilliant silence of the moonless night. Only the buildings, with tiny windows glowing like embers under glistening comforters, revealed life within. Under the streetlights the whiteness glowed.

It was nearly midnight when he opened his lab door and flipped on the lights. Though tired, he could not wait till morning to learn what had developed during his absence. The long lab had two parallel workbenches jutting out of the long wall and two windows on the opposite wall. At the far end stood the nuclear magnetic resonance spectrometer on which his work depended, and several other electronic instruments. At the end near the door stood two desks facing each other. Sam used one and Bill Estes, the graduate student assigned to the project, used the other. Opening the research notebook, he sat down to read. The first thing that caught his attention was that Bill had cleverly refined Sam's calculations, and his results were even better than Sam had anticipated. The idea Sam had planted had sunk roots and was producing shoots. He sat reading for over half an hour. Thinking about Estes's calculations all the way home, he did not notice that the naked moon tried to get his attention by laying a silver glow over the evening. Finding the apartment cold, he went to the thermostat and turned on the heat. After a few minutes, he took off his P-coat and made a cup of tea. Then he picked up the phone and called home.

"I'm glad you called, Sammy," his father said. "Is everything all right?"

"Fine. I know it's late, but I was worried about Mom."

"She'll be fine. It takes time. How was your trip?"

"The snow's beautiful. I just took a long walk in it."

"Enjoy it. You'll soon be sick of it." Then Sam heard, "Nothing's wrong, Consuelo . It's Sammy. He says the snow's pretty. Try to sleep; it's past midnight."

"Go back to sleep, Dad. Sorry I woke you."

"Good night Sammy."

The next morning Sam reported to Dalton, who greeted him warmly with a handshake. "I'm sorry, Sam."

Sam nodded.

"We've had some excitement. Estes hit pay dirt a few days ago."

"I went over his notebook when I got in last night."

Sam did not want to appear concerned in the face of success, but it must have shown.

"He's doing a great job," Dalton said.

Sam forced a smile, went to his lab and found Bill Estes there, writing in the lab notebook.

"Glad you're back, Sam. I'm really sorry about Sally."

"Thanks, Bill. I read your notes last night. Looks like you've been busy."

"With a slight variation on your idea, I think we'll get even more intimate molecular details than we expected. Maybe even differences between stereoisomers."

"Looks good, Bill, but calculations go only so far. Let's try some actual compounds and see if it fits."

"I was just about to." Bill went to the refrigerator and took out a bottle. "How about camphor? It's simple yet complex enough."

"Good." Watching Bill work, Sam saw himself two years earlier at CalTech finishing his Ph.D. dissertation. Trying not to think of Bill as a competitor, Sam recalled what his father had said about sharing ideas. I guess no one works alone anymore, he thought.

*

The night of Sammy's departure had been chaotic. Consuelo could not sleep and Pablo spent much of the night trying to calm her. After Sam's phone call, Pablo thought Consuelo had fallen asleep, but a little past two, he heard her go downstairs.

"Where you going?"

"I just can't."

A few minutes later he heard footsteps, then a door open and close, and saw a light go on momentarily and then off. He put on his robe and went downstairs and found her sitting in the living room sofa in the dark with her head lying back. The only light in the room came from a streetlight down the block.

"What are you doing?"

She turned away.

He sat beside her and took her hand. "You've got to settle down. She's gone and there's nothing we can do except go on with out lives."

"How?" The tone of her question seemed to rise from the depths of hopelessness.

"We still have Sammy and each other."

"She wasn't even my daughter. I have no reason to feel this way."

"She wouldn't have been yours more if you'd given birth to her."

"If she had been my real daughter I might not feel so bad. I'd know I had done all I could, but I let her die."

"Stop it! You know that's not true. My God! Don't you know how bad that makes me feel? I loved her too, Consuelo. Now stop torturing yourself."

She was silent. After a few moments, she said, "I'll be up soon."

The next morning the doorbell woke Pablo. At first he thought it was the alarm clock and saw it was 9:45. Seeing Consuelo asleep, he got up as quietly as he could, put on his robe, and went down.

Pablo stiffened as he opened the door and squinted to make out the figure against the bright sun.

"Good morning, Pablo. I guess I'm too early." Tony Sekul was smiling.

Pablo tried to smooth down his hair with his hands. He was dumb, wondering why this man would show up now of all times.

"Hello, Tony. Please come in. I don't usually sleep this late, but ..." Then in the living room he said, "What brings you here?"

"Elmo Starke called to tell me about Sally. This is the earliest I could get away. I'm so sorry."

"Thanks, Tony. Are you here for a meeting?"

"No. To see you."

"Consuelo's in a bad way."

"That's what Elmo said. Is she up?"

"She was awake most of the night; she's asleep now. I don't know what to do." Then looking up, "How about some coffee?"

"Sure." Pablo led him to the kitchen and put a pot of water on the stove as Tony sat at the table.

"How's Sammy?"

"It's been hard on him too. He left yesterday morning."

Consuelo walked into the kitchen in her robe. Seeing Tony rise out of his chair, she embraced him and began to sob. He looked at Pablo with obvious embarrassment. Pablo nodded approval. After a few moments, Consuelo backed away and dried her eyes.

"I'm sorry. It was such a shock seeing you. I'm glad you came, Tony." Turning to Pablo she said, "Here, let me." She took over the coffee making and opened the window shades. Taking a bottle of orange juice and the butter dish from the refrigerator, she poured three glasses of juice and then put slices of bread in the toaster. Sitting across from Tony at the table, Pablo was relieved to see Consuelo moving so energetically. It was the first time she had taken an interest in anything since the funeral. Tony's effect on Consuelo dredged up dark feelings in Pablo, but he pushed them aside.

Tony stayed most of the morning, sitting in the kitchen, sipping café con leche and talking. He brought her up to date on his job and his recitals around the state and beyond. It was the first time in weeks she had entertained thoughts not connected to Sally. Tony told her about Elmo Starke's phone call.

"I haven't been to campus much. Is he taking my students?"

Tony nodded.

"I guess I'd better call him," she said, putting her hand on Pablo's hand.

"If you're up to it," Pablo said. She put her hand on his lap.

When Tony stood to leave, Pablo asked him to stay for lunch.

"It's a long drive; I want to beat the dark."

"But you just got here," Consuelo said.

"I've got class tomorrow."

"You're a dear person, Tony," Consuelo said. "Please come back and stay a while."

"Right. We'll expect you," Pablo said. "I can't thank you enough for coming. You've been a Godsend."

Pablo surprised himself by embracing him.

Consuelo encouraged Pablo to go on to his office, that she would be fine. When he got home and found she had fixed supper, he hugged her lovingly.

That evening Sammy called.

"How's Mom?"

"A miracle!" Pablo said. "She's going back to work. You remember Tony Sekul from Tallahassee? Well, he came by. We had a good time talking; he was the tonic she needed. We're both feeling better now. I'll put her on."

"Hello, Sammy. How're you?"

"Fine. I'm glad you're going back to work."

"I can't afford to get fired," she said.

"You won't, Mom. I'm doing fine. Bill Estes is terrific."

"Truly, Sammy, I feel better, but ..."

Afraid his mother would slide back into her depression, he interrupted. "There were six inches of snow on the ground when I got here last night, and it's supposed to snow again tonight."

"Some day I'd like to see snow," she said.

When they hung up she said, "Sammy always thinks of us. By the way, it wasn't Tony who helped me. You did it."

"He helped."

"No, it was what you said last night. You were right; I've been torturing myself; you made me see it." She moved to his chair and sat on his lap. "I love you, Pablo," she said, and kissed him.

Knowing he had been the source of her anguish, Pablo embraced her. "Such an optimist."

Taken aback, she pulled away. "Are you making fun of me?"

"Don't you see? I'm the pessimist. I expect nothing from people. Knowing no one will look out for me, I have to do it. That's pessimism."

"I'm an optimist because I expect people to behave?"

"Sure. And they rarely do. It just occurred to me, but it's true. You expect kindness and generosity. That's optimism. I expect selfishness and betrayal. That's why you're always disappointed and I'm not."

"I still don't know whether you're putting me down. Do you want me to be a pessimist?"

"Ah, that's a good, pessimistic question. Of course I don't. I love you so much because you find the good in me even when there's little there. You took in Cynthia and Sally. You did what was right, and they loved you for it."

"Sounds like pessimism is the way to go," she said.

"Only if you don't mind hurting people. Jesus was the greatest of all optimists."

After thinking on that for a moment she said, "You're trying to say something quite sweet, aren't you?"

"See? That's optimism," he said, breaking into his brightest V smile.

"Enough philosophy! Let's go to bed and be optimistic."

*

Relieved that his mother had lifted out of her depression, Sam began to pour himself into his work. The next morning he got to the lab before seven o'clock and sat at his desk with Bill's camphor spectrum before him. He's right, he thought. It's even better than I expected. To test their hypothesis, Sam spent the morning running spectra on every compound he could find. By the time Bill came in Sam had four and laid them on Bill's desk for him to see.

"What do you think?"

"Wow! Let's go tell Dalton."

"Not yet," Sam said. "First we'll run all the samples we can get our hands on, especially the tough ones. When we tell him I want to be ready to publish."

"Good."

By late afternoon every sample compound had fallen into line. They were detecting differences in molecular shapes more subtle than anyone had ever seen. Dr. Dalton was bent over a manuscript when they burst into his office.

"Take a look at this," Sam said, laying the spectra on his desk. "Notice that all the predicted lines are there, including those predicted for the stereoisomers

Dalton perused them all silently. "Fantastic!" He raised his eyes to Sam. "Have you written it up?"

"We wanted to show you."

Dalton smiled maliciously and said, "You've shown me. Show me a manuscript by morning. Now go." Dr. Dalton was forty-one and was as excited as his students. He had made a name for himself with several brilliant discoveries and was in the process of solidifying his status as a leader in the field of NMR spectrometry.

Bill and Sam almost burst into a run. "Bill, you take the experimental part; you've done most of the hands-on work and know the details. I'll write up the introduction, theory, and discussion of results."

They sat at their desks and began to work. At eight o'clock that evening Sam stood. "I'm hungry."

"Give me a minute," Bill said.

They hustled to a coffee shop down the street and had a sandwich and talked about the paper. In half an hour they were back at their desks.

At half past midnight Bill said, "I'm through. Take a look."

"I'm still organizing the references. Leave it with me and go on home. I'll see you in the morning."

After Sam finished his part, he read over Bill's experimental part. It was perfectly clear and concise. It was almost two o'clock when Sam got to bed.

When he opened the lab the next morning, Bill had not yet come in. "He'll just have to wait for the typed copy," Sam said aloud as he walked the hand-written manuscript to Dalton's secretary.

"When can I have it?" he asked.

"Dr. Dalton said you'd have something for me this morning. Lunch OK?"

Sam went back and sat at his desk tapping his pencil, as if trying to make the time move faster by rushing the tempo of the tapping. It was 9:15 when Bill came in.

"How was it?"

"Great. Mrs. Chapman has it."

Bill said nothing and went to the lab bench to run more samples. Sam could not think of new experiments until the manuscript was in the mail.

"I proofread both parts and they look good. Dalton will love it," Sam said.

At 11:10 Mrs. Chapman called. "Your paper's ready," she said. Both of them hurried down the hall to her office and took the two copies, thanked her, and returned to the lab to reread them. Sam had not attached the spectra, but he had noted where they would go in the manuscript. He put Dalton's name first, followed by Bill's and his.

Within twenty minutes, they finished proof reading and took it to Dr. Dalton's office, where they found him reading.

"Looks excellent, Sam. I've made a few changes. Here, look them over; then we'll talk."

"I didn't know you had a copy," Sam said.

"Hope you don't mind."

"Not at all." Standing over his desk they read through the changes. Within a few minutes Sam said, "Looks good, but you've rearranged the names."

"Iglesias, Estes, Dalton. That's the way I want it. Any objections?" Dalton asked with a smile.

"I hope it isn't because of what I said before."

"You were right, Sam. I always put authors' names in alphabetical order, but I guess that's self-serving for a man whose name begins with a D. They should be in order of contribution."

"Thanks."

That evening Sam called home again. "Hello, Dad. How's everything?"

"Fine, Sam. Mom returned to work this morning. They were all glad to see her. They've been very understanding."

"That's great, Dad. My work's going great too. We just finished a paper on the results of the idea I told you about. Bill Estes was great. This is important stuff."

"What about Dalton?"

"He's as excited as Bill and I. He put my name first on the paper. Shocked the hell out of me."

"Good. Geniuses are only people. They can be just as ambitious and driving, and sometimes as greedy and conniving as the rest of us."

"I expected them to be above pettiness," Sam said.

"You should try to be, but remember, you're human too. Son, you're moving into the stratosphere. It's competitive. I compete against other businessmen in Tampa; you're competing against the greatest minds in the world. You'd better be ready for a rough ride."

Sam was silent for a few seconds. "Thanks, Dad, you're pretty smart."

"I wish I'd had been when I was your age."

29 – THE FOLLOWING NOVEMBER

*

In An Unprecedented Act, One Million Cubans Ratify The Revolutionary Government

*

Cuban 'War Criminals' Executed In Havana

*

State Department Says Top Cuban Rebels Are Not Reds

*

De Gaulle Austerity Strips $500,000,000 In Subsidies From Business And Farmers

*

"*On a small group of men, with Fidel Castro at their head, rests at this moment the future of six million persons. Never before in all her history has Cuba arrived at a moment so charged with transcendence. The air is filled with optimism. The people are confident. We have won! It is over! We have killed half a dozen animals and have rid ourselves of so-called police agencies who invented methods of torture that even the Nazis did not dream up. But we are awake; the nightmare is over finally! Finally we can speak freely to the press. But beware! Our romantic euphoria carries more risks than the field of battle. What the dictator's tanks and bombs could not smash can easily be leached away to leave us defenseless in the face of a vigilant enemy who sits crouching, watching the great rhetorical exuberance toward which we of the tropics lean.*

"What Cuba has been needing, what she has received, is a group of young Creoles whose hands do not tremble, men who can tear out the roots of the evils that our colonial fathers planted into our Republic. We will eliminate the lottery, reduce the standing army, democratize public life, and return stolen property and goods to the people through land reform.

"We shall never smother in the emotion of triumph!
La Revolución Popular"

*

Havana bustled with activity as the new regime settled into the everyday work of governing. With Batista gone the Cuban people rejoiced. Castro's fatigues and scruffy beard had become the symbol of freedom from repression and of the restoration of the people's voice. Cubans hungered for the banquet of purity and truth they knew would follow.

Zoraida celebrated for weeks. Her life to that point seemed but a prelude to the movement that would sweep capitalism away and restore the land to workers who sustain themselves in the sweat of their brows. She fought and worked for Castro with a dedication and energy she had never known. Seeing her fervor, Fidel put her in charge of a committee on public responsibility. It was her job to keep the people from sliding back into old thoughts and ways. She appointed three trusted, old-line associates from Sierra Maestra days to her committee and plunged into her new work, giving life to her vision of Cuban growth and prosperity.

Before long she had become a symbol of idealistic self-sacrifice that infected all within her sphere of action. Her subordinates revered her.

Matilde had become an advisor to Castro. His assignment was to organize the poorly trained Cuban Air Force into an effective war machine with which Castro could spread his program to Latin American neighbors. Though Matilde still did not believe an air force was important to a free country under no threat, he did not object and enjoyed working on problems he understood with people who admired him for his courage under fire. His fame as a pilot had grown during the march to Havana. Camilo Cienfuegos saw in him a budding revolutionary hero. Being near Castro gave him his opportunity to influence the direction of the new government. Still, his proximity to the Maximum Leader did not wipe away his skepticism, especially Fidel's dedication to creating a war machine and his fascination with Marxism. It especially bothered Matilde to see Fidel argue against his own professed ideals. Perhaps he did it to strengthen his position by trying to demolish it, but Matilde suspected more. Castro's order to unions to keep communists out of leadership positions, relieved Matilde but not completely. His skepticism grew months later when Castro rescinded that order and formally embraced communism. From that point on, Matilde resolved to remain silent on the general subject and to stick to the concrete problems of implementing a pilot training program to improve basic skills as well as tactical, battle skills. Matilde's insecurity was heightened by the ever-present Evelio, whose job, he suspected, was to spy on Fidel's associates. Evelio was a small man, undistinguished in appearance or personality. He did not seem overly intelligent, as did most of Castro's close associates, and he was far from a physical threat.

Intellectual differences were only part of Matilde's worries that November. Batista, the cold hard man from the lower classes, had ferociously clawed his way to power leaving a long, bloody record of torture and murder. In his last years he had amassed great wealth. Castro cast out Batista's followers, and Matilde had approved. Within his first few weeks in power, with popular approval, Fidel ordered the execution of dozens of Batista's men after trials that mocked due process.

Before the end of Fidel's first year in power, Camilo Cienfuegos died in an airplane crash. When Matilde asked what happened, Fidel said, *"Quen sabe? He was a little crazy, you know."* Then, as an afterthought, " If you hear anything, you must tell me." Now, a year later, with his position consolidated and his communism unsheathed, Fidel began slashing out at subversives among his subordinates. In a speech he told the people, "We will not tolerate subversion from within. Traitors in our midst are the worst enemies, cowards who smile with mock loyalty as they undermine our hard-fought revolution."

Watching Fidel's metamorphosis, Matilde's worries deepened. He agreed that subversives were intolerable, but argued against execution. It was not the typical heated discussion that afternoon.

"Exile them, imprison them, but don't kill them," Matilde pleaded. In Castro's expansive office, with Evelio sitting silently in a chair at the far wall, Matilde felt he must speak freely, for the stakes were as high as they had ever been.

Looking at Matilde with the squint that held in his anger Fidel said, "Why not? From our midst they turn on us. They hide in offices down the hall. Why are you so concerned about filthy traitors?"

"I don't care about them, Fidel, but about you and the revolution. Batista killed his enemies and the people hated him for it. You've turned Cuba in a new, clean, forthright direction." Fidel listened patiently, thoughtfully, with his cheek on his fist, puffing his cigar, shaking his head or nodding as Matilde's words poured out. He did not look at Evelio for judgment. "Executions are not worthy of a great leader like you."

"Thank you, Matilde. You're always eloquent, and I appreciate your directness. I'll ponder what you have said, and we'll talk again." Then he picked up some papers and began to read.

Obviously dismissed, Matilde left feeling hollow. Fidel's words did not carry the sound of conviction and respect, but of doubt and deception. At first they had argued strongly until one had convinced the other. Now, Matilde said his piece and Castro would dismiss him. Their disagreements had become matter-of-fact and lacked emotion.

When Matilde was out of the office, Fidel called Evelio to him. "What do you think, my friend?"

"He's dangerous, Fidel. I've told you before; you can't trust anyone that addicted to logic."

"He knows airplanes, and he's done a good job organizing our air forces."

"I didn't say he's incompetent or evil," Evelio said. "It's his righteous attitude that worries me."

"I disagreed with you in the Sierra Maestra, Evelio, but I'm beginning to wonder. He may be too devoted to abstract principles to serve the revolution. If his devotion is as strong as you think, he could become dangerous."

Evelio nodded. "He has a large following among the Negroes, Fidel. They look up to him. That is not good."

Fidel shook his head pensively and said, "At first I hoped he would help solidify the lower classes, but we can't tolerate devotion to any individual, Evelio. You are right."

*

The bright February morning shone clear and mild. Matilde and Zoraida were still in bed as the sheer, window drapery billowed in the breeze. Their fifth floor apartment overlooked the boat-filled harbor and the curving drive of El Malecón. Herds of Batista's followers and others who did not like the revolution had left Cuba in that first year. Not long after the exodus began, Castro announced, "Batista's thieves have abandoned their country. It is only right that the property they have stolen from the people be returned to the people. For that purpose I am instituting the Ministry of Recovered Property." He assigned his top advisors and commanders to the best of those confiscated homes and automobiles. Matilde's apartment was one of these, the most luxurious he had ever seen.

Hearing a volley of rifle shots, Matilde's smile sank. "He did it!"

"Of course," Zoraida said. "What did you expect?"

"But he said he would think it over."

"Why shouldn't we treat them the way Batista treated us?"

"Because we aren't like Batista. We're supposed to be changing things."

"*Que inocente.* You never change."

"Did you know this execution was scheduled?"

"Of course!"

"Can you justify everything in the name of the revolution?"

"Absolutely everything!"

"You know, Zoraida, we've argued many times, about the war, cigar strikes, segregation. Those things didn't matter because we were powerless. But we're in the government now, and our opinions matter."

"And about time!" She got out of bed and began to dress. "I want my opinion to count."

"Where are you going?"

"To meet with my committee."

"What about breakfast?" he asked, getting up and following her to the door.

"I'll eat with the committee." She opened the door and walked out.

*

That morning, the uniformed guard stopped Matilde in the anteroom to Fidel's office. Matilde hated that large, ornate, official-looking room with its high ceiling. It seemed degenerate for the leader of a popular movement. The only good thing in the anteroom was the large window that overlooked the busy square below. Except for the guard's desk and chair and one chair along the wall on either side of the desk, the large room was bare.

"I have to see Fidel."

"He's left orders not to be disturbed."

"When can he be disturbed?"

Looking down at his newspaper the guard said, "Later."

Never having heard that tone, Matilde stood there for a few moments glaring down at the man, then turned and walked out. Instead of going to his office he walked out to a nearby café, bought a newspaper, and sat at a table near the sidewalk. *Café con leche y pan tostado*," he said to the waiter. The lead article on the front page described that morning's executions and the trial that led to it. The article, obviously written before the event, described the accused men's crimes. Matilde had known them in the eastern provinces. According to the article, they had turned against the revolution by joining remnants of Batista's followers. Details were scanty, unsupported, and disconnected, but Matilde deciphered the message: don't make trouble.

He could not comprehend the turns the revolution was taking: first Zoraida, now the execution of friends as loyal to the revolution as he was. Instead of going to his office, he strolled around the city thinking about Zoraida, about Castro, about the revolution. At the waterfront he stopped for a beer and went home to meet Zoraida. After two hours he realized she wasn't coming and walked to a nearby restaurant and ordered a bowl of garbanzo soup and a *medianoche* sandwich. It was two o'clock when he sat at his desk, took the first letter off the stack of mail, and opened it. He had not finished reading it when two soldiers wearing fatigues, each carrying a rifle at port arms and an automatic pistol on his side, walked in unannounced.

"Come with us," the smaller one said.

"Where?"

"Let's go."

Matilde stood. "I demand to see Fidel," he said. "I take my orders from him."

"The order came from him. If you don't come calmly, four others outside will help us see that you do."

Matilde walked around the desk. "All right, let's go."

The smaller man came up behind him and held his arms behind his back while the larger man placed handcuffs on his wrists. Recalling his Army training, Matilde offered no resistance, for to do so would lead to a severe beating, possibly death. He would wait until he could confront someone with authority. With rifles pointed at his back, the two men marched him out of the office, down the stairs, onto the sidewalk, and into a waiting jeep. Matilde could feel all heads turn to watch as he was led into the jeep in handcuffs like a criminal. As soon as he got in, the jeep sped off.

*

His mind thundered under a siege of thoughts: What offense have I committed that they bring me to *La Cabaña*, where Batista put rebel soldiers awaiting execution. How could he? The man has gone crazy. What offense have I committed? I told him my opinion. Does that merit this hole after fighting across six hundred miles? I gave him my best. But this is no mistake. He doesn't make mistakes. I'm here because he ordered it. Why is he afraid of me? It can't be the disagreement over executions. We've disagreed and argued before. He always insisted on frankness. But he sensed my doubts. I guess he wouldn't have to be a mind reader. I can't think in this place. Think, Matilde! Forget idealism and promises. He's crafty. Being here means my life is over. In his mind, doubt means treason. I've got to get out of here. Zoraida! She'll get me out somehow. But how to tell her? She doesn't know ... or does she? The guard outside ... maybe he knows me.

Matilde walked to the small window in the door. The man had fought with Camilo and Matilde. After a moment he remembered his name.

"Oye, Manolo!"

When Manolo came, he stood beyond arm's distance and waited.

"It's me, Matilde. I was with you in Las Villas. Don't you remember?"

"I remember."

"Can you get a message to my wife?"

"What message?"

"Tell her I am here. That's all. She doesn't know."

"She will soon enough."

"Please. What can you lose?"

"I'll see." Manolo walked back to his post.

*

"I have a serious problem, Zoraida," Castro said.

"I'm at your service, Fidel." Accustomed to the perennial figure of Evelio at his chair near the far wall, Zoraida noticed that he was not there. It was her first time alone with Fidel since the mountains. Her eyes found the biographies of Jefferson and Lincoln in the bookcase by his desk and the large portrait of Camilo Cienfuegos on the wall. The windows shaded by Venetian blinds opened to a square with a huge memorial to José Marti

"You know we have traitors very close to us," he said.

"It is inconceivable after all we passed together," she said.

"I've arrested a man who lacks confidence in the revolution. He fought with us and knows much, but I can no longer trust him."

"A traitor?"

"Could be, and he's bright enough to do serious damage."

"You must eliminate him."

"What if he were someone you know?"

"Who?" Her face hardened.

"Your husband." Castro lit a cigar as he waited for the words to settle and for her to compose herself. He trusted Zoraida and knew she was loyal, but he was curious to explore the depth of her loyalty.

"Matilde questions everything. It doesn't mean he's planning treason. That's his way. He feels it's his job to make you face tough questions. It's his way of helping you."

"I know that, Zoraida, but with his access to our Air Force, he could easily escape with men and planes and do serious damage."

"He doesn't think that way," Zoraida said. "He's completely loyal."

Sensing from her tone a degree of objectivity and detachment not expected in a devoted wife facing her husband's imprisonment, Fidel smiled. "Why aren't you in a panic? Could it be that I am correct?"

"No, Fidel. I just know you prefer intelligent, calm talk. I know how important the revolution is to you. As much as it is to me."

"We'll talk again tomorrow."

"Yes, I'd like to talk with him first."

"You can't. He's in prison."

"On what charge?" Her voice trembled as reality hit her.

"Suspicion. Come back tomorrow," he said, leading her to the door.

When Zoraida got home, she found a message under her door. Nervously she opened it. It was written in an unfamiliar hand and said merely, "He is in *La Cabaña*."

She walked to the balcony and sat. Before her, spread like a banquet, Havana vibrated with life. She thought of the new direction her nation had taken. Matilde's going to spoil it the way he's spoiled everything, she thought. She knew he was incapable of treachery, but she also knew he did not trust the new regime. She knew communism worried him and that Fidel knew it. But prison! The thought of her husband in that miserable hole was too much. Turmoil clawed her insides. The mixture of pity and fear and anger and his unending questioning was boiling over. Only such an intelligent person could be so stupid, she thought. His predicament recalled the other opportunities he had ruined, but she knew he did not deserve to die for stupidity. Her imagination raced: he cannot end his days in a hole waiting to be stood against a wall and ripped to shreds by cold metal. What to do? I can't go against all I've lived for and believed in, but I can't betray the only man I've ever loved. Perhaps the times require looking beyond selfish love. How simple it would have been just a few years ago. I would have broken him out with my own hands. But I cannot give up everything. How could I betray my friends, the only people who have ever tried to free my people from oppression?

She slept little that night thinking about the probable outcome and how she would react. Awaking early the next morning, she returned to the Presidential Palace. The guard stopped her, but then said, "Oh, yes. Go in."

"Fidel, I have a proposition," she said, after sitting opposite his desk and noting that Evelio was again absent from his usual place at the far wall. The grand space befitted a head of state with its expanse of government-designed, baroque ceiling and large windows opening onto a broad balcony. The Persian carpet reflected the wealth, opulence, and arrogance of Castro's predecessor. In his neatly pressed fatigue uniform and smoking a long cigar, Fidel was dwarfed behind his huge desk. His dark eyes bored into hers as he drew a long puff of smoke and blew it into the space over their heads.

"You know how strongly I hold the revolution," she said. "I am with it and with you to the end. But I do not want to see my husband killed. After living with him twenty-five years, I know him. He is loyal to you and the revolution. I also know he is incapable of treason. He questions and argues only because he's brilliant and he knows you are too. He wants to understand everything and to do things right." Then dropping her eyes to the floor, "But also I know you have lost confidence in him. If you let him go, I promise you I'll work with you for the rest of my life or as long as you want me. The revolution means everything to me, more than anything; do you understand? Anything! It has been my life's dream, before Batista or Matilde or you. I would rather die than abandon it."

"I'm moved, Zoraida. But I cannot free him."

"Will you execute him?"

"Of course not. He will merely rot in La Cabaña."

Zoraida stood and put her head in her hands. "I know I'll hate myself, but I am with the revolution." She began to sob and turned away.

Castro watched her for a full minute. He rose, walked around the huge desk and turned her toward him. "You have nothing to cry about, Zoraida." She looked up perplexed. "He will escape. No one will know except you and me and a few others. I've excused Evelio, so even he will not know."

"I don't understand."

"My men will take him out and make it appear that traitors helped him. It will be an admission that he has joined the traitors."

"But he hasn't."

"There is no other way. I cannot release him openly. My men will take him to an isolated beach and put him on a boat. From there he'll be on his own."

"May I see him?"

"You will be driven to the beach. You may leave with him. If you decide to stay, I will receive you gratefully. If not, I will understand."

"When will they come?"

"Go home and wait."

*

Early the previous evening, Matilde was sitting on the floor of his cell wondering if word had reached Zoraida, when he heard a key enter the door lock. In a moment the guard shoved a man in so hard he fell to the floor. When the man lifted his head, Matilde saw who it was. His first impulse was to pick him up and knock his teeth out, but instead he asked, "What the hell are you doing here? Doesn't the big cheese love you anymore?"

Evelio did not answer. He got to his feet and went to the door and looked out the small opening. "*El coño tu madre, hijo de puta!*" he yelled.

"So, you can talk," Matilde said.

"Go to hell. Haven't I had enough for one day?"

The guard returned to the door and looked in. Seeing Evelio looking at him he laughed and walked away.

"Well, my little ass-kissing comrade, how did you manage to get a room in this hotel?"

"It's not funny. Fidel was my friend. He trusted me with everything until you came along. He saw you looking at me every time you talked with him and he got the idea we were in cahoots. He's had me tailed for

409

weeks. I had the misfortune of having a girlfriend who was on his hit list. They picked me up in her apartment just as I found her dead in her bed."

"And it's all my fault. How wonderful. Glad to be of service, louse."

"You fools thought I was his bodyguard, but I was much more. I was his closest confidant. He asked my opinion on everything, especially people's loyalty. I was his bloodhound, sniffing out traitors. I don't know how many came to this place because of me. You might as well know; I advised him not to trust you."

"Bastard!"

"I also told him you had no bad intentions, but he didn't listen to that. His creed is, 'If there's doubt, there's no doubt.'"

"So what awaits you now?" Matilde asked.

"The wall, I suppose." With Evelio's voice dropping to a whisper, Matilde thought he was going to cry.

"Maybe they'll shoot us together," Matilde said. "That should cheer you up."

"And four others; the bastard has been working overtime."

"You deserve some of the credit, *maricón*."

"They'll never shoot me," Evelio said through his teeth.

"Planning on staying?"

"No. Pills. Works in seconds; I'll feel nothing."

"You know from a satisfied user, I suppose." Matilde forced a laugh.

"I'm not as stupid as everyone thinks. I studied chemistry in the university before I quit to join Fidel. They won't put me against that wall like a criminal. Not for doing my job."

"What are you talking about?"

"Sodium cyanide," Evelio whispered.

"How many do you have?"

"Enough." Evelio looked at him with hatred. "Why?"

"I don't know. I can imagine situations that could be worse than a pill."

"Why should I give you one?"

"Have I asked for one?"

"No, but you want one. Right now you're thinking that having a way out is better than not having one."

"You said one thing right, Evelio. You aren't as stupid as I thought. Yes, I'd like one."

Evelio's mouth curled into a malicious smile. He looked at Matilde for a long time before he reached into his trouser cuff, ripped the seam a little, and pushed out a small test tube. Removing the cork, he shook four pills onto the floor. Matilde stared at them transfixed by their enormity—the ultimate power of death. He thought of the bullets he fired from his P-51 and their power packed into small cylinders that could propel a deadly projectile across space and rip a machine or a human body to shreds. Matilde reached out, took one, and stuffed it into his shirt pocket.

"Take two and keep them in different pockets. No room for error."

Matilde took the second and put it into his trouser pocket.

*

Zoraida did not sleep wondering if Fidel had told her that story to calm her until Matilde's execution. But she could not imagine why he would, knowing she would find out, and Castro would have another disloyal follower to deal with. The more she considered Fidel's plan, the less reason she could find to doubt it. And if true, would she go with her husband or stay? The more she pondered it the more she knew there was no real choice.

The church clock had just struck three in the morning when the knocking came. It was not the usual, loud, police pounding, but a light tapping with one knuckle. She jumped out of bed, dressed and alert, and opened the door to two men she did not recognize.

"Ready?" one asked.

She followed them to the elevator and went down with no words spoken. Out on the barren street, illuminated only by periodic streetlights curving seemingly to infinity, they got into a dark sedan whose color she could not make out.

After the city lights had disappeared behind them, Zoraida felt she was rushing headlong into the mouth of a ravenous wolf. After nearly an hour, winding along a lonely beach, they turned off the road and stopped beside another car parked on the sand about a hundred feet from the water. The half moon had risen far enough to cast shadows across the silvery sand. Three men emerged from the other car; one was Matilde. He was not handcuffed. "Go to him," her driver said. "We'll shove him off in a few minutes."

Zoraida ran to her husband and put her arms around his neck and kissed him. "They wouldn't let me see you until now."

"I don't get it. Are they going to shoot us out here?"

"They were going to leave you to rot in prison, but I talked with Fidel. It is supposed to look like you escaped. Fidel said he could not release you publicly."

Anger crept over Matilde's face. "What did you have to do?"

"I told him you were loyal. He still does not trust you, but apparently he has enough doubt to let you go."

"I asked what you had to do."

"I told him I would stay if he let you go."

"You're not coming?"

"He said I was free to go if I wanted."

"Good. You had me worried."

"I'm staying, Matilde." She looked directly into his eyes.

"I see. You've chosen him."

"No, my love, the revolution."

"I understand." He turned toward the boat.

"No you don't." She pulled him back. "Not for him. There has never been another man for me, and there never will. It is the revolution, my life's dream. This is our country, but you must go even if only to fail again. They will kill you if you stay, *mi amor*."

Matilde looked at her as if she were a stranger. He knew her leanings, but he had not comprehended the depth of her devotion. "This is worse than leaving me for another man; it's perverted. You're leaving me for what? An abstraction, a dream?"

Sobbing, she reached for him, and embraced and kissed him as her streaming tears drenched his face. And just as suddenly, she pushed him away and ran back to the waiting car and stood by it to watch.

Matilde climbed into the boat. Beside the outboard motor were two gallons of water, two Mae West life jackets, a small, hand compass, and two, five-gallon cans of gasoline. As one of the men pushed him off, he reached for the starter cord. After three pulls, the motor started. Without looking back he turned the boat north. Zoraida could see his upright form against the blackness. In the moonlight, an aura seemed to engulf him as he drifted into the darkness. She ran into the water up to her knees, screaming as if she were watching her soul depart her body, "Matilde, come back, come back. Don't leave, please."

One of the men on shore called to her, but she did not hear. Finally, she stopped yelling, dragged herself back to the sandy beach, and fell to her knees with her head in her lap. When she looked up, Matilde had disappeared into the black morning.

30 – THE SAME DAY

*

New State University Slated To Open In Tampa This Fall

*

Clear Weather Predicted For All Of Florida

*

33 Influential Cuban Nationalists Reach Key West
Seeking Political Asylum

*

Angry Rebels Jeer Cuban Refugees In Florida

*

U.S. Ships Anchored Off Havana
To Bring Americans Home, If Necessary

*

Matilde's war experiences had taught him to remain cool and rational under extreme conditions. Keeping the rising sun over his right shoulder he headed north wondering if the past few weeks had been real. In his state of exhaustion the past hours had slithered past like a hallucination from which he would, at any moment, wake screaming. The vibration of the motor traveling through his arm and frame to his brain mesmerized him. Through the rattling and slapping of the waves, he fought to stay awake and rational repeating aloud, Stay awake; head north. Keep the sun to my right.

The calm sea was a cradle, rocking him monotonously. Periodically the bow would rise out of the water and fall with a jarring slap, and he would thank God for even the slightest noise that would keep him awake. Occasionally he would spot a seagull gliding overhead, warning him with its serene cawing.

As a wave splashed over him he came to and said aloud, what bastards! At least they didn't take my wallet. But what can I do with a wallet out here? He slipped it out of his pocket to check: U.S. Air Force Veteran card, Cuban Army ID card. He had wanted to throw them out once, but was glad he had not. These could keep them from throwing me out as an alien. But this is not the time to think of that possibility.

Besides, he thought, they may want me to give them information.

Suddenly he said, Damn! No food. Zoraida could have brought something. Her and her revolution! She knew what was going on and that I would be sent out on this boat. How could I not have known her after twenty-five years? What happiness seeing her at the beach, thinking she would go with me or die with me. But no! I've been wrong about many things, but I never suspected she would be like this. How could I have been so fooled? I should have killed her with my bare hands, but I couldn't. How can I hate her so much? I loved her so. Incomprehensible! How easily anger turns to hate. Those two impostors must be made of the same stuff ... two sides of the same coin ... like sugar: delicious, but useless. I thought I knew her as well as any man could know a woman, but I never dreamed ... she's made of devotion. It is the substance of her life, her body, her dreams. Devotion fed her through all the poverty and troubles I dragged her through. Yes, devotion to me, a man of flesh.

With the boat slapping the water, possibilities came and went in rhythm as his mind churned: Offering to stay if Fidel would let me go; then he says she can leave. More lies? Fidel might have let me go only if she stayed. For sure, those four cutthroats could have easily stopped us and they didn't. She knew I'd fight them off guns or no guns. I must face it; she chose the revolution over me. She has courage, all right. And she loves me, but the revolution burned in her soul ... gave her life meaning, made her somebody. She had never been anybody except the wife of Matilde Gómez, *la gran mierda!* Fidel has made her somebody; she could become president one day. And why not? Such beauty and dedication and lust for work? Strange to be filled with such desire bouncing like a cork on this Godforsaken water. She knew I'd never succeed. Maybe the *caracoles* told her. Those damn *caracoles*, the one thing I couldn't abide about her. Her political ideas were quaint, rational, even charming and rational in a way, but voodoo, ugh! It always irritated me.

*

The overhead sun was pounding. Only the sea spray kept him cool. He looked down at his trouser cuff and remembered the pills. He reached down to throw them overboard, but instead lifted it out and the other one in his shirt and wrapped them in a piece of cellophane and tied it to one of the gasoline cans. Then he realized he had better loosen the caps so the fuel doesn't build up pressure.

The shadows had dissolved into pure pounding energy, and the glare was excruciating all around the boat. There was nowhere to look without pain. He smiled thinking he was lucky to have African skin. He tried to think of other blessings of being black, but could not. The thought of being black in a white America tightened his chest as thoughts churned in his mind: Like the court marshal at Selfridge Field and the white, bomber pilots who wouldn't thank the Negro pilots who'd saved their lives. And the teachers and parents who turned on me because I wouldn't keep the kids in line, and the police calling me "boy," ready to smash my head in, and the way the smelly Crackers at the Café Cubano sneered when I came home from the war and dared to sit with my white friends, and Pablo wouldn't even show me property because the locals wouldn't stand it, and not offering me a job in his bank. Now he was yelling: *Cabrones! Cabrones!*

What's the use? Only the fishes and the birds can hear me. Calm the rage or this blinding sun will drive you crazy. But he kept yelling at the sky and the waves and the boat and failure. After he felt spent he took a little water. Not too much, he said aloud, or you'll run out.

Forcing himself to push aside those dreadful American memories, he thought of the day he and Zoraida arrived in Cuba. Such high hopes; the hopes of a fool, happy finally to enter the classroom again. The kids were great, but so were the Cuban rebels, my people rising in defense of their … <u>my</u> people. And the trek to Havana with Camilo. Wonderful Camilo. Poor Camilo … to die in a plane crash. Probably set up by his good friend and *comandante*, Fidel. Wouldn't dare shoot him like he did the others … no, Camilo was far too popular for that. Such vanity … enjoying the role of insider, sharing ideas with the Maximum bastard? But I did like it. It was exhilarating … while it lasted. Why couldn't he understand the difference between questioning and disloyalty? Just another petty tyrant like the rest, doing anything for power. And stupid I was so disappointed. I could have seen it sooner. And I did, didn't I?

*

When the motor began to sputter he tried to remember when he had filled it, hoping it was only out of gas. He screwed the cap off the fuel can and filled the tank. He spilled a little because the wave motion was tossing him in all directions. After four pulls he was off again.

"*Gracias a diós!*" he muttered.

While he was filling the tank he realized the sea had become rougher. At times the swells rose like mountains around him, and he could not see the horizon. Ah! The Florida Strait. It will push me out into the Atlantic, so I have to correct for it.

Reaching down he pulled the compass out of his pocket and turned the boat northwest to compensate for the current. With the waves dwarfing the boat it would not be easy. Matilde imagined flying over the tiny boat in his P-51 and seeing what looked like a cork bobbing up and down, side to side.

The compass … in my hand … hold my bearing.

After he had composed himself he reached for the water bottle and took a long drink and remembered he was hungry.

"To hell with it!" he yelled. "Not the first time I've missed a meal.

His mind again drifted to the thirties, when the factories froze him out, and days passed with only black coffee and stale bread for breakfast and corn meal and garlic for supper. I put her through rough times, he thought, too many.

With the spray and the motion his stomach began to feel queasy. With all the flying he had done he could not believe he might be seasick. He tried to think of other things. He took out his handkerchief and dipped it into the gulf and put it over his head. Before he realized what happened he was heaving over the side, though he vomited little.

Hold on! He told himself. Don't fall in.

In a moment he felt better. With the heat and the splashing and pitching and rocking, his brain churned. Zoraida hovered above all other thoughts: She accepted my uselessness all those years. She's finally part of something successful. Success, after so many years, and how she loves it. Every time I lost, she paid; she never failed, but she paid anyway and never complained.

The confusion of hating her in one breath and wanting her desperately in the next was driving him crazy.

What will I do without her? Even with her I failed. Without her I'll be lost. Oh, God, what will I do?

The boat pitched and rocked so much he had a hard time holding the tiller and watching the compass and keeping his balance.

If I have to vomit again, I'll fall overboard for sure. Oh, God!

He thought he saw two fins on the starboard side for an instant. Then they disappeared. He wondered if he had seen phantoms, though he knew sharks infested those waters.

*

He almost fell asleep sitting with his hand on the tiller. He slapped water on his face. With the churning, he knew he might fall in if he fell asleep.

Night brought relief from the beating sun. He saw lights on the horizon, but they disappeared almost immediately. Hallucinations? After a few hours the splashing felt cold, and he looked forward to the sun. Polaris kept him on course when the clouds cooperated. As night deepened he could not focus on any thought for long, and he was seeing more fins alongside. He wondered if they were following him.

*

When the sun appeared over his right shoulder he knew he was still on course. He discovered his lips had cracked when he wiped them with his sleeve and saw blood. When he tried to cool his face with a handful of seawater he felt the burning. He had not urinated since yesterday and knew that was not good.

The sun inched across the sky slowly until he felt the heat on his left side and thought he would feel better when it set. But then worried that he might not see the shore unless there were city lights. He had planned on five to ten miles an hour, but with the waves he was grateful for any forward motion. He was not sure if it was the second day. God! He thought. I could be here a week.

Trying to picture in his mind the relative positions of Cuba and Florida on the map, he thought, Must be a hundred miles from Key West to Miami. I should be able to hit that target after all those tiny ones I hit from my P-51. What days those were! Instead of soaring I'm bobbing on this silly sea. Strange, I haven't seen a single boat, not even the Coast Guard. They'd probably send me back. That might be best. It would end my failures. How ironic if, even with a boat, water, and gas, I fail my escape. No, I won't do that to her.

417

*

As the sun dipped into the water he tried to think clearly: heartburn; that's new. The current is not as rough now, and I'm still moving like a rag doll, but I feel more tranquil. God, I'm hungry.

He had emptied the water bottle and filled the gas tank about an hour ago.

Feeling a surprising serenity enveloping him, he pushed Zorida and his litany of failures out of his mind and ruminated on his destination and the new barriers he would face: Failure is a seductress, and she has made me a two-timer. I think of it more than of her. *Ay, Zoraida, el amor de mi vida.*

With the compass in his right hand, he held the tiller with his left and aimed north-northwest to counter the current. Calmer water meant the current has slowed, so he decided to turn north. Calm water meant the worst of the Florida Strait was over, but it did not mean he would find a calm life ahead. As tired as he was, old memories sparked like flashes.

*

It was almost dark when the motor stalled. He had emptied the second gas can hours ago and kept them for floats. He rubbed his aching left arm. Holding the tiller involved little strain, yet it hurt and his shoulder too. He realized the pain was not new. It had been there all day.

"Enough!" he yelled, and let go the tiller and rubbed his arm and shoulder.

As he sat bobbing on the restless water, something rose into his throat that he had kept down for thirty years.

Why now? Has the time finally come? But I want to think about him. I was so angry I couldn't before. How could I hate him? No, it was not him, but Zoraida and myself I hated for letting him die, so small and beautiful, just starting to talk. How could God be so vile? All those years I knew He had punished us for Zoraida's sins, but why would God punish a smiling child for his parents' sins? He looked nothing like me. Even lilly-white Pablo would have loved him! I despised myself for wanting him to look like my father. Such voids in my heart: the father I never saw and the son I saw only long enough to mourn. The past and future are gone. I am a cog with no wheel, rotating in stellar silence. I know only that heaven is where that little boy is. God, or whatever rules the universe, can guide me the rest of the way. I've got to sleep.

He tried to calculate the hours since he slept, but could not. He thought it might be three days. The trip and the rough water had frayed his brain, and the heartburn and the pain in his arm and shoulder had worsened. Slipping into the bottom of the boat until his thighs were under one of the seat boards, he rested his head on a life jacket. Lying down, the life jacket he was wearing felt uncomfortable so he took it off. The water in the bottom felt mildly cool; not comfortable, but he would get used to it. With the large waves, the sky moved arabesque-like, creating patterns that made him faintly dizzy. If he held his head steady the wispy clouds danced lightly, round and round and back and forth in beautiful syncopation. Beyond them the brighter stars joined in. He no longer felt the water beneath him; he wanted only to lie still and watch the heavenly display. The celestial dome's expansiveness enveloped him. Dark blue behind him blended gradually to lighter blue overhead and to pink running to blood red over his feet. When the bow tipped down, the western clouds became massive flames. Colors mixed like the extremities of life: red-screaming youth slides through life until it confronts blue reality; from there it yawns to blackness.

Matilde felt the knot in his throat loosen. He recalled a flight over Germany with enemy fighters coming at him from all directions. His center of calm rose from the thought that the worst that could happen was he would die.

He reached back to an empty gas can without looking, untied the crumpled paper, and took out the capsules. He held them high, staring at them between his fingers, wondering how it would feel to die. For the first time he wondered why Evelio had brought so many with him. Then he smiled. So that was a sham too, he said and laughed aloud. He reached over the side and dropped them into the water. Enjoy them, sharks. They are from your brother, Evelio. Returning his gaze to the heavens he fell asleep

Jack Eugene Fernández

31 – TWO DAYS LATER

*

Lone Man Found Off Florida Coast
A man was found dead yesterday in a motorboat drifting five miles off Fort Lauderdale. It is not known how long the boat had been adrift or when the man died. He was lying on his back with his head resting on a life jacket. The cause of death is believed to be exposure and dehydration. Identification on his person gives his name as Matilde Gómez. The Immigration and Naturalization Service has determined that he is a naturalized American and a U.S. Air Force veteran of World War II. His uniform, military insignia, and Cuban Army ID suggest that he was a Castro functionary trying to escape. The INS is still investigating.

*

"You can read that after breakfast, Edwin," Pearl said, facing the back of his open newspaper.

Edwin Pitt did not answer. "What is it, Dad?" Harold asked.

Finally lowering the newspaper, Edwin looked into his cereal bowl.

Pearl stopped eating when she saw his face. "Edwin?"

"It's Mat Gómez, the guy I flew with who wrote all those letters from Cuba. He's dead."

"Oh, God?" she said.

"He was found drifting off the Florida coast in a boat. They figure he was escaping."

"But wasn't he one of Castro's lieutenants? Remember, we saw him on TV when the rebels took over Havana."

"Poor guy. There's nothing about his wife. She must have drowned or else stayed behind. Such a good guy." Edwin's eyes overflowed. "After all the close calls we had, he dies in a boat. He really had guts. It wasn't like him to run out like that, even to save his life."

*

"Just coffee, Consuelo. I almost forgot; I have a meeting in ten minutes."

"There's always time to eat, Pablo. Sit down."

"Can't. I've got to go. See you for lunch. Don't forget, we're eating with the Burkes."

"Shall we meet at the restaurant?" she asked.

"I hate to arrive in separate cars. Pick you up at 11:45 sharp."

"I'll be ready."

*

His meeting went as he expected. Andrew Hopkins, a handsome but overweight developer from Baltimore, was seeking funding for a new shopping center in South Tampa. His arguments were clear and his delivery animated and excited, but Pablo was not convinced. "We already have two shopping centers in that area."

"This one's completely indoors and designed to resemble a small town business district, except that it'll be air conditioned and have all the amenities—security, parking, coffee houses, restaurants, large department stores, specialty shops, everything. They're the rage up north where people can't shop outdoors in winter. It'll be a big hit here too, with your hot summers."

"How much is your firm willing to put up?"

"One-fourth and we'll do the construction. But we want to build and move on. It's a great long-term investment for a local entrepreneur."

"I'll have to consult my associates, Mr. Hopkins. I'll get back to you."

"I don't mean to pressure you, Mr. Iglesias, but other investors are waiting."

"Thank you, Mr. Hopkins. You'll hear soon, I promise."

When Hopkins left, Pablo called his secretary. "Alice, bring some coffee, doughnuts, and a newspaper. I haven't had breakfast." When she returned, he took a sip of the coffee and opened the paper. The major headline dealt with the new state university that had opened that fall in north Tampa. Then he saw the smaller headline beneath it about the man found in a boat off the Florida coast. Curiosity led him to read further. When his eyes stopped on the name, Matilde Gómez, he shuddered and continued with trembling hands. His secretary came in and said something he could not decipher; he absently asked her to come back later.

Turning to the window and looking out across the river at the University of Tampa, his thoughts raced. Remembering the TV coverage of the rebel take-over and Matilde riding with Cienfuegos, he could not imagine how he could end up adrift in the Atlantic Ocean. The phone rang, but he did not answer it. A minute later, his secretary again came in. "I'm sorry, Mr. Iglesias, but it's your wife. Will you take it?"

He picked up the phone. "Have you heard?" Consuelo said, her voice broken by sobs.

"Just did."

"I can't believe he's dead," she said.

"I'll be right home."

*

Still crying, Consuelo embraced him at the door. "I was thinking of the first time I saw him, that night he brought you home," she said. "He was so revolting and sloppy, but so kind and courteous. I've never forgiven myself for misjudging him."

"I know. He was always ready to help anybody. What lousy luck."

"He must've been desperate to leave like that, alone in a small boat."

"We don't know if Zoraida was with him," Pablo said. "If she was, she must've drowned.

"Oh, God!"

"I'll call the INS and see what they know."

After several minutes talking with the operator, he reached the INS office in Miami. "All we know was reported in the newspapers. We know nothing about any other person, except that there were two life jackets in the boat. But that could have been a precaution; he was a pretty big man," the agent said.

"Any idea what he died of?"

"We're not at liberty to say anymore than what was in the papers. We're still investigating."

When Pablo told Consuelo, she said, "Let's try Zoraida in Havana."

It took several minutes to get a Cuban operator and then several more to get Zoraida's phone number, but the operator finally found it.

"She wouldn't be home in the middle of the morning, Pablo. Maybe we should call later."

"Now," he said, waiting to be connected.

"What if she hasn't heard?"

After four rings, a weak voice said, "*Dígame.*"

"Zoraida? This is Pablo Iglesias in Tampa. Consuelo's here with me."

She broke down and could not talk for several seconds. "*Ay, Pablo. Que horrible!* I don't know what to do."

"What happened?"

He left alone before sunup three days ago."

"But why?"

"Please, Pablo. It's too horrible. Poor Matilde. He was so good. He helped everyone, but it didn't matter. It was always the same, *pobrecito.*" She sputtered her words between deep, wrenching sobs.

"I can't tell you how sorry we are, Zoraida. Can we do anything?"

"Can you bring him back?" Unintended anger seeped through her sobs.

"If only there were something we could do."

"Thank you, Pablo, but there is nothing."

"Are you all right?"

"I can't think. I'm too confused and angry."

"Angry?"

"Thanks for calling, Pablo. And thank Consuelo for me. I know how good she is and how terrible she feels."

When Pablo related their conversation, Consuelo began to cry again. "Poor woman. They were always lovers."

They sat quiet for a while. "I asked him once if he had ever been unfaithful," Pablo said. "Know what he said? 'None of your damn business,' but I knew from the smile on his face that he hadn't. I remember thinking, 'How strange, for a Cuban mulatto.'"

"Because he was Cuban or mulatto?" she asked.

"Both, I guess. I don't know."

"Maybe he was too much of a man to be unfaithful."

"You're right. He was always more of a man than me."

When Pablo began to sob uncontrollably, Consuelo sat beside him and pulled his head to her breast. "Not always, Pablo. You're not the boy who brought me here so many years ago."

Pablo raised his head. "I had the feeling she couldn't talk. She may be in trouble."

"Think we should go?"

Without calling Zoraida, they booked a flight to Havana on Pan American Airlines for the following morning. The plane landed in Havana through a light drizzle that soon dissipated into a bright, cloudy, breezy day. They took a taxi to the Hotel Nacional on El Malecón and took a room with a view of the bay and the Morro Castle. As they stood on their balcony looking at the city, Pablo brought Consuelo closer. "With the wind blowing your hair like this, you look like that girl I fell in love with." He kissed her. "Come on, we have another purpose first," he said. They went in and he dialed Zoraida's number. No answer. "I'll call later. Let's take a walk. It's been a long time."

They walked down El Malecón across the street from the water and, after an hour, stopped for a fruit punch. "Such a beautiful city," Consuelo said.

"Sitting here, seeing it all after so long, I admire Matilde for coming back."

"I don't think that's why he moved."

"I know," Pablo said. "It had to be something pretty bad to make him leave the way he did."

"It's almost five o'clock and I'm getting tired," Consuelo said. "Let's go back and try her again."

This time Zoraida answered. When Pablo said they were in Havana, she was silent for a moment; then she said, "You shouldn't have come."

"We had to see you. We're at the Hotel Nacional. How about supper tonight here?"

Zoraida hesitated again, "Seven o'clock?"

"Fine. Where do you live? We'll pick you up."

"It's close by. I'll come to your hotel."

"We'll wait in the lobby."

*

In her crisply pressed fatigues with a cap over her hair, Zoraida looked as stunning as ever as she strode into the hotel lobby. She had put on weight, but the pounds and the years only added dignity to her sensual stride. Wearing his white linen suit and feeling Cuban for the first time in years, Pablo was startled by this fiftyish woman who looked twenty years younger. Her uniform contrasted starkly with Consuelo's pleated red dress, red shoes, and matching broad-brimmed, red hat with white band.

Zoraida immediately embraced and kissed Consuelo and then Pablo. "Only good friends would come like this."

"We wanted to be with you," Consuelo said.

Zoraida tried to hold back tears. "*Vamos.* I have reservations. We'll walk; it's only two blocks."

"The hotel restaurant is very good," Pablo said.

"I know a better one."

She led Pablo and Consuelo into the *Restaurante El Mojito*, a large restaurant filled with palms, crotons, and flowers in profusion and soft lighting to simulate tropical moonlight.

When the waiter embraced Zoraida she said, "The small room if it's available, Miguelito."

"Yes, you'll be private there," he said.

"*Gracia'.*"

"It's been a long time since our last trip," Consuelo said. "You gave us an excuse. What can you tell us?"

"With all that's happened, I haven't even been able to mourn him. The waiter is Matilde's cousin, Miguelito. We can relax here. I couldn't talk on the phone or in the hotel. Miguelito is the only one who knows what I've been through. I haven't dared talk with anyone else."

"Why not?" Pablo asked.

In hushed tones Zoraida told them what she knew. "The Cuban news had an article about traitors who helped him escape. It said his location was unknown. Yesterday's news said he died of exposure during a cowardly escape. Can you believe they called him a coward? And exposure: Bah! He was too strong and smart for that. They murdered him."

"Who and why?" Pablo asked.

"I can guess."

"I talked with the INS agent in Miami," Pablo said. "He said the news report was accurate." Consuelo looked as puzzled as he.

"Maybe I'm paranoid," she said. "*No importa;* he's dead and nothing can change that. If I had gone with him, he might be alive now."

"Or you might both be dead," Consuelo said.

"That would not be so bad," Zoraida said.

"What will you do now?" Consuelo asked.

"You cannot tell it to anyone. Miguelito is urging me to escape. He has friends who can get me out."

"Why don't you just leave? There are flights to Florida every day."

"Fidel would never let me. I don't think he trusts me now that Matilde's dead. He's not ready to eliminate me, but he could anytime."

"But you're the only person who can identify the body and make funeral arrangements," Pablo said. "Fidel couldn't object to that."

Zoraida stared at Pablo. "I've been too distraught to think clearly. Of course; funerals are sacred to Cubans."

"You may have to convince him you'll come back."

"Since Matilde died I've had a hard time getting in to see him, and never alone."

"He probably thinks you'll try to kill him."

"How long are you staying?"

"As long as necessary," Consuelo said.

"I'll try to see him tomorrow and then I'll call you. If you're not in the hotel, I'll leave a message. Don't expect me to talk openly over the phone. Now let's order our food and change the subject. I don't feel safe even here."

The supper was good and well presented, and Zoraida was the perfect hostess. Her affluence was apparent. On the way to her apartment she told them not to talk about any of these things inside her apartment. "I'm sure they've bugged it."

Both Pablo and Consuelo were impressed with her apartment. She showed them around and explained how she got it. "You should have let me know you were coming. Look at all the room." When they sat on the balcony she asked about their children. "I'm ashamed that I haven't even asked about Sammy and Sally. How are they?"

"Sammy's fine. He finished his doctorate at CalTech, and is doing research in Harvard University," Consuelo said. "Sally died ... of leukemia."

"Zoraida looked down for a moment as if praying. When she looked up, her eyes were moist. "You didn't have to tell me."

Consuelo looked at her quizzically.

"Her aura. I saw it that day at the airport."

"I don't understand," Consuelo said.

"When I looked into her eyes that morning, I could barely keep from crying. It was so clear, the aura I had seen only once before. I knew God had touched her and would soon take her. I saw it again the other night when Matilde left." She was struggling to hold back tears.

Consuelo could not control herself. Reliving Sally's illness and her dying days was unbearable. She went into the living room.

Pablo explained how badly Consuelo had taken Sally's death. In a few minutes, Consuelo returned to the balcony. "I'm sorry. It's still very hard. You may not understand, Zoraida; no tragedy can match the loss of a child." Then seeing the pain in Zoraida's face, she said, "I'm sorry, Zoraida. That was stupid."

With stunning composure Zoraida said, "But death cannot wipe out the happiness a child brings. We had a baby boy. He died of diphtheria six days before his second birthday. It was just before you came to Tampa."

"Oh, Zoraida. I didn't know." Consuelo felt too ashamed to look into her eyes.

"That was the first time I saw the aura. I didn't comprehend it then." She was silent for a moment. "Matilde would not discuss the boy. Every time I tried, he would fall into a deep depression and start drinking until he became senseless. The superhuman effort he made to erase the pain only made it worse. I could do nothing."

Pablo recalled an old conversation. "I once asked him if he had children. Without emotion he said no."

"It was more than the child's death. I had performed several abortions in Havana before I met Matilde. When I told him, he was so horrified I thought he would kill me. Instead, he left me without saying a word. To him it was such a terrible act that he could not allow himself to think about it. He would not let me explain the plight of those poor women. Only after I promised to stop did he take me back. I think the birth of our son redeemed me in his eyes. He was wonderful; you have never seen a man treat a baby like that; he fed him, changed his diaper, even bathed him. I thought the boy's death would kill him. I think he blamed the abortions. He never said it, but I knew. Only after the war, when he began to dream of becoming a teacher, did he finally accept the loss."

"You're right, Zoraida," Consuelo said. "I'm glad we had Sally; it must have been the same with your baby. What was his name?"

"Ignacio. He would have been thirty-three, 'the age of Christ'." Zoraida made the sign of the cross.

"That was my father's name," Pablo said.

"Yes, Matilde told me. It was his father's too. Matilde's father was the son of Spaniards. That was all he knew, except that he owned a sugarcane plantation."

Pablo could not bring himself to ask Matilde's father's surname.

"Is the 'aura' you speak of part of your Negro religion?" Consuelo asked.

"I suppose so." Then after hesitating a moment, "I was thirteen years old when I became a Negro." When she saw Pablo and Consuelo look at each other she continued. "My parents were bad. Especially my mother. She didn't even pretend to like me." Zoraida hesitated, looking down at her feet and passing her hand over her hair. "I have never told this to anyone, not even Matilde. I was a very unhappy child. One night at supper I'll never forget. My parents were drunk as usual; almost they could not talk, but they were not too drunk to fight. I was only ten, and I remember words and brightness. I could not swallow my food with the arguing and yelling. It just would not go down. My eyes darted back and forth between them. I prayed that Nina would bring in the next course so they would stop at least for the few moments she served us. I liked Nina. She was our Negro cook; she cared about me more than my mother. When she saw my plate she said, 'You haven't eaten any of your soup, Zoraida.' Before I could say anything, my mother jumped in and said, 'When she gets hungry enough, she'll eat. Don't beg her.' She did not care if I ate or not. Papá looked at me with droopy eyes, trying to smile. 'Come, Zoraida, eat a little,' he said. 'Nina prepared your favorite—roast hen.' But my mother said again not to beg me. She said she didn't want me to think I was doing them a favor by eating. Then she told Nina to fill her wine glass. I wanted to run out to Mamita's hut, but I wouldn't give my mother the satisfaction. She must have known what I was thinking because she stared at me as if daring me to go.

"Mamita?" Consuelo asked.

"She was more mother than the one who bore me. A servant, but she was my friend, a Negro."

"You mean your parents were white?" Pablo asked.

"As white as yours. Papá's grandparents came from Valencia and Asturias; Mother's came from Toledo. My mother always said I looked like a Valencian Moor. Anyway, my mother turned to Papá and continued her harangue. I looked up at the chandelier thinking how wonderful if it would fall and smash the table and all the hateful words. My mother yelled, 'Stop begging.' Papá said he wasn't begging. 'What I ask is only reasonable,' he said. Then she said, 'Forget it! Fuentemayor Manor: what a ridiculous name.' Then she started to laugh, but it was a forced, angry laugh. 'My grandfather broke the ground in this wild country with his hands and strong back, and when he died my father continued as his father had taught him. This has been Finca de Burgos for over half a century. What have you done to merit pasting your name to it?' Papá objected, 'I have rights as your husband.' She looked at him with hate and told him that he would never own or inherit the farm. 'You accepted both the farm and me as we were, and you'll change neither.'

"Papá's voice began to tremble, and it gave me shame. He said his friends called him a fool who was not even the head of this family."

Zoraida stopped.

Consuelo and Pablo stared at her, waiting for her to continue.

"My mother said he was head comedian and no one should care what those worthless trash think. 'I don't understand why you associate with them now that I have introduced you to respectable Cuban society,' she said. Then with her ugly smile showing her teeth, she said, 'Think of yourself as the queen's consort.' My heart was pounding. I could not stand it. Staring into her eyes, Papá said, 'To sire your heirs and oversee your business?' She looked at me with hatred. 'If you call this spoiled ninny my heir, and if by overseeing you mean squandering my money, yes. I didn't marry you for your business talents, little man. You have a nice body, a charming smile, and a taste for liquor and the good life. Indulge yourself and thank God for the good fortune you have stepped into.' I knew he felt terrible. All he said was, 'You're a hard woman, Lydia.' My mother was feeling her power now. 'But I am also soft and warm, and with strong appetites, Arturo.' Then she reached over and put her hand between his legs."

"In front of you?" Consuelo asked.

"What did she care? After a long silence, Papá said, 'Must you do the seducing too?' Know what she said? 'When I need it.' 'I'm not a husband or even a consort; I'm a whore,' he said, looking down into his plate. She said, 'And that excites me most of all.' I could stand it no longer and put my hands over my ears and shut my eyes tight and got up and ran to my room. I was in my bed crying for a short time when I heard footsteps in the next room. I heard a bottle fall to the floor and roll. Soon, rhythmic bed sounds became louder and louder. After what seemed like eternity—silence. A while later I heard their door open. I went to my door and opened it slightly. My mother was dressed and rushing down the curving staircase. When Papá begged her not to go, she turned and said she would get what she wanted and she knew where to get it. Then she opened the front door and disappeared. I ran to the window by my bed and saw her step into the carriage. Pascual, our Negro driver, slapped the reins on the horse, and they fled toward town. I didn't have to ask where she was going. When their bedroom door opened and closed again, I again looked out into the hall and saw Papá in his robe walking slowly down the stairs to the living room.

"For a long time I tried to sleep, but couldn't. Finally, I got up and silently walked downstairs. I was afraid and wanted him to stop drinking because when he passed out he looked dead. The sight would make my stomach ache and I would get sick. Sometimes I even threw up. I hoped my mother would never return. After looking around the living room, I saw him swirling a glass on the terrace. With one hand he was holding himself upright on a chair. He said something through thick lips about not seeing me enough, and called me his beautiful daughter. I told him I had been helping Mamita. He swayed so much I thought he would fall. When he said he was glad I came down, I asked why Mamita didn't live with us in the house. He looked at me sternly with one eye closed and said, 'Because she is a Negro.' I did not like that. I told him she was like family and how hard she worked and how much she loved me. He explained how well he paid her, enough for someone in her station in life, and if she was unhappy she could leave. 'She would never leave,' I said. He turned away to refill his glass and said, 'Of course not. She'd never make it on her own.' That was too much. I turned and ran toward Mamita's hut. He said I shouldn't become attached to a servant, that they work only for money,' and things like that. I didn't hear the end of what he said. When I got beyond the light, I turned and saw him look around for me, shrug, take a long sip of brandy, and walk to his humidor inside and take out a cigar."

"Where did you go?" Consuelo asked.

"To Mamita's hut. I loved it. It was always warm and cozy. Even the roof of its bamboo frame was made of palm fronds. The moon made designs on the dirt floor as it filtered through the palm fronds vibrating in the breeze. I put my arms around Mamita's waist and hugged her tightly. I loved her smell, both sweet and sour. She asked what was the matter, patting my back. 'Nothing,' I said. She understood and unfastened her hammock and threw it in the corner. She took my hand and sat with me in front of a small wooden table that held a small statue of Saint Barbara, a tureen, and five flaming candles. I still have the statue and the tureen. On such a night the candles cast pretty shadows on the walls. She began to recite what she had told me many times: 'Orúnmila was there when Oloddumare created man, so he knows the destiny of every human person. He can guide and help you improve your fate, Zoraida. He knows all the other gods and what they like. He'll help you talk with them.' Snuggling nearer her warm, soft, aromatic body and holding on to her, I felt something brush the fuzz on my arms and legs. When I rubbed my leg with one hand, she said, 'Don't pull away. Let him in.' After the first shudder I let my arms hang limp on my crossed legs and felt warm inside. '*Si, Mamita*. I feel him,' I said. For the first time that evening I felt happy. Mamita hugged me. 'You have accepted him, haven't you?' she said. I nodded. She asked me how I felt, and I said, 'Good, Mamita. Very good.' From that moment the spirit of Orúnmila never left me. I could walk, run, eat, or be sick, but the spirit was always with me. When I wanted to converse with it, I would find a banana plant, one with fruit hanging, and I would embrace one of the hanging bunches, holding onto a banana as he spoke to me. I never heard voices, but the answers to my questions would grow in my heart like the memory of spoken words.

"The next morning Mamita and I were talking in her hut when my mother's voice shrieked out. 'Zoraida!' Gooseflesh crept over me as I ran out of the hut. When I got there she yelled, 'Bring me a towel. I'm cold. The idiot maid forgot to put one out for me.' My mother was sitting in her tub with a cigarette dangling from her mouth, her left eye closed against the thread of smoke that snaked up her face. When I ran in with the large towel, she stood by the tub and told me to dry her, 'And be careful,' she said. 'I don't feel well.' I laid the towel on her shoulders and patted it against her back. When I had dried her back and buttocks, she turned. I hated the next part. Lifting the towel against her chest I dried her neck and breasts and belly. When I got down farther she spread her legs. 'Dry it well and carefully,' she said, a smirk on her face. I patted her dry and then moved down her legs and feet. 'Good, good,' she said. When I finished, she said, 'My kimono.' I laid the towel on the side of the tub and went to her room and took the kimono off its hanger and brought it to her. 'You're learning, child. You have the makings of a good maid, maybe even a wife.' I was not sure what she was trying to tell me. She served no one and was a terrible wife. Did she want me to choose one or to become, like her, one born to be served. Anyway, I knew she did not care what I became. I put her kimono on her inside out. It was one of the ways I had of getting back at her. As I walked down the hall I heard her yell, *'Cabrona!* One day I'll break your neck.' I was scared, but laughed all the way to Mamita's hut.

When I got there I asked Mamita why she was a maid. Mamita was stirring a small pot of soup she had made for us to share in her hut. 'Poor child,' she said. 'Why do you worry about things like that?' I told her I loved her and didn't want her to work so hard. She said she had been the property of my grandfather and was born to work. 'I have no choice,' she said. When I said, 'You do,' she laughed and put her arm around me. 'I was born in another world; it is too late to change,' she said. 'Besides, liberty brings its own disenchantments. One of the memories I cherish is helping your mother bring you into the world.' I told her what my mother had said about becoming a maid or wife. Her face drooped. After a moment she said, 'Your family is rich. You can become anything you want.' When I said I didn't want to be like my mother, she looked at me sadly and said, 'It is not good to judge others, Zoraida, but it is good to be observant.' When I asked what she meant, she said I had to find the answers within myself, because that is where all wisdom lies. I asked if Orúnmila would help, and she said, 'Of course.'"

"You were lucky to have had Mamita," Consuelo said.

Pointing to her heart she said, "She is with me here."

"What happened to her?"

"On my thirteenth birthday my mother left the farm forever. I didn't know at the time that I would never see her again. We were eating breakfast on the terrace. After Nina had served the coffee and juice and brought me a special cake she had made, my mother blurted out, 'That bastard of a banker says if I don't pay the note by the end of this month, they'll foreclose. What was he talking about, Arturo?' 'Nothing earth-shattering,' Papá said. 'I borrowed the money to pay for the house renovations you made last year and your new automobile. Didn't you want them?'"

"I had never seen my mother so angry. She said she did not want to mortgage the house for them. She said, 'You know business is rotten. How could you borrow money on property that is not yours?' He reminded her that she had given him power of attorney. With eyes aflame she said, 'I must have been drunk.' Papá smiled and said, 'Quite drunk as I recall.'"

"Her next reaction was very strange. She must have realized that he had done it to hurt her. She said calmly, 'You knew I couldn't pay.' She acted calm, but I could tell she was seething. Papá said it would all work out. He had the upper hand so rarely; I could tell he was enjoying it. She asked how it would work out and he said, 'Either you will find the money or we'll have to move.' 'You bastard! You'd like that wouldn't you?'"

Consuelo could see Zoraida's chest heaving. She put her hand on Zoraida's to calm her, but Zoraida continued: "My father shrugged. 'It's not my farm,' he said. 'Maybe your friend in town can help.' At that, my mother stood, picked up a table knife and threw it at him. He moved slightly to avoid it and smiled. Then she stood and walked out the front door and called Pascual to drive her to town. I thought she was going to ask her friend for the money, but she never returned, not that day or the next or ever. We never heard from her again. Father tried to find out where she had gone hoping she would prevent the foreclosure, but no one knew or would say.

"For the rest of that month Father stayed drunk day and night. I thought he would die. When the man from the bank came to foreclose, he brought his lawyer and a court official expecting Father to put up a fight. Papá merely invited them in, went to his room and, in a few seconds, returned with a suitcase. 'I'm leaving, Zoraida. I'm sorry, but you'll have to make your own way.' He kissed me on the forehead and walked down the road. I called after him, but he did not even turn to look back. He just kept walking. I ran after him for a distance, but finally stopped and watched him disappear. Although I loved him, something inside told me I would be better off without him. When I got back to the house, the men were coming down the stairs. The lawyer was asking the bank man how much they could get for it. The bank man said it was hard to tell, but certainly more than the amount of the loan. They talked as if I were not there. I asked what would happen to me. The bank man said I should go after my father because they could not help me. The man from the court, an elderly man, asked if I had any other family. I told him no, only Mamita. He seemed relieved and said he would take me to her. When I pointed to her hut in the Negro quarters, he said, 'Oh,' and shrugged his shoulders at the other man. 'I don't think she'll be able to help you. She needs more help than you.' I never thought I could help anyone and realized I wanted to help Mamita. I walked to the hut and put my arms around her. She asked what had happened. I told her everything would be all right, that I would take care of her.

"The man from the bank let us stay on the farm for about seven weeks, when the new owners moved in. They kept Pascual and Nina, but they didn't want Mamita because she was too old. It was raining the morning we left. Mamita and I took a train to Havana by way of many towns I lost track of. Havana was hot and humid, but I was excited to be in the big city for the first time.

"Mamita's niece, Graciela, met us at the train and walked us to her house in a neighborhood not far from the train station. We looked for a house, but with no money we soon gave up and stayed with Graciela until she and her husband could help us build a little hut on a narrow dirt road that wound between the other tin and palm huts that had been thrown up against trees and other huts. A tiny stream flowed not far from our hut, but some days it was so dirty that I did not even want to step in it. You might think that moving from a mansion with many servants to this hovel would be terrible, but it wasn't. For the first time, I felt like a person. I helped Mamita get settled and found a job in a hospital near our neighborhood. The pay was almost nothing, but I did not care. I had to scrub floors and sweep, and when I could I helped make the patients comfortable. Before long I was helping feed and bathe them. I must have done a good job because the head nurse gave me more and more work with patients.

"Even though poor Mamita was old and tired, she washed clothes for a family across the big street that surrounded our neighborhood. She did the washing and ironing at their house and could barely stand when she got home. Because I always called her Mamita, people thought she was my grandmother, and I never corrected them, so people assumed I was a light-skinned mulatta. My dark, wavy hair and features fit the mold. I was happy not to be white like my parents. Like savages they squandered the wealth they had been handed. I hated the unfairness. Anyway, I learned to cook and soon was fixing our meals on a small wood stove. In the evenings we would sit by her little altar to pray and make plans for my future.

"One night she looked at me with a serious face and said that I shouldn't be living there with her. 'You are white,' she said. 'You should be living with white people in a better neighborhood.' I hugged her tight and said, 'I'm black, Mamita; if not by blood like you, at least in my heart. I belong with you. You are my mother.' Wiping away tears, she said it was her lot in life to live like that, but it was not mine. She said I was wasting myself. 'You're white and beautiful. You could have and do anything you want,' she said. I told her I had what I most wanted, to be with her. Mamita was intelligent and understanding. She said I should not be so easily satisfied, that I was a better person than my miserable parents. 'Go, Zoraida. I can hope for no more for myself.' That was the only time I got mad at her. Why should a few ingrates own everything while so many good people willingly suffer, starve and die of disease? It made no sense, but I knew I would never convince her.

"Five years later we moved to a nice house in a working class suburb. It was not *El Vedado*, but it was clean and pleasant, and the street was paved. We had two coconut palms in the front yard and mangos and avocados in back. Most of the neighbors were black, and I liked that. They had become my people.

"With my job at the hospital expanding, I was helping in the maternity ward and had saved enough money so that Mamita no longer had to work. I was going out a few evenings each week and had many friends."

"You were very good to her," Consuelo said.

"I tried, but one day I came home and found her in her chair, dead. She never told me her age; I do not think she knew for sure. It did not matter. I had lost the only person who ever cared for me, and I knew I would miss her forever." Consuelo and Pablo looked at each other, Consuelo through teary eyes.

Zoraida went on, "I continued my job and became a midwife. Eventually I met Matilde. The first time I saw him I knew he was for me. He was beautiful with a physique like a god. He was the only other person who ever loved me."

"It's sad to feel that way, but I know of one other who loved you," Consuelo said. "Your baby, Ignacio."

"Yes," Zoraida said, and she started to cry.

*

During the next hour, the conversation eventually turned to more pleasant topics and to the beautiful city below them and the bay beyond. Pablo and Consuelo talked about the life they had left and mused over the twists life takes. "No one can predict which turn we'll take next," Pablo said.

Zoraida looked at him with pity. "There's more in life than what we perceive with the senses," she said.

Finally, they got up to leave, and Zoraida walked them to the front door. "Are you sure you won't stay with me?"

"Thanks, but we already have a room," Consuelo said. Then, thinking about the bugging device, "Next trip we will."

As they stood at the open door Zoraida said, "Thanks again for coming. I'm sure they'll let me go for the funeral. Perhaps I can spend a few days in Tampa before returning. It would be nice to see my old friends.

"When will you see Fidel?" Pablo asked.

"I'll try tomorrow."

"We'll stay as long as it takes and fly back together," he said.

"You don't have to do that," Zoraida said.

"It'll give us more time to see our old city and some of the improvements Fidel has brought."

"That's right," Consuelo said. "Good night, Zoraida."

*

The next morning, Pablo and Consuelo were sound asleep when the phone rang. "*Hola, Pablo.* I've spoken to Raúl; he's given me a two-week furlough. When can you leave?"

"Anytime. Today, if you wish," Pablo said.

"Good. We have much to do in Miami."

"I'll check out of the hotel and pick you up in an hour."

"It's easier if I come to your hotel. I have only one small bag."

In less than an hour, Zoraida arrived at the hotel wearing a simple black dress, small pearl earrings, and a thin gold necklace. Pablo and Consuelo were in the lobby with their luggage. They took a taxi to the airport with few words about Zoraida's furlough. Mostly they talked about the weather and how Tampa had changed. After checking their bags, they walked to the boarding terminal to wait for their Pan Am flight. Zoraida talked nervously and seemed exhilarated. When the boarding call came, she was the first up. As they approached, a soldier standing beside the attendant stopped Zoraida and said, "Please step aside."

"What is it?" she asked.

"A small matter," the soldier said. "Come with me."

Pablo and Consuelo had been standing behind Zoraida and followed her and the soldier. Pablo said, "Our luggage is on board. We haven't much time."

"Please continue into the plane," the soldier said. "We'll just be a minute."

"We're not leaving Mrs. Gómez," Pablo said, as he and Consuelo followed closely behind them.

Softly the soldier said, "I have orders to take you to police headquarters."

"Here's my furlough signed by Raúl Castro. I'm going to my husband's funeral."

"I'm sorry; those are my orders."

"We're not leaving without her," Pablo said.

"As you wish," the soldier said.

"I demand to see Fidel," Zoraida said.

The soldier said nothing, but led her out of the terminal and into a police car and drove off. Pablo and Consuelo got into a waiting taxi. "*Jefatura de Policía,*" Pablo said.

When Pablo and Consuelo emerged from the taxi, Zoraida and the soldier were disappearing into the building. Pablo and Consuelo ran up the stairs and inside to look around.

"There she is," Consuelo said, as the soldier led Zoraida into an office.

The office led to a small room where the soldier left Zoraida pacing and stomping around the room. Finally she sat down and tried to think.

Pablo and Consuelo remained in the hall outside the door where they had last seen Zoraida. "We'll just wait until she comes out," he said, walking to a row of chairs down the hall.

"What do you want?" a uniformed guard asked.

"Nothing. We're waiting for somebody," Pablo said.

"This is not a waiting room. You'll have to wait in the lobby."

Pablo and Consuelo followed the guard to the lobby and sat down. "We can see from here," Pablo said.

When the soldier returned to the detention room half an hour later, Zoraida was furious. "I'm chairman of one of Fidel's most important committees. You've seen my furlough paper. Now I demand that you either release me or take me to him."

"That's where we're going. Come."

For the first time since being detained, Zoraida relaxed. As the soldier led her down the hall and into the lobby toward the front door, she saw

Pablo and Consuelo. With a tilt of her head, she motioned for them to follow.

When they reached the front door, Zoraida was in the police car, and it was driving away. Pablo and Consuelo ran to the curb and called a taxi. They did not know where Zoraida was being taken, so Pablo told the driver to follow the police car.

The ride to the Presidential Palace was only a few blocks. When their taxi stopped behind the parked police car, Zoraida was striding out ahead of the soldier with the determination of one who knows her rights. It was a tactic Matilde had taught her years before: "When you're in danger or where you don't belong, don't sneak around; act like you own the place." Pablo and Consuelo kept a good distance.

Armed guards stood at every door of the palace. The soldier told Zoraida to wait and walked to the guard at the door to Castro's office. After talking with the attendant guard, he returned. "They'll show you in soon."

Keeping the door that Zoraida entered within sight, Pablo and Consuelo walked around the lobby trying to look like tourists.

Inside Castro's office, Evelio was reporting the events in Matilde's cell.

"Everything went well then?" Fidel asked.

"Exactly as planned.,"

"And he took the pills?"

"He asked for them. What could I do?" Evelio said with a sardonic smile.

"I can always depend on you, Evelio."

Three hours later Zoraida stood as if to walk out. She had seen long delays when Fidel didn't want to see a person or when he wished to let them dangle. It was one of Castro's exquisite forms of torture. Finally one of the guards answered the intercom and then called Zoraida and held open the door to Castro's office.

"Come in and sit down, Zoraida," Fidel said, in a pleasant tone.

"Why did you stop my trip after approving it?" she said, in a tone curt with authority. After ignoring Evelio in his chair, she sat down with her hands clasped in her lap. The expression on her face and her tone emitted defiance and anger. She had squeezed her hands together until the skin on her knuckles outlined the contour of each bone.

"Who are those people?" Castro was sitting, relaxed, smoking a cigar. He took the cigar out of his mouth and held it to the side, where a thin stream of smoke rose gently as he spoke.

"They're old friends from Tampa. They're concerned about me and came to express their sympathy and to help."

"Help you do what?" he asked, in a raised eyebrow gesture that infused the question with dark intent.

"With my grief, Fidel. My God! What are you worried about?"

"I do not worry. I act."

"Then why are you acting like this?"

"Because, Zoraida, I have reservations about you."

"After I abandoned my husband for the revolution? How dare you doubt me?"

"We've been watching you. We know all your friends and associates."

"So? Is one of them a problem?"

"Most of them. You're becoming a liability."

"Stop talking in generalities."

He took a deep puff and looked at her. "I always enjoyed Matilde, but I never trusted him."

"He thought you did."

"Matilde imagined himself free and open to ideas, but in reality, he lacked the conviction and devotion essential to the revolution."

"We always considered you an intellectual," she said.

"I am intelligent," he said, pronouncing each syllable with exaggerated emphasis. "That is not the same. I gave up on intellectuals back in the university when I learned how weak-minded and useless they are. It takes a strong mind to stick to something without being distracted by possibilities. No, Zoraida, he was the typical, weak intellectual, more interested in questions and nuances than action." Zoraida stared at him trying to understand. "I had great hopes for you, Zoraida. You aren't like that. You're a woman of action, but in your heart you're weak too."

"I don't agree, but I don't expect to change your mind."

"I can understand your sadness at losing your husband, but your behavior has changed. You told me one man's life, even your husband's, was insignificant compared to the revolution, but now you blame me for his death."

"I never said that." Zoraida was instantly sorry she denied it, but she felt weak and helpless in the presence of this man.

"I saved him from execution. Have you forgotten that?"

"The execution you ordered."

"Ah-ha! You have just condemned yourself. Case closed." He faced away and took a long draw from his cigar.

"What does that mean?" Zoraida's tone of authority fell limp.

"I'm sure you understand treason, my devoted revolutionary."

"You are the only traitor in this room, Maximum Leader, *Asesino!*"

"Please go on. You're doing very well."

"You removed a murderous dictator and became just like him. Kill me if it pleases you. You've killed my husband and my dream. You've left me nothing to live for, and that is your worst crime, you dream-killer."

"I see Matilde taught you well."

"Yes, you killed him, but you can't kill truth. Kill me. It will only bring you down sooner." Zoraida was calmer now as new strength rose in her breast, as if she had been reborn into a new life to which her imminent death was prologue. "And please be sure to eliminate everyone who disagrees with you. The more you kill, the sooner you'll fall." Then turning to Evelio, "He'll kill you too, little man, when it suits him."

With the cigar clamped between his teeth, Fidel put his chin on his fist and glanced at Evelio, who was smiling, and then at the blazing woman whose eyes glowed like hot coals, and whose thick, wavy hair seemed to be standing on end. He sat for several minutes, puffing. Imagining that he was planning the most cruel and excruciating death, Zoraida felt she could not stand another second of his iron stare. Finally, his calm voice shattered her erupting panic. "You're right, Zoraida. Executing or jailing you would only rally your followers. They aren't many, but they could become dangerous. You're going to disappear without a trace. We'll arrange for your friends to think you've defected." He turned his chair to face the intercom on the table behind him. "Send in García."

As he turned around, he heard noises in the outer office, sounds of loud talking and scuffling, then yelling and a sound like that of a chair toppling. Evelio jumped up and went out the door. Turning again to the intercom, Castro said, "What the hell's going on out there?"

The crackly voice said, "There's a man and his wife here. They demand to see you, and they won't leave. He punched a guard and threw a chair at another before we could stop him."

"You know what to do," Castro said.

"They're Americans."

"Better yet! What the hell do they want?"

"Zoraida."

"That's right, Señor Castro. And I won't leave without her." Pablo was standing several feet away from the intercom with a soldier holding his arms, but his shouting came over clearly on the intercom.

"Handcuff and search them and escort them in under armed guard," Castro said, calmly. "I want to see what these crazies look like."

439

A few moments later, the door opened to Pablo and Consuelo followed by two uniformed guards with rifles trained on them. Pablo's shirt hung out in front, his tie was torn, and his hair was ruffled. One of the guards was tucking in his own shirt as he walked in.

Seeing the middle-aged couple standing before him, Castro smiled. "Who the hell are you?"

In English Pablo said, "I am Pablo Iglesias and this is my wife, Consuelo. I demand Zoraida Gómez's release. In any civilized nation she would be allowed to attend her husband's funeral."

Speaking with resigned impatience, like a teacher trying to make a pupil respond, Castro said, "I'll ask again, who are you?"

"American citizens, good friends of Matilde and Zoraida Gómez."

"You're a Cuban."

"I was a Cuban, thirty years ago."

"To us you're still Cubans and still subject to Cuban law."

"You try to enforce your laws on us, and you'll have the U.S. government to deal with." Pablo said.

"You're not in the U.S., my little, big-mouth American."

"You have already caused the death of one U.S. citizen, and that is under investigation. This woman is also an American citizen. You will not harm her."

"Tough talk," Fidel said, his smile turned to mock fear. "I assume you have a plan to enforce your demand?"

"I've alerted the U.S. embassy. They know who and where we are, who Zoraida is, and what we want. You will be hearing from them soon if you have not already."

"Enough of this comedy, *Señor Americano*. I had already decided to release her; although your Hollywood comedy act is tempting me to change my mind."

To the guards he said, "Get them the hell out of here." Then turning to Pablo, "If you're still in La Habana tomorrow night, you'll be arrested." Then he picked up some papers, turned his chair away, and began to read.

Pablo would not let Zoraida out of his sight. As they walked out of the Presidential Palace and stopped a taxi Consuelo asked when he had called the embassy.

"As soon as we get to the hotel."

"*Buenas tardes, Señor Iglesias.* Did you leave something?" the concierge asked.

"We're staying another day and want a room with two double beds," Pablo said.

"And your luggage, Sir?"

"It's on a plane to Tampa."

"I can stay in my apartment," Zoraida said.

"You're staying with us, and no argument."

"But what about my clothes and all my things?"

Pablo tilted his head in a quizzical smile. Zoraida smiled sheepishly and said no more.

When they walked into their room, Pablo picked up the phone, called the American embassy, and asked for the ambassador. The man on the line asked him to wait for the ambassador's deputy. Pablo told the deputy what had transpired since their arrival, including his audience with Fidel Castro. "There may be trouble when we leave tomorrow with Zoraida Gómez. Though she's a subordinate of Castro, she's an American citizen. It was her husband who died in the Florida Straits a few days ago. She wants to return," he said.

"You actually talked to Castro?"

"Yes, now will you help?"

"Does she have written permission to leave?" the deputy asked.

"Castro gave her a furlough, then had her picked up, I think to get rid of us. Mrs. Gómez says he was going to have her executed, but in our presence, Castro just told her she's free to leave."

"We'll call his office and tell him we expect no trouble when you leave and that we'll have someone at the airport in case you need help," the deputy ambassador said. "After his recent fiasco at the U.N., I don't think he needs any more embarrassment."

When he hung up the phone, Pablo told them what the deputy said and then poured three glasses of cognac from the bar, and they toasted each other, laughing the nervous laughter of people who had just walked away from the gallows. "Had he really decided to let you go?" he asked Zoraida.

"He had just told me I would disappear without a trace."

"So he lied to save face. But why did he give up so easily?" Pablo asked.

"His stay in New York was pretty embarrassing," Consuelo said. "Arresting an American will bring the international press down on his head."

"The why doesn't matter," Zoraida said. "If not for you two I'd be in jail now or dead. You saved my life, Pablo. He could have thrown us all in jail. Even if you eventually got out, it could have been ugly."

"That occurred to me," Pablo said.

"I couldn't believe it when you hit that soldier," Consuelo said. "I thought they would kill you."

"For once, I wasn't thinking. I just had to get in his office somehow."

"I've never been so scared." She embraced him.

They did not leave the hotel that day, but spent much of the time on the balcony looking at the city. It turned out to be an exhilarating and surprisingly pleasant evening, celebrating their courage and bravura with champagne and a sumptuous supper in the hotel dining room. They laughed more than they had in months, but their laughter lacked conviction. Mixed with the laughter were occasional tears when they remembered what had brought them together. Zoraida wanted to know about Sally, what kind of child she was and what were her favorite pastimes. Consuelo was glad to tell her. Zoraida had a way of calming taut nerves. After supper they returned to their room, not wanting to risk being arrested on the street.

*

At the top of the steps leading to the airplane, Consuelo put one arm around Pablo and the other around Zoraida and squeezed them. "He's quite a man, Zoraida and you're quite a woman."

"Reminds me of someone I knew well," Zoraida said.

As the plane lifted into the sky, Pablo leaned across Consuelo to peer through the small window at the receding land and mountains of their birth. "Think we'll come back?" he asked.

"*Quien sabe?*" she said, hoping that one day they would finally be able to return in peace to enjoy their lovely island homeland. She could not help recalling trips home to attend funerals and to get away from Pablo, trying desperately not to relive those bad days. Looking out over the water, images of his father's funeral welled up: the black-veiled woman arriving late and sitting in the back pew and doña Inez's frozen stare at what had to be her husband's mistress. Does anything ever change? she asked herself. Yes, we trade our youth for the wisdom we needed much earlier.

Across the aisle Zoraida was looking sadly into her lap. "You're missing a gorgeous view," Pablo said.

"That land is no longer Cuba."

"I'd like you to work in my bank," he said, putting his hand on hers.

She forced a sad smile.

"And plan on staying with us until you get settled."

"You're very kind."

"Thinking about Matilde?"

"Just wondering how much a woman can lose and still keep her humanity."

"You must look ahead," he said lamely.

"Matilde gave a wonderful speech at his graduation," she said. "I was recalling the end: 'Now the work begins.'"

END

About The Author

Since retirement Jack Eugene Fernandez has devoted himself to a lifelong passion—writing. He published two poems and one story in University of South Florida publications and, in 1998, received the English Department award for best short story and for best poem in their student competition. During his teaching career at USF he authored five chemistry textbooks, fifty research articles, and was a Fulbright Scholar to the University of Madrid and the Universidad Nacional de Colombia. Jack's grandparents came to Florida in the 1860's and 1880's and settled in Tampa. Born and reared in Tampa, Jack loved the old Ybor City, its scents and flavors, and the factories where he watched his grandfather roll cigars.